THE OXFORD INDIA ANTHOLOGY OF
Modern Urdu Literature

FICTION

Edited by
Mehr Afshan Farooqi

OXFORD
UNIVERSITY PRESS

OXFORD
UNIVERSITY PRESS

YMCA Library Building, Jai Singh Road, New Delhi 110 001

Oxford University Press is a department of the University of Oxford.
It furthers the University's objective of excellence in research, scholarship,
and education by publishing worldwide in

Oxford   New York
Auckland   Cape Town   Dar es Salaam   Hong Kong   Karachi
Kuala Lumpur   Madrid   Melbourne   Mexico City   Nairobi
New Delhi   Shanghai   Taipei   Toronto

With offices in
Argentina   Austria   Brazil   Chile   Czech Republic   France   Greece
Guatemala   Hungary   Italy   Japan   Poland   Portugal   Singapore
South Korea   Switzerland   Thailand   Turkey   Ukraine   Vietnam

Oxford is a registered trade mark of Oxford University Press
in the UK and in certain other countries.

Published in India
by Oxford University Press, New Delhi

© Oxford University Press 2008

The moral rights of the authors have been asserted
Database right Oxford University Press (maker)

First published 2008

All rights reserved. No part of this publication may be reproduced,
or transmitted in any form or by any means, electronic or mechanical,
including photocopying, recording or by any information storage and
retrieval system, without permission in writing from Oxford University Press.
Enquiries concerning reproduction outside the scope of the above should be
sent to the Rights Department, Oxford University Press, at the address above

You must not circulate this book in any other binding or cover
and you must impose this same condition on any acquirer

ISBN-13: 978-0-19-569217-4
ISBN-10: 0-19-569217-9

Typeset in Lapidary333 BT 11.5/14
by Eleven Arts, Keshav Puram, Delhi 110 035
Printed in India by Roopak Printers, Delhi 110 032
Published by Oxford University Press
YMCA Library Building, Jai Singh Road, New Delhi 110 001

To my parents,
Jamila and Shamsur Rahman Faruqi

CONTENTS

Preface	xi
Introduction	xv
MIRZA MUHAMMAD HADI RUSVA (1857–1931)	3
The Gentleman (excerpt from the novel *Sharifzadah*)	
RASHIDUL KHAIRI (1868–1936)	8
Bride of the Whirlpool	
PREMCHAND (1880–1936)	13
Nirmala (excerpt from the novel *Nirmala*)	
PANDIT BADRINATH SUDARSHAN (1896–1967)	20
Raunaqi, the Devoted One	
HIJAB IMTIAZ ALI (1903–99)	29
And He Had an Accident	
RASHID JAHAN (1905?–52)	34
A Visit to Delhi	
GHULAM ABBAS (1909–82)	36
The Clerk	
AHMED ALI (1910–94)	42
Our Lane	
KRISHAN CHANDER (1912–77)	56
Irani Pilau	
AZIZ AHMAD (1914–78)	65
The Shore and the Wave (excerpt from the novella *Aisi Bulandi, Aisi Pasti*)	
RAJINDER SINGH BEDI (1915–84)	75
The Eclipse	

AHMAD NADEEM QASIMI (1916–2006) 85
  Sultan
MUHAMMAD HASAN ASKARI (1919–78) 93
  The Bitch
BALWANT SINGH (1920–86) 111
  Alleyways
INTIZAR HUSAIN (b. 1925) 121
  A Chronicle of the Peacocks
ZAMIRUDDIN AHMAD (1926–90) 131
  The East Wind
QURRATULAIN HYDER (1927–2007) 142
  Sita Betrayed (excerpt from the novella *Sita Haran*)
KHADIJA MASTOOR (1927–83) 151
  Inner Courtyard (excerpt from the novel *Angan*)
BANO QUDSIYA (b. 1928) 160
  Within the Circle of a Wave
GHIYAS AHMAD GADDI (1928–86) 173
  Sunrise
HAJIRA MASROOR (b. 1929) 181
  The Monkey's Sore
SURENDRA PARKASH (1930–2002) 189
  Scarecrow
ABDULLAH HUSSEIN (b. 1931) 196
  The Tale of the Old Fisherman (excerpt from
  the novel *Udas Naslein*)
ASAD MUHAMMAD KHAN (b. 1932) 212
  Harvest of Anger
IQBAL MAJEED (b. 1932) 226
  Two Men, Slightly Wet

JEELANI BANO (b. 1936) Some Other Man's Home	234
ENVER SAJJAD (b. 1934) Scorpion, Cave, Pattern	248
BALRAJ MAINRA (b. 1935) Composition One	254
SHAMSUR RAHMAN FARUQI (b. 1935) An Incident in Lahore	257
NAIYER MASUD (b. 1936) The Weathervane	276
KHALIDA HUSAIN (b. 1938) Adam's Progeny	290
MUHAMMAD MANSHA YAD (b. 1938) The Show	300
SALAM BIN RAZAK (b. 1941) Ekalavya—The Bheel Boy	309
SYED MUHAMMAD ASHRAF (b. 1957) The Man	316
Glossary	324
List of Translators	335
Acknowledgements	339
Select Bibliography	341

PREFACE

It was Professor C.M. Naim who first approached me to edit an anthology of modern Urdu literature. He felt I was the right person to take on this Oxford University Press (OUP) project and asked me if I was interested. To be truthful, I felt so privileged to be approached by Naim sahib that I accepted at once without even pausing to consider the enormous challenge and commitment that such a project would entail. The scale of the task ahead did not actually hit me until I was asked to prepare a table of contents.

My engagement with Urdu literature began in the family home, almost synchronically during childhood. I imbibed a lot of the discourse on *jadidiyat* (trend for modernity) simply by being born in a family where such esoteric terms became epithets drifting into my six-year-old ears even as I skirted the precincts of our family drawing room where vociferous and lively discussions on the subject held forth and where the journal *Shabkhoon* was conceived and brought out in 1964. My mentioning *Shabkhoon* is only to show how baffled I was at the prospect of how much or how little I knew of the modern in Urdu.

I decided to tackle the table of contents as a teacher embarking on a syllabus for a full-scale 'survey course'. At the outset, my reading list was endless. After a year of frenzied and focused reading, I felt confident enough to broach the subject with scholars of Urdu and arrived at what I called my 'master list'. This was basically a list of writers who lived and worked during the period 1905–2005. My reading made me aware of the challenge of representing certain genres that had been ignored by most anthologists of Urdu literature. Prose, especially of the non-fiction variety, attracted me the most. Prose in Urdu has trailed behind poetry for reasons which I need not go into here. Urdu's early modernizers such as Sayyid Ahmad Khan, Muhammad Husain Azad, and Altaf Husain Hali were brilliant prose stylists. Following the development of Urdu prose from the late nineteenth century onwards, unfolds a remarkable graph of highs and lows. Some genres, for instance, the literary sketch (*khakah*), essay (*inshaiyah*), humour and satire (*tanz-o mizah*), autobiography (*khudnavisht*), and travel writing (*safarnamah*) blossomed, while critical prose was slow in developing. The extraordinary success of the short story (*afsana*) in Urdu has marginalized the other prose genres. I felt that a comprehensive anthology must include the relatively lesser known works. Despite strict adherence to my own criteria for selection, I struggled to achieve a balance. The problem was how to balance the importance, significance, and historical value of the selections.

My initial contract with OUP was for a four hundred-odd page book. However, it became impossible for me to stay within the page limit and be satisfied with the question of balanced representation. Fortunately, OUP agreed to raise the page limit and we ended up with two volumes instead of one. Anthologists, especially those dealing with contemporary literature, cannot expect their exclusions and inclusions to satisfy all writers and readers. I have made the arbitrary decision of representing each author only once. In the interest of fairness, I chose from the work of each author an example which reveals something new about the literature, and also gives us a persuasive sense of the writer's work.

I have incurred so many debts in the form of advice, ideas, help, and encouragement, from seniors, colleagues, and friends that a few words here by way of acknowledgement cannot be sufficient to express my gratitude to them. Professors C.M. Naim, M.U. Memon, Frances Pritchett, Carlo Coppola, Robert Hueckstedt, and Geeta Patel offered comments and suggestions on various aspects of the anthology and read my drafts of the Introductions to the two volumes. My father, Shamsur Rahman Faruqi, allowed me to raid and rummage through his personal library, and never complained once when I asked him to mail me innumerable photocopies of poetry selections from out-of-print books, which I had overlooked when I was collecting material. He often rescued me when I was stuck in writing the introductory note on an author. In fact, this simple task was quite frustrating for me because there was precious little information to be had on many of the writers included in the anthology. His comments on my work were incisive and helpful. I am truly grateful to my translator friends who found time from their academic pursuits to translate new material for this anthology. I want to especially acknowledge Guriqbal

Sahota for doing not one, but three new, not so easy translations for me. Geeta Patel, Shantanu Phukan, Tahira Naqvi, Akbar Hyder, Griffith Chaussee, Moazzam Siddiqi, Moazzam Sheikh, and Baran Rehman all did new and difficult translations at my request.

The University of Virginia awarded me a faculty research grant in the summer of 2006 to work on the anthology.

These volumes could never have been completed without the unstinting support and collaboration of my husband Richard Cohen. Not once did he protest as I spent countless weekends hunched over the computer, irritable and uncompanionable; all the precious summers we stayed at home, with me immersed in the anthology, struggling with deadlines, racing against time. As the project developed, it became more complicated and so unwieldy that had Rich not stepped in to help me streamline with sensible editorial advice and support, I would still be floundering. I do not have words to express my gratitude for all he did in addition to the above: for endless cups of tea, the commute between Pittsburgh and Charlottesville, errands when he visited India, the list could go on forever. His optimism sustained me during the most frustrating times.

My editors at OUP, New Delhi, cheered me on and provided all kinds of logistical support and help. Nitasha Devasar was very accessible whenever I needed her help. She gave me a lot of space to articulate my ideas, and showed great understanding and sensitivity for the requirements that a project of this nature entails. In my meetings with her I always came back energized; her infectious enthusiasm kept me going even as the intricacies of editing sapped our endurance in the hot humid summer of Delhi. Mitadru Basu's meticulousness in editing, layout, and designing was incredible. I would like to thank them both for their tremendous help.

One last debt remains. My mother, my first teacher, who taught me the magic of letters, who always took keen interest and motherly pride, is not here to see the work in its final form. She is with us in spirit though, cheering me on, smiling.

The shortcomings, which must be many, are entirely mine.

Mehr Afshan Farooqi
Charlottesville, Virginia

INTRODUCTION

The development of prose narrative in Urdu, in particular, the novel and the short story, has received inordinate attention from historiographers. The advancement of these genres, indeed of Urdu prose itself, has been attributed to the textual production that was undertaken under the aegis of Fort William College. The college was established in Calcutta in 1801 for teaching India's classical and vernacular languages to the employees of the British East India Company. However, historians of Urdu have been dismissive of (a) the prose narratives that were in circulation before Fort William College was established, such as the translations and commentaries on the Quran, and (b) prose genres such as the *dastan* (story/tale in Persian). Dastans are gigantic cyclical stories comprising marvellous tales in the romance style meant for oral narration. These gained currency simultaneously with the didactic texts that were being produced at Fort William. The former were rejected as 'elementary' or 'religious' while the latter were declared to be 'puerile', 'immoral', and 'unrealistic'.

Literature cannot be produced on order, but good, distinctive prose can be created through a free translation of classic texts. Something similar to this was attempted at Fort William College by John Gilchrist who collected together a band of individuals from the Urdu 'heartland' and assigned to them the task of producing prose texts in Urdu by translating them from Persian and Sanskrit sources. Among the books they translated was a fair amount of fiction: *Bagh-o Bahar* (Garden and Spring) by Mir Amman, *Araish-e Mahfil* (Adornment of the Assembly) by Sher Ali Afsos, *Mazhab-e Ishq* (Religion of Love) by Nihal Chand Lahori, *Shakuntala* and *Baital Pachchisi* (Tales of the Ghost) by Kazim Ali Jivan and Lallu Lal, all of which received wide circulation with the backing of the College's printing press and gained immense popularity, and in fact, are still read with pleasure. *Bagh-o Bahar*, a creative translation of *Qissa-e Chahar Darvesh* (Tale of the Four Derveshes), is unique among them both in language and story-telling style. All these translations contributed to the popularization of prose romances.

Besides the translations at Fort William, there were other fictive genres that were translated into Urdu around the same time. The establishment of the Naval Kishore Press in Lucknow around the middle of the nineteenth century boosted the production of popular literature. It is an interesting twist in the history of Urdu literature that in the late nineteenth century, the Naval Kishore Press gave the dastan a new fillip and a new audience by getting the oral narrative Persian 'originals' translated and edited into publishable texts. The 'endless' cyclic stories known to us as the *Dastan-e Amir Hamza* (Tale of Amir Hamza) and the *Bostan-e Khayal* (Garden of Imagination) were rendered from Persian into Urdu at the request of Munshi Naval Kishore by a team of talented dastan narrators (*qissa khvan* or *dastan go*), Mir Muhammad Husain Jah, Ahmad Husain Qamar, and Sheikh Tasadduq Husain. However, the end of the nineteenth century saw the marked decline of this fascinating genre. Critics of the dastan have held that the 'novel style' narratives that began to flood the market edged out dastan literature, eventually leading to its obsolescence. But as Shamsur Rahman Faruqi has convincingly shown in his masterful work on the dastan,[1] this was not the case. The two genres had distinct, separate readerships. The popularity of the 'novel type' fiction had practically nothing to do with the decline of the dastan. In fact, the earliest proto-novels were sort of 'modern dastans' except that their purpose was almost 'anti-dastan', because they poked fun at the culture that had nurtured the dastan and its imaginative world.

The first 'original' romance (original in the sense that it was not a translation or adaptation of a Persian romance) in Urdu is Rajab Ali Beg Surur's *Fasana-e Ajaib* (A Tale of Wonders). Its rhymed prose and literary conceits make it difficult going for the modern reader. The ideas, incidents, and characters are modelled on those found in the cyclical romances;

---

[1]Faruqi, Shamsur Rahman, *Sahiri, Shahi, Sahib-Qirani: Dastan-e Amir Hamza ka Mutali'a*, Vols. 1–4, New Delhi: Council for the Promotion of Urdu Language, 1999–2006.

nevertheless, it represents a departure from the adaptation and translation of dastans. Both *Bagh-o Bahar* and *Fasana-e Ajaib* were not dastans, but they were perceived and read as dastans. The contrast they provided with the world of the *Dastan-e Amir Hamza* was extremely significant because these new dastans represented the new moral and social order, and more importantly, they were narratives meant to be read not recited. The written version of the oral dastan now appeared static and dated.

With Pandit Ratan Nath Sarshar's (1846–1902) *Fasana-e Azad* (The Saga of Azad, first published in 1880), we come nearer to the domain of the novel. The miraculous and supernatural are left behind, and the principal characters are recognizable people from nineteenth-century Lucknow. But the mammoth four-volume saga of the adventures of its eponymous hero, Azad, are still a 'thousand and one' stories woven together into an unwieldy narrative. Modelled loosely on the adventures of Don Quixote and his sidekick, Sancho Panza, Sarshar's remarkable achievement is the creation of a unique 'Indianized' version of characters, especially Khoji, who copies his master in comically endearing ways. Sarshar's blustering faithful friend, Khoji, has traits of both Sancho Panza and Amar the Artful of the dastan tradition.

Nazir Ahmad (1836–1912) established that ordinary events in the lives of common people could be worthy of generating a deeper response in readers. He wrote extensive tracts on morals and manners for the edification of his daughters. These didactic, elaborate, novel-length narratives were outstanding for their depth in characterization, and lively, idiomatic prose. One could call his works precursors of the modern novel in Urdu. Nazir Ahmad's *Mirat ul Arus* (A Mirror for Brides), 1869, predates Sarshar's *Fasana-e Azad* by a decade. His vigorous prose and keen sense of a realistic message made a strong impact on his readers. His control over the Delhi idiom notwithstanding, an important reason for his success as a writer lay in his epistemic stance. He represents western knowledge as superior to knowledge flowing from the eastern tradition. In his third and most popular work, *Taubat un Nasuh* (Repentance of Nasuh), there is a horrific, hair-raising scene when Nasuh destroys the entire library of Kalim and dismisses a lifetime's collection as 'a few books'.

Abdul Halim Sharar's (1860–1926) canvas and conceptions are grand. He attempted to write the historical novel and drew his inspiration from the eventful history of Islam. Sharar was extremely prolific, crafting some twenty-five historical novels. *Firdaus-e Bareen*, translated into English as *The Assassin's Paradise* (Tariq Mahmud, 2005) is perhaps his best and most ingenious. He also wrote several social novels.

Nazir Ahmad, Ratan Nath Sarshar, and Abdul Halim Sharar were so successful in launching the fictional novel in Urdu that one would expect that the genre would have risen to great heights in succeeding years. Yet, even half a century after Sharar's death, the important names associated with the novel are essentially those who wrote in the 'Nazir Ahmad style'. The most important amongst them was Rashidul Khairi (1868–1936) who was the most prolific of the Urdu novelists. He produced some eighty books, most of them novels. Khairi's tone is distinctively didactic and inordinately concerned with the miserable lives of ordinary Muslim women. The author seeks to ameliorate their condition by advocating social reform.

I have alluded to the literary dynamics of the late nineteenth century earlier in this essay. One reason for the plateau in the sphere of the novel's development could be the arrival of competing readerships for other genres such as those that were being transferred from the oral to the written through the establishment of publishing houses such as the Naval Kishore Press. It is around this time that English education began to be promoted with forceful earnestness; translations from English and via English of other European languages also become popular at this time. Journals of all stripes and colours began vying for readership. Above all, the short story appeared on the literary horizon as a tour de force, and began to grow at a remarkable pace.

Early Women Novelists

With all the hype about social reform for women and the launch of journals such as *Tehzeeb-e Niswan* (a weekly that lasted from 1898–1949) that were especially meant for women writers and readers, it does not come as a surprise that women novelists emerged in this period. Muhammadi Begum (d. 1908), the first woman to edit a journal, began by writing manuals on subjects of domestic interest. She branched into full fledged novels, leading the way for other women writers. Her early death from influenza at the age of thirty was a loss to the genre. Noteworthy among those who followed Muhammadi Begum's lead are Nazar Sajjad Hyder, Abbasi Begum, and Valida Afzal Ali. The latter, who chose to be known through her son's name, was the author of a three-volume saga titled *Gudar ka Lal* (The Ruby Among Rags). As Aamir Hussein has pointed out in his illuminating essay on Muhammadi Begum,[2] the pioneering presence of women in the Urdu novel's evolution is remarkable and worthy of canonization. These women's contribution to fiction had a tinge of feminist colour at a time when such a practice could not even be conceived of in Europe. Though Nazar Sajjad Hyder's novels are now forgotten, her fame lives on through her daughter, Qurratulain Hyder, one of contemporary India's most acclaimed and leading novelists who passed away in 2007. Hijab Ismail, the daughter of Abbasi Begum, a budding writer herself, was married to Muhammadi Begum's writer-dramatist, filmmaker son, Imtiaz Ali Taj. Hijab's work has recently received the renewed attention that it deserves.

Hussein raises an important question based on his study of the writings of Muhammadi Begum and her successors: that is, the extent to which the oppression of people by regimes imperial, colonial, or neo-colonial parallels the subjection of women by society, and the discontinuous coincidence of the rise of women's movements and those of national liberation. All too often, the latter appropriates the former and, in the aftermath of Independence, dismisses it as a secondary agenda. Then the demand for gender equality rises again, to be faced with fresh hostilities, political, social, and religious; it is reformulated with ever more radical words of resistance, for which the documents of self-determination are essential material.

---

[2]Hussein, Aamir, 'Forcing Silence to Speak: Muhammadi Begum, *Mirat ul Arus* and the Urdu Novel', *Annual of Urdu Studies*, 11, 1996.

The First 'Modern' Novel

Mirza Muhammad Hadi Rusva's (1858–1931) *Umrao Jan Ada* (published 1899) is generally regarded as the first 'true' novel in Urdu. Though Rusva wrote several other novels besides *Umrao Jan Ada*, for example, *Zat-e Sharif*, *Sharifzada*, *Akhtari Begum*, to name a few, none of them are as charming and convincing as *Umrao Jan*. One of the characteristics of the narrative in the nineteenth century novels was the presence of the narrator, which in most cases was the author him/herself. This narrative device enmeshes the author in the text and makes the text subservient to the author's direction. The authorial voice makes the novel's discourse monologic. In *Umrao Jan Ada*, there is a twist in the narrative device. The story unfolds through a series of flashbacks in which the narration is a first-hand report, a negotiation between a woman's narrative voice and a man's recapitulation. This gives it an authenticity as well as complexity that make it deeply interesting for the reader. The authenticity of the narrator is so compelling in *Umrao Jan* that almost all its readers identify the narrator Mirza Muhammad Rusva as the author himself, even though Rusva's *nom de plume* was Hadi not Rusva! Many believe it to be a true story, and there has been speculation about Umrao Jan: that there was such a courtesan who lived and befriended Mirza Hadi.

The great strides made by the Urdu novel in the nineteenth century were outdone by the popularity of the short story in the early decades of the twentieth century. However, in Premchand, Urdu and Hindi found a writer whose genius straddled both the short story and the novel. Premchand (born Dhanpat Rai, 1880–1936), occupies a very special place in modern Urdu and Hindi literature. Of the about twelve novels he wrote, *Godan* (The Gift of a Cow), 1935, his last novel, is the most widely read and appreciated. Premchand's didacticism is tempered by his humanism; his dialogue is polyphonic, and the seemingly simple plots of his novels become complex and unsettling as Premchand artfully weaves into the narrative many subplots. The absorbing narrative of his novels is buttressed with passages of tender poetic quality as he builds tragic characters trapped in the complexities of a milieu for no particular fault of their own. Premchand's novels initiated a discourse on aspects of national identity. The true or real Indian was not the person who lived in the city; cities were centres of corruption and moral degradation. Real India was in its villages; the sufferings of Hori, the hero of *Godan*, symbolized the struggle of the honest land labourer. Premchand also showcased the dilemma of the lower middle class Indian woman: the effects of poverty, widowhood, child marriage, etc. The pristine image of rural India established by Premchand continues to influence and inspire writers who followed in his wake to the extent that even the modernist short story evokes Hori in a manner that shows the connection with Premchand's legacy.

Progressivism and the Urdu Novel (1936–47)

Social change, particularly economic individualism leading to the creation of a middle class and thereby a new class of readers, and changes in women's role and status have provided impetus to the development of the novel in the West and to a great extent, in our own culture. One would expect the Marxist Progressive Writers' Movement (PWM) to produce an array of novels that engaged with these issues. The movement did produce exemplary short fiction, but no great novelists. The first significant novel-length work produced by the PWM is Sajjad Zaheer's (1917–79) novella, *London ki Ek Raat* (A Night in London, 1938). It followed closely on the heels of Premchand's *Godan*. Written in the stream of consciousness style, the novella prefaced with an illuminating introduction received critical acclaim way beyond its merit, probably because of its style that was new to Urdu.

The only exception among the Progressive writer's Marxist-Socialist fiction is Ismat Chughtai (1915–91), whose second novel *Tehri Lakir*'s (The Crooked Line), 1947, fiery heroine Shamman (modelled loosely on Ismat herself), was a bold portrayal of the psyche of a female child born as the tenth offspring. Fecundity has driven the child's mother to a state of callous indifference towards her many children. The tenth child's emotional anchor is her much admired older sister. In a poignant but unsentimental manner, Ismat explores the emotional scars that such an upbringing inscribes on the person, the skepticism that becomes almost second nature. Ismat continued to write novels but her crisp, earthy prose style was comparatively more powerful in short fiction. Ismat's *Tehri Lakir* is nevertheless a landmark in the Urdu novel's history.

Krishan Chander's (1912–77) first novel *Shikast*'s (Defeat), 1943, importance lies in its being the first in Urdu to present the misery, loneliness, and dehumanization that results from urban expansion and industrialization. Krishan Chander was extremely prolific. He churned out novel after novel, most of them of indifferent literary merit. He stands out as a remarkable prose stylist. The simplistic plots of his novels unfold in the most elegant, effortless, and almost mellifluous prose.

An important name among the novelists of this period is that of Aziz Ahmad (1914–78). His first novel, *Havas* (Lust), showed him as an experimenter of the psychological novel in Urdu. *Aag* (Fire) and *Gurez* (Abstinence) further established his preoccupation with the Freudian approach towards sexuality and its role in shaping an individual's life.

Partition and the Urdu Novel

Urdu writers' initial response to India's partition was an outpouring of poems and fictions that were based on real life experiences and heard stories hastily clothed in literary form. The heart-wrenching pain of permanent loss and displacement seeped into poetry and fiction slowly, but surely many years later. When the mixed feelings of euphoria at the so-called triumph of Islam and sadness at the horrors and bloodiness of Partition eventually receded, left behind were numbness and a void, much like the deep, un-healable wound that is often described in classical Urdu poetry.

The heartache of displacement wrought by Partition was the source of some great novels in Urdu. Qurratulain Hyder's (1927–2007) *Mere Bhi Sanam Khane* (I Have My Temples Too), published in 1947, is a semi-autobiographical account narrated in the stream of consciousness style. Written when she was nineteen years old, the novel expresses her grief over what she perceives as the end of the *ganga-jumni tehzeeb* or the composite Indo-Muslim culture; it reflects on the betrayals and tragedies that Partition brought in its wake. Of the twelve novels she wrote, her biggest in terms of the sheer sweep of range and subject is *Aag ka Darya* (River of Fire), 1959. As C.M. Naim has pointed out in his introduction to her two novellas, *Sita Betrayed* and *The Housing Society* (from *A Season of Betrayals*, 1999), in almost all her writings, Hyder has been concerned with Time, that faceless presence which transforms all appearances and which we ignore only at our own peril. Though this inevitability of change is our only permanent reality, Hyder persistently urges us to recognize both its faces, one of gain and the other of loss. A linearly progressing time brings about changes. Should we then take sides? Should we say that change is progress? Or should we say it is decline? Either, according to Hyder, would be simplistic and perilous, for such issues are not settled by a reference to the material world alone. What counts for her is the human spirit and relationships it generates and nurtures. That is where the linearity of Time seems to curve into a spiral, urging us to recognize a past that never quite disappears.

Intizar Husain (b. 1927), Hyder's contemporary, approaches Partition in a somewhat similar but more experimental style. In both his short and long fictional work Husain breaks the linear chronology of events and the horizontal movement of time to capture and encapsulate the ephemeral world of childhood with all its fantasies and enchantments in order to express the inner turmoil of the protagonist. *Basti*, published in 1979 (English translation, 1995), the finest of his three novels, is a story that weaves the present and the past through a labyrinth of history, myth, memory, and imagination. The 'present time' in the novel is presumably the last few months of 1971, preceding the fall of Dhaka and the break up of Pakistan. The events are narrated through the evocation of memory and poignantly articulated through inaction, which is an outcome of the grief and suffering of the narrator who is separated from his beloved at the time of Partition.

Abdullah Hussein's (b. 1931) novels, as M.U. Memon has shown in his scholarly introductions of the translations of Hussein's works (*Stories of Alienation and Exile*, 1998), explore themes of alienation and exile. Hussein, an only child, who lost his mother while still an infant, grew up to be a withdrawn, sensitive young man. A chemical engineer by profession, he took to writing during the long isolated spells in the laboratory as chemical analyst at the Dalmia Cement Factory located in an obscure village called Dandot. His first novel, *Udas Naslein* (The Sad Generations), 1963, was a phenomenal success. Beginning in 1857, *Udas Naslein* moves at a leisurely pace taking in the events of the First World War, the Jallianwala Bagh incident and the gathering storm over India, and the gory events of Partition culminating with the migration of Indian Muslims to Pakistan. Its protagonist, Naim, is a peasant's son who is initially smitten by the sophistication of the West and later increasingly drawn towards the 'cause' that is Pakistan. Ironically, Independence and the creation of a new country fail to bring freedom from old ties of caste and loyalty to an old order. It is this that causes the weariness of spirit, the sheer hopelessness of a battle fought, then lost to the enemy within. Hussein's melodic prose is like a breath of fresh air in Urdu's stagnating pool of canonical, novel-length fictions. *Udas Naslein* was recently chosen for translation in the UNESCO's collection of Representative Works in World Languages. For selection, a book must be at least 25 years old and in continuous print. Rendered into English by Hussein himself under the title *The Weary Generations* (2000), it disappoints the reader who has read it in Urdu.

The State of the Contemporary/Modernist Novel

An observer of the contemporary/modernist literary scene in Urdu may well ask, why the dearth of canonical novels in Urdu? Why did the promise of the richness of the earliest novels peter out in the post-Partition era? Why did the modernist trend (*jadidiyat*) that produced remarkable changes in the complexion of Urdu poetry as well as the short story, not have a significant impact on the novel? Aamir Mufti,[3] addresses the first two questions through finding linkages between the Urdu writers' articulation of selfhood within the culture of Indian nationalism. According to Mufti, the discourse of cultural difference that

[3]Mufti, Aamir, 'A Greater Story-writer than God: Genre, Gender and Minority in Late Colonial India', in *Community, Gender and Violence, Subaltern Studies XI*, P. Chatterjee and P. Jeganathan (eds), Delhi: Permanent Black, 2000.

lies at the heart of the national community pushes the 'Muslim' into minority culture and history.

Urdu literary production in the decades before Partition is ironically 'the most secularist'. The writers who came into prominence in this period were mostly those who were affiliated with the PWM. Thus, Manto, Ismat Chughtai, Krishan Chander, Miraji, or even Faiz did not see themselves addressing a primarily Muslim audience. This aggressively 'nationalist' stance in Urdu literary culture was a paradox to the separatist or communal posture that was assigned to Urdu during the period under question. As Mufti puts it, 'The foregrounding of the short story at the cost of the novel is to be understood in terms of the ambivalent relationship of Urdu to the discourse of Indian nationhood, in terms of the particular location of Urdu within the larger space of Indian literature(s). The privileging of the short story in modern Urdu literature is a function of this problematic minoritization.' Drawing upon Georg Lukacs' work (*The Theory of the Novel: A Historico-Philosophical Essay on the Forms of Great Epic Literature*, 1989), Mufti suggests that Urdu writers take recourse to the short story as a preferred genre because the short story, being a 'minor epic form', focuses on a fragment of social life rather than its totality, letting the whole enter 'only as the thoughts and feelings of the hero', thereby presenting 'completeness' in entirely subjective terms. The novel on the other hand is the epic of the modern world; it narrates the socialization of the individual in ethically meaningful ways. The Urdu short story represents the ambivalent relationship of Urdu to the national culture; the fragments it isolates from the stream of life do not merely point towards a totality of which they are a part, but also put this totality in question.

Mufti's essay conflates Progressive Urdu literary culture with 'Muslim' literary culture and assigns it a minority consciousness. Undoubtedly, Urdu writers played a leading role in the development of the PWM, but Urdu literary culture was not synonymous with 'minority' culture, at least in the decade following Partition. In the newly created state of Pakistan, issues of national culture were a subject of debate within the intellectual community. The articulation of selfhood and the sociology of the formation of national identity could have been the material for epic forms such as the novel. Indeed, writers like Intizar Husain, Qurratulain Hyder, and Abdullah Hussein did find the novel a medium for their engagement with what constituted the Indo-Muslim identity and despair of displacement. In my opinion, the disappearance of the novel form in Urdu has much to do with Progressive-Marxist culture as well as the location of the movement in a space and time where a shorter narrative form was the ideal vehicle for conveying the message of social liberalism that was the role their ideology assigned to literature. Their zealous and overbearing concern with man's role in society was at the expense of the individual. Individual consciousness was not a part of Progressive writing. With a few exceptions, the fiction produced by the Progressives was structurally quite simple. What drew a whole generation of brilliant minds to the movement was its anti-imperialist, pro-nationalist secular stance. In fact, major strides in the short story were made by writers who were outside the Progressive fold or only nominally associated with it; for example, Saadat Hasan Manto, Rajinder Singh Bedi, Muhammad Hasan Askari, Ahmad Ali, Upendra Nath Ashk, and Akhtar Husain Raipuri. In the period 1936–55, which was the height of the Progressive Movement, no major novels were produced. In short, the Progressives made almost no contribution to the novel form and left no paradigms for the next generation of writers.

The modernist trend introduced important changes in the fictional narrative. Enver Sajjad, Surendra Parkash, Balraj Manra, and Khalida Hussain are some of the major writers associated with modernist fiction. Besides, there were fiction writers who wrote in the modernist mode such as Naiyer Masud, Zamiruddin Ahmad, Fahmida Riaz, and so on. It is not easy to determine why the core group of talented fiction writers mainly stayed with the short story, producing the occasional novella such as Enver Sajjad's *Kushiyon ka Bagh* (Garden of Happiness) or Parkash's *Doosre Admi ka Drawing Room* (The Other Man's Drawing Room). Perhaps the abstraction and intensity of the narrative that is the hallmark of jadidiyat could not be sustained in a longer narrative form. In *jadid* fiction, the immediacy or directness of sharing the experience fuses the form with the content. Almost all modern writers make an effort to understand the nature of experience in order to share it as organically as possible with the reader.

Looking for ways to linguistically capture experience, modernists have also excavated links with the classical past in search of poetics that help better define themselves and the literary tradition which connects them seamlessly together. Languages grow or languish depending on the emergence or decline of new cultures and subcultures within which they flow. This is not the space to go into the semantics of Urdu's decline as a language of distinction, or to juxtapose it with the absence of a canonical novel form in Urdu. The case of Urdu may be unique among the modern literary languages in the way in which the hierarchical relationship between the 'major' and the 'minor' genre, that is the novel to the short story, is reversed. Urdu takes pride in the great strides it has made in the short story, and one hopes that the re-linking of the modern with classical will result in the creation of phenomenal novels.

Urdu *Afsana* or the Urdu Short Story

The history of the short story or afsana (fiction), also sometimes called *mukhtasar afsana* (short story)—the name *kahani* (tale, particularly oral) is also gaining popularity now—in Urdu goes back just a hundred-odd years. But the genre grew and flowered at an amazing pace, passing through several short phases of transformation over a period of fifty years or so. The earliest short stories were written and published during the first decade of the twentieth century. Although there is some debate as to who is Urdu's very first short story writer, there is no doubt that Premchand was among the earliest and most successful, who dominates the first quarter century of Urdu fiction, and in fact, still towers as a colossus in the world of Urdu.

Among Premchand's senior or nearly exact contemporaries were Rashidul Khairi (1868–1936), Sajjad Haider Yildrim (1880–43), Sultan Haider Josh (1884–1966), and Niaz Fatehpuri (1886–1953). All of them became pioneers of the short story, though not necessarily in the Premchand mode. Premchand's style was inspired with a genuine zeal to portray the plight of the rural poor, especially from eastern Uttar Pradesh (then known as the United Provinces of Agra and Oudh). He was a nationalist who was influenced by Tolstoy and Gandhi, who also welcomed the formation of the Progressive Writers' Association (PWA) and presided over its first session. His stories, nevertheless, have an element of the human, rather than the mechanistic, and this elevates them from ordinary social commentary to sensitive narratives about the human condition. He had a sense of humour too and he wrote in a relaxed, deceptively easy-flowing style that became the despair of his imitators.

Yildrim and Fatehpuri were often described as being among the 'Romantics' of Urdu, although it is a moot point whether there was such a thing as 'Urdu Romanticism'. They wrote an artificial, 'poetic' prose and were influenced by an assortment of foreign writers. Much more important than the foreign affinities of Yildrim and others, this was a time when a spate of translations (mostly through English) from English, French, and Russian literature engulfed the Indian, particularly the Urdu, literary scene. Both Premchand and Yildrim started their writing careers as translators. One might say that in fiction the writers who most influenced Urdu writers and who were translated most were Maupassant and Chekhov. These two, and especially Chekhov, provided Urdu writers with paradigms, perhaps because Russian fiction was perceived to be more 'eastern', with an element of spiritualism with its realism tinged with a sort of introspective subjectivity.

The influence of Premchand's didactic-humanistic style was both widespread and deep. It became the link to a more powerful and invasive movement in Urdu literature known as the PWM. The PWA arrived on the literary scene with the publication of a collection of short stories titled *Angare* (Embers), which was at that time radical in both tone and content. The writers of the *Angare* group were passionate advocates of what they described as socially engaged literature. Their primary concern was not with form, style, or language, but with 'socially relevant subjects'.

The 1930s were a time of great political and social turmoil in India. The influence of Indian nationalist leaders, particularly Mahatma Gandhi, almost changed the Indian worldview in many important respects. The passing of the Government of India Act in 1935 aroused as well as disappointed Indian nationalist yearnings for full freedom. Their Marxist-Leftist leanings notwithstanding, the Progressive writers more or less consciously stepped into the nationalist slot on the Indian literary scene. However, they were not concerned so much with specific issues thrown up by colonial rule as with championing the cause of the rural and urban poor and urging that it was the society, not birth or parentage, that determined a person's character. With their agenda for literature to be fashioned as a weapon in the battle for social and political change, they found much to interest them in the portrayal of the downtrodden, as exemplified by prostitutes, factory labourers, and domestic servants. In most Progressive fiction, delineation of character gave way to the plot, which generally moved in a linear fashion.

The *Angare* group led by Sajjad Zaheer (1917–79), Ahmed Ali (1910–84), Rashid Jahan (1905–52), and Mahmuduzzafar (d. 1956) expanded rapidly as more and more poets and writers with nationalist, and not necessarily Marxist, leanings joined the movement. Despite a severe political agenda that limited and hampered the flow of creativity, the PWM produced a host of brilliant fiction writers such as Upendra Nath Ashk (1910–96), Saadat Hasan Manto (1912–55), Krishan Chander (1912–77), Rajinder Singh Bedi (1915–84) and Ismat Chughtai (1915–91). From 1936 to 1957, the PWA had a virtual stranglehold over the literary scene in almost all modern Indian languages. Yet it was the Urdu writers who provided the leadership to this movement. Nevertheless, some writers did not succumb to the rhetoric of political and social change; notable among them are Qurratulain Hyder (1927–2007), who until her recent death was regarded as the greatest living Urdu fiction writer. Many writers who were initially somewhat loosely identified with the PWA broke away or distanced themselves from it. Among the earliest of such writers were Muhammad Hasan Askari (1919–78), the ideologue and Francophile critic and fiction writer, and Ghulam Abbas (1909–1982), and a few others like Hayatullah Ansari (1908/1912?–99), who was a Gandhian and broke away very early from the Progressives, but who retained their social concerns.

A forum known as *Halqa-e Arbab-e Zauq* (Circle of those of Discerning Taste) was convened at Lahore to provide an alternate space for poets and writers who had a different take on the meaning and the meaningfulness of literature. Some members of the Halqa had begun their careers as admirers of the Progressive ideology, but were now moving away from its claustrophobic hold and seeking a breath of fresh air. The Halqa encouraged criticism and debate, but would have nothing to do with politics or political or social ideology. It thus provided an extremely valuable forum for writers with different views, and especially those who were interested in experimenting with new forms and ideas.

Much of the Urdu fiction produced in the decade after Partition was inordinately concerned with the horror stories of the rioting and the heartbreaking miseries of displacement. At this time, 'realism' as a fictional device was also popular. But the Progressives were apparently more concerned with narratives of individual loss and pain of displacement and the atrocities that attended it. They did not seem aware of the greater human tragedy of the cultural loss and destruction of ways of life that had taken centuries to evolve. They also seemed to be concerned with 'fair play' and tried to represent both Muslims and Hindus/Sikhs as equally bad and equally good.

Among some of the new writers who emerged in the mid-1940s were Muhammad Hasan Askari (1918–78), Mumtaz Shirin (1924–73), Khadija Mastoor (1927–82), and Hajira Masroor (b. 1929). The latter two were sisters who remained vaguely progressive throughout their careers. The names of Suhail Azimabadi (1911–79), Ahmad Nadim Qasimi (1916–2006), and Balwant Singh (1920–86) became notable early in the 1940s as story writers of the rural life of Bihar and Punjab, respectively.

In the 1950s, the influence of the Progressives began to wane. Some of their group professed boredom or disillusionment with writing stories that carried an explicit, unidimensional message and dealt with the same topics over and over again. Manto died in 1955, creating a vacuum in the Progressive fiction that could not be filled, especially because Rajinder Singh Bedi, the other great story writer in the Progressive camp, gradually drifted away from the PWA. In fact, even Manto had been frowned upon by the PWA establishment as not being radical enough.

The late 1950s and early 1960s saw the beginning of jadidiyat or modernism. Jadidiyat was a global literary phenomenon in Urdu that affected all creative writing and devised an elaborate literary theory, and tried to find ways to understand and reinterpret classical literature in a more positive way. The jadids were not simply seeking new subjects for literature; they wanted to experiment with both form and content, break the structure of the story or bend it out of shape so much so that it needed much intellectual effort and thoughtful unravelling by the reader to make sense of the narrative. The jadids also used symbolism and allegory to add more depth to the meaning of their individual experience, and invited the reader to make the act of reading a participatory affair, and make the experience of self-exploration mutual. In both poetry and prose, the jadids struck a note that was clearly anti-Progressive and thus invited the obvious criticism of being a negative and 'unhealthy' reaction against Progressive literature by relegating themes of social change to the background. They were also accused of being destructive of 'tradition', oriented toward the 'West', and working from a poetics borrowed blindly from the West.

The first name in the modern Urdu short story is Intizar Husain who began writing stories using symbolism around 1958. His short story, *Akhri Admi* (The Last Man), was published that year. Though Intizar Husain has a barely concealed contempt for the Progressives, he would not like to identify himself with the jadids either. The Progressives regard him as a near reactionary, given to nostalgia for a past that is hardly existent as far as the Progressives are concerned. The jadids have however tended to regard both Intizar Husain and Enver Sajjad as cult figures of modernist fiction. Born in 1934, Enver Sajjad regards himself as strongly left-wing, but has written stories and novels that are extremely dense and full of abstract images. His prose is carefully crafted and often reaches the condition of the prose-poem. His first anthology, *Chauraha* (Crossroad), 1964, established him as the leading exponent of the *tajridi* (abstract) and *'alamati* (symbolist) short story. In India, Surinder Parkash (1930–2002), Balraj Manra (b. 1935), and a host of other writers switched to the jadid mode, discarding the descriptive, plot-bound narrative of the Progressive writers. Surinder Parkash has candidly explained his disillusionment with the Progressives in an essay, '*Naya Urdu Afsana, Meri Nazar Mein*':[4]

I had complete faith in the Progressive Movement earlier (before the 1960s), and was convinced that a writer can accomplish with his pen what a soldier can with a sword or gun. My chest puffed with pride at the thought that the stories I would write would bear the seeds of political and economic revolution; but suddenly a strange thing happened. Khruschev came to power in the Soviet Union. The Soviet Union's friendship with India was strengthened even more and the enthusiasm of the Progressives to bring about a revolution [in India] cooled off. What had happened? My dream of using my pen as a sword looked like a useless thing to me now. It was a period of extreme boredom. People's ideals were shaken and nothing seemed clear. Writers who were used to following [Party] directives turned to commercial writing and some just gave up writing altogether. There was no alternative for people like me except to face reality instead of shirking away from it.

[...] Then in the silence I began to hear murmurs and I realized that there were many melodies that were restlessly waiting, impatient to be given a voice, to be sung. When those notes found given words, to our ears came an entirely different song from the ones that we were accustomed to. This time the 'new' writer (*naya adib*) was not talking about merely experimenting with new usages but also with the content of the work.

[...] But it is wrong to imagine that the modern short story is the property of some individuals belonging to a certain age group or those who are experimenting with new forms and usages; or that it is a deliberate attempt to make fiction difficult to comprehend. A story written in a straightforward, traditional style can also be modern provided its narrative is reflective of the mental state of the individual living in the present times.

The modern short story does not deny social realities; it tries to present them with more truthfulness so that it does not seem that someone's [other

---

[4]Parkash, Surinder, '*Naya Urdu Afsana Meri Nazar Mein*', in *Urdu Fiction*, Ale Ahmad Suroor (ed.), Aligarh: Department of Urdu, Aligarh Muslim University, 1973, Translation, mine.

than the writer's] personal biases or judgements have been thrust between the truth and the reader. The story is closer to life and the modern writer refuses to advocate an agenda.

The modern story is certainly not an attempt at thrusting its writer's half baked experiences, prejudices, complexes on the reader. I do not regard literature as a means of expressing myself but as a means of self-exploration and I invite my reader to participate in it so that whatever result may emerge from it, it can be equally shared by both.

Not all the fiction writers of the 1970s and 1980s resorted to abstraction, obscure, personal symbolism, or allegory. Many (including Intizar Husain) used light symbolism or none, and eschewed abstraction. Outstanding among the 'mainline' story writers are Ram Lal (1923–96), Iqbal Mateen (b. 1924), Zamiruddin Ahmad (1925–90), Qurratulain Hyder, Abdullah Husain (b. 1931), Iqbal Majeed (b. 1934), and Naiyar Masud (b. 1936). Many of these would not call themselves 'modernist' in our sense, but none of them, except Qurratulain Hyder, gained recognition under the Progressive dispensation. It was modernism that provided them their due space in contemporary literature.

FICTION

Mirza Muhammad Hadi Rusva
(1857–1931)

Mirza Rusva was a man of many interests and accomplishments. He knew several languages and had a deep interest in philosophy, mathematics, and astrology. He worked as an engineer for some time, and developed a special passion for chemistry, purchasing and collecting an array of scientific instruments from abroad. Born in the year of the great rebellion of 1857, Rusva grew up in a cultural and political milieu which raised many questions about the direction society was taking.

His novel, the well-known *Umrao Jan Ada*, was published in 1899, and later received considerable recognition for being the first novel in Urdu. *Sharifzadah* (The Gentleman) is his second novel, and is yet to be translated into English. It was first published in 1928, and has been in print ever since. The novel is semi-autobiographical. Its principal character, Mirza Abid Husain, is a typical new-style, Anglicized Indian gentleman. Of respectable family, impecunious but honest, he is partly self-educated and completely self-made. Mirza Abid Husain hates Urdu poetry, as well as the lifestyle and most amusements of the average city dweller. Through his character one is introduced to Rusva's own feelings and biases with respect to the 'progress' of Indian society during his time. In a style he felt quite competent and comfortable in, Rusva reveals a deep, rather sophisticated analysis of the fabric and failings of the culture he knew best, yet rejected.

The Gentleman

A wise man has said that there are two constituents in the development of intellect: one is external and the other internal. Each of these has two elements. The internal includes the person's genetic makeup plus his or her readiness, while the external includes the conditions that surround one from birth to maturity. In addition to the above, society too plays a role. All of these are vital in the shaping of a person's character. Now let us see to what extent Mirza Abid Husain's personality was shaped by these elements. Laying aside the internal factors, when we examine the external ones we see that he was not very different from the citizens of Lucknow. It is true that his father, Mirza Baqar Husain, strove as best as he could to educate him. No one in his family was as well educated or what we can call well educated as Mirza Abid. His father's Persian was perfect. His grandfather had some basic education, as was expected of gentlemen in his times. But the rest of his ancestors were unlettered (I hope Mirza sahib will pardon my saying so). They were proud but illiterate soldiers. They looked down upon those who tried to learn how to read and write. It would be best not to probe his ancestry further than this. Who doesn't know the reputation of the Qazzaqs of the desert of Kazakhistan?

As for the society Mirza grew up in, not one of his peers from his neighbourhood is worth including in this story. Some families belonging to the *kahar* caste (they fetch water or serve as palanquin bearers) lived near his parents' house. Among their sons, Durga learnt how to read and write and became the supervisor of the palanquin bearers at Sarfaraz Mahal. Debi, the grocer, lived in the same neighbourhood. His son Mahku Lal worked as a broker for merchants in Sa'adat Ganj. Fida Ali belonged to the cultured stock and he and Mirza played together as children. Upon graduating from high school, Fida Ali became a pigeon fancier. Mirza went for higher education. He passed the entrance exams while Fida Ali's brood of pigeons flew up to Navaz Ganj, fought and scored a victory over Qurban Ali's well trained brood, killing fifteen. Mirza became an engineer. Fida Ali was appointed Shahenshah Mirza's official pigeon fancier. When Mirza retired, took his pension and came back home, Fida Ali had quit his job. He now supplied duck, partridge, pigeon and geese to Matiya Burj. A notable resided in the neighbourhood. He had family ties with Bahu Begum sahiba. His son Sultan Mirza became an expert distiller of the local brew. I never saw a lump of opium suspended in any syrup except the one he produced. Among his relatives was a lad named Chuttan. He fixed quails' beaks in a way that made him famous in the city. Ali Husain was also among Mirza's peers. He liked to exercise. He grew up to be a matchless bully. Renowned tyrants were afraid of him. He controlled the area from Sa'adat Ganj to Nakkhas, and all the way from there to Aminabad. His replica of the spearheaded banner of Hazrat Hasan and Husain that is carried out in the procession of the festival of Muharram was the highest ever seen in the city. The symbolic water bucket and the ropes that Ali Husain tied were unsurpassed as well. He had two cousins: one was a reciter of elegiac poems and the other a *hadis* narrator.

Among the friends of Mirza Baqar Husain was an older gentleman, one Mirza Haider Husain, who lived in the neighbourhood. He was crazy about writing poetry. He wrote poems with the poetic nom de plume 'Hasrat' which means desire or longing. He had a son, Tassaduq Husain who was just like the father. The latter wasn't highly educated but had begun composing verses from his early teens. His *takhallus* was 'Vahshat' (Madness). He regularly recited a bunch of poems at the *mushairah*s. In one of the *ghazal*s he recited that evening was a highly evocative *sher* which became his punch line, so to speak. He recited it over and over again through the evening on request from listeners, and people in the audience went home with the verse on their lips:

Junun-e Qais ka andaz jo tha
Use zindah kiya Vahshat hamen ne
[The manner of Qais' madness
Vahshat, we kept it going]

Although there was nothing new in the *sher*, the charming use of the takhallus created a word play. The listener's enjoyment was further heightened by hearing it from the young poet's lips.

Our Mirza Abid Husain sahib had no interest whatsoever in the aesthetics of ghazal poetry. It wasn't that he couldn't understand it, for he had studied Persian thoroughly with his father. When on the very next day Miyan Vahshat proudly recited his couplet before Mirza Abid Husain, the latter expressed his comments in the following manner: the meaning he derived from this sher is that no one could boast of a passion like Qais' until Vahshat came and revived the same intensity. Mirza added that he could not enjoy such a couplet because there was no truth in it nor did it express a real human emotion. For, as far we know, according to Mirza, Qais or Majnun was a poet and his contemporary was a female poet named Laila. The Arabs in pre-Islamic days indulged in composing vulgar poetry of this kind. They often had gatherings similar to what we call mushairah in our times. Majnun and Laila participated in these gatherings and one could say that there was a competition of sorts between the two. Laila wasn't a great beauty; she wasn't plain looking either. Women have a natural suppleness in language. Majnun was at best competent in his art. He simply loved Laila's poetry. That was the real basis of his love for her. If Qais had been content to leave it at that, all would have been well. But he had the desire to be united with Laila. So he sent a proposal of marriage through his father. Laila's father rejected the proposal for some vague reason. It is believed that he did so because the story of Laila and Majnun's love for one other had become common knowledge and if they were to marry, people would assume they had had an illicit relationship. Laila's father couldn't bear this shame. Qais was completely devastated. He could not control his passionate yearnings, so he became a crazed lover or *majnun*. Had Qais had strength of character he would have been able to control his emotions. In fact, he should have checked his feelings. Therefore why should anyone take pride in comparing their emotions to those of a weak character such as Qais?

In this narrator's opinion, Mirza Abid Husain's understanding of this sher is incorrect, because Mirza has declared the historical Qais to be the subject of this sher. There is a world of difference between the Qais who actually lived and wrote poetry and the Qais of the poet's imagination (what philosophers would call the exemplary Qais). The exemplary Qais has been perceived as the perfect lover. The object of perfect love need not necessarily be a woman. Spiritual love's goal is of the highest order and certainly merits reverence. The perfect man is one who has reached the stage of gnosis. Mirza implies that the poet is singing his own praises, and criticizes him for doing so. This censure is incorrect too, because whenever a poet refers to himself he is not referring to his actual self, but simply using it as a model or what is called 'ideal' in English. That is, if one was actually what the poet supposes, according to the nature of the messenger (the poet), then pride is justified. For example:

Larati hai falak se mujh ko meri himmat-e a'li
Tamasha dekh lein zor azmai dekhne vale
[My indomitable courage gives me strength to fight the heavens
Let the bystanders watch this trial of strength]

In the above sher, the poet has taken pride in his supreme courage, but here too he hasn't described his present or actual state. He has delved into one of the purposes of creation. Thus the meaning of the sher is something like this: I should be so strong that when the heavens send troubles my way I can face them with fortitude.

The fact is that from a very young age, Mirza sahib was engaged in realistic pursuits because of necessity and inclination. He seldom had the opportunity to think about the world of imagination. Then, his interest in agriculture made him even more used to seeking the practical side of things. He stayed away from philosophy and poetry. He was literally a man of experience.

We are not surprised when people whose interests are in business and commercial knowledge show no interest in philosophy and poetry. It has been observed that such people often don't care about religion too. But our Mirza sahib was not like this. His faith in religion was very sound. He said that he didn't find religion opposed to commercial enterprise in any way. This makes it obvious that he practised what he believed in. He was brought up to believe in a faith whose tenets were based on beauty and intellect. He did not find in his religious beliefs anything that he could not understand, or that he was compelled to follow blindly. His religious beliefs were therefore not a problem for him.

As for the matter of faith, he thought that if the origins of the religion are correct, then there should be no obstacle in observing piety.

Mirza had no interest in writing poetry, hanging out in tea stalls, lying around smoking hookah, listening to *dastan*s, pursuing civil suits; all these were for the most part favourite pastimes for city folk. In the city he had no friends who shared his interests. Therefore, he felt out of place. He owned a farm that he had laid out himself, based upon his professional training. There was a house to stay on the farm. Attached to the women's quarters was a small annex. This was his laboratory, equipped with agricultural tools, apparatus associated with chemistry experiments, as well as chemical samples. Close to the farmhouse several acres of land had been earmarked for cultivating plants that would be useful for botanical knowledge. Adjoining it was the summer house that boasted a collection of ferns, herbs, and a variety of ornamental trees. In their midst was a silvery tank; there were models of hills and mountain tracks in and around the summer house. There was an observatory near the laboratory with weather forecasting apparatus installed by the side of the summer house that were protected by a shed-like structure. A 'model house' that is a sort of display room for various tools and such was next to the shed. Farther away from these buildings were the stables and the animal house, and some distance from there were the servant quarters. Although this farm was not exclusively meant for experiments in agriculture, any green field that has Mirza Abid Husain as the agriculturist can be assumed to be an area for high yielding crops.

Mirza performed all the farm chores himself: tilling, levelling, weeding, and irrigation. There were no difficult and complicated tasks that Mirza did not perform along with the workers and servants, and always with enthusiasm. The workers he had hired were unique too. They never grumbled, lazed around, or argued.

Translated by Mehr Afshan Farooqi

Rashidul Khairi

(1868–1936)

Rashidul Khairi was born in Delhi. He is generally regarded as Urdu's first short story writer, whose story *Nasir aur Khadija* (Nasir and Khadija) was published in 1903, in the journal, *Makhzan*. He was an extremely popular and prolific writer of melodramatic novels about the domestic life of women. In his novels he argued for women's rights in Islam, particularly the right to education. Among his well-known works are *Dilli ki Akhiri Bahar* (The Last Spring of Delhi), *Tarbiyat-e Niswan* (Education of Women), *Subh-e Zindagi* (Life's Morning), *Gudri men La'l* (Ruby among Rags), etc. He launched a number of journals, including three especially for women: *Jauhar-e Niswan*, *Banat*, and most importantly *Ismat* (Honour), which was a literary journal. Most of the contributions to the journals came from Muslim women.

This excerpt from *Bhanwar ki Dulhan* (Bride of the Whirlpool), a melodramatic love story in which the hero and heroine's marriage ceremony is performed on a boat before it capsizes in a whirlpool, is from the collection *Jauhar-e Ismat*, published in 1920. Khairi employs rhetoric reminiscent of the florid style of an earlier period. His complex sentences are laden with strings of adjectives, independent and dependent clauses, and adverbial phrases. The Urdu original rewards the reader, literate in the tropes and specialized vocabulary of the piece, with a sense of nostalgia and grandiloquence. The translated text, however, fails to convey exactly the cultural sensibility of the original.

Bride of the Whirlpool

Badshahi Bagh that had witnessed the glory of the great, heroic Mughals up to the last ineffectual emperor, Bahadur Shah, and had welcomed the visits of the Mughal princes for generations, is situated four miles from Delhi's Shahdara Station. One would be hard-pressed to find an example of another pleasure garden such as this that had been continuously nurtured for more than five centuries. In the rainy season, the heavily shaded part of the garden became a magical world. Leafy *jamun* and mango trees formed such a dense canopy that let alone ordinary gardeners and horticulturists, even the most skilful experts of the art were astonished to see this long avenue of trees stretching for nearly ten miles, creating such a thick canopy that not a drop of water from a torrential downpour could reach the ground. The eastern part of the shady side of the garden touched the waves of the river Yamuna. The Mughals spent most of the days and many nights of July and August in this garden. When purplish grey clouds filled the sky, lightning flashed and the sound of thunder echoed, those fun lovers would indulge themselves in the seasonal sport of swinging. Gold and silver swing-seats were suspended from the trees with multicoloured silken ropes. The fairy princesses of the Red Fort dressed in red and green garments, propelled the swings, and the sonorous voices of the swingers would rise from the ground and mingle with the song of the bulbul and the plaintive call of the koel. But now, the garden has shrunk to a small cluster of trees, dilapidated pavilions, and crumbling walls. The Begum Pasand Well still has fresh water, but no one bothers to give it a passing glance. Jackals roam where once upon a time there were crowds of people and one couldn't find a place to sit. In the middle of the garden is the hut of Feroze Khan Tatari Baloch, the garden's caretaker, who is living out his days there with his young daughter, Feroza.

(2)

The lamp flame of the sun was glimmering slowly before dying, and the corpse of the bright day was about to be interred. The trees of Badshahi Bagh, now standing on their last legs, were bewailing the passing of their prime. The music of the leaves and the songs of the birds were announcing the evening hour when Feroza emerged from the hut, carefully wrapping her soiled dupatta around her shoulders. Her humble shack was not spoiled by the artificial luxuries of this pretentious world and the goods that had become a part of the lives of the rich. A silent joy of contentment enveloped this shack made of grass and hay. This figure of youthfulness before which beauty prostrated itself was untainted by the anxieties and pains of life. She was completely unaware of the passions of youth. Yet an unfamiliar restiveness gripped her heart, searching for what, she didn't know.

(3)

Husain Ali Zamindar's son, Ahsan, had been hunting on the banks of the Yamuna all morning. Piles of water fowl and geese lay here and there; servants, friends, a group of eight or ten people, with five or six rifles, accompanied Ahsan. He was pleased with his success, the companions' unstinted praise of his marksmanship, and intoxicated by his father's wealth and position. Every page from the book of his life said that failure existed in this world only for the poor. The table spread for the afternoon meal was laden with a variety of delicacies of every kind. Water carriers, cleaners, porters, all kinds of menial labourers availed themselves of the bountiful meal, expressing utmost servility by repeated cries of, '*hujoor, hujoor.*' Like flower buds that are surrounded by buzzing honey bees and winged insects as soon they open, that have never even by mistake seen the face of a flower gatherer, Ahsan's 'wealthy' ears were filled with the buzz of flatterers. The arrogance of youth filled his veins. Excessive riches made his days Eid and nights Shab-e barat. In villages, a zamindar is no less than a god and the workers are his slaves, not his tenants. Their money, homes, honour, material goods, all virtually belong to the zamindar.

Ahsan was born and raised in such a family. In fact he was the king of the village though his father was the zamindar. He was the only child. No one could dare to disobey his orders. Two weeks ago he had ordered a dhobi to be evicted, and had allotted his house to one of his policemen.

(4)

When evening drew near, Ahsan washed and changed out of his hunting dress. Over tea he said to one of his companions:

Ahsan: Mir sahib, I heard that Mr Gent went hunting and came back with nothing. Manjhle Miyan ran around for three days and couldn't get even a baby bird. I'm surprised how these people can come back empty-handed. I always get so much that it becomes a challenge to bring it all back with us. Look at the heaps of game lying here and there. The fact is that my aim is always true to the mark.

Mir sahib: My lord, you are unique. The idea of your going out for a hunt spells death for the hunted. Everyone says that there are only two hunters in the whole of Hindustan, the Navab of Hyderabad and your lordship whose aim never goes astray.

Ahsan: I'm surprised that the British praise my hunting skills.

Mir sahib: Yes, sir. The Collector's head cook told me himself that he heard his master praise you.

Ahsan: These people respect good strategy. The last time we went out together and I fired along with Collector sahib. By chance I missed but the sahib appreciated my strategy.

Mir sahib: My lord, they govern through strategy. The daily parade and display by troops, it's strategy after all!

Ahsan: Mir sahib, what's the report on the dhobi?

Mir sahib: Who can disobey your lordship's orders. The villagers did not dare open their mouths to protest.

Ahsan: I know that house belonged to the dhobi, but his arrogance made me angry.

Mir sahib: Your lordship awarded him the right punishment. Now he is living under a tree with his children. This has taught him a lesson for a lifetime.

Ahsan: These low born people have to be straightened out in this way.

Mir sahib: Let us go for a stroll in the Badshahi Bagh.

(5)

The expanse of the sky and the skirt of the earth were both free from the outward manifestation of the sun and the moon. The laughter of the trees was echoing in the air. It was dusk. A light breeze was tickling the green leaves. A bird perched on the quiet bough of the jamun tree, and sang a lament for the transformation of the Shahi Bagh. It was the night of the full moon, and the eyes of the world were fixed on the sky, waiting for the moon to rise when the earthly moon emerged from the hut in Shahi Bagh. Feroza, the picture of perfect beauty, emerged from her hut and looked around. She filled two pails of water from the Begum Pasand Well and brought them to the flower bed. Flowers of all colours and hues were blossoming, and the breeze had filled the garden with their fragrance. She watered the various jasmine flowers. When she got to the rose plant she noticed that two blossoms on a branch were swaying, intertwining in the breeze. Feroza was unaware of the emotion that the flowers symbolized. But nature sparked a fire in her heart on seeing the flowers intertwine. She bent forward to touch them when a gust of breeze brought the blossoms together again, this time in a kissing embrace. A flower herself, Feroza touched the blossoms to her eyes. Her fingers played silently with them, caressing, touching them with her lips, her forehead, still not knowing what she felt and why she was behaving that way. She would hold the flower's stem and let it go, making them swing in the breeze, or she would cup them in her palms. Her actions were utterly innocent and devoid of guile. She wore no *surma* or kohl in her eyes, no powder on her cheeks, and no lavender on her clothes. Her arms were free of bracelets and her body miles away from ornaments. But she was the embodiment of qualities that nature had bestowed on her and regarded with pride. Beautiful black hair fell over and framed her lovely face as she stood, totally oblivious of her surroundings. The rose blossoms were delighted with their success. As she stood beneath the leafy mango tree, a bulbul's warning cry brought her out of this state. Quickly pushing her dishevelled hair into some order she realized that a young man stood gazing at her. He seemed to be lost in his own world. Perceiving a stranger's stares, her Turkish blood began to boil and her eyes flashed red with anger. But even as she seethed with rage, a contradictory emotion rose within her and cooled the flaming anger. She lowered her eyes, a smile played on her lips. But desire made her raise those lowered eyes again and suddenly three different emotions gripped her at once: anger was burnt to ashes and replaced with a quest; the quest took the form of desire and the last emotion that made her lower her eyes yet again was the awareness of herself as a woman. All this happened, but Feroza didn't know what had happened to her.

Translated by Mehr Afshan Farooqi with Richard J. Cohen

Premchand

(1880–1936)

Premchand, born Dhanpat Rai, occupies a very special place in modern Urdu and Hindi literature. He began writing under the assumed name of Navab Rai. Of the twelve novels he wrote, *Godan* (The Gift of a Cow), his last novel, is the most widely read and appreciated. It was for a long time the only Premchand novel available in English translation. Recently three more novels have been translated: *Nirmala* by Alok Rai (1999), *Ghaban* (Stolen Jewels), 2000, by Christopher King, and *Baazar-e Husn* (Courtesan's Quarter), 2003, by Amina Azfar. Premchand's collected works spanning twenty-two volumes have also been published by The National Council for the Promotion of Urdu (Government of India).

Writing in the early decades of the twentieth century, Premchand wrote with a nationalist-didactic fervour. Even though his fiction was mostly about rural north India and concerned with social wrongs and domestic crises in the lives of ordinary people, his plots were complex and unsettling and his humanism breathes life into his characters. The question of women's freedom was particularly relevant in the context of the Freedom Movement that was sweeping across India in those times. Dowry, or rather the lack of it, forced women into mismatched, miserable marriages.

The novel *Nirmala* is a poignant story of a young bride Nirmala who is married to an elderly widower because she does not have a dowry to offer. The jealous husband perceives the possibility of a relationship between her and his stepson Mansaram, even before it happens. This excerpt describes the old man's pathetic efforts to dress up and act young that are ironically undone when he fails to summon up courage to kill a snake that enters the house. Mansaram kills the snake. *Nirmala* was first published in 1928 and was a huge success in its time.

Nirmala

After this extravagant demonstration of his deep feeling for her that day, Munshi Totaram was confident he had secured an unshakeable hold on Nirmala's affections. Nirmala however, far from being drawn towards him, now ceased talking to him altogether in the casual, light-hearted manner which she had earlier adopted with him occasionally. Instead, she began devoting all her time to the care of the children. Every time he returned home he found her sitting with the children. Sometimes she would be feeding them, at other times helping them put their clothes on. Sometimes she would be playing with them, or telling them a story. Nirmala's thirsting heart, disappointed in the expectation of romantic love, turned to the children as a sort of solace. Spending time with them, taking care of them, laughing and playing with them provided some consolation to her denied maternal longings. Whenever she had to spend time with her husband, Nirmala found she was overcome by feelings of awkwardness, and shame and loss of desire, so much so that she found herself wishing to run away. But the honest, simple devotion of the children gladdened her immensely. Initially, Mansaram was a little hesitant about coming near her—but now he too would sometimes come and sit with her. He was roughly the same age as Nirmala, though he was five years behind her in psychological development. Hockey and football constituted the sum of his world; they defined the field of his imagination as well as the whole teeming range of his feelings and desires. He was a handsome, cheerful, and somewhat shy young man of slender build—and to him the family home was simply a place where he came for his meals. For the rest, all his time was spent gadding about all over the place. Listening to him talk about his world of games and sports, for a little while Nirmala was able to forget her own anxieties. She would find herself longing for the days when she herself played with dolls and arranged their weddings— the days which were, alas, recent and still fresh in her memory.

Like many other solitary persons, Munshi Totaram was a passionate soul. For a few days he devoted himself to taking Nirmala to all sorts of entertainments. But when he realized all this was unavailing, he returned to his solitary ways. After a whole day's worth of hard mental toil he longed for some light dalliance. But when he entered his garden of delights he found the flowers withered, the plants wilted, and dust swirling about in the flower-beds—and then he longed to ravage that garden altogether. He could not understand why Nirmala was so cold and unfeeling towards him. He tried all he could glean from the marriage manuals but without success. He was at a loss to figure out what he should do next.

He was sitting immersed in these thoughts one day when his classmate Nayansukhram came and sat with him, and after the usual greetings smiled and said: You must be having the time of your life. There's nothing like the embrace of a young wife to restore one's own youthful passion. You're a lucky fellow! Really, there's no better way to bring back one's lost youth than to marry again. Just think how irksome my existence is. My dear wife clings to me relentlessly, but I'm thinking of marrying a second time anyway. So, if you come to know of a likely bride, arrange it for me, please. I promise I'll give you *pan*s made by her own hands by way of commission some day.

Totaram replied in a sombre tone: Beware, don't ever make that mistake, else you'll regret it. Young lasses need young lads, I tell you. You and I are no good for that purpose now. I tell you honestly, I'm sorry I got myself into this mess by marrying again. I'd thought I'd get a few more years to enjoy the pleasures of life—but I've ended up being worse off.

Nayansukhram: What're you saying! There's nothing to gaining the affections of these wenches—just take them out a few times and praise their looks—and you have them eating out of your hands.

Totaram: I've tried all that. It's no good.

Nayansukhram: So, did you try perfumes, give her flowers, ply her with fancy food?

Totaram: Forget it. I've tried it all. I've tried all there is in the books. It's all bunkum.

Nayansukhram: Well then, I have one piece of advice for you. Get yourself a face-lift. There's a doctor here these days who treats people with an electric current—he can remove all signs of ageing from one's face. Not a wrinkle or grey hair escapes his ministrations. It's pure magic, I tell you—making new men from old.

Totaram: How much does he charge?

Nayansukhram: I've heard he charges five hundred rupees!

Totaram: He must be some sort of trickster, I tell you, robbing fools of their money. He must use some oils or other to make one's complexion appear smooth. I've no trust in these sleazy doctors who advertise their wares on the back pages of magazines anyway. If it had been a small sum of money I might have gone along, just for a lark. But five hundred is a lot of money.

Nayansukhram: It's hardly a lot for you. It's only a month's earnings. I tell you, if I had five hundred I'd have gone in for it right away. An hour of youth is worth much much more than a mere five hundred rupees.

Totaram: Go on, tell me some cheaper remedy, some folk medicine or herb that will have the desired effect without demanding as much of me. As for electricity and radium, they'd better be left for the rich. They're welcome to all that.

Nayansukhram: Then prepare to play the part of the young gallant. Throw away this loose, ill-fitting coat of yours and get yourself a tight-fitting achkan made up in fine cloth, and a finely crinkled pair of payjamas. You'll need a gold chain around your neck, a flashy Jaipuri turban on your head, you'll need surma in your eyes and oil of henna in your hair.

And yes, you'll need to flatten your paunch. Get yourself a double-sized cummerbund. It'll be a little uncomfortable all right, but it'll show up the achkan to advantage. As for the hair-dye, I'll get it for you. Commit some hundred-odd ghazals to memory, and remember to recite a couplet or two when you get the chance. Let your talk be suffused with emotion and colour. Let it appear as though you haven't a thought for the cares of this world, that all your attention is focused on but one object, and that's your beloved. Remain constantly on the lookout for situations in which you demonstrate your courage and manliness. Some time during the night set up a false racket about thieves, and then single-handed, sword in hand, rise to her rescue. But make sure first that there's no real thief about, else you'll be exposed as a fool and coward. If there's ever a real thief about just stand quiet as a mouse, pretend you aren't there at all, but as soon as he goes away you should leap up sword in hand and demand to know the intruder's whereabouts. Just try this out for a month. And if in that time she doesn't start worshipping the very ground you walk on, demand of me what penalty you like.

Totaram laughed these suggestions off at the time, as was only proper for a worldly-wise fellow like him, but deep down some of the suggestions seemed, well, quite appealing really. And there was little doubt they would, in time, be adopted by him. He began them one at a time so people shouldn't notice too sudden a change. First it was the hair, then the surma for his eyes—and in a month or two he was a changed man. That suggestion about memorizing ghazals was farcical, but there was no harm in bragging about his courage from time to time. From that time he carefully set up situations, each day, in which he might boast about his courageous exploits, until Nirmala began to wonder if he was suffering from some form of clinical delusion. Considering he had been a man who was hypochondriac enough to depend on sundry medicaments even to help himself cope with the barest of bread and lentils, there were good grounds for Nirmala's suspicions of his new-found penchant for bravery. It was obviously too much to expect Nirmala to be impressed by these charades, but she did begin to pity him. Pity instead of anger and loathing. A sane person may deserve anger and loathing, but someone who is so obviously touched in the head deserves only pity. Ever so often she would tease him and make fun of him, as people are wont to do with those out of their minds. But she took care to see he didn't actually catch on. She would suppose that the poor fellow was paying for his sins. After all, she thought, all this has become necessary only so that I might forget my misfortunes. But if I can't do anything to alter my fate, why should I torment the poor man?

One evening Totaram returned from his gallivantings at around nine, very much the gallant, and said to Nirmala: I found myself face to face with three rogues today. I'd stepped out in the direction of Shivpur, and it was dark, of course. As soon as I got to the road near the rail track, three fellows armed with swords appeared suddenly. Believe me, all three were fearsome dark fellows. And I was all alone with only this walking stick in my hand. And those three against me, armed with swords. I thought then my time was up, but I thought if I had to die anyway I'd at least die a hero. Just then, one of them challenged me: Give up whatever you've got and slip away quietly or else.

I steadied my stick and said: All I have is this one stick, and it's worth at least one man's head.

I'd barely uttered these words when all three fell upon me with their swords. I fended off their blows with my stick. They attacked me furiously, there was a loud report, and I reacted like lightning to ward off the attack. For some ten minutes those three tried all their skills with their swords and didn't succeed in as much as giving me a scratch. The only pity of it is I didn't have a sword with me. Otherwise not one of them would have survived. But how can I even hope to describe my exploits? My skill and reflexes beggar all description. I amazed even myself with all that agility. When the three of them realized they'd met their match, they sheathed their swords and patted me on the back in congratulation—Brave one, they said, we've never come across a fighter like you. The three of us happily loot villages of more than three hundred inhabitants in broad daylight, but you've worsted us today. We salute you. And with those words they disappeared.

Nirmala replied in all seriousness, albeit with a smile: There must be many sword-marks on this stick?

Munshiji was unprepared for this, but realized he had to say something: I kept foiling them each time. On a couple of occasions, when they did manage to hit my stick, all they gave were glancing strokes incapable of leaving a mark.

He hadn't quite finished saying this when Rukmini Devi burst into the room, wildly excited and panting for breath: Tota, where's Tota. There's a snake in my room. He's somewhere under my bed. I've run away. He must be at least two yards long. He's spread his hood and is breathing out poisonous fumes. Come with me, please, and bring your stick!

Totaram's face went ashen, he began to shake with fright, but he concealed his feelings and said: Snake, where's the snake? I'm sure you're mistaken. Must be a rope.

Rukmini: I tell you, I've seen it with my own eyes. Why don't you come and see for yourself? Shame on you, a man and afraid!

Munshiji did leave the room but stopped again on the veranda. He was quite unable to move further. His heart beat wildly. A snake is a very irritable creature, he thought, and if he bites me it'll surely be the end of me. What he said was: I'm not afraid. It's only a snake, not a tiger. But a stick's not effective with a snake. Let me go and send someone with a spear.

With these words Munshiji stepped out briskly. Mansaram was sitting at his meal. Munshiji having gone away, he pushed his uneaten food aside, picked up his hockey stick and, rushing into the room, pulled the cot aside. The snake was ready for combat, and instead of slinking away reared itself up with its hood on full display. Mansaram quickly stripped the sheet off the bed and threw it over the snake—and then registered three or four smart blows. The snake struggled and died within the sheet. Then he picked it up on his stick and made to leave. Munshiji was now returning, with several people in tow. Seeing Mansaram approach with a dead snake on his stick, Munshiji screamed aloud. But he controlled himself and said: I was hurrying back anyway, why did you rush in and do this? Let someone go and throw it away.

With these words he went bravely and positioned himself at Rukmini's door, and after carefully inspecting the room he stroked his moustaches proudly and said to Nirmala: By the time I could rush back Mansaram had already killed the snake. He's a foolish boy, rushed in with a stick. A snake must always be killed with a spear. That's the trouble with boys. I've killed any number of snakes this way. One must play a snake properly before killing it. Many times, I've simply crushed them to death with my bare hands.

Rukmini was skeptical: Go away, we've all seen how brave you are!

Munshiji was embarrassed: Oh well, at least I'm not asking you for a reward. Go and tell the cook to serve my dinner.

Munshiji went for his meal and Nirmala leaned against the doorframe pensively, thinking to herself: God! Has he really contracted some dreadful illness? Lord, do you wish to make my condition even more pathetic? I can look after him, respect him, devote my entire life to his service, but I cannot do that which I cannot do. It's not in my power to wipe out the difference between our ages. What is it he wants from me? Ah, if only I had figured this out earlier, he wouldn't have had to go to all this trouble and mount this elaborate charade.

Translated by Alok Rai

Pandit Badrinath Sudarshan
(1896–1967)

Pandit Sudarshan was a contemporary of Premchand and also a follower of his style in fiction. Sudarshan, along with Rashidul Khairi, Sultan Haider Josh, Sajjad Hyder 'Yildrim', and Premchand, shares the credit of being one of the earliest exponents of the short story and also popularizing the genre. He focused on social issues and tribulations such as child marriage, widow remarriage, gambling, and drinking. He wrote in a simple, unpretentious style but his stories had interesting plots.

Pandit Sudarshan's narrative style often deployed what can be called a contrast technique, juxtaposing the lives of the poor and rich, rural and urban milieus to bring out the disparities between them. His sympathies lay with the underprivileged and middle classes whom he characterized with sensitivity.

Jan Nisar (Raunaqi, the Devoted One) is among his well-known stories. It presents the dark side of Diwali, the festival of lights, which he describes as 'the illumined night when thousands of greedy people lose all their possessions in the hope of getting wealth.'

Raunaqi, the Devoted One

It was the night of Diwali and the earth was decked out like the sky. There were *diya*s everywhere as far the eye could see; countless like stars. Yet this is the illumined night when thousands of greedy people lose all their possessions in the hope of getting wealth. Then they weep at their folly. There are people who want to taste the sweet fruit of labour without working for it. Hope tricks intelligence. Puran Chand was among those who are drunk on such hopes. He gambled day and night. When Diwali drew near, he even forgot food and sleep while gambling, in the passionate hope that one day he would get lucky and his fortune would shine. Even though each time hope would take the form of craving, Puran Chand did not lose heart and kept throwing his dice on fortune's chessboard. He worked as a treasurer in an office. As Diwali drew near he began to absent himself from work. But he had to report for work towards the end of the month because he had to prepare the salary bills of the employees. As luck would have it Diwali fell on the first of November that year. Money for the salaries arrived on 31 October, but at 4 p.m. All the employees had gone home by then and the money could not be disbursed that day. Puran Chand, however, took out his own salary and went home happy that he was ready for the big gambling on Diwali night. After the Lakshmi Pooja on Diwali night he set out on the pretext of watching the illuminations and reached the gambling house. Bad luck was waiting for him there. He lost all his money very soon after his arrival. Now his state was like the bird whose wings have been clipped before getting a chance to fly. Its helplessness is heart wrenching. It wants to fly. But it looks at its clipped wings and sighs restlessly, unable to do anything. Puran Chand felt that he would lose his luck forever if he didn't do something tonight. He looked around but didn't see any possibility of borrowing money. Suddenly he had an idea and he saw a way to keep his hope alive—the money for the salaries was there in the office and he was the treasurer.

Puran Chand was possessed by this idea. He proceeded to his office in a state of near madness. It was ten o'clock and the garden of delightful diyas was now showing signs of autumn. The bustle in the bazaars had diminished. But Puran Chand had turned a blind eye to everything. He was almost running as if he was on his way to call a doctor for a sick friend or relative. He noticed the watchman as soon as he got to his office and his resolve weakened a little. The watchman called, 'Who is it?'

'It's me, Ganga Din. How are you?'

Ganga Din at once recognized his voice and stepped forward, saying, 'Come on in, Babu sahib. The bazaars are humming with activity, what brings you here tonight?'

Puran Chand's heart was racing but he was in control of his mind. He laughed and said, 'I forgot some papers. Open the office for me.'

Ganga Din complied immediately. If it had been someone else he might have refused. But Puran Chand was the accountant so he did not ask any questions; sometimes, advance funds were needed. Puran went inside, switched on the electric light and sat at his table. His mind was agitated like a pigeon in the grasp of a hawk. He thought repeatedly of the risk involved in what he was about to do but he caught the occasional glimpse of the enticing face of hope in the darkness. Eventually the magic of hope prevailed on him. He opened the safe, extracted four hundred rupees and thrust them in his pocket. Then he locked the room and came outside. At that moment he felt he had crossed the first hurdle in the path of success even though every step he took was taking him farther away from the land of prosperity.

In a short while he was back at the same gambling house where fortunes are ruined and misfortune smiles. Hope was showing him the way but misfortune stood by smiling. Puran Chand placed his bets again and lost everything once more. Now there was darkness all around but more terrifying than the darkness was the light of dawn which was slowly, slowly creeping near. Puran was so terrified of this light that the mere thought of it made his soul shudder and he wished there was a way to stop the sun from rising. But how was that possible? When he walked home his legs were stumbling like a drunk's. His father Rai Sahib Srijan Mal was a rich man. However, he was more famous for his miserliness than his wealth. Puran considered confessing his losses to his father and asking him for a loan of four hundred rupees. But he felt that if his father were generous he would have set him up with a factory and a good income anyway, and now he would gain nothing but humiliation by asking. He couldn't sleep all night but when morning came he was relatively relaxed, and ready with another dishonest idea to cover up his misdeeds. He was thinking about his servant Raunaqi.

(2)

Puran's father, Rai Sahib, had three servants. Raunaqi had served him longer than anyone else. In fact he had spent most of his life in serving Rai Sahib. His employer too respected his senior status and did not scold or berate him. Raunaqi had a sour tongue. His speech was so abrasive that it seemed he was fighting instead of talking. He avoided work as much as he could, and loved scolding other employees and disciplining them. Often servants would complain about his high-handedness but Rai Sahib always took Raunaqi's side. This made Raunqi's face light up. He would boast, 'See, you couldn't touch me!'

But whatever Raunaqi's faults might be it was true that he was willing to lay his life down for his master. Rai Sahib also trusted him with money. He was convinced that Raunaqi would rather die than steal even a paisa of his master's. There had been numerous opportunities for the servant to steal hundreds of rupees but Raunaqi was never tempted by the golden net. Another's man's money was like dust for him. This good quality covered all his shortcomings.

(3)

On the morning after Diwali, Raunaqi was sitting in his room smoking a hookah, eyes closed and deep in thought, when Puran Chand rushed in and said, 'Raunaqi, save me!'

Puran's tone of voice carried a nervous appeal and the hookah fell from Raunaqi's hands. He had a deep affection for Puran and had watched him grow from an infant to an adult. Raunaqi never sacrificed his sleep. But if Puran ever fell sick Raunaqi would spend nights sitting by his bedside. In fact, he had turned down prospects of better paid jobs for the sake of being near Puran. He had no children of his own and loved Puran as a father would. Just as a person who nurtures a plant and begins to love each leaf and every branch of the tree it grows into, so did Raunaqi care for Puran's future. He drew spiritual satisfaction in watching him grow and mature. He always thought of Puran when he was alone; in fact, at that moment he was thinking about him. Why was Rai Sahib delaying Puran's marriage? He felt that his employer's miserliness had something to do with it. His heart sank on seeing Puran Chand rush into his room so suddenly. 'What's wrong, *sarkar?*' he responded, worried.

(4)

As he spoke, Raunaqi picked up a heavy stick lying in a corner and got ready to attack the terrible bandit who he imagined to be in Puran's pursuit. A smile played on Puran's troubled face for a second like a firefly flitting it the night sky. He sighed deeply and said, 'Put away the staff, Raunaqi, we don't need it.'

Raunaqi felt as if a load had been removed from his chest. Putting away the stick, he said, 'What calamity then has made my sarkar look so dejected?'

Puran Chand cast his eyes around like a thief before a crime. He was beside himself with anxiety and was afraid that someone would hear him. He spoke in a low tone. 'Truly I've been struck by misfortune. You can save me, Raunaqi. Will you do something for me?'

Raunqi puffed his chest and replied, 'I am ready to jump into hell for you. Just give the order.'

Puran Chand's face lit up. A ray of hope shone through the darkness of despair. He took out a valuable necklace from his pocket, thrust in into Raunaqi's hands and said, 'Take it to the market and sell it. I'm in desperate need of money.'

Raunaqi was stunned. The necklace frightened him. He looked like a man who had been bitten by a snake. He was rendered speechless. Thousands of questions crowded his mind. What dire need had prompted Puran to sell a gold necklace? He wasn't poor. His father Rai Srijan Mal could buy half the city if he wanted. Why would his son have to sell a piece of jewellery? It then dawned on him that Puran was hiding something from his father; that his father did not know about the necklace. He just couldn't understand why such a need had arisen. He gave Puran a bewildered look. The look gave away his feelings. Noticing his hesitation, Puran immediately became nervous. The ray of hope vanished.

Raunaqi asked, 'What can be the matter that you want to sell this necklace?'

Puran Chand's eyes filled with tears. He did not reply, just put back the necklace in his pocket and began to leave. He was the very picture of despair. Raunaqi's heart sank. He ran after him asking how much money was needed. Like a thirsting rice field that had been watered Puran responded in a voice filled with hope. 'Four hundred.'

'When do you want it?'

'Right now.'

Raunaqi had saved up some six hundred rupees which represented his lifetime's savings. He sent all but three or four rupees from his salary back home to his family. The savings he deposited in a box which he buried in a corner of his room. He thought that instead of selling the necklace he would give Puran the money from his savings. Puran wouldn't be so hard pressed for cash in the future; eventually he would return his money and Raunaqi would give him back the necklace. So he took the necklace and said, 'Sarkar, consider your work done.'

Puran breathed a sigh of relief. He felt Raunaqi was not a servant but an angel of mercy.

(5)

After a little while, Raunaqi shut the door of his room and began to dig the ground in the corner. His heart beat wildly. Even though he hadn't committed a theft or done anything with a wrong intent, still he was shaken to the core of his being. He desperately wanted to help Puran, and save him from the humiliation of admitting his misdeed in front of his father. Even though he was an uneducated man he realized that Puran's offence, about which he was still in the dark, would affect Puran's prospects and standing in his father's estimation. This thought made his heart squirm. He dug the ground as fast as he could, counted and took out the money and levelled the earth again. Once again his face regained its former complacency. Shortly after this Puran Chand came back looking hopeful and scared at the same time. He asked hesitantly, 'Raunaqi?'

Raunaqi sat smoking his hookah. He did not reply but gestured towards the head of his bed. When Puran saw the money he was so relieved, almost as if he was a dead person who got life again. He looked at Raunaqi with eyes full of gratitude and left.

But Raunaqi was jolted from his soporific state like someone who all of a sudden discovers the loss of a precious thing. He had forgotten to bury the necklace. He shot to the bed like an arrow. The necklace lay by his pillow. He thought it would be best to wait for the night for it wouldn't be safe to bury it in the middle of the day. What if someone got suspicious? He tucked the piece of jewellery in the cloth he wore around his waist and busied himself in work. But he felt restless all day.

When night fell he shut the door of his room and started digging in the corner. But his hands were lifeless and his heart was racing as if there were police chasing to arrest him. He felt tired and worn out as if suffering from a long illness. All these symptoms foreshadowed the events to follow. Poor Raunaqi, unaware of these omens, kept on digging, compelling his lifeless fingers to burrow into the ground. Suddenly there was a knock on the door. He felt his worst fears were coming true. Nervously he got up and listened, hoping that the knocking might just be a figment of imagination. But the knocking persisted. Beads of sweat appeared on his face. It was a cold night but he felt he was going to suffocate. Summoning up courage, he inquired, 'Who is it at this time of night?'

'Open the door.'

The colour drained from Raunaqi's face. It was Rai Sahib's voice. Raunaqi's state was like a goat cowering on hearing a lion's roar. He saw dishonour dancing before his eyes. He tried to speak but his words stuck in his throat.

'Open the door!' Rai Sahib said in a stern voice.

Raunaqi hid the necklace under the mattress, snuffed out the flickering earthen lamp and opened the door. His feet felt like lead.

'What happened to the lamp?' Rai Sahib said, stepping inside.

'I snuffed it out, sarkar,' Raunaqi replied.

'I saw the light a moment ago. Why did you snuff it out? Light it again.'

Raunaqi's fears were becoming tangible. He began to make excuses, hoping to tide over this bad moment so that he could offer an appropriate explanation for his behaviour later. Time is crucial in covering up crime. But Rai Sahib did not give him the slack of time. He took a matchbox from his pocket and lighted the lamp himself. Looking at the mound of disturbed earth in the corner he asked, 'What were you doing?'

Hands folded in supplication, Raunaqi replied, 'Sarkar, I save a part of my salary and bury it here for hard time's sake.'

'But what were you burying today? You haven't been paid yet!'

The tongue of falsehood was silenced. Rai Sahib stepped forward, pushed the loose earth aside and saw the little bundle. Then he shook the mattress. He presumed that Raunaqi had been gambling because he could never imagine, let alone suspect him of dishonesty. He was taken aback to find the necklace under the mattress. He began to shake from head to foot. Had this crime been committed by someone else Rai Sahib might have reacted differently, even forgiven the perpetrator. But Raunaqi's betrayal made his blood boil. He spoke in the coldest of tones which is more dangerous the worst of tempers, 'How did you get this? I bought it only a few days ago.'

Raunaqi may have had a hundred faults but he was not a thief. In fact, Rai Sahib often praised him for his honesty. The reputation he had earned in a life's work was about to crumble into dust. Now is the time to make a clean breast of the whole affair, he thought. After all Puran Chand is Rai Sahib's son, he wouldn't punish him too harshly. Having thought this through, he lifted his head, joined his hands in supplication and began, 'Sarkar, the matter is....' Then he saw Puran Chand who stood there shivering as if gripped by high fever. He looked at Raunqi in a strange manner, then lowered his gaze. Raunaqi felt as Puran had said: I trusted you but you have betrayed my trust. I wish I had known so that I would have saved myself from shame.

Just as a paper kite changes direction with the flow of the breeze, that look from Puran changed Raunaqi's resolve. He decided that he would take the blame and save Puran's reputation. He said, 'Sarkar, I stole the necklace.'

Rai Sahib sat down on Raunaqi's bed. He felt as bad as though he had suffered a loss of thousands of rupees. Puran Chand on the other hand was exultant. There is no dearth of people in this world who can tell lies for their own sakes but how many can lie for others?

Rai Sahib was quiet for a while, then he said, 'Get out of my house before daybreak. That's your punishment.'

Both Raunaqi's and Puran's eyes filled with tears.

(6)

Rai Sahib Srijan Mal died a year after this episode. Now Puran was the sole heir of his father's wealth. After the cremation ceremonies had been taken care of, he sent a money order of four hundred rupees to Raunaqi with a letter asking him to come back. The money order came back undelivered after a week. There was a letter from Raunaqi's brother with it. He wrote that Raunqi had passed away almost a year ago. He was always sad, wrote his brother; it seemed as though he had a malady but no one knew what ailed him.

Puran Chand was deeply affected by the letter. He mourned Raunqi's death; his tears wouldn't stop. He gave up gambling and built a charitable boarding house in his memory. There is a life-size portrait of Raunaqi in the building. People laugh at this and think Puran Chand a fool. Only Puran Chand knows that this tribute to Raunaqi's loyalty and sacrifice is a mere particle of dust compared to the sun.

Translated by Mehr Afshan Farooqi

Hijab Imtiaz Ali
(1903–99)

Hijab was born in Hyderabad, India. Her mother, Abbasi Begum, wrote for women's journals. Inspired by her mother, Hijab began writing at an early age and became famous by the time she was twenty. She married the writer-publisher Imtiaz Ali Taj and moved to Lahore where she lived until her death a few years ago. Known for her boldness, she was the first Indian woman to earn a pilot's license.

Hijab's work shows the strong influence of French Romanticism and Turkish fiction. The recent republication of her work has generated renewed interest in her writing, especially as a prose stylist and feminist. Her known works are the novella *Meri Natamam Mohabbat* (My Unrequited Love) published in 1932, and the Freudian novel *Andhere Khwab* (Dark Dreams), 1950. The heroine of *Meri Natamam Mohabbat*, modelled on Hijab herself, is a woman of indomitable spirit, who revolts against traditional values such as arranged marriage. Hijab creates a world which is populated by strong-willed women and weak males. There is tragedy, though, since it has the requisite sombreness of the exotic environment in which her characters live. But the tragic characters are males, not females! She also published several collections of horror stories.

In the story presented here, a dejected husband falls off the balcony of his house in order to attract his wife's attention.

And He Had an Accident

Laid on a stretcher, he was brought to the operating theatre. Today, he had been looking around, standing on the balcony of the upper storey of his house. The morning was brilliant and extremely beautiful, when all of a sudden he fell several feet to the ground. Apparently no one had pushed him, neither had the floor of the balcony been so weak that it had given way under his weight. Then how had he fallen down? By the way, what was so strange about it? It was an accident like the ones that keep on happening every day. Even he himself was not conscious enough to think over this matter. Nor was he the nit-picking sort. It's obvious that it was a slip of the foot that made him lose his balance and fall from such a great height. As far as words were concerned, this explanation seemed good enough: he had fallen due to loss of balance, and accidents do happen that way.

When he was brought to the operating theatre, although his body was unfeeling and motionless like a corpse, his mind bore the vast agitation of the ocean. The same ebb and flow, the same stormy billows—the human brain is never devoid of anxiety and strife. He was totally unaware of his surroundings. He could see neither the white caps of the nurses nor the masked faces of the doctors. His eyes were sightless to the glare of the bright lights of the operating theatre and his ears deaf to the sound of scissors and scalpels. It was so because when we behold even an ant in our past, we are unconscious of a mountain in the present. He had no knowledge of why he was brought there, yet the ears of his memory and his mind's eye could see far in the distance.

'Munoo! Munoo!' The voice fell in his ears. He wondered whose name it was, still reverberating in the deep valleys of the past. And suddenly he remembered that Munoo was a puppy that he had borrowed from his friend and lovingly looked after. Munoo was so tiny that it could not even suck milk and so the whole night long it would moan in its pain-filled voice which disgusted the neighbours. And quite apart from the neighbours, his own mother had an unreasonable hatred for the puppy!

So many times his mother had scolded him angrily, 'Get rid of this puppy or I'll poison it! The wretch keeps on screaming the whole night through!'

But today, after so many years, why was he reminded of Munoo? He was now thirty years old and Munoo was a forgotten silliness of his childhood!

Then it so happened that Munoo was not poisoned but nature itself turned against it. While romping on the road, it was run over by a bicycle. After this accident, Munoo became the apple of his mother's eye. Ointment was bought for Munoo's wounds, from the market. The puppy was treated and bandaged. A new bed was made and its untimely wailing was tolerated with fortitude. Poor puppy! It was injured. He realized that this dangerous accident had made the puppy pitiable in the eyes of his mother.

Gradually the sound of Munoo's wailing faded and another incident of recent years rose on the screen of his mind. That day, on Friday, he got leave from the office a little early. On the way home, he decided to go boating with his wife Feroza and take some refreshments along as well. Enroute was the house of a good friend. He went there and invited him to join them. Momentarily, he thought that the friend he had invited was disliked by his wife. She might be displeased, but then, he thought that he would persuade her. After all, Ahmad was not as bad as she thought. No denying that he was a liar but who doesn't lie? He bought chicken sandwiches and cheese fingers from a restaurant and hurried home.

Carrying bags of snacks, he wanted to shout with joy like a child while hugging Feroza, and tell her that he had got an extra holiday. On reaching home he cried out, 'Feroza! Feroza! Look what I've brought! We were let off from the office early today!'

His wife, leaving her chores, came into the room.

'Whatever have you brought?'

'Chicken sandwiches and cheese fingers! We're going boating!' he said laughingly.

'A holiday from the office makes you as excited as a kid escaping from school,' she teased him.

A little offended, he said, 'If you went to the office everyday, you'd understand that its rules and regulations mean the same to us as school and captivity mean to a child. OK, put all these things in a tiffin basket and fill up a thermos flask with tea. We have to rush as I've told Ahmad to arrange for a boat. He'll be waiting for us on the beach.'

'Why do we need Ahmad to accompany us?' she said, somewhat displeased. 'The boat could've been arranged easily once we'd reached the seaside. I don't like Ahmad's loud ways.'

'You're being unreasonable. He's all right. Why are you so put off by him?' he said.

'Well, because he's a tittle-tattle! He carries a tale from one person and relates it to another. Isn't this enough? I hate such dangerous people!'

He laughed. 'Such people are the life and soul of the party. Just forgive him this time and don't show your displeasure so obviously. He noticed it last time too.'

'Still he agreed to come today? Who would like such shamelessness?' Feroza said scornfully.

'OK! OK! Put up with him just for today. I'll never invite him again. He'll be waiting for us on the shore right now.'

And they reached the seaside.

By pure coincidence, this small party had been boating for not even half an hour when a dark cloud rose, a strong gale blew, and the gusts of wind hit so hard that they lost control of the craft and it overturned.

After an hour, he and his wife reached the shore safely but Ahmad was not to be found. Everybody thought he had been drowned. Somebody said that he had been eaten by the fish. Someone else said that he must have fainted from loss of breath and been carried away by the waves.

He felt that this tragic accident had had a great impact on Feroza. She said in a sad, tearful voice, 'Alas! Who knew that Ahmad would be separated from us like this?'

'I thought you'd be happy!' he commented sarcastically.

'I wasn't his enemy.'

But the next day, the fishermen found an unconscious Ahmad. Before bringing him to his house to be looked after, he first spoke to his wife. 'If you don't disagree, may I bring Ahmad here? He can go back to his own home after he feels better.'

Feroza answered emotionally, 'Do bring him here. This accident in the water has washed away my hatred.'

And Ahmad was brought to his house.

He noticed that this accident had changed his wife's attitude completely. Earlier, she couldn't even tolerate Ahmad's presence but now the same Feroza felt pleasure in looking after all his needs.

He thought that this accident had made Ahmad someone deserving of pity in the eyes of Feroza.

He felt a certain similarity between his mother and his wife. Munoo's incident and now this event! Both women were similar in this respect, but poles apart in others. Who would tolerate a woman who did not resemble his mother in some ways? If Feroza had been a totally different woman from his mother, as different as day is from night, she could have been acceptable. But his perplexity was that although seemingly alike they were still dissimilar. Alas! This had caused conflict. The heart's perturbation had increased.

A few days before today's accident, he had started feeling a little aggrieved with his wife. He loved her deeply but at the same time his heart was full of complaints against her. He could never see his grievances in a practical way; how could he? He was himself unaware of the reason for these grievances. Then how could he quarrel with his wife or complain about her?

He remembered. One night he and his wife had argued over some small matter. When he got up in the morning he felt ill. He was sure that his wife would be anxious because of his pain and maybe even massage his head. But it didn't happen that way. Feroza gave him a frowning look and said, 'It's time for the office. Get up, have your breakfast and leave.' And he didn't know how his fever vanished and his headache disappeared.

In minutes he was ready and gone. But sorrow and depression made him slack and idle. In the afternoon a friend took him along to his house. He played cards with him all evening and his dejection apparently dissipated. But when he was climbing the steps to his own house, his anger resurfaced unconsciously and a sea of despair appeared in his eyes. In low spirits, he passed by his wife and went to his room.

'What's wrong with you, darling? Come to me!' His wife's loving words echoed in his waiting ears. Forgetting everything, he was about to run to his wife when he realized that this was not her voice but the sound of the radio on the upper storey. A play was being broadcast—perhaps his ears had heard what they were yearning for. Whatever it was, it wasn't his wife speaking. He stood still and depression swept over him.

Next day, he was standing on the balcony of the upper storey, looking around. The morning was brilliant and extremely beautiful when suddenly—all at once, no one knows how—he fell several feet to the ground. And his wife left all her numerous tasks to sit by his bedside—yes! By his bedside!

And that is how accidents happen!

Translated by Atiya Shah

Rashid Jahan
(1905?–52)

Rashid Jahan, the eldest daughter of Shaikh Abdullah, founder of Aligarh Muslim Girls' College, was a physician. More importantly, she was one of the four young writers whose contributions made up the so-called provocative collection of short stories, *Angare* (Burning Coals), 1932. The writers of the *Angare* group were passionate proponents of socially relevant literature. Rashid Jahan became a core member of the Progressive Writers' Association. As a physician she was dedicated to serving poor and socially repressed women. Her fiction reflects her intimate knowledge of the lives of Indian women. Her early death from cancer cut short her literary career.

'*Dilli ki Sair*' (A Visit to Delhi) is about a woman who eagerly accompanies her husband in the hope of getting to see the famous sights of Delhi. However, her husband leaves her at the station with the luggage and goes off with a friend he met at the station for lunch. When he returns several hours later, she has no desire left for sightseeing and wishes to return home. The irony of the situation is not lost on the reader, neither is Jahan's intention to make a strong statement on the subject of the husband's thoughtlessness.

A Visit to Delhi

'Oh please! Wait for me.'

This voice came from the veranda and a young girl emerged, wiping her hands on her *kurta*. Among all her friends, Malka Begum was the first to have travelled in a train. And that too all the way from Faridabad to Delhi! Even the far-off neighbours had thronged to hear the tale of her journey.

'Come quickly, if you must. I am tired of repeating everything again! May God not let me make up stories. I have related this story a hundred times already. Well, we sat in the train from here and reached Delhi. There "he" met some wretched station-master acquaintance of his. Leaving me near the luggage, "he" vanished. And I, perched on the luggage, wrapped in a *burqa*, there I sat. First this damned burqa, and then these cursed men. Men are no good anyway but when they see a woman sitting like this they just circle around her. There is no opportunity even to chew pan. One damn fellow coughs, another hurls a remark. And I...breathless with fear, and so hungry...only God knows, and the Delhi station! Bua, even the Fort would not be as huge. Wherever one looked, one saw nothing but the station, the railway lines, engines, and goods trains. And what scared me the most were those blackened men who live in the engines!'

'Who live in the engines?' someone interrupted.

'Who live? How do I know? Wearing blue clothes, some bearded, some clean-shaven, swinging with one arm from the moving engine. And the onlookers...their hearts leap into their mouths. And the sahibs and memsahibs; there are so many of them at the Delhi station, Bua, that one loses count. Hand in hand they walk by, talking *gitpit gitpit*. And our Indian brothers...they stare at them so wide-eyed that I wonder their eyes don't pop out! One of them even said to me, "Just show your face." At once I...'

'Did you?' someone teased.

'Think of Allah, Bua! Did I go all the way to show my face to those wretches? My heart started pounding madly.' She added angrily, 'If you want to hear, don't interrupt me in mid-sentence!' Everyone became quiet. Such delightful events rarely occurred in Faridabad. And women had come from far to listen to Malka's experiences.

'And the hawkers, Bua, not like the ones we have. Clean khaki clothes, sometimes white, but the dhotis of some were quite dirty. Carrying baskets, "*Pan-Bidi-Cigarette*"...or "Toys!" "Toys!"...Selling sweets in closed boxes, they run all around. One train came in and there was so much noise that it tore the eardrums. Coolies shouting at the top of their voices and hawkers howling in the ears. And the passengers...piling over each other. In all of this poor me perched on top of the luggage! How many pushes and shoves did I suffer! And in my nervousness reciting *Jal tu jalal tu aiyee bala ko tal tu*. At long last the train started moving. Then started the bickering between the coolies and the passengers: "One rupee." "No, two annas." One hour of bickering before the station cleared. Did I say cleared? The damned scoundrels hung on. After two hours "he" came along twirling his moustaches. With what nonchalance he said, "If you are hungry shall I get you some *puris*, etc...yes? I have just eaten at the hotel."

'I said, "For God's sake take me back to my house. I have had enough of this 'visit to Delhi'. May no one ever go with you, not even to paradise. What a great trip you brought me on!"

'The train for Faridabad was ready. He found a seat for me and pulled a long face. "It's your wish. If you don't want to enjoy a tour of the city, don't. Don't blame me!"'

Translated by Syeda S. Hameed and Sughra Mehdi

Ghulam Abbas
(1909–82)

Ghulam Abbas was born in Amritsar, in the Punjab of undivided India. He began writing while he was still in high school and also received early recognition of his talent. He was the editor of the important and popular children's journal *Phul* (Flowers) from 1927 to 1938. *Phul* published children's stories written by well-known authors. He worked for All India Radio as editor of its programme journal, *Awaaz*. After Partition he worked for Radio Pakistan in almost the same capacity as editor of its journal, *Ahang*. He also worked for the BBC as producer for Urdu programmes from 1951 to 1954.

Abbas's forté was writing unpretentious, effortless, uncomplicated prose. He did not write many stories (only thirty-nine in a long career), but occupies a significant position in the canon of the Urdu short story for many interesting and important reasons. Some of his short stories became extremely popular among readers, especially the title story of his first collection, '*Anandi*'. In a career spanning five decades he came into contact with at least two important and persuasive literary movements but he held his own and refused to be drawn into identifying his art or thought with any given political or philosophical position. He chose to write about the (extra) ordinary lives of the common man. The plots of his stories are more in the nature of observations than concrete events.

The short story '*Chakkar*' (The Clerk) reminds one of Chekhov's stories but it has an interesting, unusual twist to it: a wish for rebirth.

The Clerk

Seth Channamal's clerk Chelaram worked from morning to mid-afternoon at Sethji's mansion, engaged in bookkeeping and other secretarial work. Right after that, he would go for debt collection. One June afternoon, he picked up his cloth bag in which he kept papers and such, and went by Sethji's front room. Sethji was reclining against stuffed bolster pillows, taking drags from a long-stemmed hookah. Noticing Chelaram, he called out from behind the hanging bamboo screen, 'Hey Munimji, don't forget to go to the warehouse, and remember the money has to be deposited in the bank today. And those registered letters, they are important. I assume you have my doctor's prescription and the list of books?'

Chelaram replied 'Yes' to all of these reminders and set off.

He was fifty or so years old and still strong-limbed. It was obvious that he must have been a well-built and healthy man in his youth. He always wore the same kind of clothes in all seasons: a long loose shirt made from homespun cotton, a thick *mulmul* dhoti, a checked cloth coat, black *topee*, and kid leather shoes. Since he walked a great deal, these shoes were more durable than boots or open sandals. The shoes pinched his feet a lot at first but gradually after the ankle joints and toes developed dark calluses, the pain went away.

Other than the above clothing, an old umbrella with a fashionable ivory handle had also become a part of his attire. This umbrella once belonged to Sethji's oldest son who had discarded it some time ago. Seth Channamal, perceiving that the umbrella would no longer be of any use at their house, gave it to Munimji. But Chelaram had to pay heavily for the umbrella, as we shall see. In the past, Sethji may have had some qualms in dispatching Munimji on frequent errands to remote sites in the harsh summer months. But now, having presented the umbrella, his conscience was totally guilt-free.

When Munimji set out, the sun was right in the middle of the sky and shadows from the walls had receded to a mere line that brokenly followed the road's edge for miles. The sun beat down so strong and intense that one's eyes squeezed shut almost instinctively. But even through closed eyes the light seeped in under the lids and darkness tinged with red floated inside them. Although Chelaram had unfurled his umbrella, the hot rays filtered through its worn cloth and leapt on his face like fevered breaths.

Chelaram walked on, holding the umbrella at an angle to protect his head and chest from the slaps of the hot June wind. He must have walked two hundred yards from the *kothi* when he hung the cloth bag on the curved handle of the umbrella and fished a packet of *bidi*s and a matchbox from his coat pocket. He lit a bidi and contemplated how to organize the different tasks assigned to him so that he would have to walk a little less.

Today, he had to collect money from six different people. Two of them lived nearby but the remaining four lived in separate corners of the city. He could not go to the bank until he collected money from them, and the cashier at the bank shut the window at 3 o'clock. Then there were some important registered letters that had to be dispatched that day. Sethji had reminded him of those as he was leaving. Post offices were usually crowded these days and it might take an hour to send those letters off. He had to go to the warehouse at the railway station; this would take him at least an hour or an hour-and-a-quarter. In addition to all this he had to get Sethji's wife's prescription filled and buy schoolbooks for their second son who had passed the sixth grade this year.

By 6 p.m., he had run his errands thanks to his kid leather shoes, his packet of bidis and the cool water that was provided in the wayside sheds that had been set up by the municipal committee and also by a few kind-hearted businessmen in front of their shops. He had toured the capital just like a wilful tourist from a far off land who considers it obligatory to walk every street and every bazaar in a famous ancient city. When the hot wind bothered him he would smoke a bidi to distract himself. When the bidi's smoke parched his throat he would soothe it with water from the wayside sheds. When his shoes got filled with dust or it simply felt too hot, he would stand under some shade and shake the dust out of his shoes. And if there were a municipal tap at hand he would wet his feet as coach drivers cool the wheels of their carriages when they get heated.

When he had set forth from the *kothi,* the day's errands loomed like a mountain before him, but now he was amazed at how he accomplished all those tasks, not just anyhow but in a manner that would please his employer. Only one defaulter had made him wait for ages and not paid up. He also had to stand and wait for the prescription to be filled because the chemist at the dispensary where Seth Channamal had his account did not like Chelaram and deliberately served him at the very end. But he didn't have to wait long at the post office because he had selected one in a less populated, remote area; most people were not even aware that there was a post office there. The warehouse job had been a walkover because the expected goods hadn't arrived yet.

When he got back to the kothi the sunlight's intensity had paled. A steamy heat was rising from the roads as they were sprinkled with water. Instead of a cooling effect it created a stultifying humidity. Sounds of laughter and conversation floated to him from Sethji's front room and when he reached the doorway, he paused just outside by the hanging screen. He could identify the voices very well. One voice was Seth Banke Bihari's who was a neighbour and a distant relative of Seth Channamal. He was a moneylender too, though his was a smaller business. Seth Banke Bihari would generally close shop at 6 p.m. and come over to chat with Channamal. On most occasions, Banke Bihari brought along his friend who was a business contractor. This friend was well known in élite circles for his engaging small talk and repertoire of jokes and witticisms.

Then there was Sethji's brother-in-law. He was a good-for-nothing fellow and bankrupt to boot. He lived off Sethji's scraps. The brother-in-law loved to join in these informal gossip sessions. And Sethji enjoyed these meetings tremendously because he was tired of sitting alone or sleeping in his room all day and this small gathering at home provided him with much entertainment.

Chelaram coughed discreetly from the door several times but Sethji was so engrossed in talking with his friends that he did not hear him. Seth Banke Bihari's contractor friend was holding forth on the cycle of births and rebirths. He was saying—

Gentlemen, let us give this some serious thought. Now most of us believe that this is the *kaliyug* and that the world is full of sin and only sinful people live here. If this is true then the world's population should decline because when a sinner dies s/he cannot be born again in human form but in the form of some lower species like a bird or animal. Thus there should be more animals and fewer humans. But this is not the case; in fact it is the opposite. So it's obvious that we are not committing sins; we are performing acts of goodness and therefore we are reborn as humans.

Suddenly, the contractor looked towards the doorway and stopped in mid-sentence. Then every one looked at the doorway. Chelaram, not being able to stand much longer at the door, had in an impulsive moment lifted the hanging screen and stepped inside.

He was in bad shape. His legs were shaking and his face looked strangely haggard. His salt and pepper moustache, eyelashes and eyebrows were layered with dust. His eyes were so red they seemed to hurt. His skin was an unhealthy reddish black from the slaps of the hot wind and the rigours of an entire day spent in the sun. His face was like that of a corpse on a pyre as the flames begin to lick the flesh.

The base of his cap was dark with sweat and he had perspired so much at the armpits that his coat was drenched from the chest to the elbows. His dhoti was speckled with crusted mud and he looked so exhausted that it seemed he would fall down at any moment.

Realizing that conversation had ceased and all eyes were focused on him, he became a little nervous. But he stepped forward, put the cloth bag on the floor and proceeded to pull out books, receipts, medicine bottles, prescriptions, and other papers, arranging them before Sethji. He wanted to report about the goods that hadn't arrived when Sethji motioned him to be quiet and said with a degree of kindness: 'Munimji, you go home now. We'll talk about it tomorrow morning.'

Chelaram's house was some two miles from his employer's kothi. When he finally staggered home it was late evening. He went inside, took off all his clothes save his dhoti, and stepped out into the open area in front of his house. There was a bamboo cot leaning against the wall near his front door. Without bothering to ask whom it belonged to, he lowered it to the ground, and numb with exhaustion he collapsed on the cot.

Perhaps his ailing wife, who was crouching near a wood stove preparing the evening meal, said something. But he heard nothing. His younger daughter came and put her arms around him but he brushed her off harshly or perhaps she withdrew involuntarily upon noticing his terrible state.

For fifteen minutes he lay still with his eyes closed. Slowly he regained his senses. And with the awareness of his body came the sensation of a slow ache and cramps in different parts, particularly his ankles and lower back. He began to groan softly. He turned this way and that, stretching his legs fully, then pulling them in close to his body. He straightened his shoulder blades, tucking them behind his head. He pulled up his ankles to nestle against his thighs, flexing his hands and then his toes, spreading them out and pulling them in. If any of these movements made his joints pop, he would feel a great measure of relief. Thus tossing and turning he began to feel better and fell asleep. But he had not slept long when a noise near his bedside woke him up. It was his neighbour Rolu, returning home after a long day of work driving his horse carriage. He had unhitched the horse from the carriage, removed the harness and yoke, and put a loose rope around its neck, the end of which was in his hand. A masseur with a thick wad of cloth was giving the horse's back and hind legs a good massage. It seemed that the masseur was exerting himself considerably because he was grunting with every stroke. Rolu held a cloth too and was busy wiping off sweat from the horse's neck, joints, and stomach.

The rope around the horse's neck was studded with brass rings with tiny bells on them. The horse shook its mane, flipped his head restlessly and with each movement the bells would tinkle and flash in the dark with a silvery sound. Every now and then the horse stamped his hoofs; occasionally he would neigh loudly and kick out with his hind legs. Rolu would then soothe him with clicking noises and loving words: 'Come now, my baby, my precious, we are almost done.'

Chelaram observed this display with absorption. However, he tired of it quickly and turning over, shut his eyes once more. His wife called out from the stuffy room: 'Come and eat.'

Chelaram did not respond. He lay still with his eyes shut. After a few minutes his wife came to the door and said, 'Food is waiting, do come inside now.'

Chelaram remained silent.

What was he thinking? Was he thinking about the cycle of birth and death? Was he silently wishing that he be born a horse in his next life....

Translated by Mehr Afshan Farooqi

Ahmed Ali

(1910–94)

Ahmed Ali, distinguished short story writer, novelist, poet, translator, critic, anthologist, and diplomat, was born in Delhi. After his father's death in 1919, he lived for a few years with his uncle in Azamgarh, Uttar Pradesh, from where he was sent to Aligarh for higher studies. From Aligarh, he transferred to Lucknow University for his M.A. in English literature. In Lucknow, he met Sajjad Zaheer and Mahmuduzzafar and the three of them along with Rashid Jahan formed the core of the All India Progressive Writers' Movement (PWM) in 1936.

Out of the nine stories published in *Angare* (Burning Coals), the book that initiated the PWM, two were Ahmed Ali's. His first collection of Urdu stories *Sholay* (Flames) was published in 1936, the same year in which the PWM was launched. However, when the Progressive ideology became synonymous with the ideology of the Communist Party, Ali moved away from the group. He continued to write in his own romantic-realistic style and published a novel in English, *Twilight in Delhi* (1940) that is perhaps his best and most well-known work. Some of his other collections of Urdu short fiction are *Hamari Gali* (Our Lane), 1942; *Qaid Khana* (Prison House), 1944; and *Maut se Pahale* (Before Death), 1945. Among his important translations are the *Al-Quran* (1984), *The Golden Tradition* (1973), which is a critical anthology of Urdu poetry, and *The Flaming Earth: Poems from Indonesia* (1949).

Ali migrated to Pakistan in 1948, served in the Pakistani Foreign Service and died in Karachi. In 1981, he was awarded the *Sitara-e Imtiaz*, the highest honour conferred by the Government of Pakistan, and in 1993 the degree of doctor of letters from Karachi University.

'*Hamari Gali*' is generally regarded as his best work in Urdu. Ali has translated many of his Urdu stories himself. His translation is a free interpretation of the Urdu original. I have taken the liberty of touching up his translation of '*Hamari Gali*' to make it more contemporary.

Our Lane

I used to live in Koocha Pandit. The door of my room was divided into two halves. By closing the lower one the upper half was turned into a window. This window opened on the narrow road. In front was the shop of Siddiq the grocer, and adjoining it the shop of Aziz the carpenter; and all about were the shops of the palanquin bearers, the chemist, the pan sellers, and a few others, like the butcher's, the general merchant's, and the sweet seller's.

People could go to other localities through our quarter; all sorts of men passed below my window. Sometimes a person dressed all in white went by, finding relief from the scorching summer sun under his umbrella. Sometimes a person dressed up in English clothes went by, stepping lightly over puddles of water or jumping quickly away as someone threw more on the road, avoiding the urchins or glaring at them angrily for gazing and staring at him. Sometimes the passer-by would get exasperated and raise his stick or umbrella to strike the boys, but the urchins would run away and shout, 'See, what a sight, boys!'

Then the gruff voice of Mirza the milkseller would be heard, 'What are you up to, you brats! Don't you have anything to do at home?' And if someone were nearby, Mirza would complain, 'Look at their mothers. They leave their children to roam like consecrated bulls. And these brats have nothing better to do besides uttering profanities and tomfoolery.'

His small red eyes would glow and, scratching his triangular beard, he would turn to some customer and take curds out from the earthen pot or milk from the cauldron and, putting a little cream on top of it, pass it on to the customer.

They said that Mirza came of good stock. His father had turned him out of the house when still a boy for not doing well at his lessons, and after roaming about aimlessly for some days, Mirza opened a shop. His father asked him a number of times after that to forgive him and come back home, but Mirza refused. Then he got married, and his business began to flourish. His milk *peras* were known for their excellence, and his milk was always delicious. Whenever a person came to buy milk, Mirza tossed it from an earthen cup into a bowl and back again with a swinging movement until it swished with froth and bubbled. Then he extracted a fraction of cream from the top of the milk in the cauldron with a flat spoon so skilfully that the milk was not disturbed.

Sometimes his wife sat in the shop. She had become old. Her face was wrinkled, her back bent, and her gums toothless. Her broad forehead and fair complexion proclaimed that she belonged to a good family.

But now their business had become slack; they had grown old and could not work as hard. With their only son dead, there was no one to lend them a hand.

During the days of the freedom movement when non-cooperation was surging like a wave from one end of the country to the other, Mirza's son took part in a procession with his friends. The very air was ringing with shouts of '*Bande matram*' and '*Mahatma Gandhi ki jai*'. A battalion of 'tommies' stood at the Clock Tower fully armed. The superintendent of police, the deputy commissioner, and a few other Englishmen watched nervously the fury of the mob and that demonstration of national anger. The crowd surged forward but was pushed back by the soldiers. Some rushed through the line from the side, and the deputy commissioner authorized the commanding officer to open fire. Many were killed in the shower of bullets, Mirza's son among them.

When after a long time they were allowed to take away the dead, his friends brought home the body of Mirza's son.

All the shops were closed and the lane was desolate and quiet. The winter sun shone ashy and pale. The smell of putrefaction rose from the gutter, which had not been cleaned. When the dead body was brought in, Mirza and his wife were stunned. They could not believe that their son, who was alive a while ago, who had been laughing, and that very morning had prepared the sweets and rinsed and washed the cauldron, changed into clean clothes and gone to see his friends, was no longer alive but was dead! They looked at the blood-smeared corpse over and over again, and Mirza's wife hugged the dead body and her loud laments rent the air. People tried to take her away from the corpse, but she would not part with her dead son's body.

'My darling, my loved one,' she wailed; and sometimes a lament burst from her lips and she moaned, 'May God destroy these foreigners. They've murdered my loved one. May they die!'

Mirza rushed out of the house like one demented. Siddiq the grocer had just started the day's business and when Mirza passed by, his hair dishevelled, Siddiq called out to him and enquired, 'What a pity, brother. What happened, after all?'

There was no sign of tears in Mirza's eyes, but his face was a picture of pain. 'I'm done for. My world, my son, is dead.' And he walked away towards the house.

The customers who were standing in front of the shop asked Siddiq the cause of the boy's death. Siddiq bent forward and cast a glance at the receding figure of Mirza. A strong gust of wind blew, and the lane was filled with dust. A tattered bit of paper rose in the air and, tumbling and tossing, came down to earth again. Mirza's trimmed hair waved in the wind; then he vanished in the alley.

'Happened? He'd gone for that non-cooperation thing, got shot and died. Why won't they mind their own business? Serves them right to rebel against the government! He was a good-looking young man but he fell prey to those ants from hell and the khadi clad fellows.'

As he talked he put a ladle in the mouth of a pot. Many pots were fixed side by side in the wall and looked like a dovecot. Taking out a cup full of puffed rice Siddiq pushed it towards the customer. The customer, who was listening to Siddiq, nonchalantly began to tie it in a piece of cloth. Suddenly his eyes fell on the puffed rice and he said, 'Say, King Basha, what's this you're giving? I asked for *arhar* lentils. Hurry up or my wife will fume and shout...'

In the house, Mirza's wife was beating her breast and lamenting loudly, cursing both the English and Gandhi. When Yasmin's mother heard of the incident, she rushed to offer condolences. She had also lost a young son who was crushed under the debris of a falling wall, and she was bringing up his children by working as a seamstress. Both of them hugged one another and wept; and Mirza's wife was consoled a little...

At last they took him away for burial. The night was dismal and dark. The wind blew cold, and the lanes were chilly on account of the damp. In the dim light of kerosene lamps the place looked desolate; and not a living soul was about...

For some time after this, one could hear the sad voice of Mirza's wife singing one of Mughal Emperor Bahadur Shah's sad poems:

abruptly the winds have changed course
my restless heart has no peace

Eventually she fell silent and kept herself busy in the shop with odds and ends.

In the vestibule of my house was an old date palm tree. At one time it used to be heavy with fruit, and the bees flocked round it, descending to the ground in search of food. Birds came and perched on its expansive branches, and stray pigeons rested there at night. Now its branches had withered, the leaves had seared and fallen, and its trunk, ugly and dark, stood like a scarecrow in the darkness of night. No more did the birds flock nor were the bees attracted towards it. Only now and then some raven perched on its bare top and croaked itself hoarse, or some kite sat there crying its shrill cries and flew away. In the growing light of dawn its trunk stood out against the sky, but in the sunset it gradually faded from sight and was lost to the darkness. Often as I entered the house at night my eyes fell on its thick and ugly trunk, and followed it up to the sky. But the tree trunk stood between me and the heavens, its top in line with the end star of the Great Bear, blocking the expanse of stars.

A mad woman frequently came to our quarter. Someone had shaved her hair, and her head looked like a walnut on her heavy and well-built body. God-fearing people often dressed her in clothes, but soon she would become naked again. Either some one took off her clothes or she herself tore them away. Saliva ran down her mouth, and her arms hung stiff by her sides. She often pranced and capered on the road, and mumbled incoherently as speech-impaired people do. The moment she set foot in our quarter a crowd of boys gathered and followed her clapping and jeering, pelting her with stones, shouting '*Pugly, Pugly.*' The woman cried helplessly, '*Ain, ain,*' and hid in a corner...

Whenever this happened in front of Mirza's shop, he shouted at the urchins, 'You good-for-nothings, do you think you won't die one day? Get away from here. Go away.' But after a while the urchins would collect again.

Even adults often made fun of her. She was rather ugly, but she was not old. Her belly was bulging, and every now and then Munnoo, who belonged to a well-to-do family but had now turned a loafer, put his hand on her belly and asked, 'When are you going to have a baby?'

The mad woman would utter a wild and anguished cry and, thrusting her hands forward, would turn to a passer by or shopkeeper and point at Munnoo. In her cracked, ugly voice was a request and prayer, the request a helpless person makes to their superior or someone stronger to forgive and save them. But others also joined in the fun and laughed merrily... They said that some men had dragged her away to the Old Fort one night, and her belly had started bulging after that...

There are millions of people in India who are unaware of any reality besides eating, drinking, and dying. They are born, they grow up, work, eat, drink, and then die. There is no benevolence about them nor have they any sense of the dignity of life, like slaves who are not conscious of anything except labour and death. The days for them are meant for work and nights for sleep. That is their life and the reality of their existence, death alone can bring them salvation from living...

Other conspicuous beings in our quarter were dogs, sickly and starving. Many suffered from mange, and their flesh showed through their skins. They bared their sharp teeth and scratched their backs, or closed in mortal combat over a bone in front of the butcher's shop. They came stealthily, sniffing the gutters with their tails between their legs, and quarrelled over offal. But often it happened that just as they saw a piece of meat or a bone, the kites swooped down and carried it away. Then, tails between their legs, they sniffed at the spot, like a man who becomes conscious of being laughed at, or to hide their shame they quarrelled with each other.

Early in the morning was heard the voice of Shera the hawker of parched gram. He went about from lane to lane, hawking his grain which he carried in a bag slung across his back. He was about forty, very lean, and thin. Wrinkles had already appeared on his face and grey hair in his close-cropped beard. His eyes, which had dark hollows around them, reflected hunger and poverty, misery and squalour. He had thin, red lines in his eyes, the kind that appear with intoxication or fever and starvation for days, which were visible from a distance. He wore a dirty cloth cap; his back was covered with a tattered shirt, and through his meagre loincloth showed thin and bony legs.

Years ago he had come to our city from a neighbouring village in search of a job. At night he used to sleep in a mosque and wander on the roads during the day. But like the towns and countryside, the cities had no jobs to offer, and Shera could not find work.

Mir Amaanullah used to go to pray at this mosque. Shera related to him his woeful tale. Mir Sahib took pity on him and took him to his house. Shera was honest and industrious; after a few weeks, Mir Sahib gave him five rupees.

'I'm giving you this money,' he said, 'so that you can start some trade of your own. You may return it when you have some; otherwise, don't worry.'

Shera started hawking parched gram and *dal seo*. In a short time the people of the locality came to know him, and he began to sell briskly. Within a year he returned Mir Amaanullah's money, brought his wife and children from the village, rented a small house, and was happy.

Just then Abdul Rashid was condemned to death for the murder of Swami Shradhanand, leader of the Hindu Revivalist Party. The Muslims of the city were angry and excited. On the day of the execution thousands of men had collected outside the jail. They wanted to rush through its gate when there was delay in handing over Abdul Rashid's corpse. When the police refused to hand it over, the fury of the mob knew no bounds. They wanted to destroy the jail and to bury that martyr in a manner befitting a saint...

Shera had happened to go to the Jama Masjid that day. The sky was overcast with dust, and the roads were empty and desolate. He met only a few angry dogs licking refuse and offal. In a gutter lay a dead pigeon, its neck bent to one side, its stiff, blue legs sticking upwards, the wings soaked in the dirty water, and one of its eyes, which was still visible, ugly and sickening. Shera was drawn to the sight as by the force of deformity and ugliness. He was still engrossed in the scene when he heard the resounding cries of the Muslims chanting the *kalima* coming from a turn off in the direction of another road. He looked up to see people carrying a dead body on their shoulders, and a crowd following the funeral which grew thicker as it emerged into sight so that it seemed the whole population of Delhi had come out. People had run away with Abdul Rashid's corpse. Shera joined the procession. Just then the police came rushing down from the other direction and stopped the funeral. Shera was then lending a shoulder in carrying the bier and was arrested with others. He was eventually sentenced to two years' rigorous imprisonment for taking part in the 'riot.'

Now he had come out of jail, but his customers had forgotten his once-familiar voice. He had no money left either, but a few old acquaintances advanced him some, and Shera restarted his trade. Now he hawked parched gram and went from lane to lane. But his voice had lost its resonance, and misery and sorrow were heard in every cry he uttered. Still, as they heard his voice, children rushed to buy gram, and he took it out by handfuls from his bag, weighed, and handed it over to them...

Another frequent visitor to our quarter, one who came every night, was a blind beggar. He was thin and small, and his short beard was always encrusted with dirt. He carried a broken bamboo stick in his hand with the help of which he felt his way. He looked insignificant and mean, like a swarm of flies over a dirt heap or the skeleton of a dead cat. But his voice had a sadness and pathos which spoke of the transience of life. It came from far away on winter nights, bringing with it gloom and hopelessness. I have never heard a sadder voice and hear it still ringing in my ears. Bahadur Shah's poem that he sang brought back the memory of olden days when Hindustan had not been shackled in its new sorrows. His voice conveyed the lament of India's slavery:

> I'm not the light of any eye
> I'm not the balm to a tortured soul
> I'm simply a fistful of dust
> Not of use to anyone.

But the well-to-do people of the quarter shrank from giving him alms for they said he was addicted to drugs...

About ten o'clock on a summer night I was sitting in my room. Most of the shops were shut, but the kebab seller and Mirza had not shut theirs. On either side of the road men lay on their string cots. Some had gone to sleep, but some were still chatting. The air blew dry and hot; and the smell of putrefaction rose from the gutters. Underneath the wooden plank jutting out of Mirza's shop sat a cat as if waiting for prey. A man came and bought an *anna*'s worth of milk, and, after drinking it, threw the earthen cup on the ground. The cat stole out of her place of hiding and began to lick the broken pieces of the cup.

Just then Kallo passed beneath my window followed by Munnoo. Kallo was young. She was dark complexioned; nevertheless she looked radiant and bright in her youthfulness. She swayed her body as she walked; drunk with life, her slim figure was lithe with bursting youth. She was a maidservant in the home of Munsif Sahib, whose wife had brought her up since childhood. Kallo had been widowed but the young men of the quarter had their eyes on her.

When she reached the corner of the lane, Munnoo caught her by the hand. Furious, Kallo shouted, 'You lump of flesh! God's scourge on you! How dare you lay hands on a defenceless woman!'

'Do you mean to waste your youth?' asked Munnoo.

'Get away. Let go of my hand.'

Nearby on a roof two cats began to fight. Kallo jerked her hand free.

'You good-for-nothing, I hope you die young! Think I have no strength? I'll have you beaten so that you'll remember it all your life.'

Mirza, who had gone inside for a minute, came out just then. He heard Kallo's last sentence, and asked her, 'What's the matter, Kallo?' But without once looking back, she vanished in the alley.

Aziz the carpenter, who was sleeping in front of his shop, was awakened by the noise. When he saw Munnoo standing there he asked, 'What's wrong, Munnoo?'

Munnoo stood crestfallen and indignant. His face had gone expressionless, and looked drawn and pale. His eyes shone poisonous and sharp like those of a snake.

On a heap of refuse the eyes of a cat gleamed in the dark and vanished. Munnoo turned to Aziz and said in a hurt voice, 'Nothing. It was just Kallo.'

'Could you strike a bargain?'

'No, couldn't get her. She ran away. But where will she go?'

The cats were still quarrelling on the roof. They purred fiercely, then screamed and caterwauled, as if they would devour each other. Then one mewed loudly and ran away, the purring tomcat following at her heels.

Aziz the carpenter asked Munnoo to sit down on his bed, produced a hand-rolled cigarette from under his pillow, and pushed it towards Munnoo. But Munnoo took out a silver cigarette case from his shirt pocket. 'Here's a cigarette,' he said, 'which you'll never forget for the rest of your life.'

And taking out a cigarette he gave it to Aziz.

'Say, whose case have you pinched this time?'

'Oh, well, what is it I lack? Whom God refuses, Asifuddaula provides. And if I had relied on Allah, life would have been hell.'

'Come on, talk sense. Fear Him. You'll have to pay for this by burning in hell. Repent.'

'Go away. Don't be an ass. Eat, drink, and be merry. That's all I know. What's more, my master never taught me. I believe in twirling my moustache and idling away my time. Even if hell exists, we'll see when we're there. Why worry now?'

'Shut up. Don't blaspheme. Everything comes to pass. Then you'll forget this boasting.'

'Now that you've started talking like this, I'm off.'

'Just a minute. You see, something's been worrying me for a long time. Swear that you'll tell me.'

'Fine, you won't have cause to complain. By Allah, I'll tell you.'

'Why do you steal?'

'Oh, no; this wasn't what we agreed on.'

'Look here, you can't go back on your word.'

'All right, I've lost. To tell you the truth, I would never have stolen. You know that my relations are rich.'

'That's why I wonder so much.'

'I had a cousin. The boy was rather handsome. It was about ten years ago. We had a falling-out over a kiss. We used to be in the same class, and he went and told the master and had me punished. The devil got into me. I said, 'All right, if I don't take my revenge, I'll shave my moustache with urine.' One day I stole his satchel. It contained expensive things. That's how it began. Another time I took a fancy to an uncle's cigarette case. Ask him for it I could not, so I pinched it. After that I became adept. And, if you ask me the truth, these people will never give anything to the poor.'

'But if you are caught?'

'You've started asking those silly questions again. I'm off, or there'll be a row for nothing at home.'

Saying this he got up and, slapping Aziz loudly on the back, walked away...

Nisar Ahmad used to call the *azan* in the mosque of our district. He was a well-built man with a dark complexion and beard dyed with henna. His head was bald, but on the sides and on the nape grew long, well-trimmed hair. A callous had formed in the centre of his forehead as a result of always touching the floor during prayer, and it shone conspicuously from a distance. He often passed below my window, clearing his throat loudly. He wore a loose payjama and shirt of home-spun *khaddar* and carried a bandana on his shoulder. There was a remarkable resonance and charm in his voice. His azan was famous far and wide, and could be heard in several districts. Even his clearing the throat before calling the prayer was audible. The beginning of the call expressed the exaltation and solemnity of the command to prayer, and as it neared the end, he lowered the pitch, and the sentences, sonorous and reverberating, ending in a deep silence, were lost in the air. They called him Bilal Habshi after one of the Prophet's companions, an African renowned for the beauty of his voice. They had many things in common—their glorious voices and dark complexions.

One evening I was sitting alone on the roof of my house. Thin clouds were spread over the sky. The sunlight fell over them, dyeing them a muted red, for the dust and dirt of the city and the smoke of far-away chimneys were floating in the atmosphere. The hum of the city came from a distance like the buzzing of flies. There was everywhere a poignant hopelessness, that painful gloom which is a distinctive feature of our towns, which conveys to us the sense of misery and filth, of the hollowness and despondency of life. A pigeon flew across the dust-covered, dirty clouds, and was lost in their toneless colours. From afar sounded sirens and railway engines. Flocks of pigeons rose from the rooftops and minarets of the mosques, circled, towered above, and settled down again. Far and wide, wherever the eye could see, ugly buildings jutted their heads out to the skies. Far and wide, wherever the eye could reach, there was a sense of death and indifference. Here and there some two- or three-storey structures were being built and their scaffoldings stood between the vision and the sky. But the colours of the bamboos and girders did not jar on the vision and were lost in the tones of the clouds, looking hazy and dim.

Just then, Nasir Ahmed cleared his throat, and his ringing voice filled the air with its golden resonance. There was such sadness yet peace in the voice that my boredom was turned to a silent gloom. With its glory and richness the voice communicated a sense that life was ephemeral and passing, that the world was fleeting and impermanent, and its lovers were dogs, that everything was meaningless and vain as the dust and the dirt and the smoke on the face of the clouds. A prey to my thoughts, I listened to the azan until it neared the end and the fading cadences of the last notes, inviting the faithful to prayer and life eternal, began to ring in the ears, producing with their dying fall the sense and certitude of the meaninglessness of this transitory world. The notes of the azan came to an end so gradually that one did not feel the voice had ceased. Its echoes still reverberated and whispered in the ears that somewhere far away, beyond the pale of existence, there was another world in which the Beginning and the End were one, and that this universe was meaningless and vain. The voice was lost in the ether, where the earth comes to an end and the sky begins. It was still striking against the eardrums, but it seemed that silence had always reigned over the earth and was buzzing in the ears...

I sat thinking how well the azan symbolized our life. There was the same ecstatic silence which has become a part of our minds, the same despair of hopelessness and gloom, the same fear of reality which forces us to lead subjective lives. Ignoring the world, we dream inflated dreams of Creation and the End; forgetting man, we spend our time in the quest of God. And everything of our life leads us to Him—our songs sing the same lullabies. Our feet are shackled; our hands are fettered. There are iron collars round our necks, but we have become so used to them that they seem part of our anatomy. Our bodies have become numb, our souls lie asleep, yet we are happy in our helplessness and lead a senseless life of indifference, until Death thrusts her claws and drags us into her lap and oblivion. Our glory and shame are alike, and, like the azan, we change from life to death so quietly that none can say we were indeed ever alive, or that our being was a mere delusion, and we, the loved ones of Death, drunk on her lullabies from time immemorial, have been sleeping a sound and dreamless sleep...

One night a few people were talking at Mirza's shop. One of them was Aziz, the carpenter, the other was the kebab-seller, and some more had collected in the shop. The hookah was placed before them at which they were pulling by turns. 'Well,' one of them was saying, 'I see his glory in everything and wonder.' My curiosity was aroused and I began to listen attentively. In the meantime a customer came and asked for five paisa worth of milk, and stood aside. Mirza took an earthen cup and reached his ladle to the cauldron to take out the milk.

'The other day I was going through Chandi Chowk,' the voice said, continuing its story, 'when I saw a young cow approaching before me. Just there lay a small child. The cow stopped when she came to the spot where the child was lying. I said to myself: Let's see what she does now. But to my surprise she put all her four feet together and jumped clean across the child. There was manifestation of His glory in the animal's wisdom!'

One of Mirza's hands was near the cauldron; in the other he held the earthen cup and was staring into the speaker's face. 'Great is His glory,' said Aziz with reverent amazement. Mirza filled his bowl with milk and began to toss it.

'Mysterious are His ways,' another began. 'Once upon a time, the Prophet Suleiman was ordered to build a palace. Suitably, he began to make preparations. The jinns collected huge stones and slabs in no time; and the work began. You know how quickly the jinns work. Every day it rose a little bit higher. Within a few days the palace climbed to the skies. Hazrat Suleiman went every day to supervise and see if anyone neglected his work or wasted his time. Now then, one day the palace was ready. Only the bits of stone and pieces of slabs remained to be cleared. The next day Hazrat Suleiman was there as usual, propping himself up on his stick, and he issued the order to clear the lumber away. In the meantime some other order had come from above. Now, see the manifestation of His glory—while the palace was being cleared of the lumber, the worm set upon Hazrat Suleiman's stick. He stood there firmly, until the worm had eaten the whole of the stick and had begun to work on its handle. But he was oblivious of it. The stick crumbled, mere dust and ashes, and he fell down, dead. The jinns vanished, for the one they obeyed was no more. But what I am wondering is...who will now throw out those pieces of stone and bits of slabs?...'

Aziz held the shaft of the hookah near his mouth without smoking, and gazed at the speaker, engrossed in his words. One of Mirza's hands which held the bowl was still raised in the air, the other with the earthen cup was lower down near the floor, and he was lost in the story of Solomon's death...

I burst out laughing, but then began to think who would really throw out these 'pieces of stone and bits of slabs'?

A strong gust of wind blew the kerosene lamp out, leaving the road in total darkness. Slowly the men came out of Mirza's shop and began to disperse, and I too went inside the house.

Translated by the Author

Krishan Chander
(1912–77)

Born in Gujranwala, into a Punjabi Khatri family, Krishan Chander was an ardent Progressive, and among the most famous and prolific short story writers of Urdu in the 1940s and '50s. He earned an M.A. in English literature followed by a law degree from Punjab University in 1937. Krishan Chander worked for All India Radio from 1939 to 1942. He resigned and moved to Pune to work for a film company as a script writer. From Pune he went on to Bombay, where he lived till the end of his life. In a forty-year literary career, he wrote nearly five thousand short stories, dozens of novels, many plays, and other works of prose. He was awarded the *Padma Bhushan* in 1969.

Krishan Chander's writing was devoid of any depth or complexity; he could and did write on a variety of subjects only in a charming superficial way. He has been called a 'romantic' because of the unabashed sentimentalism that colours his work. But he was a remarkable prose stylist; lyrical, almost too mellifluous at times, his work has a naïve quality that appeals to readers. Some of his important novels are *Shikast* (Defeat), *Asman Roshan Hai* (The Skies are Bright), *Tufan ki Kaliyan* (Blossoms of the Storm), *Mitti ke Sanam* (Idols of Clay), *Chandni ka Ghao* (Moonlight's Wound).

Most of his fiction revolves around the life of the poor and homeless Bombay slum-dwellers. He also wrote about the sad, horrific events of

Partition. '*Irani Pilau*' represents Krishan Chander's sensitive storytelling style as well as his Marxist-Progressive stance. Irani Pilau is not the aromatic pilau that the name suggests but an euphemism for leftover food: the pieces of bread, meat, chewed bones, bits of rice, parts of omelettes, slices of potato—all of this uneaten food is mixed together in a watery stew which is sold for two annas a plate at the back door of the restaurant. Usually even the poor people do not eat it, yet every day two or three hundred plates are sold. Ironically, its consumers are young men who earn a living by polishing shoes.

Irani Pilau

The night was mine because I didn't have any money in my pocket. When I have money in my pocket, the night doesn't seem like it's mine. That night, I saw the cars strutting down Marine Drive; I saw the glittering flats and the dancers on the roof of the Ambassador Hotel. Yet that night was completely mine. That night, all the stars in the heavens were mine, and all of Bombay's streets were mine. When there's even a little money in my pocket, the whole city seems to subdue me. Every object scowls and rebukes me, forces me to sit far away from myself. From ordinary pants to lovely radio programmes—everything says, you are far away from me. But when there isn't a coin in my pocket, the whole city seems made for me. It's as if 'Built for Bishan, a Starving but Cheerful Writer' is written on every stone, on every turn in the road, on every electricity pole. On those days, I don't worry about the lockup, about being hit by a car, or about eating dinner. There's a vast, intoxicating mood of freedom and good humour that spreads out for miles. That night, I wasn't walking by myself. That night, the streets of Bombay were carrying me. Every curve in the road, every turn in the markets, every dark corner invited me: 'Come here, look at us. Join us, friend. You've been living in this city for eight years. Why are you walking around like a stranger? Come, take our hand.'

That night was mine. That night, I wasn't afraid of anyone. Fear comes to those who have money in their pockets. In this country of people with empty pockets, only those with full pockets need to be afraid. What did I have that anyone could snatch away?

I've heard that the government has made it illegal to walk around on the streets after midnight. But why? What is there in Bombay after midnight that they want to hide from me? I was going to find out. That night, I wasn't afraid of anything—not of any minister, not of any lockup. That night, no matter what, I was going to go exploring and take my friends' hands.

With that thought in mind, I went past the road in front of Churchgate Reclamation and into the University grounds. My plan was to pass through the middle of the field, come out in front of the big, dark houses on the other side, and from there go on to Flora Fountain. But while I was passing through the field, I noticed a few boys had formed a circle in the corner and were singing:

You and I have fallen in love
You and I
You and I
You and I have fallen in love

Two or three of them were clapping. One was trying to make a flute sound come out of his mouth. One fellow was shaking his head from side to side and making a tabla out of a wooden box. All of them were swaying with pleasure and singing in voices that were sharp and flat, high and low. I came closer to them and asked, 'Hey guys, whom have you fallen in love with?'

They stopped singing and looked at me for a moment. I don't know what people think when they look at me. But I do know that after looking at me for a moment, people quickly warm up to me. They become so intimate with me that they start to tell me every secret of their lives, every picture of their own little universes, every pain and sorrow in their hearts. There's no greatness in my face; there's nothing special about it. I don't have a commanding personality or any majesty; there's no special flair to my dress. My clothes don't have the look you get from a black coat with a red rose or from a sharkskin suit. I wear ordinary sandals, above them cotton pajamas, and above them a cotton shirt. The back of my shirt often gets dirty, first, because I usually sleep on the ground in my hut, and second, because I have a bad habit of always putting my back to a wall whenever I sit. Why so many dirty walls come into my life and why so few clean ones is another story. Shirts quickly fall apart at the shoulders of those down on their luck, and there you'll see stitches. The real reason is that these people try over and over again to stitch together old, torn clothes. Not every man can stitch a red rose onto his black coat. What's the difference between one stitch and another? It's true that no two people are alike; they can't have the same face and the same form. I see different faces night and day in Bombay. Thousands and thousands of different faces, but what does it mean that all of them have the same stitches at the shoulders? Thousands and thousands of stitches try unsuccessfully to join the ends of torn lives. After reading my stories, one critic said that he doesn't see any human face in them. That's the trouble with me: I don't express my characters' faces. I see the stitches at people's shoulders; and those stitches show me their inner face. Those stitches tell me about their struggles and their hard work, without which no novel about life and no story about society can be complete. That's why I'm happy that when people see my face some think I'm a clerk, others that I'm a junk dealer, and still others that I'm a comb-seller or a hairdresser. So far, no one has imagined me to be a minister or a thief. I'm happy to be one among these millions of little people who can become familiar with one another quickly, without any formal introduction.

After a moment's hesitation, the boys looked at me and smiled. A thin lad said to me, 'Hey man, have a seat. You can sing with us.'

After saying this, he shook his hair and went back to playing his wooden box as a tabla. Then we all started to sing:

You and I
You and I
have fallen in love

All at once, the thin lad stopped playing his tabla, nudged another boy who had his head between his knees, and said, 'Madhubala! Why aren't you singing?'

Madhubala slowly lifted his head out from between his legs. His face wasn't beautiful like the actress Madhubala. There was a burn from his chin all the way down to his left elbow. He grimaced and his tiny eyes looked like two black fissures on his round face. He seemed agitated. He said to the tabla player, 'Leave me alone, *sala*! My stomach hurts.'

'Why does it hurt, sala? Did you eat Irani pilau today?'

Madhubala shook his head and said, 'Yeah, I ate it.'

'Why did you eat it, sala?'

'Why do you think? I only did three polishes today.'

There was another lad who seemed older than the rest of them; he had a bit of a beard on his chin, and he was growing sideburns. Scratching his nose, he said, 'Madhubala, get up and run around the field. Come on, I'll run with you. After two rounds your stomach ache will go away.'

'No, leave me alone.'

'Get up, sala. Otherwise I'll hit you!'

Madhubala brought his hands together and pleaded, 'Cuckoo, just leave me alone. My stomach ache will go away, I swear.'

'Get up! Why are you ruining our band?'

Cuckoo lifted Madhubala up by his hands and then they both started to run around the university grounds. I watched the two of them running for a while, then the boy sitting next to me scratched his head and said, 'If you eat Irani pilau, it's a problem. If you don't, it's a problem.' I said, 'No, man, Irani pilau is good food. Why would it give you a stomach ache?' Hearing my words, they all started to laugh.

One boy, whose name was Kuldeep Kaur, and who was wearing a torn jacket and torn shorts, chuckled and said to me, 'It seems you've never eaten Irani pilau.'

Opening the buttons of his jacket, Kuldeep Kaur told me that Irani pilau was their special slang. They don't eat it every day. But on those days when one of them doesn't polish many shoes or when he doesn't have much money, he has to eat it. The pilau is available at the nearby Irani restaurant after midnight. The food that people leave on their plates during the day—the pieces of bread, meat, chewed bones, bits of rice, parts of omelettes, slices of potato—all of this uneaten food is mixed together in a watery stew and this stew is sold for two annas a plate at the back door of the restaurant. Usually even the poor people around there don't eat it, yet every day, about two or three hundred plates are sold. The people who buy it are usually shoe polishers, furniture cleaners, doormen, poor people working in the nearby buildings, and people doing construction.

I asked Kuldeep Kaur, 'Why is your name Kuldeep Kaur?' He took his jacket completely off and started to rub his black belly with a lot of pleasure. Hearing my question, he had a big laugh. When he was done, he said to his friend, 'Bring me my box.'

Kuldeep Kaur's friend brought him his box. He opened it and inside were shoe polishing materials. On the bottles of polish was the picture of Kuldeep Kaur. He then had his friend open his own box and all of its containers were covered with pictures of Nargis cut from magazines and newspapers.

Kuldeep Kaur said, 'This sala does a Nargis polish. That guy does Nimmi, and that one Suraiyya. All of us cut out pictures of some film actress and put them on our containers, and then rub their polish.'

'Why?'

'Customers love it. We say, 'Sir, what polish would you like? Nargis' or Suraiyya's, or Madhubala's?' Then the customer chooses the polish of the actress he likes, and we send him to the guy who has Nargis' polish, or Nimmi's, or some other actress'. There are eight of us, and we sit over there behind the Churchgate Parsi Bus Stand. Whichever actress's polish one of us has, that's his name. That's why our business goes so well, and we have a lot of fun, too.'

I said, 'If you sit over there on the footpath doesn't the policeman bother you?'

Kuldeep Kaur had been lying on his stomach. He stood up and then flipped an imaginary coin into the air. He said, 'What would that sala say? We give him money. And the people who sleep in this field, they give him money too. Money?' Saying this, he flicked another imaginary coin into the air, followed it with his eyes, and then pretended to catch it. He opened his hands and looked inside, but both hands were empty. Kuldeep Kaur smiled with a pleasant bitterness. Saying nothing, he lay down again.

Nargis asked me, 'Do you polish shoes over in Dadar? I think I might have seen you in front of the Yazdan Hotel.'

I said, 'Yes, you could think of me as a type of polisher.'

'A type of polisher?' Kuldeep Kaur raised his head and then sat up. He looked at me observantly. 'Sala, speak clearly. What do you do?'

He called me sala. I was very happy. If someone else called me that, I would have hit him. But when this boy called me sala, I was happy because here sala is not a term of abuse, it's a word for brotherhood. These people included me in their brotherhood. So I said, 'Friend, I'm a type of polisher, but what I do is polish words, and sometimes I scratch at old, dirty leather and see what's in its rotten depths.'

Nargis and Nimmi both spoke up at once, 'Sala, you keep talking gibberish. Tell us what you really do.'

I said, 'My name is Bishan. I write stories. I sell them to newspapers.'

'Oh, you're a writer,' Nimmi said. Nimmi was a small lad. He was the smallest among the circle of boys here, but there was a gleam of intelligence in his eyes. He became very interested in me because besides polishing shoes he also sold newspapers. He advanced towards me and said, 'What newspapers do you write for? Free Press? Central Times? Bombay Chronicle? I know all the newspapers.'

He came right up next to me.

I said, 'I write for Shabab.'

'Shabab? What's that?'

'It comes out of Delhi.'

'From Delhi? What?' Nimmi's eyes scrutinized my face.

'And I write for Adab-e Latif,' I said, to awe him.

Kuldeep Kaur started to laugh. 'What did he say? He writes for Badbe Khaltif? Sala, that sounds like some English film actress' name. Badbe Khaltif! Ha-ha! Nimmi, change your name to Badbe Khaltif. It sounds like a great name! Ha-ha!' When all the boys had finished laughing, I said with great seriousness, 'Not Badbe Khaltif. Adab. Adab-e Latif. It comes out of Lahore. It's a very good paper.'

Nargis shook his head indifferently and said, 'All right, sala. Say you do work for Adab-e Latif. What do we care? We'd just sell it over there and get paid a little money for it.'

Kuldeep Kaur looked at me and then started to laugh again. He said, 'But look at you. You certainly don't seem like a writer. You look like a shoe polisher, like us!' Then they all started to laugh again. I started to laugh with them since there was no other recourse.

Kuldeep Kaur kept laughing, and then became serious for a moment. He turned towards me and said, 'And for these...stories...how much money do you get?'

'I get just about as much as you get, often nothing. When I have finished polishing words, then the publisher says thanks, takes them for free, and then makes his own magazine or newspaper shine with them.'

'Then why do you wrack your brain for nothing? Why don't you polish like us? I mean it. You can come into our brotherhood and we'll call you Badbe Khaltif. Give me your hand.' I shook hands with Kuldeep Kaur.

Then he said, 'But you'll have to give four annas a day to the policeman.'

'And if one day I don't have four annas?'

'I don't know. Get it from someone. Steal, rob, but make sure you give four annas to him. Oh, and you'll have to go to the lockup two days a month.'

'What? Why?'

'I don't know why. We give the policeman four annas a day—every shoe polisher does—but still two times a month he grabs us and takes us away. It's his rule. He says, "What can I do?"' I said, 'Okay, so I'll stay in the lockup for two days a month.'

Then Kuldeep Kaur said, 'Also, you'll have to go to court once a month. You'll have to get a ticket from the bailiff to go to court, and then you'll have to give them two or three rupees as well.'

'Why? If I had already been giving four annas a day to the policeman...'

'He also has to seem like he's doing his job. So what do you say, sala Badbe Khaltif?'

I winked at Kuldeep Kaur and said, 'Sala, I get everything.' We both started to laugh. Just then Madhubala and Cuckoo both came back from the field, dripping in sweat.

I asked Madhubala, 'Has your stomach ache gone away?'

He said, 'The pain's gone, but now I'm really hungry.'

Nargis said, 'Yeah, me too.'

Nimmi shook his head and asked, 'Should we get Irani pilau?'

'So you can get a stomach ache and then run around the field and get hungry again?' Kuldeep Kaur said bitterly.

Nimmi said, 'I can give two paise.'

I said, 'I have one anna.'

We had four annas all together. Nimmi was sent to get the Irani pilau because he was the youngest. The cook at the Irani restaurant liked him too. If the cook saw Nimmi, he'd maybe give three plates for the price of two, or at least three plates worth of food.

When Nimmi had gone, I asked, 'Do you guys sleep here at night?'

'Except for Madhubala, we all sleep here,' Cuckoo said, 'Madhubala usually goes home, but he didn't today.'

I asked Madhubala, 'You have a home?'

'Yeah, there's a hut in the billboard. My mother lives there.'

'And your father?'

Madhubala said, 'Father? What do I know of my father? That sala is probably a big honcho in one of these buildings around here.'

Suddenly they all became quiet, as if someone had slapped them. These boys—defenceless, homeless, and nameless—tried through film songs to fill their lives with the love they would never have.

'*You and I have fallen in love*. Where is your love? Father! Mother! Brother! Who are you? Why did you bring me into this world? Why did you leave me to be kicked from door to door on these mean, hard footpaths?' For a moment their pale, plaintive faces were stricken with an unknown fear. They grabbed each other's hands forcefully, as if they couldn't get help from anywhere else. It was as if every building, every footpath, and every footstep in the city was trampling them, forcing them, in the darkness of the night, to hold each other's hands. They seemed so afraid and innocent to me, like forgotten children lost in some unknown, endless jungle. Bombay sometimes seems like a jungle where society's nameless children are groping around trying to find their way out of the labyrinth of the streets; and when they don't find the way, they sit down under a tree and close their eyes. Then I think, no, it's not like that at all.

Bombay is not a jungle. People say it's a city. It has one Municipal Corporation; it has one government and one system. It has alleyways; it has markets; it has stores. There are roads and there are homes. All of them are joined to one another in the way that things are connected to each other in a civilized and cultured city. I know all of this. I recognize Bombay's roads and homes. I give them honour and respect. But despite this honour and respect, despite this love, why do I see in this city of Bombay so many alleyways which have no way out? There are so many roads that don't go anywhere, so many children for whom there is no home. Suddenly, Nimmi broke the silence. He came running toward us. In his hands were three plates of Irani pilau. There was a warm, sweet-smelling steam rising from them. Only when he brought the plates and laid them on the grass did we see that there were tears in his eyes. 'What happened?' Kuldeep Kaur asked.

Nimmi said in an angry tone, 'The cook bit me really hard here.'

Nimmi turned his left cheek towards us.

We saw there was a big mark on his left cheek.

Kuldeep Kaur started cursing the cook and said, 'Bastard...'

But after that, they all dug into the Irani pilau.

Translated by A. Sean Pue

Aziz Ahmad
(1914–78)

Aziz Ahmad was born in Hyderabad, capital of the former princely state in central India, which forms the background of many of his novels. He was fluent in several languages: Arabic, French, Turkish, Italian, German, and translated from these languages into Urdu. His translation of Dante's *Divine Comedy* was published in 1943. He moved to Pakistan in 1949. Aziz Ahmad was educated in Hyderabad and London, and taught in the Universities of Osmania (Hyderabad), London, and California at Los Angeles. He was Professor of Islamic Studies at the University of Toronto.

A leading Urdu novelist and short story writer, he also wrote a number of books on Indian Islam, on which he was considered one of the foremost authorities. He published numerous collections of short stories. His first novel *Hawas* (Lust) appeared in 1932, the second *Gurez* (Abstinence) in 1943, followed by *Aisi Bulandi, Aisi Pasti* (Such Highs, Such Lows), 1948, *Shabnam* (Dew Drops), 1951, and *Teri Dilbari ka Bharam* (The Illusion of Your Charms), 1985. He also wrote a couple of novellas in the historical mode that were based on themes drawn from Mughal history.

Ahmad was an exponent of the realistic-subjective trend in novel writing. He gave true to life, touching portrayals of the decaying feudal order. The present excerpt is the opening chapter from the novel *Aisi Bulandi, Aisi Pasti*, translated by Ralph Russell under the title 'The Shore and the Wave'. This novel in particular presents a picture of an important but too little known section of Indian social history. Ahmad's fictional Farkhunda Nagar, the city in which most of the scenes are set, is in fact Hyderabad. In the novel he talks about the impact of westernization on the educated, well-to-do sections of Hyderabad society.

The Shore and the Wave

Love cannot develop to the full without separation, they say, and no landscape is perfect without heights and depths. That is why there is a hill near every big city, and if God has endowed the citizens with good taste, they build their houses on the hill as well as in the plain. If He has not, they build a temple or two on the hill or discover somebody's shrine there, and go and visit it from time to time. From the top of the hill, they gaze down for a while at the city below, admire the scene, and then return to their narrow streets.

Near Farkhunda Nagar, capital of the princely state of that name in central India, lies the hill which now bears the name of Kishanpalli, but which in former days was called Gipsies' Hill. From the air it looks like a great spider, a spider with three symmetrical, linked bodies, and numberless legs reaching out in all directions. All around is flat country, stretching away until in the distance it once more meets the hills, and dotted about the plains are muddy bluish pools which from the air look like big pieces of blue glass set in the fields of green-waving paddy. In former days there were only tracks on Gipsies' Hill, winding their way through the trees of thorny babool and bitter-leaved neem, among rocks of every shape and size. There is a legend that when the Creator had fashioned the world, He flicked His fingers to free them of the clay still clinging to them. The lumps of clay fell on the Deccan plateau and formed the rocks which litter it today. Most of these rocks are black, like the Deccan's Dravidian inhabitants, or like the stone-hewers whose vigorous young women Josh Malihabadi immortalized in his verse. These rocks occur in the most curious shapes. One stands upon another, almost as though it were suspended above it. The lower rock is often small, while the upper one is very large and barely in contact with the lower. You would think that the slightest shock would bring these great rocks crashing down, but far from it; even earthquakes have failed to move them, and these jugglers of the world of stone stand fast still poising their weight as before.

These days there are houses among the rocks. Look for instance at the house of Wali Chalak Jang, a small five-roomed building of so-called 'German' design. Wali Chalak Jang was no slave to tradition, and he made changes when he moved in. He had the name of the house, which had been engraved on the gate like the inscription on a tombstone, written in Kufic script on an old-fashioned Chinese lantern, suspended like a streetlight on the front veranda near the bougainvillea creeper. He changed the name, too. The house had been called 'Gulkada'—the 'Flower House'—perhaps from the deep pink flowers of the bougainvillea, but the 'Flower House' reminded him of the Eid greeting cards fashionable in Farkhunda Nagar twenty-five years earlier. His family had played a great part in changing this old-fashioned style with its profusion of flowers and leaves, and introducing a simpler taste, so he dropped the old Urdu name, and on the Chinese lantern was now engraved in a sort of English Kufic script: 'The Rock'. Not that this referred to the house itself, which looked more like one of those modern Urdu poems in free verse, descending in stages from front to rear until it came to a stop, at the edge of a pool. No, what gave the house its name was a huge rock some fifty feet high, which stood confronting it like a virile young aborigine. By some geological freak, the breast of this gigantic rock had been cleft open; across the cleft lay a slab, ten feet long and seven feet high, and on the top of that yet another much smaller one.

Today there are houses on the hill. But two hundred and fifty years ago, when the armies of the Mughal Emperor Aurangzeb marched over Gipsies' Hill, it must have been green and uninhabited. In the rear of his armies came the *banjaras*—the merchant-gipsies who supplied them, and who were to give the hill its name. They were still there when the Mughal Empire fell and the Marathas overspread the land, levying tribute wherever they went; and when the Afghans invaded and far to the north defeated the Marathas at Panipat and cut off their commander's head; and when the Sikhs rose to power in the Panjab; and when the Dogras conquered Ladakh; and they were still there when the soldiers' tread was heard no more on Gipsies' Hill, roaming as before and trading where they could. There, where the smoke rose from their huts near the sheer rock, three hundred feet high, that curves towards the valley like the thigh of a giant negress, the poet Nazir warned them of their approaching doom:

Give up your worldly gain, your ever-restless wandering.

'Oh, shut up!' said the banjaras, and went on with their trading. Nazir tried again, at the place where you suddenly find yourself looking down over the plain below, where the great rocks come to an end, and give way to hundreds of thousands of useless little stones, littering the slopes like little tombstones. He tried to frighten them:

Your wealth will lie abandoned there when Death the Trader goes his way.

'Oh, go away', said the banjaras; and they went on their accustomed way, roaming from town to town and from village to village. They came down from the heights of Gipsies' Hill towards the valley; they knocked at the door of Amir Karim Khan, and spread out the wares they had brought from Delhi:

The screens and curtains, carpets, rugs, the carved and painted beds of state.

They bowed low before the gatekeeper of the Rajah of Rajahs, *Himmat Shamsher Singh Bahadur*, were granted audience, and paraded before him:

> Fine horses, saddles chased with gold, and elephants with trappings red.

Nazir again tried to frighten them:

> Your sons and grandsons—yes, your wives, will shun your corpse when you lie dead.

And in fact not all of them waited so long—these banjaras' wives, decked in the jewellery they had brought with them from Tibet and Central Asia, wearing in their ears, on their arms, on their ankles, in their noses, on their foreheads, ornaments of brass which jingled as they walked. It was a banjara's wife who deserted her husband to enter the harem of the Rajah of Rajahs and to become the grandmother of the present Rajah. But the banjaras went on trading, selling their wares, their women, themselves, until the day when the Honourable Englishman entered the market and prospered to such an extent that Nazir's prophecy came true, and not only Nazir's banjaras, but all the banjaras were wiped off from the slate of history. The footpaths of Gipsies' Hill fell silent. Their children ceased to be their own. Even the Khan Hazrat, the ruling prince of Farkhunda Nagar, stopped buying their vessels of gold and silver and went over instead to the glassware displayed in the English-style shop windows.

> Your wealth will lie abandoned there when Death the Trader goes his way.

Then came the aborigines from the nearby plains: stone-hewers, bird-catchers, and eaters of carrion flesh. It was they who robbed the hill of its trees, so that today there are no trees on Kishanpalli except those which the new residents have planted in their gardens or those in the avenues laid out by Dr Qurban Husain. The aborigine women lopped and felled the trees and uprooted the thorn bushes for fuel. That is why in the summer months Kishanpalli is burning hot, and the earth on the hillsides seems to turn a deeper black, and the ringed snakes come out from under the scorching black rocks, those rocks which, in Josh's poem, suckled dry the young Dravidian women of the Deccan plateau. Here and there you can see a pair of mongooses courting, or you may hear the cry of the hares, with their deep blue eyes, as they run past the bird-catchers' huts...

It would be about a hundred years after the last banjaras departed from Gipsies' Hill that one afternoon early in the rainy season Ahdi Husnkar Jang happened by the merest chance to go walking there. The Deccan rains, the Malwa nights, evenings in Oudh, and mornings in Banaras are all proverbial, but the first two were made by God, and the other two by man. It was July, the month when in northern India it seems to be raining fire, but when in the country around Farkhunda Nagar the earth becomes a paradise. The grass was lank and green, the air cool and fragrant; and the Rajah of Rajahs, *Shujaat Shamsher Singh Bahadur*, Prime Minister of Farkhunda Nagar state, decided to postpone the business of government until the next morning and to spend this beautiful afternoon in the gardens of the Royal Tombs picnicking with his Rajput consort, one of his Muslim wives, and three of his concubines. His secretary-in-waiting, Ahdi Husnkar Jang, bowed low and asked leave of absence for the afternoon.

Ahdi Husnkar Jang drove out of the city to the foot of Gipsies' Hill and went for a long walk. He climbed to the top, and splashing through pools of mud, passing from track to track, and from hanging rock to hanging rock, made his way past the bird-catchers' mud-and-straw huts to the spot where the solitary house of Dr Qurban Husain—the first to be built on Gipsies' Hill—was already standing.

It so happened that at this moment the sky took a fancy to see what was going on in the city. It tore a gap in the clouds and looked down with its deep blue eyes. The Rajah of Rajahs' Hindu cook was soaking gram cakes in yogurt. His Muslim cook was grilling shish-kebabs on the spit. His youngest wife was thinking of the handsome young Arab who had eyed her appreciatively from the corner of the road. The British Resident was confiding to the finance minister his distrust of the prime minister. The ruling prince, the Khan Hazrat, had just taken another tablet of opium, and was picking his nose and trying to make up his mind whether to sign the papers sent by the Resident or to write an elegy on the Grandson of the Prophet, martyred thirteen hundred years ago. Near the Four Turrets the horse-carriage drivers were making fun of a group of eunuchs dressed as women. A labourer was carrying on his back a fifty-four pound sack of cement and a man was putting up a poster advertising a Charlie Chaplin film. In short, all was right with the world. Ahdi Husnkar Jang looked up at the sky and smiled his gratitude. The sky laughed back graciously and the clouds spat out the mild sun.

The view over the city was beautiful—the minarets of the mosques, the spires of the temples, the thousands of dwellings sprawled out beneath his gaze, and the great lake of Shahid Sagar, brimful of monsoon rain. At his feet lay a little pool, and on the slopes below it rolling fields of paddy with not a square inch of barren land to be seen. Grass was growing round every stone and rock, grass and creeping vines, studded with bright yellow flowers and swarming with hundreds of thousands of insects whose mingled chorus could be heard clearly in the still air.

Ahdi Husnkar Jang closed his eyes and opened them again. He had conjured up a picture of the hanging gardens of Malabar Hill in Bombay, overlooking the sea. He looked again at Shahid Sagar with its muddy blue water, and in his mind's eye he saw hundreds of houses being built among these hanging rocks on the top of Gipsies' Hill, and on its slopes and in its hollows. He saw the tracks being widened, roads being built, descending to the valleys and climbing up to the heights, hanging like lace on the skirts of the hill. The most picturesque rocks could, he thought, be left as they were or surrounded with gardens, and the rest could be broken up for building stone. He saw thousands of aborigine stone-hewers driving their wooden-wheeled buffalo carts loaded with heavy stone, their women bare from the waist up and with breasts as firm as the rocks around them, carrying baskets of stone on their heads and passing them to the masons. He saw hundreds of houses going up, modern and bizarre and exotic, combining 'German' abstract designs with arabesques and marble trellises, enclosed by hedged gardens; here and there, would be a house resembling a pagoda or even one reminiscent of far-off South America. There would be orange gardens, and tree-lined avenues....

The following day Ahdi Husnkar Jang was again on duty, laying various papers before the Rajah of Rajahs for his decision. The Rajah of Rajahs was very, very old. His false teeth were old, the eyes that peered out of his dyed eyelashes were old, his arthritic backbone was old, and held artificially straight by a surgical belt. When he had signed all the papers which had been laid before him, routine orders, orders for promotion, demotion, and transfer schemes motivated by patriotic fervour—or by nepotism—he put down the fountain pen which the British Resident had presented to him, tilted back his head, and closed his eyes. God knows what lay behind those eyelids, in the recesses and vacant space of that brain: boundless love and loyalty to the Khan Hazrat; boundless love and loyalty to the British Crown; philanthropic concern for the poor; consideration for the rich; condescension towards his courtiers; and love for every woman in the world—love for the slanting eyes of his young Rajput Rani, love for the big moist eyes of his Muslim Begum, love for European women, love for low-caste aborigine women, love for other men's daughters and daughters-in-law, love for the dark-skinned maidservants in their grubby sarees... The air was full of the fragrance of the hookah. The Rajah opened his eyes and said with dignity, 'Long may the Khan Hazrat live! Long may his Kingdom endure!'

He took another pull at the hookah and blew out the smoke, wafting the aroma across the Persian carpets. Ahdi Husnkar Jang, who had been waiting to catch his eye, bowed low, by which he meant, 'Your servant awaits your command,'...that is, wants to go. The Rajah motioned to him with the mouthpiece of the hookah to stay, and with a gesture towards a nearby chair indicated that he should sit down. The secretary-in-waiting again bowed respectfully and took his seat. The attendants saw at once that the Rajah of Rajahs was in a gracious mood.

With his eyes half-closed, the old man said, 'Call them in.' This was the signal for audience. Courtiers and petitioners who had been waiting outside far an hour or more in the cool, spacious veranda, patiently gazing at the Kashmir carvings on the wooden columns, were now brought in. Each of them bowed deeply and salaamed as he entered. The Rajah acknowledged each salutation with a nod; for the senior officers such as Zijah Jang, the home secretary, Araish Jang, the chief engineer and Khaqan Jang, the royal physician, there was a gracious smile as well.

One of the petitioners—a somewhat untidily dressed young man who looked as though he drank heavily—was presented to him: 'This gentleman has brought a letter from Iqbal. He is himself a very promising poet.'

'God be praised! God be praised!' The hookah gurgled and the aroma again filled the room. 'So you have a letter from my friend Iqbal. He knows me for a mystic like himself, whose soul is not with the things of this world.'

'Your Lordship is indeed a mystic,' said the Royal Physician, bowing deeply. 'A most just, a most true observation.'

The Rajah smiled contentedly. The petitioner was about to hand over Iqbal's letter to the Rajah of Rajahs, but the great mystic was now in a mood of abstraction, pulling at his hookah and reflecting an the vanity of vanities. With an understanding smile Ahdi Husnkar Jang took the letter from the petitioner's hand.

The hookah again gurgled. Zijah Jang and Khaqan Jang were whispering together, and the Rajah of Rajahs returned from the ecstasy of Life Divine to the banalities of this world. He laid the mouthpiece of the hookah on a silver dish and asked kindly, 'What is it, Nawab?'

'Your lordship, Zijah Jang was telling me about his case.'

'What case, Zijah? Let us hear it.'

Zijah Jang was an impressive figure. Six feet tall, fair-complexioned, haughty, and an aristocrat by birth, he never adopted a humble tone with anyone except the Rajah of Rajahs, and, of course, with the Khan Hazrat.

'May your lordship live forever! The finance minister, who, as your lordship knows, does not like me because of my devotion to your lordship, had made two complaints against me: First, that by my order the two parts of the Secretariat have been connected by a bridge between their upper storeys; and second, that there is an inscription on the bridge saying that this was done by my order.'

'Excellent! A bridge with an inscription. A most fitting plan. I must be sure to come and see it one day. Eh, Ahdi?'

The Rajah of Rajahs had already seen it half a dozen times at least; in fact, it was he who had laid the foundation stone.

'Indeed,' said Ahdi Husnkar Jang, 'your lordship should most certainly see it.'

Zijah Jang continued. 'The finance minister has refused to sanction the expenditure.'

'Set your mind at rest. I shall speak to him about it.'

'God grant your lordship long life.'

'Well, Ahdi, what has Iqbal written to me, his unworthy mystic friend?'

Ahdi Husnkar Jang began to read out the letter. As he listened, the Rajah of Rajahs began to doze, and before the letter was finished he had fallen fast asleep in his chair. The petitioners tiptoed out. Ahdi Husnkar Jang whispered to the bohemian poet who had brought Iqbal's letter of recommendation: 'That is all that was needed. I shall write to the Education Department to find you a post as lecturer.'

A little later the Rajah of Rajahs awoke. 'Yes, Zijah,' he said, 'you were saying about Averroes that there was no greater scholar in Sicily. What, Ahdi? Have they all gone?'

'Yes, your lordship. It was time for your lordship's luncheon.'

'Very well. Have you anything else to tell me?'

'Nothing of importance, your lordship. But yesterday when I was out walking I saw a wonderful sight. I went to Gipsies' Hill. The summit commands a beautiful view over the city, and it occurred to me that if your lordship felt interested a fine suburb could be planned there for the nobility and the higher government officers. Have I your lordship's permission to submit a scheme?'

'Do so by all means. I shall take it personally to the Khan Hazrat, may he live forever, and obtain his approval. Tell me something of the scene on Gipsies' Hill. You know that romance I am writing these days?'

'*The Magical Tale of the Magnet and the Straw*? Yes, your lordship.'

'You know Munshi Gyan Chand? He told me that Sri Krishna had appeared to him in a dream and handed him some parts of this romance, saying to him 'Give these to Rajah Shamsher Singh; they are his work written in a former birth.'

'Just so, your lordship.'

'Well, describe the scene on Gipsies' Hill to Munshi Gyan Chand. I may have described it somewhere, I don't remember. Munshi Gyan Chand will receive his instructions from Sri Krishna...'

In *The Magical Tale of the Magnet and the Straw*, reckoned among the masterpieces of the Rajah of Rajahs, *Maharaja Sir Shujaat Shamsher Singh Ji Bahadur*, Munshi Gyan Chand, in accordance with the instructions received in his dream from the blue-bodied god, Lord Krishna, describes Gipsies' Hill in these words:

'The storytellers of olden time and the chroniclers of the traditions of ages long past tell that on Gipsies' Hill in former days there stood a great city, the twin in splendour and in population of its neighbour Farkhunda Nagar. Such was the charm of its dwellings and its gardens that the dwellings were gleaming white as the faces of the *houris* of paradise, while the dense shade of the trees of the gardens was as black as their long tresses—the envy of the long black night of separation. Only the great and the noble dwelt in the city. Commoners could not enter and no barking of dogs grated upon the ear. There was no market place, no commerce. It seemed an enchanted city where none laboured, yet all were blessed with wealth and high estate. If there were any who worked, they worked in Farkhunda Nagar, and the sweet-tongued chroniclers relate that they too dozed in their offices. In this earthly paradise, women would sit adorning their beauty at eventide, and the younger among them would sigh for the love of some swain. The *peri*, Gulandam, would sit writing love-letters or reading lovers' tales in the old romances, and would keep secret tryst with her demon-lover, Khanna Dev, behind the black rocks. But the fairest among these peris was the enchantress Nur Jahan. Her skin was like ivory, her cheeks bloomed like the rose, her delicate body was slender as the cypress, and her fragrance was the fragrance of musk; and the sweet-tongued chroniclers tell her story in this wise.

Translated by Ralph Russell

Rajinder Singh Bedi

(1915–84)

Rajinder Singh Bedi was born in Lahore. He worked as a clerk in the post office from 1933 to 1943, after which he took up a job with All India Radio. After Partition he moved to Delhi but he eventually settled in Bombay where he began a successful career in writing film scripts.

When Bedi published his first collection of short stories, *Dana-o Dam* (Of Grains and Nets), 1939, the PWM was at its height. Since his stories were about the joys and sorrows of the common man and written in a realistic style, he was labelled a Progressive, a tag that he accepted willingly because he felt that the Progressives were spirited revolutionaries and would infuse into literature the spirit of nationalist-socialistic reform. When the Movement became explicitly Marxist, in such a way that it restricted the flow of creativity, Bedi moved away from it.

Bedi's forte was writing about human relationships, particularly within the bounds of the lower middle class. Since he is much concerned with sex, domesticity, and marital complexities, women characters are central to Bedi's stories. He created a number of arresting, memorable characters such as Lajwanti, Kalyani, Holi, Ma, Rano, and Sita. His realism is infused with imagination. He draws upon the enormous corpus of Indian literature, especially the mythic, for metaphors to enrich his narrative. His Urdu is peppered with regionalisms, which set him apart. Each word in every sentence is placed after considerable thought, making his prose extraordinarily compact and powerful. The chronological order of his fictional works is as follows: *Dana-o Dam*, 1939; *Garhan* (Eclipse), 1942; *Kokhjali* (Burnt Womb), 1949; the novella, *Ek Chadar Maili Si* (A Sheet Somewhat Soiled), 1962; *Apne Dukh Mujhe De Do* (Give me your Sorrows), 1965; *Haath Hamare Qalam Huey* (Our Hands were Cut Off), 1974; and *Muktibodh* (Understanding Freedom), 1982.

The story presented here, '*Garhan*', is the title story from the second collection. Its distinctiveness lies not in the apparent pathos it evokes, but the parallelisms it creates to convey the irony inherent in the story of the Indian woman's suffering. It is the first among many stories in which Bedi maps the Hindu myths associated with planets, and raises them from the level of mythic astrology to the level of mythopoeic metaphors so as to read tragic meaning in the average Indian woman's life.

The Eclipse

Rupo, Shibbo, Katthu, and Munna—Holi had borne four boys to the Kayasthas of Asarhi village, and the fifth was about to be born in just a few more months. Deep dark circles had begun to form around her eyes; her cheekbones stood out and the flesh stuck to them. Holi, whose mother-in-law—*maiyya*—in the past used to call her *chanda rani* (moon princess) and whose radiance and beauty were the objects of Raseela's lust, had become pale and withered like a fallen leaf.

This was the night of a lunar eclipse. With the onset of dusk the moon transitions into the phase of its eclipse. Holi did not have permission to tear any cloth, lest the ears of the child in her stomach be torn as well. She couldn't sew, otherwise, her child would be born with its mouth sewn shut. She couldn't write a letter to her *maika*, or her bent and crooked letters would be written on her child's face. She deeply longed to write a letter to her parents.

As soon as the name of her maika came to her, her entire body would shake with a single peculiar sensation. When she was living at her maika, she desired to go to the *sasural*, but now she had become so fed up with living at the sasural that she wanted to run away from there. She even made up her mind to do so, but every time remained inopportune. Her maika was at a distance of twenty-five miles from Asarhi village. On the bank of the ocean in the port of Harphul, one could catch a steamer in the evening, and after a journey along the shore for about two hours, the large, rather rusted spires of the temple in the village of her maika would begin to come into view.

Today, before sunset, Holi must finish cooking and washing up. Her mother-in-law insisted that she must eat before the eclipse; otherwise, every movement in her bowel would affect the child in her womb, not just its physical being but also its destiny. As if that ugly woman with a frog-like nose expected Holi to be a Hamida Bano who was going to give birth to another Akbar the Great.

The family was large; four children, three men, two women, and four buffaloes with Holi alone to do the work. It took her all afternoon to clean up the pile of dishes. Then she went to prepare the feed for the cattle; soak correct proportions of oil cake, cotton seeds, and gram. Her haunches were tearing with pain and the rebellious child in her womb began to protest, albeit ineffectually, but nonetheless caused Holi more discomfort than anything. Tired and defeated, she sat down on the wooden seat, but she couldn't sit too long on a wooden seat or the floor, because according to her mother-in-law, if one sat too long on the broad and flat wooden seat, the child's head would become flat. If at all Holi must sit, it should be on one of those circular, woven stools made of bamboo strips. Once in a while, avoiding her in-laws' scrutiny, Holi would lie down on the string bed, yawn and stretch her legs to the fullest extent, like a well-fed bitch. Then, with trembling hands she would massage her swollen belly which held her little tormentor.

She couldn't bring herself to forget that she was the daughter of Seetal, a prosperous moneylender of Sarangdev village. Peasants from villages twenty miles around went to Seetal to borrow money on interest. In spite of this, she was humiliated by her in-laws who were Kayasthas. Holi was treated worse than dogs. The Kayasthas wanted children. Holi could go to hell for all they cared. As though in the whole of Gujarat, only these Kayasthas understood the real meaning of *kulvadhu*: the proverbial woman, the family's symbol of fecundity.

Every year or year and a half, they were pleased to see a new critter crawling in their courtyard. Due to her continuous child-bearing, all the food that she ate did not show in her appearance. Perhaps she was fed only because the child in her stomach wanted food, and that is why as soon as she became pregnant she was allowed savouries and assorted fruits in generous measure.

Holi would think to herself, even my younger brother-in-law beats me. But her mother-in-law's jibes were a lot worse than those beatings; and when her father-in-law lost his temper, she would feel the ground slip beneath her feet. What right did they have to oppress her so?... Raseela was another case altogether. The *shastra*s have given a husband the status of a god. Blessed is the knife with which he stabs... But has any woman had a hand in the writing of the shastras? And maiyya, she is a class apart. If a woman had written the shastras, she would have imposed stricter regulations on her fellow women...

Disguised, Rahu was blissfully savouring the divine nectar. The sun and the moon informed Lord Vishnu of this sacrilege and God Vishnu with his divine discus sliced Rahu into two pieces. The head and torso flew up into the sky and became Rahu and Ketu. Now twice every year, they wreak vengeance on the sun and the moon. Mysterious are the ways of the gods, Holi would think… And how strange is Rahu's visage! A black demon mounted on a lion, he appears so fearsome. Raseela also looks just like Rahu. She had yet to take her fortieth day's bath after Munna's birth when he started demanding his conjugal rights. Did she have to repay a debt to him too?

Just then, she heard the mother and son's footsteps. Supporting her stomach with both hands, she quickly got up and put the griddle on the low flame of the hearth. She found it increasingly difficult to bend and blow at the embers to stoke the fire. She had tried, but felt as if her eyes would pop out of their sockets.

Raseela entered the kitchen, holding a newly repaired winnowing basket. Mumbling, he washed his hands. His mother followed him in and immediately asked, 'Bahu, have you stored away the grain?'

'Yes, ye-yes…I have—no, I haven't. I forgot, maiyya…' Holi replied in a faltering voice.

'Then what are you doing sitting here, my dear lady.'

Holi looked at Raseela with beseeching eyes and said, 'I can't move the sack of grain in my present condition, can I?'

Maiyya was speechless. She was more concerned about the child in the womb than she was about Holi. Perhaps that is why she looked pointedly into Holi's eyes and said, 'Why have you put *kajal* in your eyes, woman? You slut, don't you know that there will be an eclipse tonight? What if the child goes blind? How will a slut like you bring up a child like that?'

Holi became silent. With her eyes rooted to the ground, she began mumbling to herself. She could endure all abuses, but she couldn't bear to be called a slut. Seeing her mumbling, maiyya continued her tirade, all the while aggressively searching for the bunch of keys. A mortar and pestle for grinding collyrium was kept near a dirty candle stand. Fishing out the bunch of keys from there, maiyya went towards the storeroom. Holi was now alone. Raseela threw a lascivious look at Holi and tugged the edge of her sari suggestively. Apprehensive, Holi pulled back the sari end and began to call out to her younger brother-in-law as if she wanted the presence of another person in the kitchen. Spurning a man's advances is not a simple offence. Raseela was incensed. He spoke through clenched teeth, 'What was the rush, I say?'

'What rush?'

'This,' Raseela pointed to her belly. 'You are a bitch, a bitch.'

'How am I to blame for it?' Holi said in a trembling voice.

With these simple words Holi had made out Raseela to be uncouth, lecherous, and a brute. The arrow found its mark. Raseela was at a loss for words. A speechless man's weapon is a slap, and the very next moment Holi's cheek bore the mark of his fingers. Just then, maiyya emerged from the storeroom with a basket of lentils and rebuked her son for his poor behaviour with his wife. Holi was indifferent towards Raseela's slap, but she was indignant at her mother-in-law's platitude—the slut, she could say whatever she wanted. And when her son abused Holi, she offered inanities, what did she think...

Yesterday Raseela had slapped her because she hadn't offered a reply, and he hit her today because she had answered back. She knew why he was annoyed. Why he kept bad mouthing her, why he found fault with her cooking, everything that she did...and her condition. She was utterly fed up. Men put women into this state, and then distanced themselves. These men!

Maiyya piled some rice, lentils, salt, etc., on the kitchen floor, and proceeded to weigh them on a scale. The scales were wet. She must have known. When the rice grains stuck to the bottom of the scale, she blamed Holi for being careless. And then began to wipe the mess with her clean *dupatta*. When the dupatta became dirty, she threw it in Holi's direction with the injunction, 'Go wash this.'

Now Holi didn't know whether she should cook the rotis or wash the dupatta. Whether she should speak or be silent. If she should move or stay put. A bitch or a lady, she thought it better to wash the dupatta. The moon was about to enter the orbit of the eclipse. The baby would be born scrunched up like the cloth she was washing. And if she was accused of having produced an ugly child, was she to be blamed? But it wasn't a question of her fault or her innocence. No one cared about that anyway. All blame was Holi's.

At that time, the memories of Sarangdev village came to her. How she would dance the *garba* with other women at the beginning of the month of Asauj, and light would gush out from the holes in the water pot her sister-in-law carried on her head, illuminating the entire hall. Meanwhile, all the women would clap their henna-covered hands and sing:

The henna shrub grows in Malva
But it has coloured Gujarat
Henna touches everything

At that time, she was a young girl bouncing and jumping like a poem without the restrictions of metre or rhyme. She would get whatever she wanted. She was the youngest in the house. She was not born of nobility, and her girlfriends…they must have been married off already.

In Sarangdev village on the event of an eclipse, charity was doled out generously. Women gathered together and went to Trivedi Ghat for ritual bathing. Flowers, coconuts, and sweet sugar cakes are set afloat in the ocean. The gaping mouth of a cresting wave comes and takes away flower petals. At the time of bathing, everybody's sins, both men's and women's alike, are forgiven. These sins are those that people committed throughout the past year. With the bath, sin is washed away. The body and the soul become pure. The ocean's waves sweep away everybody's sins, taking them far, far away across an unknown, uncrossable, unbounded ocean. One year later, people's bodies again become stained with sin; they become scarred. Then another wave of clemency washes over them, and all is pure and clean again.

When the eclipse starts, and the radiant honour of the moon becomes stained, for several moments there is silence everywhere. Then the chanting of 'Ram, Ram' begins; then, the gongs and the conches simultaneously begin to sound. After bathing in the midst of this cacophonous uproar, all the men and women return to the village, singing and chanting as one.

In the midst of the eclipse, poor people run throughout the markets and back alleys. Twirling their crutches and holding their sacks and begging bowls, the lame scurry around like plague-stricken rats, falling over one another in the process. Because Rahu and Ketu have taken the beautiful moon completely into their clutches, the kind-hearted Hindu gives charity so that the poor moon will be released. These scurrying beggars go through a journey of many miles in order to receive charity, all the while chanting 'Let go! Let go! It's time for charity!'

The moon was about to transition into its eclipse. Holi left her children with the elders of the community, tied on a filthy old dhoti, and set out towards Harphul port with the other women for the ritual bathing.

Maiyya, Raseela, the oldest boy Shibbo, and Holi were heading towards the ocean. Flowers, garlands, and mango leaves were in their hands. In Holi's mother-in-law's hands, besides her string of *rudraksha* beads, there were cubes of camphor that she wanted to light and place in the water so that her path would be illuminated in the next life. Holi was afraid—would *her* sins be washed away by the ocean's water too?

There was a steamer docked at the ocean's edge about three-fourths of a mile from the ghat. That was the part of Harphul port, on the port's uneven shore and tiny dock, where some workers were making small, inconsequential efforts against the backdrop of the struggle between light and darkness at sunset, and where a soft-flickering light from one of the cabins in the steamer was dancing on the mercurial water's waves. Eventually, the waterwheel was seen spinning around. Several indistinct shadows began to pull up a large coiled rope. The steamer's final whistle sounded at 8 o'clock. Then it would depart for Sarangdev village. If Holi were a passenger, then about two hours later those temple spires of Sarangdev, bathed in the moonlight for centuries, would again come into view—and then her mother, she, Holi, unmarried and dancing the garba.

Holi glanced towards Shibbo. Shibbo was perplexed why his mother crouched down in the crowd and kissed his forehead, and from where that warm drop fell on his cheek. He ran up and took hold of Raseela's hand. They came together to the ghat where men and women were separated. Not forever but merely for a few hours...this water would bear witness to the times when women were tied to men. What mystical, unknown power was in the water? From afar, the flickering light from the steamer was reaching Holi.

Holi wanted to run, but how could she. She tightened her flimsy sari firmly. The sari kept slipping down... In half-an-hour she was standing across from the docked steamer. She wasn't across from the steamer; she was across from Sarangdev village...Holi remembered the spires, the temple bells, the steamer's whistle, and then she remembered that she didn't have money for a ticket.

She sat down in one of the corners of the steamer and was motionless for a long time. A worker came at a quarter to eight, and demanded Holi's ticket. On not getting her ticket, he slipped away silently. A little while later, the whisperings of employees began to be heard; then in the darkness, there was the sound of stifled laughter and conversation. Holi recognized some of the words, 'Chicken... Take more... I have the keys... There's too much water.'

Afterwards, several wild bursts of laughter cut the silence, and moments later, three or four men began to push Holi into a dark corner of the steamer. At that time, one of the inspectors came aboard. Just as Holi's world was becoming dark, there was a ray of hope. That inspector was certainly one of the boys from Sarangdev village, and therefore was like her *bhai* or brother. Six years ago, he left the village with great ambition, and crossing the Sabarmati River, set out for some unknown destination. Sometimes, at the time of misfortune, a person's senses become heightened. Holi immediately recognized the guard's voice, and quite bravely spoke:

'Kathoram!'

Kathoram recognized the sweet voice of his childhood friend too. He used to play with her when they were young.

Kathoram spoke:

'Holi!'

Holi was filled with reassurance, but spoke in a strained voice: 'Katho, take me to Sarangdev village.'

Kathoram came close. He glared at one of the workers and said, 'Holi, will you go to Sarangdev?' And then, Kathoram spoke, addressing the man standing across from him, 'Why did you place her here, bhai?'

The worker standing the closest said, 'She's some troubled, distressed woman. She doesn't even have money for a ticket. We were thinking, what can we do to help her?'

Kathoram took Holi by his side and got down from the steamer. Setting his foot on the dock, Kathoram said, 'Holi, have you run away from Asarhi?'

'Yes.'

'Is this how well-bred women behave? If I were to inform the Kayasthas, then...'

Holi shook with fear. She was born of a family that was neither noble nor high-status. In this place and in such a condition, she could not say anything at all to Kathoram. Feeling weak, Holi silently listened to the sound of the ocean's rolling waves. Ahead of her, the steamer's rope was loosened. There was a low whistle, and Sarangdev village ominously vanished from Holi's sights. She looked back once. A long streak of foam following the steamer could be seen in its soft light.

Kathoram spoke, 'Don't be afraid, Holi. I will help you in every way possible. There's a boat docked not too far from here. I'll lead you there in the morning. Don't worry so much. Stay with me at the inn tonight.'

Kathoram took Holi to the inn. The owner of the inn stared at Kathoram and his companion with great bewilderment. When he could no longer stay quiet, he asked Kathoram in a deliberately slow voice:

'Who is she?'

Kathoram softly replied, 'She's my wife.'

Holi's eyes glazed over. The next moment, she clutched her stomach and sat down leaning against the wall. Kathoram rented a room in the inn. Holi fearfully set foot in the room. After a while, Kathoram came inside. The smell of alcohol was on his breath.

A huge and heavy wave came from the ocean. All of the flowers, sweet cakes, mango tree stems, garlands, and lighted camphors were swept away. It also took humanity's terrible sins along with it...far, far away towards an unknown, uncrossable, unbounded ocean...where there was only darkness...then the conches began to sound. At that time, a woman came running out of the inn. Charging ahead...at full speed...she fell, ran, sat clutching her stomach, panted, and began to run...at this time the moon

was in its total eclipse. Rahu and Ketu had completely extracted their debt to their heart's content... Two indistinct shadows were running here and there anxious to help this woman... Everywhere there was only darkness. And from afar, barely-audible voices were coming from Asarhi—
'It's time for charity... Let go, let go, let go...'
From Harphul port, there was the voice—
'Catch [her]...catch [her]...catch [her]'...
'Let go... It's time for charity...catch [her]... Let go!!'

Translated by Mehr Afshan Farooqi and Jonathan Loar

Ahmad Nadeem Qasimi
(1916–2006)

Fiction writer, poet, essayist, and editor, Ahmad Nadeem Qasimi's prolific output and exemplary services to Urdu literature made him a legend in his lifetime. Born Ahmad Shah in Anga, a small village in Punjab, into a family of learned theologians, he received his early education at home. He lived most of his life in Lahore working as a journalist and/or editor of a fairly large range of publications. He was the editor of literary journals such as *Adab-e Latif*, *Savera*, *Nuqoosh*, and *Funoon*. A dedicated member of the PWM, he was appointed the secretary of the Association's Pakistani wing in 1949. He was jailed for two years under the Pakistan Government's Safety Act for the Association's adoption of 'extreme socialist resolutions'. However, he continued trying to resuscitate the PWM but without success.

Qasimi wrote in what is called the 'realistic' mode; his stories follow a linear chronological path that is fairly straightforward and uncluttered. In his early work he comes across as an unabashed crusader, zealous and eager for social reform. The early stories are emotional and tend to be repetitive depictions of life in rural settings. His mature work shows more restraint and polish. Even though Qasimi's basic concern in his fiction is social amelioration, he does explore the uncharted space in human nature when what can be considered oppressive becomes a need to the oppressed, the bewilderment when the freedom once longed for arrives but the sense of direction is missing.

Ahmad Nadeem Qasimi has published sixteen collections of short stories, eight volumes of poetry, and numerous essays.

Sultan

Dada clasped Sultan's head with his left hand while his right clutched a staff that made a loud tapping noise on the cement pavement as he walked.

When Sultan paused for a moment, Dada quickly uttered his practiced speech, 'O babuji, this blind fakir...'

'No Dada,' Sultan interrupted, 'its not a babu, it's a juggler's show.'

'Damn the jugg...' Dada collapsed into a coughing fit before he could rattle off the expletive. He took his hand off Sultan's head, clutched his chest and succumbed to a long spell of coughing.

By the time his breathing steadied, Sultan had watched the juggler transform the rags under his basket into two plump sparkling white pigeons.

Dada waved his left arm in the air and called, 'Where are you?'

Sultan immediately placed his head under Dada's crustacean grip and they started walking down the pavement again.

When Dada's staff hit a lamp post the pillar rang out and Sultan called, 'Dada, did you hear? The lamp post rang!'

'Yes.' Dada stopped and tried to strike the post again but missed. 'Pillars talk. Here, you try it.'

Sultan took Dada's staff and struck the lamp post and Dada said, 'See? When I was little like you, I used to stand with my ears glued listening to the lamp posts. They used to sound like English ladies then.' Dada mimicked their voices, 'You good. You bad.'

'English ladies spoke through lamp posts?' Sultan was astonished. 'Who talks now, Dada?' Suddenly his manner changed and he whispered, 'Two babus are coming this way.'

Dada swiftly began his speech, 'O babu, in God's name give a paisa to the blind beggar to buy a roti. May you prosper. May God give you sons and grandsons.'

One of the men laughed loudly and said, 'This old man seems to be carrying on propaganda against family planning.' They passed by, laughing.

'Have they gone?' Dada asked in a low tone.

'They're gone.' Sultan whispered back. After a brief pause he swore at them.

Dada pressed his fingers into Sultan's skull. 'Stop this nonsense. What did I tell you yesterday? If they hear you they'll twist your neck.'

Sultan walked quietly with Dada; after a little while, he said, 'Dada, will you scratch my scalp, the spot just beneath your thumb? Yes, right there.'

The grandfather rubbed his thumb on Sultan's temple.

'Sultan?' Dada inquired after a long while. 'Where are all the people today? You haven't stopped anywhere so far.'

'They're dead.' Sultan replied. He suddenly paused and said, 'What day of the week is it Dada?'

'What do I know, my son.' Dada replied. 'You should keep track of the days; for me day and night are all the same.' He stopped to think, then said, 'Day before yesterday you took me to the green dome mosque, didn't you? It was Friday then; so it will be Sunday today. Curse Sundays. All babus must be staying home today, spending time with their wives and children.'

Sultan stood stock-still as though something horrible had happened.

Suddenly the sound of a coin being dropped rang out. Some passer-by had dropped a coin in Sultan's bowl.

'Got something? What was it?' Dada asked.

'It's a one paisa coin; the small one, new,' Sultan replied.

Dada rubbed Sultan's head with his fingers, 'Go buy something to eat. Go, I'll stand here.'

'There's nothing to get with one paisa,' Sultan replied, 'if we get a couple more I'll buy sugar cane chunks.'

The old man lifted his hand from Sultan's head and dug in his pocket, 'Here are two paisas saved from yesterday. Eat something. You haven't eaten all morning. Children get hungry fast. Go on.'

When Sultan took the money, Dada said, 'Come back quickly. I'll stand here. Now where am I standing?'

Sultan took Dada's hand and said, 'Move to the left; here, lean against the lamp post.'

Dada stood there leaning against the lamp post. He stood that way for some time. Then he put his ear on the post as if listening to something and smiled. All of a sudden he began to shout as though something was amiss, 'Sultan! Sultan.' Then he began to curse, 'Are you dead, you bastard. Where have you gone?' Not getting any response, he began turning this way and that pleading, 'O good people, my little grandson has gone to buy two paisa worth of food. His name is Sultan. Please tell me that the unfortunate one hasn't been run over by a car or tonga.' Then he shouted, 'O Sultan!'

'Coming, Dada!' Sultan's voice came from a distance. But the shouting had brought on a coughing fit. When his breathing steadied, he turned and asked as if talking to the lamp post, 'Had you dropped dead?'

Sultan lifted Dada's left hand and placed it on his head, 'I was watching the juggler. He was pulling balls out of his stomach.'

Dada pressed his fingers hard into Sultan's head as though he were going to lift him up, 'Take me home, I'll show you juggler's tricks there... bastard! Left this poor blind man standing by the wayside like that.'

Sultan began to walk quietly. After a little while the old man asked gently, 'What did you eat?'

'Sugar cane chunks,' Sultan replied.

'You unfortunate wretch! Sugar cane chunks are nothing but water.' Dada was losing his temper again. 'You should have bought chick peas; that would have kept you going till the afternoon.'

Sultan remained quiet.

'I hope the bowl is not hanging limp in your hand?' The old man inquired.

'No, Dada.'

'That's right,' Dada remonstrated gently, 'always keep the bowl facing up or people will mistake you for a shopper, not a beggar.'

Sultan perked up, 'Once I was going with the bowl in my hand to buy some oil and a gentleman dropped a two anna coin into it. Do you remember, Dada?'

'Yes, I do,' the old man replied, 'but that doesn't happen often. There aren't many gentlemen like that one.'

'Dada,' Sultan asked, 'please scratch me in the same spot beneath your thumb again.'

The old man rubbed his thumb hard on the boy's temple and said: 'When we get home today, I'm going to ask Zebo to pick the lice from your hair. You do something for her in return. Fetch a bucket of water or something.'

'Okay.' Sultan replied.

After they got home Sultan would lead Dada to his string bed and help him settle down. The old man would lean his staff against the cot and take his hand away from Sultan's head. As soon as the hand was off his head Sultan would experience a sense of weightlessness; his feet that felt as though fettered with iron became free as if they had rubber wheels. He would slip out from the shelter and, avoiding Aunt Zebo's vigilant eyes, run off to the playfield amidst the big houses where rich people's children played cricket and poor folk's children fielded for them. When the rich boys left, the servant children would play, usually glass marbles. At one time Sultan had joined in their game too. He played with them for several days; then, the sweeper's son broke the news that he was a blind beggar's boy. From then on he was banished from the game. But whenever a marble strayed by accident Sultan would run and get it. He would twirl the marble between his fingers before returning it. He had wept for hours once and got a few paise from Dada to buy glass marbles. But when he took them to the playground the children saw them and they snatched them from him, claiming them as theirs. Who ever heard of a beggar boy owning marbles, they had jeered. He had stamped his feet in frustration and cried. But the next day he was back at the playfield.

Once he was at the playground he was always apprehensive of going back home lest Dada clutch his head in his bony hand and make him walk through every street in town. He knew that as soon he opened his eyes in the morning he would have to go begging with Dada; that is why as soon he was up his head felt as though he wore a hat made of stone. He felt each of Dada's five fingers radiate pain that shot through his skull;

so when Dada would finish his early morning prayer, call out to him to bring his staff and then place his hand on his head, Sultan felt half dead. Asleep or awake, the hand haunted him like a ghost. The hand held him captive as he walked through the streets as handcuffed prisoners walk with the police, and finally at the prison house they stand behind the iron bars and stare at the happy faces of people passing by. But they can only look, for the bars stick to their eyes like crosses.

Walking with Dada's hand on his head he would sometimes wish he could stop to grab and eat the sugar cane chunks that had rolled off the vendor's cart and lay by the edge of the open drain. He could pick up the banana peel that had been thrown by a passer-by and lick it. But whenever he asked Dada to stop for a moment on any pretext the old man would dig his fingers into his skull and admonish, 'Did I bring you here for a stroll or are you here to help me beg? You unfortunate child, if we don't earn four-five annas by the end of the day, will Zebo prepare food for us from her own pocket? Isn't it enough that she has allowed us to live in a corner of her hut?'

Some years back when Dada, having finished his round of the bungalows, passed by the servants' quarters and was walking past Begoo the tonga driver's hut, Begoo's mother had come outside and said to him, 'Baba, pray to God that my son gets relief from the pain in his ribs. I'll give you a whole rupee if he gets well.'

Dada stood right there and prayed. After a few days he asked Sultan to take him past those bungalows again. They hadn't reached the bungalows yet when Zebo saw them. She gave Dada a rupee and asked, 'Tell me where you live Baba? I'll come by every Thursday to pay my respects.' When she learnt that the two of them slept under whichever shelter they found on the street, she had her son clear out the space beneath the awning in front of her hut and asked them to stay there. They would give her their day's collections and she would cook their food for them. These days she was asking Dada to say prayers for her son to have children.

Sultan disliked Aunt Zebo as much as he disliked Dada. Whenever he tried to slip away after bringing back Dada from the begging rounds, she would shout and say, 'Look, he's off to play, leaving his old, crippled grandfather alone.'

On days when Dada got fatigued and came back in the afternoon, and Sultan hadn't had a chance to slip out, the old man would rest for awhile, then grabbing his staff he would ask the boy to take him on another round of the chowk, saying, 'If we get more today, tomorrow you can have the day off.' But Sultan never got that day off, for they never ever got that 'extra money'.

However, what had been happening more often now was that the old man would have attacks of asthma through the night and cough and pant till daybreak and be half dead. On those days he would not go out begging, but Sultan still could not get time off because he would have to massage Dada's shoulder and ribcage all day long. If his hands paused Dada would call out in an asthmatic wheeze, 'Hey Sultan, what are you doing? Are you dead?'

Sultan would immediately start rubbing Dada's shoulder and say to himself, 'May God make you die, Dada. By God, when you die, it will be great. I wish you would die now, this very moment, and I would go to the bungalows and beg the mistress for her child's hat and cover my head with it.'

Then one day Dada did die. Throughout the night he had sat with his head between his knees, coughing and panting; his ribs ached, racked with pain. Sultan massaged his shoulder and pressed the joints of his spine for a long time, then he fell asleep. In the morning, a weeping Aunt Zebo informed him that his Dada had passed away.

Suddenly Sultan felt sparklers dazzling inside of him, and he said, 'Really?' As if he could not believe that Dadas could die. Then, Begoo the coachman gathered some people and they bathed the body and took it for burial.

Aunt Zebo sobbed intermittently and her daughter-in-law kept Sultan close to her side the whole day. When Begoo returned from the graveyard, he brought some sugarcane chunks for Sultan, and sucking on the chunks, Sultan thought it's so much fun when Dadas die.

That night, Aunt Zebo didn't let him sleep outside under the awning thinking he would be scared since he was just a child. In the morning she gave him a leftover roti and a cup of buttermilk. When he got up after finishing breakfast, she asked, 'Where are you off to, son?'

Sultan found this question odd. Why should she care where he went? Dada was dead, after all.

When Sultan was silent, she said, 'My son, beggar boys don't go out to play.' Then she took his hand and brought him out, gave him his begging bowl and said, 'If beggars won't beg, what will they eat? Try to bring back eight or ten annas tonight. I'll make a pullau for you. Go son, choose a busy street. May God be with you.'

Sultan took the bowl, but paused after leaving the shelter. He went back as if he had forgotten something. Then he began to cry bitterly. But ran out again before Aunt Zebo could envelop him in her outstretched arms.

His face was drenched with tears when he pushed his bowl in front of someone on the street. 'Babuji, in the name of God, give something to this blind beggar to buy a roti,' he repeated Dada's line. 'Are you blind?' The man asked sternly. Sultan suddenly realized his mistake and shook his head in confusion. Then he burst into tears.

'You tell lies and cry at the same time?' The man scolded him. 'Want to work?' He asked. When Sultan did not reply, he moved on.

'Babuji, give me money for the sake of God,' Sultan called out in a choked voice.

The man walked on without turning back. He had gone quite a distance when Sultan began running towards him calling, 'Babuji, Babuji.' The man stopped. Some passers-by also stopped to watch.

'Want to work?' The man asked.

'Babuji,' Sultan caught up, breathless. His lower lip pouting, he said, 'I don't want work. I don't want alms,' and he threw the bowl on the ground.

The man looked at the crowd gathering around them and said harshly, 'Then why did you call out to me?'

A flood of tears brimmed in Sultan's eyes. His lips began to quiver, and with an effort he said, 'Babuji, may God bless you. Please walk with me with your hand on my head. May God shower you with good fortune. My head hurts.'

'And what else?' The man looked at the crowd, nonplussed.

Translated by Mehr Afshan Farooqi

Muhammad Hasan Askari
(1919–78)

Muhammad Hasan Askari's given name was Izharul Haq. He was born in Saravah near Bulandshahr in western Uttar Pradesh. He joined Allahabad University as an undergraduate in 1938 and went on to get a master's degree in English literature. He began publishing his short stories while still a student and soon matured into one of Urdu's most original and brilliant literary critics, and a translator and fiction writer of distinction. His first job was of a scriptwriter for All India Radio. Soon after that he began writing a literary column titled *Jhalkiyan* (Glimpses) for the Urdu journal *Saqi* that was published from Delhi. By then he had published his first collection of short stories, *Jazire* (Islands), 1943. After Partition, he migrated to Pakistan and stayed at Lahore, working as a full time writer; he led the debate on what would constitute 'Pakistani culture'. In 1950, he moved to Karachi and worked as editor of the literary magazine *Mah-e Nau* for several months. He was appointed professor of English literature at Karachi's Islamiya College in 1950 and he taught there until the end of his career. Askari's collected works have been published from Lahore in two separate volumes, *Askarinama: Afsane, Mazameen* (Askarinama: Short Stories, Essays), 1998; and *Majmu'a Muhammad Hasan Askari* (Collected Works of Muhammad Hasan Askari), 2000.

Askari was a strong critic of the Progressive-Marxist ideology in Urdu. There is no doubt that Askari's critical prose is among the most delightful, as well as incisive and trenchant, written in the six centuries of Urdu literary production. The prose of his fiction (unfortunately, he wrote only eleven stories) is of a different type—slow, subtle and measured, and occasionally inclined to drag because of his preoccupation with detail. He has two models: one of critical prose and the other of creative prose. Askari's creative oeuvre was a conscious implementation of his thoughts on prose, usage, syntax, and language. He felt that literary Urdu was lacking in the full development of the long, complex sentence, and therefore, in his own creative writing he attempted, often zealously, to experiment with the run-on sentence.

The story '*Haramjadi*' is Askari's favourite, and it serves as a model of his many ideas on writing fiction in Urdu. The story is based on a conceit suggested by the title 'Haramjadi', which is a rustic, dialectical variant of *haramzadi*. The literal meaning of haramzadi is 'illegitimate'. But the local midwife uses the pejorative, not to imply that the Anglo-Indian, Emily, is a bastard, but an interloper, someone invading her cultural space, behaving inappropriately, a woman of loose morals. In Urdu, the implication of haramjadi is more forceful than 'illegitimate' or 'bastard', closer to the English word 'bitch'.

The Bitch

The loud thumping on the door and the continuous, stubborn shouts of 'open up!' resounded in her brain like the long drawn out groaning sound of a bucket hitting the water in a dark, deep well. Her sleep-laden and half-willing eyes opened slowly, but the very next moment the kohl-like darkness that tinged the faint light of early dawn began to fill her eyelids, and they shut again. They drooped like heavy blankets, gently pressing on her eyeballs, sending them to slumber. But her ears, out of tune with her eyes, were buzzing. They wanted to shut their windows against the new assault of the early rising invader—and yet they were buzzing.

This conflict of hope and hopelessness which perhaps sleep's torrent would have drowned quickly didn't last long enough; for now, even the door hinges were coming apart, and the voices were emanating from a throat that was more impatient, restless, harsh, and hoarse. 'Open the door, open the door,' the voices were penetrating her brain like sharp, thin needles and were tearing the blanket of sleep into shreds. She could hear the caller in between his shouts of 'Open up, open up' also muttering unpleasant things, indicating unpleasant intentions, and swearing under his breath in between pauses. And not only that, some fellow was advising him to pick up rocks and pebbles from the street and throw them at the house. Eventually she opened her eyes wide and slapping her hands on the bed called: 'Nasiban, look who's there.'

There was nothing new for her in all of this. Ever since she had been posted to this small provincial town as a midwife, this was a daily affair: the shouts, the banging, the unpleasant conflict between duty and rest, the same bitter tussle, the same annoyance, and then the same retreat—all this as usual. She had to get up and leave early and then spend all day watching newborns arrive protesting and screaming, flinging their hands and feet. Part of the day was spent inspecting the progress of the new babies and going back and forth to the town area office for registering the births and deaths. She could barely find time for lunch and a little rest in the afternoon, and that too wasn't always possible. Because babies don't care a twit about things like appropriate time or place—four o'clock in the morning, twelve o'clock noon, two o'clock at night, every hour, every moment, she had to be ready to answer the call—'Here I am, here I come.' And the babies, they kept coming so fast, like little stones hurtling along in a mountain spring. Popular talks about birth control had been unable to travel down the dirt and pothole-ridden road that connected Daulat Nagar with the city, and if somehow they could have managed to crawl there, it was a sure thing that the folks there would not regard them worthy of the least attention, for they knew very well that the birth of babies was ordained by God. And what power did man have in the matter? Eighteen year-old boys, fifty year-old men, inexperienced young girls, middle-aged women, all of them with an astounding industry and singleness of purpose, as if they were labourers toiling in the factories for the purpose of national defence, kept adding to the numbers of urchins playing in the roadside drains. And what could those poor souls do anyway? They were helpless at God's command. In short, babies were arriving: dark babies, pale babies, babies red like plucked chickens, and occasionally fair babies, thin, bundles of skin and bones, or then some plump and healthy babies, with kinky hair, others flat-nosed, soft pulpy babies like voles, others hard like wood, babies of all kind and colour.

Emily had heard her grandmother say that once when she was small it had rained frogs, and these frogs weighed as much as half a pound each. Sometimes Emily would think—and the thought would make her smile in spite of herself—that these babies were those very frogs, yellow half-pounders.

And it was just for the purpose of watching each and every drop of this yellow frog-rain dropping away that she had to wander all the livelong day through the broken cobblestone roads of the small town, through narrow, dark, and dank lanes, through dirt and dust, past heaps of garbage and red and yellow dogs that kept barking away, and shopping places chock-full of farmers' carts and grass cutters. The narrow streets always had sandy margins on both sides, and the drains, they had to be right in the middle, their blackness usurping a large part of the road like the smeared kohl from the eyes of a rustic woman. Sweepers cleaned these drains and piled the muck on the road itself. So, to protect her sari from the filth, she had to wear her high-heeled black shoes instead of her pretty light blue sandals. The high heels made her unstable because of the innumerable stones sticking out from the surface of the road. The boisterous frolic of the thoughtless brats playing tipcat on the roadside invariably caused her clothes to get stained. Thankfully, however, she always managed to get home with her eyes and teeth intact. And the heat! She felt as if she would surely melt away with sweat. Despite the narrowness of the streets the sun shone with such piercing intensity that she felt sparks dancing on her body, and her parasol printed with blue flowers became nothing but a burden. When stumbling and balancing herself on high heels, burning and roasting in the sun she walked on the road, the sound of the *alha* being sung from afar, the clack of the drum, the loud and harsh cackles of card players sitting under trees in groups seemed hateful and sneering like the buzzing of heavy flies making sleep impossible on an afternoon, and she would be lost in the memories of the city she left four months ago. But now, the city became the land of dreams that eluded recall even after a thousand efforts in the morning and the faith in its delicate beauty kept her heart restless all day. She imagined she saw a light somewhere...a sparkle, an openness, a vastness—a bit of greenery floated in front of her eyes...and then she would again be stumbling along and regaining her balance on that street of burning pebbles, drains, and gritty sand. Even imagining the room with an electric fan didn't help diminish her feverish, burning pain. Yes, if by a stroke of luck she happened to be free on a night and got the chance to stay awake lying in bed, then pictures of city life glided before her eyes, clear and bright like those on a cinema screen; she could stop any picture she liked for as long as she wanted. But if in the midst of enjoying these pictures she was reminded of the scenes she had to confront every day, her weariness and dejection would slowly rise up again. The walls of the house would close around her with their nightly darkness, her heart would sink, her breath become short and laboured, and her reeling brain would at last be drowned in the senselessness of sleep, and she would dream that she was back in her old hospital, but this time its walls and doors seemed to be oozing something like unconcern instead of friendliness, and her limbs were frozen into immobility and some unknown fear was weighing on her heart. She had this dream three or four times during the night, and in truth comparing these two lives should obviously have produced such an effect on her. Admittedly, in the city too there were dank lanes, broken roads, dust and dirt, and naughty urchins; it wasn't that she was unaware of them. Like a bird on the wing, careless and content, she would sit on the cushions of the tonga, lightly swaying, and would pass by those neighbourhoods once in a fortnight or so. Her world was in the main hospital of the district, away from those other localities. What an open place it was, she would never forget the sweetness of the air there all her life. There was a broad tar road in front of the hospital, swept twice a day, it always shone like glass. In the evenings, when she stepped out on the road for a stroll with her friend Dina, cool breezes blowing across the meadows caressed her eyes and cooled her brain. Her sari would flutter in the breeze, a lock of hair would fall and sway on her forehead and her gait would become light and brisk. How pleasant and enjoyable it used to be to talk during these walks. There wasn't a trace of dirt or dust here. The hot winds of May and June sped over the white buildings and glass structures of the hospital, headed for the city, and not even a shadow of the harshness and sadness of the afternoon could touch the rooms cooled by electric fans. When she passed by with a stately air, adjusting the hem of her sari, the servants at the hospital would greet her from all sides, addressing her as 'memsahib, memsahib,' though everyone here addressed her as 'memsahib' too. Sweepers would pause while sweeping the roads when they saw her approaching. Even the *zamindar* of these parts spoke to her using the polite form of address, 'aap'. Still one couldn't capture that ambience here. That awe, that grandeur, that feeling of authority, her presence was an unalienable part of the hospital, a living embodiment of the cool, white and grave building, its invisible but unshakable laws and principles. No one could move in protest once faced with the hospital's knife. In the same way, everything entering her zone of authority had to fall in line with her wishes. They always began preparing the wards ahead of her round of inspection of patients. She would rebuke even the paying patients, for she couldn't tolerate betel leaf juice on the walls of her clean ward. At the slightest lack of care or violation of instructions, she would rudely yell at even those who were most likely to give themselves airs. She always spoke to people using the familiar form of address: 'tum.' But the women here were very outspoken. They were scared and afraid of her, but didn't miss a chance to answer back. After trying for several days, she had given up hope of keeping them in line and let them do pretty much as they liked. And these women didn't know the first thing about cleanliness and proper management. Even in summer, a woman in labour was promptly shut up in a room crowded with winter bedding, earthen pots filled with rice and other grain, broken string beds, pots and pans, pots full of coal, bundles of cotton twine and coarse thread, and all kinds of odds and ends, while someone lighted a brazier and put a pot with a concoction of herbs on it. In some homes they would quickly begin to daub the floor with cow dung, which would get unstuck with people's feet and make the floor into a mess totally unfit for walking, and its moisture would mingle with the heat of the coals and make breathing impossible. All the women of the house, and there would be at least four, would crash into the room with their smelly clothes and in their nervousness upset all the things inside so that one couldn't find even a rag. All this clatter and the loud whispers, and the groans of 'ya allah', coupled with the constant opening and shutting of the door as the women went in and out, woke the children in the house who, not finding their mothers by their side, would start whimpering, their older sisters would try to soothe them by making comforting noises and gently slapping their backs, rocking to and fro: 'Come now, it's okay, hush...little brother has come...you'll see him in the morning...a tiny little brother.' But the hope of seeing a little brother in the morning couldn't console them and their whimpering would turn into bawling adding to the chaos in the birthing room. Anyway, on top of all this was the stench of dirty bed clothes, pillows coated with grime, rancid clothes and the reek of long unwashed hair, and these smells were heightened in the heat, making her want to throw up. Avoiding contact with everything in the room, she would keep moving around. Spending an hour in such a room was like preparing for the punishment of hell. Agreed, she didn't have to do anything but stand there, for the women of this small town were totally unready to present themselves for newfangled English experiments and allow a stranger, and that too a Christian midwife, armed with unfamiliar and suspicious looking instruments, to examine them. They trusted only the old midwife of their town and fragments of hard baked clay from broken earthen pots. However, their husbands, out of fear of the town area office, had persuaded them to agree to tolerate the presence of that new Christian midwife in the room. Thus her burden of duty was practically reduced to nil. But the responsibility was hers after all, and she was accountable to the town area committee for everything that happened, good or bad. And her discharging this responsibility was like battling with the winds. Often, young girls in first labour screamed and thrashed their arms and legs so much that it was very hard to control them, or some would be so scared that they wouldn't move at all. Mothers of three or four children with the confidence gained from their own experience were even more problematic, they certainly weren't ready to give any importance to the peculiar instructions given by this sari-clad Christian woman who walked the streets unveiled. They would even pause in between groans and start instructing the local midwife, and Emily had to keep biting her lips and remain silent. As for the local midwife, why would she listen to her? She was convinced of her own superiority and Emily's incompetence; besides, she realized that Emily's presence was a threat to her own income, so she made it her duty to contradict everything that Emily said. Emily had hardened herself to disregard the sarcastic remarks of the local midwife, but after all, her heart wasn't made of stone. And the local woman's behaviour had made other women bold as well. They would gather around the bed, paying scant attention to her, and she would be left to stand behind all of them. And all she could do was stamp her feet with annoyance and keep calling out to them, trying to get their attention.

After passing through all of these travails, each time she had to go to the town area office for registering the birth. Seeing her, the clerk's eyes would light up with a leer; in a semi-mocking way he would bare his black, betel-stained teeth from behind his small beard and big moustaches, and pushing a chair towards her, ask: 'Well memsahib, boy or girl?' The closeness of the thick, stiff, black hair of the moustaches scared her, and she felt that suddenly those hairs would be electrified, stand up and brush against her face. She would recoil with fear and revulsion, avoid meeting Bakhshiji's eyes, and try to finish her work as soon as possible.

Having dealt with these obstacles, she would usually get home around eight or nine in the evening, tired and dispirited. When your steps fall every which way and your head is tight and reeling, and when there is no coordination between the limbs of your body, then how the hell could you have an appetite? She would unbuckle her shoes and kick them off into a corner and take off her clothes with such impatience that Nasiban the maid would have to take them out for ironing the next day. After pushing some odd food down her throat she would just fall on the bed. The minute she put her head on the pillow, the walls, the trees, the whole world would start spinning around her. Her brain would throb, trying to burst out of her head. Her head kept sinking into the pillow but she felt as if the pillow was pushing against her head. Her arms would become numb. Her palms felt leaden and she couldn't raise her hands. Likewise, her legs refused to move and her back would become a lump of stone. She wanted to recall her old hospital, but couldn't recall anything in its entirety. The window pane, the iron leg of a patient's bed, wheels of a car, the tip of a neem tree, betel-stained black teeth and thick, stiff moustaches, one by one all these would flash before her eyes like lightning and disappear with the blink of an eye. She longed to add a room to the window pane, but at the most she could add a latch, in fact sometimes the leg of the iron bed would be lodged in her mind like a stake and not budge despite her attempts to get rid of it. The top of the neem tree would never have a trunk....then a drain with sandy edges would begin to flow on the green neem tree top and betel-smeared black teeth would smile through the panes and thick stiff-haired moustaches would bristle impatiently... different faces would merge with one another and fighting, jostling, colliding, trampling, racing from one end of the brain to the other... bunches of countless stars burning in the black sky streamed into her eyes like buzzing insects, dancing, her burning eyes closed slowly, lulled by the sleep-inducing tapping in her temples....and when she fell asleep those forms broke into even smaller fragments that would float in one by one and want to impose themselves on her brain. One would arrive and push the first one out. And while this tussle was going on a third one would crash in. Their competitive wrestling made her repeatedly start in her sleep ever so often and she would open her eyes with a soft groan... and then the stars, whole bunches of them, would start filling her eyes... and it wasn't until dawn that these faces tired, and left their battle field, and then a gentle breeze would begin to blow and Emily would be lost in deep sleep....but before she could sleep her fill, the continuous and stubborn shouts of 'open up' resounded in her brain—the same shouts, the same banging, the same bitter conflict between duty and rest, the same annoyance, and then the same retreat.

Nasiban returned from answering the door. Emily had been summoned to Sheikh Safdar Ali's house. And the caller had insisted that it was 'urgent', she should get there quickly. Everyone who comes along says that—'hurry'. Why should she hurry after all? Is she their paid servant or do they bestow a fortune on her? Hunh! Hurry! Are they going to die if she doesn't get there? And anyway, what will they get from having called her? Those hags declare: 'She knows damn all'. She knows nothing—nothing! These people couldn't even have dreamt of the many instruments she has seen: sparkling, sharp, with ivory handles—and Dr Carfield's lectures, how painstakingly she explained the human anatomy with diagrams and pictures, knows nothing—hunh!

A smile played on Emily's lips. At first, she felt like letting them know that she wouldn't get there quickly, she won't go at all. But then, she thought, those people are ignorant after all, their ranting doesn't harm her, and anyway, it is her responsibility. Therefore, she said to Nasiban,

'Tell them to go, I am coming.' Satisfied, she rolled over, eased her head on the pillow and closed her eyes. She stretched out one arm on the cool bed sheet, and put her hand on her face. She wished she could empty her mind entirely and lie still. But the thump thump of her heart was pounding in her ears, and every once in a while a rock would suddenly hit her brain—'quickly'—making the nerves on her forehead and temples taut and seem ready to burst. She had to go quickly—quickly—and this is what she was paid for, thirty rupees a month by the town area committee—she had to go quickly...but she couldn't really sacrifice her health for the sake of duty. Last night again she had returned very late. She was human after all, not a machine—now she felt that her head was aching, her lower back tense, her shoulders and legs lifeless. Getting up quickly in such a condition would be injurious, especially in the air of this little town where her health was steadily deteriorating. Only last month, she ran a fever for four days. And then, what will she accomplish by going there? Those people don't need her that badly—it would be better to get some more sleep.

She would have slept, but the morning sunlight was streaming through her fingers, not allowing her eyes to remain shut. She slid her hand from her eyes and shut them very tight. She was drifting back to sleep now, but, each time she dozed off, cries of 'Buy some milk,' 'Hey Kalu, Oye!' 'Get up, get off! Not going to school!' and the sounds of Nasiban breaking sticks and banging pots startled her. Trying to sleep in this way made her eyes water. Her head throbbed and her forehead became hot. Desperate, she now lay straight and buried her face in her arms. Now her limbs felt heavier and unable to move, and she began to grind her teeth at those cries, noises, the demanding summons of 'You are needed quickly!'—the morning moon and the smallness of the town. She wished she could wrap herself in some sheet that would cover up those cries, noises, the summons of 'You are needed quickly!', the morning moon and the small town, underneath which none of them could reach, and where she could lose them, forget herself, lose herself...She felt two strong and familiar arms encircling her body, holding her tight...it seemed as if someone had suddenly taken away her headache...two eyes shone from a little distance and seemed to smile and she let herself loose in the embrace of those arms...Her body was as light as the wind, her head swayed softly, softly flowing on the breeze. It was peaceful, it was quiet and she could only hear her joyful heart beating...the two arms were holding her body close...two strong, familiar arms.

She opened her eyes, slowly, fearfully. The morning's moonlight was gleaming. Nasiban put a pot on the stove. The goatherd was collecting goats from the neighbourhood, and the pulley at the well was spinning furiously. She looked up and her eyes began searching for something in the air...two almond-coloured shadows began to descend, her eyelids fluttered and slowly, slowly her lashes touched and closed, as if trying to enmesh those shadows...the shadows stopped at a little distance. They stumbled and faded gently melting in the breeze...the eyes were now seeing the colourless morning sky. Her neck sagged, and her arms fell apart—two familiar arms—but they weren't here.

After lying listless for a little while, she began to remember Williams. Long, swept-back hair, broad chest, red veined eyes, swiftly moving, thick lower lip, side burns extending to the ear lobe, dark shadow of a shaven beard on an olive skin, cheek bones raised beneath the eyes and strong arms...those arms embraced her tight so many times in a day and she would become helpless in their grip and sometimes irritated, would retort, but he would respond with more caresses...and place warm, moist kisses on both her cheeks...and many times during the course of a day...certainly a strong smell of alcohol was on his breath, but he lifted her in his arms with such ardour and madly kissed her face, hands, neck, bosom, and then laughed...'My Love, hahahaha...Emily dear, beloved, hahahaha'—how well he took care of her. Holding her in his arms, he would ask, 'What kind of sari will you get this month, my love? A red one would suit this bosom! Tell me. Do you like this? Hahahaha'—and he never allowed her to go out in the afternoon. If she was called by the hospital, he would send back a reply saying that Mrs Williams was sleeping—he would prepare tea before she woke up, and place it on a table near the bed—and how lovingly he embraced her—but he isn't here!—if he were here he would never have allowed her to go anywhere so early. If he were here she wouldn't have gone anywhere herself. He would have smashed the heads of such people who banged on the door in order to awake her. But only if he were here?—if he were with her, then why would she be here—but—some other faces emerged—it's good he's not with her—his hair was tangled and tousled, and he was chewing his lips as though he would make mincemeat of them—and how cruelly he beat her with a cane, saying, 'Want more...comes back from there thinking no end of herself...' And if Memsahib hadn't arrived upon hearing the noise, who knows how much more he would have beaten her—Emily searched for scars on her arms—it was good to be rid of such a cruel man. How bloody his eyes were—and he had begun to drink so much towards the end—but if he were here, he wouldn't have let her leave so early—admitted that he would stay out with Rosa until late at night, but his behaviour with her remained the same, or at least it seemed so. If she herself hadn't gotten so upset and berated him every hour of the day, perhaps matters would not have reached such a pass. He held her close so lovingly. How could she bear that he stay out with Rosa—Rosa, black as a griddle, bones sticking out in her face, thin as a reed, and fond of wearing a dress, thought she was a real memsahib. Learnt a few phrases of English, and became such a show-off that her feet wouldn't touch the ground—don't know what she had that he was so taken by her—she needn't have bothered, he would have tired of her anyway—would it have mattered if she had allowed things to go on for awhile as they were—but he had beaten her callously—yes—so what if he beat her once—he was ashamed of it himself and reluctant to face her—and if Dina hadn't instigated her so much, she wouldn't have filed for divorce. Dina needled her just to have fun—what kind of friend was she—she won't speak to Dina now. If she meets her by chance, she will look the other way and walk on, and if Dina speaks to her she will frankly tell her that she doesn't want to be friends with traitors. If Dina gets upset, let her. Now she has been transferred from the city hospital. Now it's not a daily matter, she doesn't have to speak to her...

In this way, she kept on agitating over Dina's treachery. Then Nasiban called out to her, 'Memsahibji. Get up, the sun has risen.' She sat up confused and looked all around. She really needed to get going. Still, she stretched her arms several times and rubbed her head on the pillow before getting out of bed.

She washed her face, and sat on the bed waiting for tea. Adjusting the kindling in the stove, Nasiban said, 'Mansain was saying, "Your memsahib is as scarce as the Eid moon, never drops by..." Why don't you visit her one day, memsahib. She remembers you a lot.'

Should she go to her place—what will she do there? One is made to sit on dirty, broken string beds—what can she talk about with these women? Except tell them stories that so and so gave birth to a still-born baby, so and so endured so much pain, and so and so suffered from such and such illness. How much longer can she produce such stories for them? It seems they don't want to hear anything else...and then these women are so uncouth. They're all over her with their stinking clothes...she feels such revulsion in accepting pan from their hands, but she has to, there is no way out...they keep half smiling as they talk to her, almost mocking her...and all the time they exchange looks, and watch over the house from the corners of their eyes as if she was a thief and would steal something the minute their attention is diverted...why are these women so wary of her? Is she not a woman like them? Or is she a monster? These women are really very silly! And when she visits them in their homes, their signal sends the young girls running inside to hide. From there they take turns peeping at her, and if her eyes meet theirs, they quickly move away and sounds of giggling can be heard from within; if they are compelled to come before her, they emerge hugging themselves, their dupattas wrapped from head to toe as if she would steal something just by looking at them, as if her eyes would defile them. She thoroughly dislikes their behaviour. Don't they have confidence in her, do they mistrust her? It's better not to go to visit them. Let them stay at home with their daughters—and those dirty children, smeared with mud, noses running, half naked, stomachs protruding. They come and stand in front of her and scrutinize her, as if she were a strange and unfamiliar animal, newly caught—and when she talks to them, they run right away—they are totally ill-mannered, like animals...absolutely—and strangely enough, on her arrival the women start sweeping the house. It becomes difficult to breathe with all the dust. They think nothing of one's health. And why should one go there at the risk of falling sick—and their men, their behaviour is so embarrassing. They always sit in the foyer, blocking the entrance, and don't move until she gets very close—'Move the hookah away, move it away.' They take so long to get up that she gets anxious—must be doing that deliberately so that she has to stand there for a while—and when she gets inside, she can hear their laughter—how uncouth they are—the English respect women so much—that old priest who used to come by, what a good man he was. He would always speak with everyone individually. In fact, he even recognized her—on Sundays we used to go to church, all of us together—she—Dina—Kitty—Mary—Sheila—and, yes, Mercy—how they would make fun of Mrs James. She would lag behind them, out of breath, umbrella in her hand. And what did she have, poor woman, she was simply a bag of bones—returning from the church was even more entertaining. We walked together laughing and cracking jokes—and Sheila, Oh my! Was she funny! What faces she used to make. When she began laughing she couldn't stop—but there is nothing like that here—one doesn't live with people here or so it seems—really, can the people here be called human? Anyway, she hardly has time to spare. She is on her feet all the time—and who wants to meet the likes of them—just animals—no one to talk with, no one to laugh and joke with. Come back from work and flop on the bed, that's all—as for Nasiban, all she can talk about is her son who ran away or that she has quarrelled with her husband—that there was a splendid *barat* at her place the other day. So what? What are they to her, how is she concerned? Or at the most Nasiban unnecessarily scares her by talking about thieves—once she told her a story of how some people had lured the midwife of the neighbouring district and what they did to her—all lies, do such things happen? But what if it happens to her—no! It's an irrational fear. People would stop going out if such things happened. And how would work get done? The old woman is crazy. Someone has misguided her—still, one can't trust this place. Who knows what may happen. She has no one, too—it would have been better if she wasn't a midwife. Personally, she wanted to become a teacher, and papa wanted that too, but mama just wouldn't agree—so much time has passed since papa died—twelve years. So many years have gone by and it seems as if it were yesterday—he loved her so—brought her to school every day—

her seat was near the table—and the English teacher, what a good man he was—never said a word, even when she didn't bring her homework—and the boys thought her to be something else. She was the only girl in the school. All the boys would glance at her covertly, avoiding the teacher's eye. That fat Karamchand stared at her too. As if she thought he was handsome—and that Azim—he was so innocent, so pale and emaciated but had such large eyes. He would gaze at her too, but if their eyes met he would bashfully lower his eyes and start wiping his face with a handkerchief. Oh! How she would secretly laugh at this. One day she happened to get to school early. He was approaching from the opposite end of the veranda. When he got near, his face was flushed and he began looking in all directions nervously. He stopped by her side and began to say something...timidly, he caught her hand and dropped it quickly. Seeing her nervousness, how distressed he had become, and how earnestly he had appealed to her, 'Don't tell anyone.' She had laughed for many days afterwards, whenever she remembered the incident—how gentle he was, really—if she could remain in school, how wonderful it would be—but those days are gone. Now she is here, alone, away from the world. There's no one to talk to—not even a letter from someone. Every day, she asks the postman if there is a letter for her, but the reply is always the same, 'No'. And if there is a letter, its only the long manila envelope—On Her Majesty's Service—instructions from the district's Health Officer—do this, do that—if someone were to listen to her, she could do this or that—an unnecessary nuisance—but where would she get a letter from anyway? If only Auntie would write from Delhi, wouldn't be such a big deal, but she doesn't care to write—it's been years—she should visit Delhi—it's a good city—such wide streets and so many cinema houses—and him—he's there—well—he—

The raucous cawing of a crow startled her. The sunlight had crept halfway down the wall, a crow was screeching 'caw, caw, caw,' and she was lying on the bed with her legs dangling below. She had to leave early and had wasted so much time lazing pointlessly. She began to vent her anger on Nasiban, berating her for not bringing the tea. Nasiban replied that she thought Memsahib was sleeping. In fact, she thought, had she really been asleep all this while, she would have been so much the better for it. She asked Nasiban to bring the tea quickly.

She washed her face again, gulped the tea somehow and went to get dressed. Opening up the large metal box where she kept her clothes, she began to think which sari to wear. White with the red border—but she wore the same colour every day—white saris get dirty very easily. They're good for just a day—are impossible to wear a second time—the blue sari caught her eye from underneath the pile—why not wear this one—but those people will leer at her if they see her in a blue sari—all of them stare at her whenever she passes by. She detests this habit of ogling—and those zamindars, they pretend to be well-mannered! Anyway, this is the way it is—when she goes past they laugh behind her back and taunt, '*Arre yaar!*—*Abey* Majid, *zara lijiyo!*'—someone clears his throat—as if she doesn't understand all this—let them try this in the city—she would have taught them a lesson—but what can she do here. She has to give in—it's because of them that she has given up wearing bright saris and wears white. But they harass her nevertheless—now if she goes out in a blue sari today, who knows what they will do—then she should wear white—wear white every day—is she afraid of them—let them laugh, they won't eat her up. What can they dare do to her?—She will start wearing bright saris again—challenge them to do what they dare—most certainly, they will laugh—so what—today she will surely wear a blue sari.

After putting on the blue sari, she sat herself in front of a mirror to comb her hair. Sleep deprivation had made her eyes red and puffy. She picked up the mirror and examined her eyes. Why was her complexion getting so dull, her skin had become rough too—when she was a young woman there was such a radiance on her face—so what if she was dark complexioned, her skin shone—her Auntie always said to mama—'You have a nice daughter'—and now—

She put the mirror aside and began to inspect her body from head to toe, astonished, like a peacock seeing its feet—the flesh on her arms was sagging and she had gained some weight and her hands so hard—her hair dry and rough, much thinner too—as for agility she has none now—

how fast she used to walk and for such long distances. But now her back begins to hurt even in a short walk.

She took a deep breath and stretched her arms. The dullness of her face and the loose flesh of her arms had an effect on the colour of her blue sari, making it fade. Half-heartedly she brushed her hair, leaving several strands floating untidily. Her hair was done now but she kept on staring at the mirror, her mind squeezed itself into the swollen eyelids that were beginning to smart from staring at one particular spot for so long.

When she put away the mirror she noticed the Bible sitting on the corner of the table close to the wall. Papa had given it to her for her birthday when she was little. She hadn't opened it in ages now and it was layered with dust. The Bible reminded her of Papa so much that she was compelled to pick it up. There was her name inscribed on the fly leaf. She had written it herself but now the ink had faded. She was in the fifth grade when she wrote it. She was amused to see her own unformed handwriting and recalled having a green fountain pen in those days. She decided she'd buy a green pen on her next visit to the city. But then she thought that the pen wouldn't be of any use to her. She didn't have to write much.

Papa often reminded her to read the Bible. She was now ashamed of her negligence and started turning the pages—Genesis—Exodus—she turned the pages faster—Book of Ruth—Jerome—Matthew—where should she begin—Adam—Noah—The Flood—Abraham—The Ark—The Cross—Jesus—church bells—we went to church together, laughing and joking—

Eventually she couldn't decide where to start; she had to leave soon and there wasn't enough time. But she made up her mind to read the Bible every morning—or at least on Sundays—but one must pray every day—it's bad not to pray—Mama never allowed her to go to bed before saying her prayers—really, it doesn't take much time—and if it does, so what—the business of the world goes on.

She tried to empty her mind and closed her eyes. But despite batting her eyes, first Mama and behind her Papa and the street in front of the church, the bells, the group of laughing friends who went to church all entered into her eyes. She opened them wide and shook her head vigorously as if trying to dislodge them. Eventually her mind became empty and quiet. Only her heartbeat was pounding in her ears and in her head. She shut her eyes again, joined her hands, and repeated the prayer: Our Father, who art in Heaven. Hallowed be thy name. Thy kingdom come. Thy will be done. On earth as it is in Heaven. Give us this day our daily bread. And forgive us our trespasses. As we forgive those who trespass against us. Lead us not into temptation. But deliver us from evil. For Thine is the kingdom and the power and the glory, for ever and ever. Amen.

Upon opening her eyes she felt a little closer to quietude and tried to smile. Once again she glanced at the mirror and wished she could pray for something special. But what?—Someone?—that she be transferred to the city—but she will have to face Williams—this small town is better than having to do that—what else?—there was a story in which a fairy had promised to fulfil three wishes of a man—but what?

Musing, she rubbed her arms, but couldn't think of anything—and she was getting delayed so she deferred her prayers and wishes for later and grabbing her umbrella stepped out.

As she walked on the street she was driven by the thought of getting there quickly. After the sluggishness and languor of the morning she felt a sense of exhilaration in the exercise. The light warmth of the sun and the brisk walk had quickened her pulse, and oblivious of the open drain, gritty sand, and pebbles, she concentrated on covering the distance as fast as she could. If she felt that her speed was slowing she lengthened her stride. The roadside urchins weren't up and about yet so she didn't have to care about the safety of her nose. When she passed beneath the shadows cast by the walls her pace quickened even more.

Soon she reached the main square. Sheikh Safdar Ali's house was a short distance from there and she began to feel reassured that she wasn't too late. As she was walking along she suddenly noticed a store owner. He was smiling and signalling his neighbour—was he doing this upon seeing her?—possibly they were laughing at something else, she was late—she had moved away from them when she heard: 'The sky is blue today...its been a long time since it was blue'—she wanted to turn back and hit that lout with her umbrella...come what may, she will stop here and tell them that she couldn't bear this any longer and she knew exactly what they meant when they made those remarks—how long could this go on?—her feet felt like lead, as if they weighed a ton, and her legs trembled, making her stumble several times as she walked—but those eyes that ogled her from all directions made her go on without stopping. She shrank into her sari, wrapping its loose border securely around her bosom and, with a bowed head pulled her feet off the road...

When she reached the house of Shaikh Safdar Ali, she saw him smoking a hookah along with some men in the front room. On seeing her he stood up, and in a complaining tone, as if she had slipped up on some rare opportunity for which he sympathized with her, said: 'Aahh Memsahib...you came very late.'

'Er...yes...I was delayed,' she said as she moved in the direction of the women's quarter. When she got to the doorway she saw the local midwife crossing the courtyard with a bundle of clothes in her left hand and a jug of water in her right. Twirling the jug, she heard her say: 'You know...that bitch hasn't stepped out from her house yet.'

Translated by Mehr Afshan Farooqi

Balwant Singh

(1920–86)

Balwant Singh was born in Gujranwala, Punjab into a conservative Sikh family. Their financial condition was not good. Balwant had a restless childhood and ran away from home several times, only to return again. His father, after changing several jobs, eventually moved to Allahabad, where Balwant graduated from Allahabad University in 1942. It was around this time that he emerged as an important short story writer of the Progressive platform. His first collection of short fiction, *Jagga*, was published from Lahore in 1943 and immediately established him in the first rank of writers of short fiction. It was followed in quick succession by the collections, *Pehla Pathar* (First Stone), *Tar-o Paud* (Highs and Lows), *Sunahra Desh* (Golden Land), and *Chilman* (Screens). For a short period he worked for the Ministry of Information, Publication Division, in the editorial team of the journal, *AjKal* and *Naunihal*. After his father's death in 1948 he moved permanently to Allahabad and looked after a hotel that he had inherited. In the 1970s, he began writing in Hindi, and produced several novels; however he had already produced his best work.

During his Allahabad years he struck up friendship with noted fiction writer, Upendranath Ashk. Ashk has described Balwant Singh in his tribute upon his death as an extraordinarily handsome man, tall and well-built, who in the last eleven years of his life became a shadow of his former self, and suffered greatly from the effects of diabetes, becoming semi-blind. His passing away went virtually unnoticed.

Balwant Singh wrote mostly about the Jat Sikhs living in remote villages of the Punjab, known for their virile, dominating, aggressive personalities. He wrote about their feelings, experiences, and world view, almost romanticizing their masculinity and machismo and creating characters that could be called anti-heroes. But his greatness as a short story writer lies in the thought-provoking stories about women; the women, who suffer at the hands of males, but remain unvanquished. In '*Galiyan*' (Alleyways), a powerful and deeply moving story, first published in *AjKal* in 1964, Singh uses the metaphor of earth for the oppressed woman; she is crushed but her regenerative power prevails; she is resilient and emerges victorious.

Alleyways

When she, beside herself, emerged from the corner room, she ran her eyes in all directions, extremely disconsolate. The alleyway was desolate in the late afternoon, and just by chance no one caught sight of her. She thus darted ahead, setting aright the collar of her kurta, buttoning it up with fingers trembling in fear.

Immediately after her, Bela Singh and Phulaila Singh too burst outside. Though they were cousin brothers, on this occasion they looked more alike than even real brothers... They wanted to tear apart a mother of three, yet she was paces ahead of their claws.

Their faces were as puffed and red as dough leavened with *gulal* over four days. Whiskers from their nostrils were peeping out like the antennae of a grasshopper. Sweat was dripping over their temples and cheeks.

They were panting heavily. Their legs were giving out. While they were trying to catch their breath, they squinted and caught the last glimpse of a fleeing woman. Then they felt defeated, dusted off their wide *shalwar*s and stamping their feet on the ground as bears do, went back inside the house.

The fleeing woman was running away as if she would surpass all the limits of this world. The winds were blowing against her face. Her light complexion had become yellow. Her lips had chapped and she kept running her tongue over them. But even her tongue had become parched. The dirt on her neck had become thick and moist. Her eyes were wide open. Her heart was beating wildly against her ribcage. She had decided to give up her own life today.

Over the last year the thought of dying had occurred to her several times, for other than death there was no solution in sight to her problems. And today she had made up her mind for good and was completely resolved to do it. About two miles from the village homes was a deep well. All that was needed was to take a leap into it and her problems would be resolved all at once.

She had been born in this very village. But to call it a 'village' would be going a bit too far. All kinds of new developments had sprung up. Just a mile away the opening of a factory had led to an increase in the village population. Many factory workers had started living in the village. Hand pumps for extracting water were installed instead of wells. Alongside the crude handmade brick walls of these homes, walls of mass-produced bricks were erected. Sewage canals had been built before home fronts. First there were the three familiar alleyways. Now the web of alleyways spread outwards. For the simple-minded country folks, from this point onwards there were just alleyways after alleyways. For a woman rushing to suicide, how could all of these alleyways not appear labyrinthine?

Her grandfather had lived for a rather long time. First thing every morning, before even rinsing his mouth, he would drink half a litre of pure mustard oil, and he would attribute his advanced age and good health to just this. Other folks who acted on his advice were not able to hold in the oil, and in some way or other it would be expelled. Being able to digest it was a secret deep within him. It was as if he was not even aware of this secret. If he was privy to it he wouldn't have desisted from telling others. He was also a poet of an older era.

[Two lines of a Punjabi folk song]

Whatever people these days may make of him, in his own times he was known as a sufi. He would say that the thinking of human beings was like alleyways, those kinds of alleyways in which a human being, strolling about, knows not where she will end up. If an idea occurs to one's mind, then think of it as an alley opened before it. Why not?—for human beings move from one alley or inkling to another by way of decision. This was a complicated matter. Grandfather would expatiate on the complications for hours. His friends would be all ears, weaving together his discourses. Yet, his little granddaughter didn't comprehend a thing. She would stand a little way away and tie up her pig tail. She had no idea what kinds of knots and what kinds of complications her grandfather was undoing or resolving. She just liked the way his face looked, despite the fact that on the cheek just next to his stringy beard there was a mole from which four whiskers stuck out like thorns, looking strange.

From the end of one house to the end of another, whether smoothened walls of mud or modern brick, within the cracks of which were the webs of plaster, skipping over one drainage channel after another—house, wall, channel, house, wall, channel—kept on streaming by.

In the dust-laden sky the sun too was writhing on account of its own intense heat.

Fearful that her foot might get caught in her *shalwar* and she would fall and hurt herself, she drew her shalwar up and drew tight the string. She saw nothing humorous in that after having resolved to call death upon herself, she should be fearful of getting hurt. Her ankles had yet to give out.

She had spent her childhood here. She had no recollection of her real mother's face. Her stepmother did not treat her badly, but that woman did not know how to love either her children or her husband. She was an unusual, obstinate woman. On her wrist she wore a thick iron bracelet. She was that kind of woman. As long as her mother and grandfather were alive, they would shower her with much affection. She never could understand her grandfather. However, she did sense love in his silence. At that time when alleyways in the village numbered merely three, the alleyways of her ideas could be counted on just one finger of her hand. Days, months, and years streamed by. The settlement's alleyways kept increasing. The alleyways in her mind kept expanding branch by branch...kept getting tangled... When grandfather died, many of the alleyways of her mind turned into graveyards.

And then that time came when her body blossomed.

[Punjabi folk song]

A close friend of hers recited the song to her and said, 'To get a glimpse of you a youth comes around your alleyway. Get out of here!' she said and took off. In her home was a small fragment of a mirror in which it was impossible to see one's entire face. Therefore she went off to a girlfriend's house. On some pretext or other she managed to put herself before the large mirror. There she looked at herself from head to toe. Feeling satisfied, she departed. First she got a good look at that heart-stricken wanderer, learned a thing or two about him, and then whenever she saw him from afar, she would slam hard the courtyard door behind her. It was certain that if she didn't get married off right away she would one day smash this door.

She didn't remember when the young man succeeded in drawing her into a relationship with him. Nor from which alleyway he came with a wedding garland tied around him, and made off with her as his bride from an assembly of weeping girlfriends of hers. Nor which alleyway she entered after bestowing upon him three children from which there was no turning back.

When her husband was living, that neighbourhood in which she lived was alive. In the mornings, along with the chirping of the birds, the brass cymbals and the drums of the distant *gurdwara* would be heard. As if from a lassitudinous ambience the words of the *gurbani* would take flight on golden-winged birds, hovering in the air, unknowing, innocent, unaware, floating through unexplored silvery alleyways, and behind them gold and silver sparks would rise and fall undulating and leave behind a path of dancing particles. In the depths of her heart was a lake of blue water upon the banks of which clouds upon clouds of fireflies would be abuzz. On the surface of the water there were lotuses, which appeared faintly through the hazy light. When one after the other she gave birth to three children, she did not indicate to anyone anything unusual about the children, but she was recognized as their mother. Whenever the children would play in the dust of the alleyways, the breast of the mother would burst with joy...How these children had come to light from darkness... 'What kind of light?' The father of the children had died, thus she would repeat this question to herself again and again.

When she came running past a small *pipal* tree, she did not realize that there were scores of parrots sitting in it. She only came to know once they became frightened of a stricken woman speeding towards her death and burst out flying from the tree like sparks from fireworks. However, we all know that parrots are masters when it comes to making conversation.

If someone had said to her before the death of her husband that a whole year can be spent stumbling from one dark alleyway to another without direction, she would never have thought it possible. But now she had herself accomplished just this series of deeds. It is a strange thing: that which she had never thought to do, which her heart shook from just thinking about, she had done. It had to be done.

By the mercy of the Great Lord, no one saw her escape from Bela Singh and Phulaila Singh's house in such an awful state. They were returning from the cattle pens. The fields around the settlement were echoing with indeterminate sounds for hours. She was smearing mud mixed with straw upon the *tandoor* oven in the courtyard and she saw big heavy shoes on the walkway to the backdoor, shoes that were buried in dirt. The lace of each shoe stuck out over it like the tail of a scorpion. Her heart started beating uncontrollably. These were the men's shoes.

Gradually her eyelids began to turn upward, as did her sight. A waist cloth of a bright green colour, a silk kurta, the end of a turban hanging below. On his chin hung a black beard. She visualized smiling lips and dancing eyes above that. One time she wanted to hold back her gaze from this point. Yet, to what avail? She looked up just then and saw lips devoid of a smile, a face utterly serious.

Bela Singh took off his decorated turban and stood there eating *jalebi*. He called jalebi '*jaleb*'. 'He took some jaleb and went over there and stopped when he saw that the door was open.' Why did he stop? He had no answer to this. But internally he knew that in a woman's mind this question can raise its head.

'Where are the kids?'

He asked this to break the silence of the woman.

How the evening became so calm so soon. Maybe all the cattle had returned to their separate pens. The woman felt as if someone was driving her out of the house.

As he was eating jalebi, Bela Singh's hand became steady and his mouth remained open. It seemed for a second as if he was going to put a woman instead of a jalebi in his wide-open mouth... But no, that wasn't really the case. The children that Bela Singh was looking for came out from different parts of the home. He went up to them right away and gave them a large bag full of jalebi: 'Here, eat these jalebs...take them...come, eat.'

She continued her work on the tandoor oven. Bela Singh kept chatting with the children. Then he peeked out of the courtyard door and carefully looked to the left and right. At that moment no one was there. He took the opportunity...disappeared in the haze of the alleyways.

As soon as the memory of Bela Singh resurfaced, her feet grew wings. Her fear and horror intensified. And she ran even faster. The sky was clear, though on the edges of this wide open clear blue lake there were several red-blue-yellow shy wisps of clouds hung about like petrified nymphs... Some women, men, children, cows, water buffalo and crows saw this absconding woman with a passing glance and receded back to their respective tasks, thoughts, alleyways.

For several days in a row, one after another, Bela Singh would appear swaying along, as if unravelled from a coil of smoke from some hazy alleyway. Ostensibly he loved her children. He gave them sweets, he looked at the children's mother from top to toe... Sometimes it seemed as if he was taking a deep breath and saying, 'Look at all the manifestations of the Creator.' Meaning, the Lord's divine play is amazing.

Now, the house was no longer hers. The numerous loans and her inability to pay the interests upon interests; it had slipped out of her hands. Bela Singh had declared: 'This is injustice.' So she continued to live there. The moneylender became silent.

How many times this kind of situation had presented itself! There was only one solution each time…escape. She had gotten tired of running away again and again. The one significant difference between Bela Singh and the others was that he seemed the very image of seriousness. One could see lust, jaws wide open, behind the dancing eyes of other men.

Now Phulaila Singh started coming by too. He was about to open a school for children. Though she was not educated she did know the *gurmukhi* script. Bela Singh and Phulaila Singh also only knew that they needed her to teach the children the alphabet. Actually, they wanted to find a way to help her. She was the mother of three children. She had no one in the world.

As she was running she saw the fortunate women who were seated on their cool porches spinning cotton on their wheels. They were winding thread on the reed. A few were sitting relaxing with their dearly loved children.

Finally, today, she made it to the corner room of their house. Fearful and hesitant, she took some steps toward the iron chair. She drew in her shalwar and sat down. Carefully she arranged her dupatta, covering the breast that fed three children. The parting in her hair was perfectly straight like the line of white herons in flight around a dark storm cloud. She draped her dupatta over her head in such a manner that her hair was well covered. Both of her lips were united so that they gave a soporific impression. She gave the impression of a great, very lovely, very experienced, and very competent mother.

Bela Singh was already seated. Phulaila Singh came a little later. His eyes were bloodshot, his face flushed. He had either come having eaten and drunk, or having gotten drunk and eaten. In the hands of each was a thorn from an acacia tree with which they were picking their teeth. They seemed very sombre as if some dire problem had come up.

She wanted to know something about the new school. Till now even the decision about salary had not been made, just that she also had these three toddlers. She did not want them to grow up in the alleyways, and become rogues by the time they came of age. She presented her questions and particulars before them. Her eyes were downcast. She did not feel the need or perhaps she felt a bit hesitant... She didn't look at them eye-to-eye as they conversed.

With her head bowed down she began waiting for their answer. Minutes passed. The silence attained an increasing depth, so much so that she felt as if both of them had left the room. Perhaps they had taken off to the fields on their black ponies... But one can wait for only so long. In the end she raised her head and saw that they were still sitting there. Large bodied, heavily built, like ogres. Now they both looked in her direction too. Their moustaches twitched. Their jaws widened. They broke out in smiles. Today was the first time they laughed freely and boldly before her.

At that pace she reached the outskirts of the settlement. She was passing by the gurdwara grounds. Facing the alleyway was a wall about four feet tall. Its bricks were stripped. The wall and the gate were being repaired. The courtyard, which was quite spacious, was in the olden times a public forum. And next to the forum was a large pool of water. This pond had not accrued any religious significance, but it did have banyan and *sharina* trees growing in it and it was cool under their leafy shade. At that moment, the priests from the gurdwara were sitting drying their hair in the shade after having washed it in boiling soapy water. Just at the edge of the bank half-submerged toads were staring at them wide-eyed. Leaves from the banyan tree would break off from their branches and flutter in the breeze before falling into the water and drifting delicately like little boats on the water's surface.

Close to the alleyway in a screened-off little marble room, Sant Avatar Singh was seated with a *tanpura* resting on his arms. He had an unpleated cloth wrapped around his head. Two deep wrinkles of contemplation and devotion were on his deep tawny forehead. Above his narrow-legged trousers, a coarse cotton tunic. Around his neck a wreath of marigold flowers. His lips half-open. He was reciting a verse to be sung during that evening's congregation. The fingers of one hand were dancing over the strings of the tanpura. His other hand would grasp the handle of his nine-inch long *kirpan* hanging down over his side after every line or two. This was because whenever in a state of trance he would begin to rock back and forth, the handle of the kirpan would press against his ribs. In his voice was a frisson of pain. The tune was as if a deep river was rushing through a half-lit passageway.

Pigeons and finches, the males red with black speckles on their breast, chirped in the garden among the flower beds of the gurdwara. To fill their bellies they pecked with their beaks at some living insect. The insect would convulse, writhe, draw back, seek escape—and ultimately give up its life. It would sacrifice its dead body to these stomachs.

She had passed beyond the boundaries of the gurdwara and was already in the fields. Now a few fields and some footpaths lay between her and the destination. On one side a stooping camel with its ungainly gait was going in circles about a wheel. On the other side was a tall wispy tree devoid of leaves and flowers. Through the cover of its thickets the worn-out edge of the well in which she wanted to leap and drown was visible.

The speed with which her glances were darting and skimming and embracing the tips of the swaying plants in the fields, reaching ultimately the horizon, was faster than the speed at which her feet were moving. Here and there the seeds that had remained buried in the fields were preparing to come out of slumber. Between them and the illumining light of day was the darkness of layers of earth and the web of unknown, unseen alleyways.

It was as if the state of woman and of earth were one. From the earth's breast too droves upon droves of restive clouds rain melted pearls and then are gone. Upon which royal roads they come and towards which destinations they pass, the earth knows nothing. She only knows how to give birth from her womb. How much power there was in that! The shoots that burst out of the seeds and which can wither on account of just one blast of hot wind fight and advance against the elements of the earth. Breaking out against these, one day they stand in rapture before the world-illuminating sun.

It is easy to be distraught and confused, cry and whine before the meaninglessness of life and of the universe, but who dares to see the illuminating beauty of this meaninglessness? This princess swings back and forth between one galaxy and another, from one star to another. She disperses meaningless smiles. But it must be remembered that if our happiness is based on some reason, for how long can we remain happy?

After a short while, darkness from the recesses of the sky will come forth in procession after procession, and her settlement will become occluded in this darkness. Her children will find the darkest alleyways more desolate than ever and cry their hearts out.

If there is a plan to drown oneself in a well, then it is inevitable that one has to run through alleyways. If one does not have to cross even one alleyway to reach a destination, what kind of destination could it possibly be? Or perhaps the destination is located on those grounds from which a human being runs to arrive at a destination.

All at once she stopped. The cloud of dust that picked up around her began to hover about her calves. She was panting. She placed her hand on her chest and tried to regulate its pulsation. She did not fear the well or the death concealed in its depths. But nevertheless she slowly turned her back to the well. Her courage had waned all of a sudden. She didn't see a bright future awaiting her. She had not come there to forfeit her principles and virtue... Thus, with great attention to propriety she wrapped her dupatta over her breast twice and pulled the edge around her head so securely that her throbbing forehead and the edge of her dupatta became one. Between sobs, she wiped away her tears and with clear sparkling eyes cast a vanquishing glance towards the settlement.

When and from which alleyway had Mother Earth come? She looked deep into her eyes and smiled. When and in which alleyway did she then recede and become lost?

Translated by Guriqbal Sahota

Intizar Husain
(b. 1925)

Fiction writer, critic, and translator, Intizar Husain is regarded as the most significant short story writer in Urdu since Saadat Hasan Manto. He was born in Dibai in the Meerut district of western Uttar Pradesh and migrated to Pakistan at Partition. He took a master's degree in Urdu literature in 1946 from Meerut College. After resigning from his job as a columnist for the Urdu daily *Mashriq* in 1988, Husain settled in Lahore where he presently lives and writes. His first collection, *Gali Kooche* (Alleyways) appeared in 1952. But it was the publication of *Akhri Admi* (The Last Man) in 1967 that established him as a leading exponent of the modern Urdu short story. *Shahr-e Afsos* (City of Sorrows) was published in 1972. *Satvan Dar* (Seventh Door) and *Patte* (Leaves) are more recent collections. He has published three novels, *Chand Gahan* (Lunar Eclipse), 1953, *Khali Pinjra* (Empty Cage), and *Basti* (Habitats), 1983; a travelogue, *Aagey Samundar Hai* (Sea Ahead); a memoir, *Naye Shahr Purani Bastiyan* (New Cities, Old Habitats); and a volume of critical essays. He has been widely translated in English and other languages.

According to Husain, Partition was the single most important event in his life; it has also shaped his creativity. As a fiction writer he grappled with the question of identity. It became increasingly urgent for him to locate his Indo-Muslim identity within his historical, geographical, political, and cultural space. In many of his stories Husain explores the relationship of Islam with India. He felt that the Urdu fiction writer was connected to the Indian tradition of storytelling as much as a writer in any of the Indian languages. His reading of the epics, the Vedas, the Panchatantra, Kathasaritsagar, the Jatakas, and other similar frame-story literature, combined with what he knew of the Indo-Persian tradition of the *dastan* and what he had read of western literature, enabled him to create something unique of his own. Husain's writings have had a tremendous impact on contemporary Indian writers.

MorNama is Intizar Husain's response to the disturbing nuclear tests that India and Pakistan carried out in 1998 in order to display their nuclear superiority over one another. 'War transforms man utterly,' writes Husain in *MorNama*. Deploying the peacock as a symbol of the link between the past and the present, he weaves stories from both Islamic and Hindu traditions into the narrative, creating multiple levels of meaning and symbolism.

A Chronicle of the Peacocks

Allah alone knows why this evil spirit is after me! I am shocked and upset. I had actually gone there to inquire after the well-being of the peacocks. How was I to know that this evil spirit would grab hold of me?

It was by chance that I came across that small news item; otherwise, in the midst of all that turmoil, I would never have found out what had really happened. Tucked away in the middle of the terrifying news about India's atomic bomb was a small note about how the explosion had so frightened the peacocks of Rajasthan that they had flown up screaming into the sky and scattered in all directions.

Immediately, I wrote a column expressing my sympathy for the peacocks and thought that, having done my duty, I was free from all further obligations. But had I really done my duty? Was I actually free? That insignificant piece of information disturbed me in the same way as that small fish had disturbed Manuji. Manuji had once caught a fish no longer than his little finger and had placed it in a pot. He, too, had thought he had done his duty and was free. But the fish started to grow and grow. It became so big that he had to take it out of the pot and release it into a lake, and then take it out of the lake and release it into a river. The fish, however, became too large for the river, and Manuji had to carry it to the sea. In the same way, a news item, which journalists thought deserved no more than two lines, overwhelmed my imagination.

The news reminded me of the peacocks I had seen in Jaipur. *Subhan Allah*, what a beautifully-planned pink city it was! I reached Jaipur late in the afternoon. At first, I did not sense their presence. But, in the evening, when I opened the window of the guest house, which was as lovely as a new bride, the view outside was breathtaking. Everywhere I looked—in the courtyard, on the parapet around the fountain, over the balconies—there were peacocks; peacocks and more peacocks; peacocks with bright blue tails! They had a quiet dignity and a royal grace and a calm elegance. I felt as if I were in the very cradle of beauty, love, and peace.

The next evening, as I was about to leave the city, I saw peacocks on every tree, rock, and hill. Their movements had the same peace, the same grace, and the same beauty. As the evening shadows deepened, the air was filled with the song of peacocks. I thought they were there to both welcome and bid me farewell.

Whenever I recall that trip, my mind is filled with the images of those peacocks. I am surprised. Did I really see so many of them? Did the peacocks of Rajasthan actually come out to greet me? I wonder how they are now.

I try to imagine that city now, but all I can see is a picture of desolation. Shocked and disturbed, I am neither able to see the peacocks nor hear their song. Where have they all disappeared? In which corner of the world are they hiding? Suddenly, I have a vision of a lonely peacock on a distant hill. He seems battered and bruised. I walk quickly toward him but, before I can reach the hill, he rises into the sky screaming with terror and disappears.

Where has he gone? Where are his companions, those countless peacocks? Why is he sitting alone on that hill, the very picture of desolation? Why is he so despondent, so terrified? The sight of that dejected, bewildered peacock suddenly brings to mind another image of desolation that I had forgotten. On the far edge of a dark, oil-soaked sea, I see a forlorn duck covered with foul effluents, watching the waves in disbelief. Till yesterday the sea was ambrosia, today it is poison. The wings of the duck are so heavy with slime that he can no longer fly. Poison flows through the veins in his body. The weary bird is a symbol of the horrors of the war between the United States and Iraq. It is sad to see a bird in so much pain. The poor duck seemed to have taken upon himself all the crimes human beings commit against each other—Saddam Hussain against his countrymen, the Iraqis against the Kuwaitis, and the Americans against the Iraqis. It is strange that whenever apocalypse is at hand, the rich and the powerful rarely ever pay for their sins; instead, the poor and weak take upon themselves the burden of suffering so as to redeem their times. The duck is symbolic of those prophets who, according to all religious texts, think of suffering as a sacred duty.

At that time, I didn't recognize the duck as a symbol of our times. I lacked the visionary insight to see that he had the grace of a prophet. It never occurred to me to write a story about him. I forgot about him completely. He was only a poor, small duck, and not a gorgeous peacock about whom I am so anxious to write a story now. What if he had been a royal swan instead of a mere duck? But there are no royal swans in the world now. Once upon a time, it was difficult to decide whether the royal swan or the peacock was the king of the universe. In those days, royal swans used to swim in lakes that were as translucent as white pearls. And princesses used to scatter pearls across palace courtyards to tempt their swan-lovers. In our times, there are no swan-lovers who can be seduced by pearls. Nor are there any royal swans that swim in the shimmering waters of Mansarovar. Now, no one even knows where Mansarovar is. The lakes are dry, the rivers polluted, and the air thick with the dust and smoke of bombs. The royal swans have flown away in search of clear air and pure water. They exist only in the world of fables and myths. Only the poor ducks and geese have been left behind to bear the burden of our times.

Until recently, the peacock, in all his grandeur, was a link between the past and the present. When the monsoon breeze cooled the evening, the song of the peacock used to fill the air. I remember that once a peacock came and sat on the parapet of our terrace. I quickly ran up to the terrace, tiptoed along the wall, and was about to grab its tail, when a shudder ran through his body and he flapped his wings nervously and flew away.

'You should never trouble a peacock, son. He is the bird of paradise,' Dadima reprimanded me.

'The bird of paradise?' I asked in wonder. 'What is he doing here?'

'He is paying for his mistake.'

'What did he do to be so punished?'

'O my son, he is innocent but he got trapped in the wiles of that wretch Satan.'

'How did he get trapped in the wiles of Satan?'

'That wretch disguised himself as an old man and went to the gates of paradise. He pleaded with the gatekeepers to let him in. But the gatekeepers saw through his disguise and recognized that the old man was Satan himself. So they refused to open the gates. A peacock, who was sitting on the wall surrounding the garden of paradise, felt sorry for the old man. He flew down to him and said 'Bade Mian, I'll help you across the wall.' Well, what does a blind man need but the guidance of someone who can see? Satan jumped onto the peacock's back at once. The peacock flew over the wall of paradise and helped Satan enter the Garden of Eden. When Allah Mian found out, He was very angry. When He exiled Adam and Eve from the Garden of Eden, He also asked the peacock to get out.'

I was upset when I heard the story and felt sorry for the peacock. Once upon a time, he used to sit on the wall of paradise, and now he sits on the wall of our terrace. When I told Dadima this, she replied, 'Yes, son, that is what happens when we are exiled from our own courtyards. Now, all he can do is find something to sit on—any wall around any courtyard—or any tree or hill where he can find a foothold.'

When I walked through Sravasthi, I saw a peacock sitting on a green hill lost in thought. It seemed as if he was waiting for someone. I had reached Sravasthi late in the afternoon, Mahatma Buddha had lived there a long time ago. The *vihara* where he used to stay with his monks during the monsoons is now in ruins. Only a few scattered bricks mark its place. The peacock on the hill was, perhaps, the last of the survivors from the days of the Buddha and still carried images of those days in his eyes. Due to the presence of that one peacock, Sravasthi seemed a place of great tranquillity.

I didn't stay long in Sravasthi. I had to get back to Delhi. But, that evening, Delhi was a sad and desolate city. At least, the *basti* around Nizamuddin was. Only a few days earlier, a caravan of migrants, whose homes had been looted, had left the area. On that rainy day, it seemed as if the silence and the gloom would never lift. Even Nizamuddin's tomb, in the middle of an unpaved courtyard, looked dismal. The tomb was surrounded by tall grass. As I walked through it, I heard a peacock call from somewhere behind the tomb. When I turned around to look, I couldn't see him, but I heard him call once more. It was a strange call, resonant of millennia past.

As my imagination moved further down the ages, I was once again startled by the call of peacocks. '*Ya Maulla*, where are those peacocks, in which garden?' Surprised, I walked a little further, and found myself in a city whose outer walls touched the clouds. Beyond the walls were orchards filled with a variety of fruits. The garden echoed with the music of birds of different hues. Two notes were more distinct than the others—the whistle of the koel and the call of the peacock...Arrey, this is Indraprastha, the city of the Pandavas! Have I really travelled so far from home? I must get back.

I have travelled far and wide. I have seen peacocks—peacocks from different ages and lands. I have heard their song. Now, it is time for me to write my *Mor Nama*—my Chronicle of the Peacocks. But, before I go back home, I must make another trip to Rajasthan and find out if the peacocks that had flown away in fear have returned.

The peacocks had actually returned in great numbers. Strangely, the moment they saw me, they were so terrified that, screaming in terror, they rose from the hills and trees and scattered in the sky. At that moment, I sensed that I wasn't alone. Someone else was walking beside me. When I looked to my left, I was so shocked by what I saw that I couldn't turn my gaze away... What! Is that Ashwatthama, the great criminal of Kurukshetra? Why is he here? Why is he walking beside me?... I don't know when he attached himself to me. Perhaps, he began to follow me when, on my way back from Indraprastha, I stopped at Kurukshetra. Yes, I am sure this evil creature attached himself to me there. But Kurukshetra was desolate. I had seen no living being there. Where had he been hiding? Had he been wandering there ever since the war?

War transforms man utterly. Take Ashwatthama, the son of Dronacharya. Dronacharya was a man of such profound learning that all the great warriors of the Pandavas and the Kauravas used to bow down to him and touch his feet. Ashwatthama, his son, had inherited many of his father's qualities, but he didn't have his wisdom. He was the most damned and accursed man of that war.

It is said that Dronacharya, guru of all the great warriors, possessed the most dreaded of weapons, the *Brahmastra*. In appearance, it was no different from a blade of grass, but its power was so great that it could reduce everything to ash, destroy all living things far and wide in an instant. Dronacharya had passed on the secret of that weapon only to his favourite disciple, Arjuna. War is so awful that in Kurukshetra, the teacher and his disciple found themselves in opposing camps fighting each other. Both, however, had taken a vow never to use the Brahmastra because it would destroy the whole world.

Before his death, Dronacharya revealed the secret of the Brahmastra to his son, Ashwatthama, but warned him sternly never to use it. After

Dronacharya was killed there was no one left to restrain Ashwatthama. So, during the last days of the war, he decided to stake everything and release the Brahmastra.

The last days of war are always the most fearful. They are dangerous and unpredictable. During those days, men are tempted to use weapons that are only meant to threaten. It doesn't matter then if a city like Hiroshima burns; at least the fighting comes to an end. The victors are satisfied; the defeated are lost in their sorrow. At Kurukshetra, it was Ashwatthama who acted foolishly and used the Brahmastra.

When Shri Krishna heard what Ashwatthama had done, he said to Arjuna, 'O Janardhan, Dronacharya's foolish son has released the Brahmastra. Now, all living things will be destroyed. Only you can counter that weapon. Act quickly before everything is reduced to ashes.'

Arjuna took out his Brahmastra and released it to neutralize Ashwatthama's weapon. It is said, that when Arjuna released the Brahmastra, the fire was so intense that its flames singed all the three worlds. Its heat even scorched the distant forest where Vyasa Rishi sat in meditation. He was terrified. He abandoned his meditations at once, went to Kurukshetra, stood between Ashwatthama and Arjuna, and raising both hands, shouted, 'O evil ones, what great injustice is this! The entire world will be destroyed. Recall your weapons.'

Arjuna touched the feet of the great soul, and at once recalled his weapon.

But Ashwatthama was unrepentant, 'Maharaj, I have released the weapon, but I don't have the power to take it back. All I can do is change its direction. So, instead of falling on the Pandava army, it will fall on their women, strike their wombs, and destroy their foetuses. The Pandavas shall have no heirs and their clan shall come to an end.'

Then Shri Krishna said angrily, 'O son of Dronacharya, you are a great sinner. By killing children you have committed a great crime. I curse you to wander alone in the forests for three thousand years. May your wounds never heal, may pus and blood flow from them always, may they stink so much that people everywhere run away from you in disgust.'

Even I wanted to run away from him as far as possible, but he clung to me like a shadow... Ya Allah, where can I hide; how can I get rid of him?... I suddenly remembered that Meerabai's *samadhi* was also nearby. I wondered if I should seek shelter there. Then, it occurred to me that the dargah of Khwaja Moin-ud-din Chishti was also in the same vicinity. If I could find it, I would easily get rid of this evil spirit. Who would let him enter the dargah? Other thoughts raced through my mind. But I didn't know how to cast him off. No matter what path I took, he followed me like a shadow.

Peacocks screamed with fear on one side; women of the Pandavas wept on the other. There was mourning in every home. In every family, a child had died. There was calamity even in Arjuna's house. Subhadra was crying bitterly. The Kauravas at Kurukshetra had killed Abhimanyu, the son born from her womb. She had mourned for him. She had hoped that Abhimanyu's wife, Uttara, would give birth to a son and ensure the survival of the Pandava lineage. But Ashwatthama's prophecy had been fulfilled. Uttara collapsed after giving birth to a stillborn child. There were no celebrations in any other Pandava household either. The Brahmastra had rendered the wombs of all their women barren. Subhadra remembered the promise her brother had made to her. Shri Krishna had promised, 'Sister, I shall not let your daughter-in-law's womb remain barren.' And, so, because he was an incarnation of Vishnu, he instilled life in the body of the dead child once more. He also predicted that Uttara's son would sit on the throne of Hastinapur and bring honour to the Pandavas.

But when Uttara's son, Parikshit, was on the throne, he asked Vyasaji who had come to the palace to give him his blessings, a very strange question. Parikshit washed Vyasaji's feet in a bowl of rose water, stood before him with folded hands, bowed his head and said, 'O wise one, with your permission, can I ask you a question?'

'Ask, son.'

'Maharaj, all the elders of our family were present at Kurukshetra. There were wise and knowledgeable men amongst the Pandavas and the Kauravas. Why didn't they understand that in war everyone has to pay a heavy price? That war destroys everything? Annihilates everything?'

Vyasaji sighed and replied, 'Son, during times of war, even the best of men lose their heads. Besides, that which is fated must come to pass.'

Then, Vyasaji went back to the forest.

In those blessed days, rishis used to live for thousands of years. Arjuna's grandson wasn't a rishi. He died when a snake bit him. But the question he asked Vyasaji, continued to live long after his death. I suddenly remembered that question when I was wandering through Rajasthan. Indeed, I encountered it at the same time Ashwatthama began to follow me. I felt as if I were walking between two shadows.

At first, I was surprised to see Ashwatthama. 'Oh, this cursed man hasn't yet completed his three thousand years.' When I remembered the question Parikshit had asked, I was even more surprised. 'Was that question still alive?' In fact, it seemed to be even more urgent in the present. It hung over India and Pakistan like a sword. But that which is fated must come to pass. Vyasaji evaded the question and refused to answer it. That is why it still hovers over us, demanding an answer. Ashwatthama's shadow was bad enough, why must I be tormented by Parikshit's question too?

I had to get rid of Ashwatthama. I tried to deceive and evade him. I changed my path suddenly and was sure I had lost him. But, after some time, I realized he was walking beside me once again.

He couldn't follow me forever. I had to get back to my country. He was the evil spirit of this land. He could follow me only up to the border. Who would let him cross it and go any further? I had to deceive him, escape from his clutches and get back home. I would be safe there.

I did finally evade his vigilant eye. I fooled him, and before he realized it, I crossed the border and heaved a sigh of relief when I reached my country. I thanked God that I had finally escaped from that evil spirit. I recalled a story from the *Baital Pachchisee*. But that was only a story. It is only in stories that evil spirits continue to cling to living beings. Anyway, I was free at last and very relieved.

I thought of peacocks from different epochs and different lands. I recalled their song. Now, I could sit in the tranquillity of my home and write my chronicle of the peacocks. I was ecstatic. All the peacocks I had met began to crowd my imagination. Their lovely songs echoed through my brain. Then I had a vision of one divine peacock. It spread its tail like a fan over the entire universe and danced. I walked in its shadow.

As I approached my house, I heard soft footsteps behind me. I quickly turned around. I was paralysed with fear. Ashwatthama had followed me home. 'Oh, the evil spirit has found me here too! How can I ever be rid of him?'

In despair, I cried out, 'O my Creator! O my Protector! When will this evil spirit complete his curse of three thousand years? When will I be able to write my *Mor Nama*, my chronicle of the peacocks?'

Translated by Alok Bhalla and Vishwamitter Adil

Zamiruddin Ahmad
(1926–90)

Zamiruddin Ahmad grew up in Fatehgarh and received higher education at Aligarh and Allahabad Universities. He was getting his master's degree in English when the turmoil of Partition struck and Ahmad decided to move to Karachi. Everyone in the family except his father followed him to Pakistan. Ahmad went back to Fatehgarh in 1952 but could not convince his father to come back with him. His failure to bring his father over to Pakistan continued to haunt him for the rest of his life. In Pakistan, Zamiruddin Ahmad drifted into journalism and became a political correspondent for the Associated Press. He was posted in Delhi from 1952 to 1956. It was at this time that he began writing and publishing his short stories, and also fell in love and got married. He continued to write through the 1950s and 1960s but abruptly stopped writing after moving to England in 1971. He resumed writing after a hiatus of ten years and went on to write some of his best fiction in the years that followed. Zamiruddin Ahmad died of lung cancer in 1990.

He wrote only forty-two stories; each one a classic. A collection titled *Sukhe Sawan* (Dry Rains) was published in 1991. His other publication, *Khatir-e Masoom* (The Innocent Heart), 1990, is a critical reflection on the idea of the beloved in Urdu poetry.

Ahmad's fiction defies categorization, neither fitting the 'progressive' nor the 'modernist' mould. His stories are mostly about the turmoil that smoulders beneath the picture of quiet domesticity; how desire is suppressed and compromises are made. The stories also reveal his love for the pre-Partition world of his native Uttar Pradesh and the self-reflexive commentary on the happy coexistence of Urdu Muslim culture with the non-Muslim cultures of India. The story presented here is about the reawakening of past desire for a lost love that may or may not disturb the status quo of the quotidian relationship of a middle-class couple. The *purvai* or easterly wind has the 'effect of making the saddest person happy for a little while', but also 'opens old wounds'.

The East Wind

The boy lifted his eyes from the copybook and looked towards the closed door behind which his father was changing his clothes.

'*Abba,* what does *purva* mean?'

But the answer came from the kitchen where his mother was frying parathas for breakfast.

'It's another word for purvai.'

'You mean the wind that blows to the east?'

'No,' said his mother, removing the paratha from the pan and placing it in the bread-cloth. 'The wind that blows *from* the east, or rather from the lands of the east. *Purab,* the East, *purba,* purva, purvai.'

'It's also called *purvaia.*'

His father opened the door and, buttoning his shirt, came out on the veranda where there was a round table spread with a stained plastic tablecloth and surrounded by one three-legged chair and three whole ones. The boy was sitting on one of these. A satchel was lying open in front of him on the table. He was bent over a copybook writing something. After buttoning his left sleeve the father asked:

'Why?'

'I have to make up a sentence.'

'What sentence have you made up?' asked his father after buttoning his right sleeve with his left hand.

The boy slowly slid his copybook towards his father.

'If the wind is blowing from the east it is called purva,' his father leaned over and read from the copybook. 'But that's just the meaning!'

'So?' the boy scratched his head.

His mother brought a plate with a paratha and a small helping of spiced scrambled eggs on it, put it in front of the boy and said:

'Write.'

The boy bent over the copybook again.

'The east wind has the effect of making even the saddest person happy for a little while, and...'

The boy took his eyes away from the copybook and looked up at his mother.

His mother paused for a moment.

'That will do. Cut the "and".'

The boy struck out the 'and'.

The mother quickly went back to the kitchen which adjoined the veranda and which had a door that opened onto the small central courtyard.

The boy shut the copybook and put it in the satchel, closed the satchel and began to wolf down his breakfast. Then he opened the spout of the water tank in the courtyard by the kitchen door and rinsed out his mouth. He wiped his hands and face on the towel hanging from the clothesline, put the satchel around his neck, said to his mother, 'I'll be back late this evening. There's a hockey match,' and, lifting the latch of the courtyard door, went out, saying goodbye.

A few moments later the wife brought another plate with two parathas and a little bit of the curry left over from the night before. She placed the plate in front of her husband who was now sitting on the same chair his son had been sitting on earlier. The husband stared at the plate.

'No more scrambled eggs?'

'There was only one egg,' said his wife on her way back to the kitchen. 'I'll bring some home this evening. It's pay-day today.'

Sitting down on a small stool in the kitchen, she took out a piece of stale flatbread from the cloth and, dipping it in the curry remaining in the pan, began to eat it slowly. But after taking three or four bites, she put the bread back in the bread-cloth.

'Aren't you going to eat breakfast?' asked her husband, wiping his plate clean with the last piece of paratha.

'I've eaten,' his wife said, lifting the kettle from the stove and pouring the boiling water into the teapot.

'When?'

'When you were having a shower.'

The husband heard the sound of the spoon against the teacup.

'Any chance of some tea?'

In answer, the wife brought two cups of tea set on saucers and, putting one before her husband and one before herself, she sat down on one of the empty chairs.

The husband took a sip and began to rub off a yellow lentil stain on the tablecloth with his forefinger.

His wife also took a sip.

'I'll wash it.'

For a while they both sat drinking their tea. Then the husband said:

'I've been wearing this shirt for the past two days!'

'We'll have to find another laundryman. He never comes on time.'

'Surely one or two shirts can be washed at home.'

'Why not!' The bottom of the teacup struck against the saucer. 'In fact all the washing can be done at home!'

The husband looked at her face.

'Why're you getting upset!'

His wife didn't say anything.

He took her hand in his and began to rub it gently.

She pulled it away.

The husband got up and stood behind her chair so that only its back separated their bodies. He placed the palms of his hands on her pale cheeks and bent down and kissed her unwashed hair. Then he ran the forefinger of his right hand over her firmly closed lips. Both his hands slid from her loose hair to her shoulders and, after resting there for a short while, they slipped further down.

His wife stood up quickly.

'There's a lot left to do...'

An embarrassed smile spread over the husband's face.

'I have to wash up, make the beds, have a bath...'

The husband put his hand on her shoulder and made her sit down. Then he pulled up a chair and sat down next to her.

'What's the matter?'

'Nothing!' said his wife fixing her eyes on her unpolished nails.

'Look at me.'

But without looking at him, his wife said, 'This is hardly the right time!'

'And last night?'

'My head was hurting.'

The husband let out a derisive laugh.

'You should give lessons in making excuses.'

The wife picked up the teacups and headed towards the kitchen.

And her swaying hips disappeared into the grey darkness of the kitchen, winking at him from under the cover of her sari.

As she stepped out of the shop, she saw a chauffeur-driven car come to a stop on the other side of the road with a man in the rear, his head resting against the back of the seat. She stopped short. The chauffeur got out and opened the door that faced the street. She hid herself behind a tree on the pavement. The man sitting in the rear stepped out. Tall, tawny-skinned, suit and tie, shoes shining. After exchanging a few words with the chauffeur, he went into one of the side streets nearby, and the chauffeur went back to his seat in the car.

She felt her throat becoming dry, her feet becoming heavy, sweat covering her forehead. Her eyes wanted to follow the man down the street into which he had disappeared. She swallowed once or twice. She ran her hand across her forehead and over her hair. She lifted her sari from her shoulder and placed it over her head. She came out from behind the tree. She stepped forward to cross the road but stopped. For a few seconds she stared blankly at the car. Then she quickly crossed the road, approached the car and stopped about two feet away from the chauffeur, as if she could not make up her mind whether to stay where she was or to go forward.

The chauffeur looked her up and down.

She tightened her grip on the shopping bag and went forward slowly. She turned to walk away but came back after taking ten or twelve steps.

This time the chauffeur looked only at her face.

She took a deep breath and came right up to the car.

'Who was that gentleman?' she asked the chauffeur the way one passer-by asks another the way or the time.

The chauffeur again examined her from head to toe.

'He's our guest!'

'Yours?'

'Yes, my boss's. He's come from Pakistan.'

She stood silent for a few moments.

'His name is Musavar Ahmed, isn't it?'

The chauffeur was lighting a cigarette. He blew out the match and flicked it out of the window. The match landed near her sandal.

'I don't know. The boss calls him Qazi Ji.'

'Qazi Musavar Ahmed,' she said as if she was talking to herself. 'His full name is Qazi Musavar Ahmed.'

'Maybe.'

And his attention drifted, as his eyes became fixed through the windscreen, on a girl in tight clothes walking by in front of the car.

A car passed close by. She saw that a young woman was driving. There was another young woman on the front seat next to her, her hair blowing in the wind, and in the back sat a thin man and a fat woman. She crushed the head of the burnt match with her sandal. She opened the shopping bag and peered into it. Then she turned and went around the rear of the car to a clothes shop on the other side and stood by the shop window. After a short while she retraced her steps back to the chauffeur and, like a child asking for something it has little hope of obtaining, enquired:

'Is his wife with him?'

The chauffeur looked at her the way ordinary people look at the crazed, insane, and demented. He did not like her coming back and asking another question but he was well-mannered and said softly:

'His wife! No madam; Qazi Sahib is still single.'

She quickly said 'Thank you,' turned to look down the side street, and then set off towards the bus station with light but rapid steps.

The boy was sitting at the table doing his homework when the father entered the house carrying a bundle of files. He put the bundle on the table, sat down on a chair, and took a look all around.

'Where's your mother?'

'She's having a bath.'

There was the sound of splashing from the bathroom which was next to the kitchen.

'At this time?'

The boy gave no response.

The father's eyes fell on the plastic tablecloth which was shining. He saw that the floor of the veranda was wet in one or two places. It looks as if it's been washed, he thought. The floor of the courtyard was also wet in places. There were only three rooms in the house and the doors of all three opened into the courtyard. He looked at the first door, then the second, and then the third. All three were clean. They've been dusted and wiped down, he guessed. The same shadeless bulb was hanging over the main table and there was a layer of dust on it as before. But nevertheless, it seemed to him as if the bulb was giving off more light.

The sound of splashing stopped. A few moments later, the door of the bathroom opened and his wife came out wearing a light-green starched payjama with a kurta of the same colour, her head wrapped in a towel.

'It took ages today!' she said stopping by her husband. 'I missed the six o'clock bus.'

A fragrant dampness was rising from her body. A rose-red tint had spread over her cheeks. And the bulb hanging from the ceiling of the veranda was lighting up the rounds of her eyes.

'Didn't you bathe this morning?' asked the husband, tearing his eyes away from her cheeks.

'I was late.'

As she moved towards the door from which her husband had emerged that morning buttoning his shirt, he said:

'Could I have a cup of tea?'

'Let me dry my hair. Then.'

She said this and went into the room. The husband took out a pack of cigarettes and a box of matches from his jacket pocket, lit a cigarette and began to puff on it.

The boy finished his homework, picked up his textbook, his copybook and his pen, and went into the middle room.

The husband took the last puff of the cigarette, crushed it against the sole of his shoe and was about to get up, when his wife came out of the bedroom. Her hair, now freed from the hold of the towel, was scattered across her shoulders. The rolls of her gathered dupatta were set across her chest. She went out to the clothesline in the courtyard to hang up the wet towel which was in her hand. Then she went towards the kitchen.

'*Ammi*!', the boy's voice came from the middle room.

She stopped.

'What is it, sweetie?'

'I'm hungry.'

'All right.'

'Hasn't he eaten yet?' asked his father.

The mother replied in the negative.

'Why?'

'He had two pieces of toast with tea as soon as he got back from school. He said he wasn't hungry.'

The boy came out of his room.

'Dinner, Ammi!'

'Come on now, sweetie, there's no need to be so impatient! Let me make your father some tea, then I'll give you something.'

The boy went back into his room. The mother went into the kitchen. And getting up from his chair, the father said:

'Forget it.'

'Why?'

'I'm hungry too. We might as well eat.'

There was a rattling of pots and pans in the kitchen. The boy turned on the radio. And the father went into his room to change his clothes. After changing, he went into the bathroom. While he was in there, the mother set the plates on the table, brought a jug of water with three glasses and then the food.

'Come along, sweetie! Dinner's ready,' she said sitting down on the middle chair.

The boy switched off the radio. As he came onto the veranda, his eyes fell on the large rice-platter in the centre of the table.

'Wow! There's pilau today!'

The husband, who had wiped his face and hands on the wet towel on the clothesline, was now on the veranda. He too said 'Pilau!' with surprise as he sat down on the first chair.

The wife moved the rice-platter towards him.

'I got off early today. Thought I'd make something special.' The husband took some pilau first and then poured some raita on top of it. The mother put more than half of the pilau that was left on the platter onto the boy's plate and, taking what was left for herself, she moved the bowl of raita towards him. The boy poured a little raita over his pilau and then placed the bowl in front of his mother.

'It's good,' the husband said after eating the first mouthful. 'Hmm,' came the sound from the boy's food-filled mouth.

The mother smiled.

When dinner was over and the plates and everything else had been cleared away, the mother brought out a cardboard box from the kitchen and put it on the table.

'Well, well!' the husband said as he opened the box. 'Today, as the man said, we really are going to have our fill. You haven't had a pay raise, have you!'

And he picked out a *gulab jamun* from the box of sweets.

'Of course not!' the wife said, looking a little sheepish. 'This little one has been going on and on about wanting sweets for days now. Thought I'd get some.' She said to the boy, 'Take some!'

The boy picked out a *laddu*.

The father also took a laddu.

The mother took a piece of green *barfi*.

Then the boy reached out his hand for a gulab jamun but before putting it in his mouth, he said:

'Ammi, Siraj Sahib said that the east wind also has another effect.'

'I know,' the mother said gently.

'What is it?' asked the father.

'He said that when the east wind blows, old wounds start to hurt. Is that true?'

The mother said quietly, 'Yes.'

'Have some more,' her husband said pushing the box towards her.

His wife said, 'Enough!'

After about thirty or forty minutes, the wife went to the kitchen but came straight back out again.

'I'll wash up tomorrow.'

The husband was bent over an open file. Without lifting his head he said, 'Yes.'

After a short while, the mother went into the boy's room.

'He's sleeping,' she said as she came back and sat down on a chair.

Again the husband said 'Yes' without lifting his head from the file.

A few moments later, the wife went into her room and started to read a magazine. But when the husband closed the file in front of him, moved it to one side and bent down to pick up another from the floor, he saw from the corner of his eye that her gaze was fixed on the darkness covering the courtyard, not on the magazine. However, when he raised his head to light a cigarette, he saw that she was reading the magazine again. She lifted up her eyes to look at him, smiled, and then went back to her reading.

A little later she closed the magazine and got up.

'I'm going to bed.'

'You go ahead; it's going to take me a while yet.'

She went back to her room and the sound of her humming could be heard for some time. Then there was silence.

When the courtyard was filled with the thick, damp darkness falling from the sky, when the noise of the traffic from the street had ceased, when a dog started whining in the distance, he closed the last file and put it on top of all the other files already stacked up in a pile. He rubbed his eyes, lit a cigarette, stood up, switched off the light on the veranda and, opening the door gently, went into the bedroom.

Two beds were laid out in front of him, their headboards against the wall. Between the beds there was a small, three-legged table. On it there was a small lamp with a yellow cloth shade that would not let the light from the weak bulb rise much above the beds.

His wife was sleeping on the bed to his right. He saw that her payjama, kurta, and dupatta had been thrown carelessly onto the armchair to the right of the bed. When he had seen his wife in that same payjama, kurta and dupatta two or three hours earlier, he had felt a surge of desire. There was also a bra. He was surprised because when his wife changed clothes she would carefully fold the ones she had taken off and place them in the cupboard.

He stepped forward and lifted the light quilt that covered his wife's body from her feet to her shoulders. All he could do was stare. Unrestrained by shame or modesty, a sleeping body was waiting wakefully for someone. He felt as if he was seeing this body for the first time.

He quickly put out his cigarette and sat down on the edge of the bed. His wife moaned and her face, which had been turned a little towards the armchair, came into the fold of the light filtering through the lamp shade. And, as the husband watched, the hint of a smile spread across his wife's closed lips.

He placed one hand on the pillow beneath her head and the other on the one she held under her arm. He bent down over her face. But his open lips stopped as they came near his wife's closed lips. He thought for a moment that her lashes were wet. Then he saw a moist patch on the pillow by her head and his doubt turned to certainty.

He sat up straight and for some time looked at her face and at her breasts turned towards him. Then very gently he ran his forefinger along his wife's lips. The rhythm of her breathing and the rise and fall of her breasts changed and the smile disappeared from her lips. He held his breath and waited a few seconds; when the rhythm of her breathing and the rise and fall of her chest became steady again, he got up very carefully. For a few moments he stared blankly at the warm, radiant body stretched out on the bed. And then he began to fold his wife's clothes. He folded the dupatta, the kurta, the payjama, and the bra. He placed them on the armchair and went and sat down on the other bed.

His wife turned over a few moments later. Her face was now towards him. A smile that seemed like an answer to a lover's entreaties was beaming from her lips and the corners of her eyes, fanning the redness of her cheeks, and she had clasped the other pillow tight against her breasts.

The husband reached out and covered his wife's nakedness with the quilt, switched off the table lamp, and lay down.

Translated by Aquila Ismail

Qurratulain Hyder
(1927–2007)

Qurratulain Hyder was born into a wealthy, aristocratic family of writers. Her father, Sajjad Hyder 'Yildrim' was among Urdu's earliest short story writers; her mother, Nazar Sajjad Hyder, also wrote fiction, both novels and short stories. Qurratulain was educated mostly in Lucknow, at the famous Isabella Thoburn College, then at Lucknow University, where she obtained a master's degree in English literature. Hyder migrated with her mother to Karachi in December, 1947, after communal riots broke out in Dehra Dun where she was living at that time. From Pakistan she moved to England where she worked for the BBC. In 1961, she returned to India and lived in Bombay, first as the managing editor of *Imprint*, then as assistant editor at the *Illustrated Weekly of India*. Since 1984, she has lived in Delhi and has held visiting professorships at Aligarh University and Jamia Millia Islamia. She was awarded the Jnanpith, India's highest literary award, in 1989. Qurratulain Hyder died in August 2007 after a protracted lung illness.

Qurratulain began writing as a young girl, and published her first story while still in her teens. Though she is a great writer of short stories, what distinguishes her from her contemporaries is her contribution to Urdu as a writer of novels. She has written six major novels. Her first novel *Mere Bhi Sanam Khane* (I Have My Temples Too), published soon after Partition, is a moving account of the lives of individuals whose world was destroyed by tragic division. Her most remarkable and well-known novel is *Ag ka Dariya* (River of Fire). Published in 1960, it established her as the leading Urdu novelist in the Indian Subcontinent. Her two-volume semi-fictional autobiography, *Kar-e Jahan Daraz Hai*, is an account of her family's history from the time her ancestors arrived from Central Asia up to 1978, the time of her writing it. Hyder is the most prominent among the notable writers who had a different perspective on the meaningfulness of literature and did not succumb to the Progressive rhetoric of literature as a tool for political and social change. Qurratulain was more interested in the past and the cultural manifestations of it in modern times.

This excerpt is from her novella *Sita Haran*, generally regarded as her finest work, first published in 1960, in the journal *Naya Daur*, Karachi. The novella is undoubtedly one of the more complex engagements with the Partition in fiction; the question of personal loyalty within the context of political shifts, the experience of exile, and the follies of misplaced trust are some of its themes.

Sita Betrayed

The rest house was on a rise, in the middle of a dense forest; below it, over a flat bed filled with purplish rocks, rushed the Kalini Ganga, filling the air with noise and spray. The birds returning to roost in the trees were raising their own chatter. A strong breeze rustled through the swinging fronds of the palms. Sita sat quietly at the window and gazed into the slowly darkening current of the river.

On their return from Nuwara Eliya, when Sita and Leslie had reached the rest house, Leslie had bade her farewell and rushed off to Colombo. He had received a telegram in Nuwara Eliya that asked him to return immediately and proceed to Calcutta. After Sita saw him off, she went back to the room and closed the door. This rest house, unlike the others, was not a glittering modern affair with fancy fixtures. Its furniture was heavy and old; its floors were covered only with coir mats; and the mirrors on its dressing tables had turned dull. There were no other tourists staying there; Sita was all alone. The driver from American Express had put the car in the garage and had gone to the servants' quarters. At dinner, the lonely waiter displayed his teeth ingratiatingly and said, 'Madam, this is where they shot 'Bridge on the River Kwai'. That gorge over there, that's where the bridge was built. Alec Guiness. William Holden. All the big stars stayed in this rest house. It was so wonderful...madam?' But Sita had not been listening. Afterwards, she returned to the room and sat by the window looking out. Then she turned off the light and lay down on the bed. Early next morning she too had to return to Colombo.

The night continued to grow darker: the night, which was set loose in the forests of sandalwood, slumbered on the bushes of cardamom and cloves; it lay on the white flowers spread over the steps of the temple in Kandy; and rustled like a snake in the grass by the banks of the Kalini Ganga. Silent as the Portuguese and Dutch churches tucked away in forests, the night hid in the smooth rocks at the bottom of the river. The night, proud and regal like the mahouts of the state elephants in Kandy, was dark and heavy-footed like the bathing elephants in the Mahaveli Ganga. The night which was the crack of the lash, the melody of the flute, the reel of the bagpipe, the ripple of the sitar...

In Kandy a torchlight procession is going down the road. The procession of the Buddha's Tooth. The tooth is in a box studded with diamonds and emeralds, and the box is being carried by an elephant who is also covered with gold and silver ornaments. But the Buddha who is sprawled on the grass is laughing, showing his teeth. He has false teeth. The Buddha has one set of teeth for eating, and a different set just for show...

Priyam Mayurah Pratinrityati. The peacock dances and comes close to its beloved. *Priyam.* God, I've forgotten all the languages I used to know. How many do I know now? Not one. I'm dumb...

King of Words! O King of Words! I salute Vani and Vinayaka. They created words and meanings. I am Vishakhadatta, son of Maharaja Bhaskaradatta. Clouds are thundering overhead. My beloved is far away. What has happened? What is going on? The herbs of immortality grow on snow-covered peaks. A coiled snake sits on the head of Shiva. A coiled snake...

What was that song by Chandidasa that that fool Qamarul Islam Chowdhri sang to me? 'It's a dark night; the clouds are heavy. How did you manage to come? He stands among the flowers, getting drenched in the rain. My mother-in-law is most cruel, and so are my sisters-in-law. Chandidasa says: Dear friend...dear friend...'

And what was that lyric by Vidyapati that the great artist Projesh Kumar Chowdhry explained for me? 'The pupils of Radha's heavy-lidded eyes are like the bumblebees on lotus flowers. The gusts of wind tickle the petals. After her bath she puts collyrium in her eyes. Why would someone gild a lily...?'

And then she puts on a sari, dark as night itself, and goes off to meet Krishna...

Please Krishna, let me listen to your flute. Please, please Krishna...

Tulsidas has written in his *Ramacharitmanas*: A young woman is like the burning flame of a lamp. O my soul, do not become a moth to that flame...

But no son of a bitch listens to Tulsidas now...

If only I could find in Ratanpura that magic diamond that fulfils all wishes...

All the mountains in Sri Lanka are leaning...

May Autumn, which is pale like the body of Vishnu, remove all your problems...

I receive your command with bowed head, just as one receives a garland of flowers...

But who shall receive the garland that I'm offering? Yes, friend, who shall...?

Maharaj, may you be victorious. There was a man without a passport. He was trying to leave our camp with a letter. He has been put under arrest...

How do they give someone the third degree? The third degree. F.B.I. C.I.D. Ph.D. K.L.M. Pan Am. Air India International...

The trees, bare of all leaves, have lined up, as if getting ready to escort someone's coffin...

Now I go to burning places and invoke the spirits of love's magic words. May Kali of Calcutta be victorious. There was a Hindu burning place on the way to Maripur near Karachi. When Muslim refugees arrived from India they set up their huts there. May Kali of Calcutta be victorious....

'The beginning of the Universe is a dark secret, dark like the body of Kali. The red in the sky at sunset is the wrath of Kali; the typhoons, plagues, and death are her companions. We in Bengal have seen her wrath for centuries.' Shri Projesh Kumar Chowdhri gives a statement to the press. A fraud. A painter of fake Expressionist paintings. Fraud. Fraud. Fraud. The concept of Kali is 'expressionistic'. Fraud...

They drew a line on the ground to protect me, but it didn't work...

Anasuya said: Listen, O princess...

Virtue...devotion to one's husband...innocence...fidelity...Alas, alas...Ladies and gentlemen! Comrades! Brothers and sisters! I beg to inform you that Sita is lost in the dreadful jungle of today's world. She was abducted by the Ravana of today's world. This world of ours which is divided in two camps. The world which is prey to Anglo-American imperialism; in which innocent people are tortured but no Hanuman comes to rescue them...Lata dear, the microphone is dead...Kailash... Kailash Nath Mathur, please get the power turned on quick...So, ladies and gentlemen, as I was saying, in today's world where the demons of hydrogen bombs are ready to destroy human habitations, where the Sitas of Asia and Africa are daily abducted....You frauds, you who read the *Ramayana*, how many Muslim Sitas did you abduct in 1947? Just count them for once. And you Muslim holy-warriors, you whose tongues never tire of cursing the tyrants of the seventh century, you tell me...

Sita Mirchandani. Roll number 963...?

Yes please...

Yes, I am Sita...

My beloved Sita...My darling Sita...

Sita, my love, my darling...

Sweetheart. More precious than life

Tell me what you wish for most...

What do I wish for? I only want all the diamonds in Ratanpura. Then you'll see how I shall put you in your place...

What a petit bourgeois...! Hello, hello, hello! Noises, sounds. What sounds? The humming of telephone wires. The rumble of train wheels. The sputter of the motor boat engine. The roar of the airplane. Whrr, whrr. Phat, phat. Bang, bang. Shloop, shloop. Is that the washerman? Has he brought the clothes?...Bilqis *bitiya,* please check the clothes... Begum sahiba, what do you want me to cook for dinner...

Ah, those wonderful sounds...the shehnai players in Banaras...the band at Qaisar's wedding...On the island of Capri...the drum players at Muharram...hurry, it's, Ja'far Bandi singing the *nauha:*

'The nightingales love the roses, yes they do;
the roses love the morning breeze, yes they do;
but we who love Ali, Father of the Dust,
love only his grave's dust, yes we do....'

Yes, I do...

Ravana is burned. Sita is burned too. All of Lanka's land is burned to ashes...

Was that Rahul laughing?...Rahil's gay laugh. Jamil's loud laughter. The tinkle of wine glasses...There was an old couple on the Brooklyn Bridge; they were whispering to each other and laughing like children...

I shall die. Death will come to me. My feet will be turned towards the West so that my soul can get on board a boat and cross the ocean of Sindh...The flames of the bier...The candles dripping wax. Fresh flowers. The graveyard in Tulsipur. That's where we buried Jamila Baji. Who was Jamila Baji?... Then there was her husband; he was wailing and crying so loudly. Bilqis told me he remarried next month. The swine. They are all swine, the men...Jamil darling, I still sometimes have that awful dream. That I'm taking my M.A. exam., but the questions are set in a language I don't know. And the allowed three hours are ticking away. Two hours left! Now one. Twenty minutes. Five minutes. One...

Give me five minutes more
Only five minutes more
Only five minutes more of your charms
Give me five minutes more *In-your-arm*...

The rock looked exactly like an elephant. When you climb a high rock you are likely to slip and fall. I can go and hide on a rock twice as high as Sigiriya, but they'll find me...

May I have the pleasure...?

Who me? I am Mrs Beach Luxury Hotel. And you? Mr Ashoka Hotel? How nice! Please take a seat...

India, that is Bharat, discovered the pillar of the mighty King of Kings, Ashoka; discovered the Chakra of Ashoka; discovered the Ashoka Hotel...

May I have the pleasure...?

Of course. This is my sister-in-law. Quite something. Bilqis Anwar Ali. A-1 actress. Producer of great plays. Super intellectual...Hey you, Jamuni Begum, are YOU listening? Umrao Begum? Khetu Begum?... Where the heck have they all disappeared? What the hell is going on? Hey you, Jamil's wife, look at the soles of your feet. That will protect you from the evil eye. Hey you, Bhuri Begum, what's making you so itchy? Why do you want to rush off so soon. Hey you, Bundi Bua, Jamil Bhaiya is not feeling well...I think I'll go crazy from worrying. Last night I washed Lord Ali's medallion to give us protection...Just listen to what Khetu Begum has done—she's accusing poor Bundi of all sorts of things, as if she herself is the most virtuous of wives...You know, Urooj's wife lies like nobody's business. Don't ever let yourself be fooled by her, Mother...What can she give to anyone? She shivers in winter and starves in spring...Jamil Bhaiya, last night the Lord Ali himself appeared in a dream to me. Are you listening, Jamil Bhaiya...?

I'm a cow...

Mr Sandman...Mr Sandman...Step into my heart's Vrindavan...

In my little corner of the world
Tonight my love—tonight my love...

The night has come down on the Buddhist shrines...

Why has the night attacked me again...?

The wind has turned violent...

The wind blows over Parakrama Samudra. It floats over Kalini Ganga. It dances away towards Colombo...

The wind...

The moon...

The moon sleeps in sandalwood branches...The eyes of the people snoring in dusty cottages are filled with the sleep of centuries...Don Fernandez da Costa Samrasinharuna Mudaliyar... Ratansinha Jaisurya... Gunapala Gunawerdene...Their eyes are filled with the sleep of forests... Portuguese covered with armour attack Dutch castles. The spirits of English planters line the road to Mahahinya and beg for sugar and butter from American GIs...The moon swims in Mahaveli Ganga...These elephants are nothing but spirits that were held captive for thousands of years in the jungles...

The moon...

The night...

The night is the hair of Queen Sita. The dark-hued body of the Lord, Rama Raghurai. The face of Mother Kali...The darkness before all creation...We are always caught in that primordial darkness, though we might deceive ourselves and think that a great evolution has taken place...

Dark, dark, dark. Night...

I lost my sleep in New York...The palm trees in the forest have shot into air and are touching the blood red sky...the ruins of Lanka Tilaka are like a mouth full of teeth gaping open in a hideous smile...the pond of lilies is open like a sleepless eye...Lilavati... Rupavati...Sitavati...

The bones collected in the stupa of Rana Vihar are busy discussing the international situation...Parakrama Bahu I is urgently writing the fifth chapter of *Communism in South Asia*...I was devoured by the forest...

God, how beautiful were the ornaments that Bari Khala gave me at my wedding...the bride's jewels...The goldsmiths of Ratanpura are busy making a diamond-studded necklace...All that glitters...Light...light... The sounds of the jungle...the sounds of the birds, the ocean, the roads and the highways, the sounds of the harbour, the sounds in the stillness of the mountains...

The sound...

There is only one...

Come here...come here, near me...come near me...come...

(ii)

'I just got back,' Sita spoke into the mouthpiece of the telephone in her room in Mount Lavinia. 'Any news?'

'Oh, hello, Sita,' Irfan replied. 'So you're back. How wonderful! May I come up to your room?'

'Please do...'

He arrived five minutes later.

'Well, well. You look very cheerful. I'm so glad the forest air did you some good.'

'Please sit down.'

This was his first time in her room and he seemed rather nervous. He paced the room once, then sat down on the sofa in one corner. She remained seated on the edge of her bed, busily knitting something.

'What's that?'

'A sweater for my son. I started it so that I could give it to Jamil to take back with him for Rahul...But now I don't even know how big Rahul is. It may not even fit him. I've been going by my memory alone.'

Irfan remained silent for several moments, then he asked, 'What else? Tell me more.'

'More?' she asked with a smile.

'For the whole week I thought of you all the time. I couldn't get interested in the conference at all. God knows what I finally wrote in my report. But tell me, was your trip interesting?'

'Very interesting.' She picked up a new set of needles.

'How were the doddering American widows?'

'I didn't meet any doddering American widows. Though I met an American...a man. But he wasn't even old.'

'Bitch,' Irfan muttered under his breath and fell silent.

Some moments passed, then Sita said, 'You didn't ask your usual question: what happened next?'

'Tell me yourself....'

'He was an archaeologist.'

'Then you must've had a great time discussing Ceylonese history with him. The way you had lectured me on the history of Sindh.'

'Sure.' She went on knitting, unconcerned.

Irfan stared at Sita for a while. Suddenly he jumped up from the sofa and, striding up to her, slapped the needles and the knitting out of her hands. Then he grabbed her by the shoulders and pulled her off the bed.

'What else did you do besides discussing history?' he snarled.

Sita turned white.

'I asked you something. What else did you do?'

'Shut up!' Sita's face was flushed with anger. 'What right have you to ask me that?'

'None,' Irfan hissed between clenched teeth. 'None at all. Perhaps even your husband has no right to question you—since you ran out on him two years ago.'

'Shut up, Irfan!' Sita screamed. 'Get the hell out of here. Get out before I call the manager.' She was trembling with rage.

For a long moment Irfan stood silently watching her, then turned around and slowly walked away. At the door, without looking back at her, he spoke once again in his normal, calm voice, 'I finally managed to get an appointment with Jamil. He has agreed to talk to me tonight. I'll be meeting him for dinner at Galface Hotel. Afterwards, I'll call you. Good night.'

Sometime after midnight the phone by Sita's bed rang persistently, but she didn't answer.

Translated by C.M. Naim

Khadija Mastoor

(1927–83)

Khadija Mastoor was born in Lucknow into a family that cherished learning and political awareness. Her mother wrote for women's journals, and both Khadija and her younger sibling, Hajira, showed early promise as budding writers. The death of her father when she was ten years old put the family under extreme financial distress but they bore the hardships with fortitude. Khadija worked actively for the Muslim League. The family migrated to Lahore after Partition. Khadija and her sister Hajira were among the younger group of Progressive Writers. Inspired by Ismat Chughtai, Mastoor too wrote with passion about the anguished lives of women who strive for equality and social justice. People who read her stories were surprised when they saw her for the first time: a slender, simple, and bashful young woman who wore the traditional burqa, she seemed quite unlike her fiery heroines.

Mastoor published five collections of short stories and two novels, *Angan* (Inner Courtyard) and *Zamin* (Earth). She was awarded Pakistan's highest literary honour, the Adamji Award, for *Angan*.

Angan is written against the backdrop of Partition, but it is above all the story of Aliya, the young, determined woman who will not let the challenges of the turbulent times break her fiery spirit. Mastoor's narrative style is direct and uncomplicated but remarkably effective.

Inner Courtyard

It rained heavily all night and at daybreak the sky was still overcast and black rain-laden clouds drifted across the sky. Washed clean by the rain, the trees in the school compound had acquired a pristine freshness. Hidden in the foliage of some tree, the koel called dementedly. The smell of mango peel lying in the street below wafted up in the air; the newspaper vendor walked swiftly by, shouting at the top of his voice:

'Bomb exploded. Japan's back has been broken. Hiroshima destroyed! Victory imminent for Allied Forces! Today's news! Hiroshima...'

So, the bomb had destroyed an entire city. What will happen after this? Jamil would come back. Having put away the tools of British propaganda, he would return empty-handed. But what of those who were killed by the fire of war? What of those others who waited for their return? What would become of them? Finding no answer to her queries, she got out of bed. She was eager to read today's news.

Barre Chacha had already gone to the *baithak* and the pages of the newspaper lay scattered on the bed. She picked them up impatiently, 'Hiroshima invisible behind a wall of fire...'

She put down the paper and sat there in stunned silence. 'Dear God, why did governments target cities during war? What fault was it of the people that they should be sent to their deaths in this manner? But this was the way history was made. It had never smiled on the aspirations of ordinary people. Each word that she read was like a drop of blood. What all had been destroyed in the fire that raged in Hiroshima? What had the people been doing when the bomb exploded, what dreams, what aspirations had they set out with, what tasks had they been in the process of bringing to completion? With what plans had they stepped out of their homes that day? Perhaps even at that moment, some Japanese child had stepped into a shop to buy a doll or a toy? And then the bomb had exploded...and...'

'Hurry up and have your breakfast, Aaliya Bitya, the school tonga will be here soon. What are you thinking of sitting there,' scolded Kariman Bua and she came quickly and sat down to drink her tea. She still had to change and get ready for school.

'Japan is on the verge of defeat. An entire city of theirs has been destroyed.'

Stepping out of the bathroom, Amma gave her the news with an air of great complacency.

'Yes,' she said coming out into the courtyard after finishing her breakfast. Barri Chachi was sitting at the tap, washing her face. Flattened by the rain, the plants in the flower bed crouched close to the ground. She had dressed for school and was combing her hair when the cry of 'the teacher's tonga is here' was heard outside. Burqa in hand, she moved towards the stairs to find that Najma Phuphi was there before her, precariously negotiating the stairs in her high-heeled sandals.

'Teacher, your tonga is there!' Her lips upturned in an amused smile, she turned and looked at Aaliya.

'Both of us belong to the same profession, the only difference is that you are called a lecturer and I a teacher. Even if this difference is never erased, the sky won't fall, Najma Phuphi,' Aaliya responded sharply.

'Yes. Nor can this difference ever be erased. You haven't got a Master's in English. There is a marked difference between a horse and a donkey, you cannot deny that.'

Najma Phuphi sat down to have her breakfast, when the cry of 'teacher, the college tonga is here,' was heard from the street.

Aaliya laughed, 'It appears that for the tonga-wallahs you and I are the same. Why don't you explain the difference to them?' She went and sat in the tonga and did not hear Najma Phuphi's reply.

On returning from school she saw somebody standing in the courtyard. As her back was towards her, Aaliya didn't immediately recognize her, but she had only taken a couple of steps forward when Chhammi turned and clung to her. 'Chhammi! You've come!' Aaliya hugged her tightly; 'And who is that? Lying in the cot in the veranda?'

'I don't know,' was the mumbled reply.

'It's Chhammi's little daughter. Who else?' Barri Chachi answered joyfully.

Forgetting to remove her burqa, Aaliya ran towards the baby.

'Oh, how pretty she is. She's just like you, Chhammi.' She wanted to pick up the sleeping child and cuddle her. It occurred to her that had Tehmina Apa lived, she too would have been the mother of one or two children by now.

The dupatta that covered the face of the child slipped off and a fly came and settled on her cheek. She brushed it aside and covered the child's face again. 'I'll buy a little mosquito net for her on my way back from school,' she said. 'Then she'll be safe from flies.'

'Now who can escape from flies? They are seasonal butterflies where I come from, Bajiya,' laughed Chhammi. 'If anyone speaks like you in our village, everyone makes fun of them. After all, who can escape from flies?' She laughed again but there was pain in that laughter. She had lost weight as well. It made her look lovelier than before. As she took off her burqa, it occurred to Aaliya that Jamil had made a big mistake in losing Chhammi.

'Have you met Barre Chacha?' she asked folding up the burqa.

'How could I? He's not been home since I've come,' then turning to Barri Chachi asked after him like a venerable matron: 'Barre Chacha is well, isn't he?'

'He's well enough. He's grown weak,' Barri Chachi replied.

'Have you eaten, Chhammi?' she asked.

'No Bajiya, I was waiting for you.'

The baby woke up and began to cry. Barri Chachi picked her up and held her against her shoulder, patting her lovingly. Amma was on the *takht*, snipping betel nut. She hadn't deigned to look at Chhammi even once. Ever since Aaaliya had got her job in a school, a new contempt for those around her had taken birth in Amma's eyes. As for Chhammi, she had always disliked her.

'Your husband hasn't come, Chhammi?'

'No Bajiya. He couldn't get away, his buffalo had fallen ill. He just put me in the ladies' compartment and asked an old woman to keep an eye on me.' She began to laugh.

'I've missed you very much, Chhammi.'

Looking affectionately at her, Aaliya realized that she didn't seem content with her situation. It was a painful thought.

'I've come especially for you, Bajiya.'

'Hmm! There was peace in the house after you left, that is why she was tormented by your absence.' Amma taunted her with words.

'Really?' Chhammi laughingly endured the jibe.

What? Had Chhammi lost all her fire? Aaliya couldn't believe her eyes. There was such a look of weighty seriousness about her.

'Chhammi, give your little daughter to me. I'll bring her up. Looking after her will help pass the days that are still left to me,' Barri Chachi said again and again as she kissed and cuddled the child.

'Take her, Barri Chachi.'

Chhammi made the routine response each time, but her face paled as she uttered the words. Perhaps she was reminded of her own childhood and the circumstances under which she had been nurtured. She too had been left here to be raised and cared for.

The baby began to cry in earnest. Leaving her half-eaten meal, Chhammi washed her hands and took her in her lap. Barri Chachi went inside. Amma had already taken her *pandan* and retired to Chhammi's room. Perhaps she was afraid that her niece would settle in there once again.

The heat was stifling and the still, breathless air added to the humidity. The endless afternoons, impossible to live through, went by on leaden feet.

'Kariman Bua, take these toys for the little daughter of the house and convey my blessing to Chhammi Bitiya. If everyone has eaten, then...' Israr Mian made his request from behind the half-shut door, and Kariman Bua collected everyone's leavings in a bowl and made preparations to settle his fate with a bout of cholera.

Aaliya stretched a hand to take the toys from him and Kariman Bua broke into a frenzy of recriminations:

'Glory be! It is the sign of the times that now Israr Mian should bring toys for Chhammi Bitiya's baby!'

She slapped down the bowl of food and rotis in his outstretched hand.

'You won't gain caste this way, Israr Mian! Strutting about and giving yourself airs. Don't you know your true status?' Kariman Bua had moved to the veranda but her grumbling continued unabated.

Kariman Bua, may death claim Israr Mian for its own and may God strike you dumb, she prayed silently in her heart as she sat down near Barri Chachi who was riffling through bundles of silk cuttings and braid to stitch a cap and kurta for the baby. She talked unceasingly as she worked: 'What is your mother-in-law like, Chhammi? She doesn't quarrel with you, does she? And your husband? He must love you very much?'

Chhammi laughed and answered in the affirmative to all the questions, but Aaliya noticed that she avoided meeting their eyes.

'Why do I love her so much, Bajiya?'

In an attempt to save herself from all the questions, Chhammi changed the subject.

'Because she is your daughter.'

'Ever since she's come before my eyes, the rest of the world has receded to nothingness.'

She sighed deeply, then holding her daughter to her breast, lay down with her.

'Her father and grandmother don't care for her at all. They wanted a son.'

In a little while, Chhammi dropped off to sleep, and in her sleep continued to sigh. Aaliya sat up with Barri Chachi all afternoon, stitching the kurta and cap.

That evening Barre Chacha came home when everyone was having tea. Chhammi saw him and turned her face away.

'Barre Chacha is here, Chhammi,' chided Aaliya.

'Oh, it's Barre Chacha is it? I didn't recognize him.' She laughed sarcastically.

'Greetings Barre Chacha, tell me how is your Congress party faring? By the grace of God, Gandhi Mian's life is being prolonged indefinitely.'

Good heavens, this was the same old Chhammi! The only difference was that now she had a little baby in her lap! Aaaliya couldn't believe her eyes.

'I hope all is well with you and your household?' Confused, Barre Chacha turned towards the baithak: 'Kariman Bua, have my tea sent out.'

'He needs a long life doesn't he, poor man? He dreams of ruling India in his loincloth!'

Pleased with the tenor of her talk, Amma began to talk to Chhammi. In such matters she was fully in agreement with her niece. And then, she was all but willing to lay down her life for the English rulers. The reason for this being that ever since Aaliya had got a job, Amma's English sister-in-law had begun to write long, loving letters to her. She wrote about many things in these letters. For instance she had written that if all the women of India were to become economically independent, this country too would be as good as England.

'You're a grown woman now, Chhammi; you've become a mother, surely you could have shown some consideration for Barre Chacha.' Despite her efforts to say nothing, Aaliya could not stop herself from chiding her cousin.

'I don't know what happened to me. I'll beg his pardon.'

She bowed her head and began to think of something.

'I'll leave tomorrow. Kariman Bua, tell Israr Mian to get a tonga for me tomorrow morning and put me on the train for home.'

'What? Will you go back so soon, are you angry with me, Chhammi?' Aaliya went and stood near her.

'Come, don't be absurd, Bajiya, how could I ever be angry with you? You don't know with what difficulty I got permission to come for one day. You don't know Aaliya Bajiya, you don't know...' Her eyes filled with tears. 'I would like to stay forever, but I have my little daughter now. Come, suggest a nice name for her Bajiya. Her grandmother's named her Tamizan!' She collapsed in a heap of giggles.

'Why can't you stay? Stay for at least eight or ten days, it feels so good to have you back; it's as if you've brought the Spring with you!' Aaliya became quite emotional. 'Such a stillness came upon us when you left. The silence made my gorge rise, Chhammi.'

'I'll come again Bajiya,' she replied, patting the baby with great concentration.

A tonga stopped in the street outside and Najma Phuphi entered settling her sari pallu.

'Ah! It is Chhammi! How are you? And this is your little daughter? She's very pretty, hasn't taken after the father at all.' She patted the baby's cheek. 'Give her a good education, Chhammi, otherwise she too will grow up an illiterate like the rest.'

'I'll send her to you, Najma Phuphi. You educate her!'

The arrow loosed by Chhammi brought a frown to Najma Phuphi's forehead. 'All right then, we'll talk later. I'm tired now,' and she tip-tapped her way up the stairs.

'Any news of Shakil?'

'No, Chhammi,' she replied softly.

'And do you ever hear from my father?'

Aaliya was silent. She began to stroke the baby's cheek gently. On getting no reply, Chhammi began to look about her restlessly. She had asked after everyone but forgotten to ask about Jamil. There was no reality in this love, Aaliya thought, feeling very strange.

The clear night sky was bathed in mild white moonlight. A small cot had been added to the row of beds in the courtyard. The gurgles of the little baby lent an added charm to the already beautiful night. Yesterday's rain had brought down the temperature and the weather was pleasantly cool. Instead of sleeping on the rooftop, Aaliya had made up her bed next to Chhammi in the courtyard. She experienced a strange indefinable sense of belonging tonight. Everyone was sitting together in one place and Chhammi's little daughter gurgled contentedly. Only Najma Phuphi wasn't there. Eschewing the company of ignoramuses, she slept alone on the rooftop. After that one encounter with his niece, Barre Chacha too hadn't set foot in the house. He had eaten his dinner in the baithak and his bed had been made up outside on the terrace. He was lying there now, talking to somebody.

Her chores done, Kariman Bua came and sat on the ground near Amma, crooning lullabies to the baby.

a ja ri nindiya, tu a kiyun na ja
come this way sleep, why don't you come

'Kariman Bua, tell us a story,' requested Chhammi, looking like a little girl herself.

'I find it hard to remember any now, Chhammi Bitya,' she replied and began to think.

'Any story, Kariman Bua! I do love listening to these tales.'

Aaliya joined Chhammi in pestering her. Tired of the world of books, she longed to lose herself in a tale of simple innocence.

'Come on, Kariman Bua, begin with the one that starts with: Once there was a king who had seven daughters. One day he called all seven of them to him and asked, "Whose kismet is it that you live off?" Six of them answered: "Yours, dear Father," but the seventh and youngest daughter replied, "I live off my own kismet," and the king had her cast in the jungle, saying, "Then go and live off your kismet." And then, when she was sitting alone in the jungle, crying away, a *jinn* came and conjured up a palace for her! There, that's the kind of story you must tell us, Kariman Bua, I've reminded you of so many stories,' said Chhammi, sitting up.

'All right then, listen. Once upon a time there was a king—God is the King that you and I know—yes, as I was saying, this king had seven daughters. One day he called all seven of them to his presence and asked...'

Kariman Bua's tale began to unravel, but Aaliya did not hear a word of it, she was wondering why Chhammi had remembered this particular story. Was it because she still hoped that some event or person would change her luck? She had been lost and wandering in a jungle for such an age, but no jinn had come to save her. Chhammi, why won't you understand, it is those who have lost all in life who find comfort in these innocent stories; there is no reality to them.

Long before the story drew to a close, the sleep-fairy wafted Chhammi away to some enchanted place and placed her next to who knows which handsome prince.

Chhammi left early next morning. On her way to school Aaliya was strangely depressed. She felt she wouldn't be able to do justice to her lessons that day. It wouldn't have done any harm if Chhammi had stayed on for a few days.

Translated by Neelam Husain

Bano Qudsiya
(b. 1928)

Bano Qudsiya was born in Ferozepur, East Punjab. She earned an M.A. in Urdu literature from Government College, Lahore, in 1950. In college, she met and married Ashfaq Ahmad, a well-known fiction writer with whom she shares her many literary pursuits. She and Ashfaq Ahmed were publishers of the literary journal *Dastaan-Goi*. They live in Lahore.

Bano has written plays for the stage and television both in Urdu and Punjabi. Her important collections of short stories include *Bazgasht* (Recollections), *Amar Bel* (The Clinging Vine), and *Aatish Zer-e Pa* (Fire Beneath My Feet). Her novel *Raja Gidh* (King Vulture), 1981, was critically acclaimed. Her televison play collections are *Aadhi Baat* (Half a Story), *Sitamgar Tere Liye* (For You, My Tormentor), and *Footpath ki Ghas* (Footpath's Grass). She was awarded the *Sitara-i-Imtiaz,* Pakistan's highest civil honour, in 1983.

Qudsiya's fiction engages with socio-psychological problems such as loneliness in a world shrunk by globalization, the challenges of displacement, and disillusionment in marriage.

The story included here is a striking example of Qudsiya's genius as a writer and social critic: she presents the usual dramatis personae caught up in a South Asian marriage, in such a way as to leave it to the reader to decide who is in the right.

One can perceive shades of Ismat Chughtai, the great Progressive fiction writer who wrote on women's sexuality, in Bano's writing. At times it seems that Bano continues the story of the middle-class woman where Ismat left off, albeit with even greater sensitivity and thoughtfulness. There is much left unsaid which, in the end, is the message.

Within the Circle of a Wave

In the morning she felt as if she had drunk from a bottle of soda with sand in it. The bedsheet next to her was wrinkled. Rehan had left the room early. She rubbed her teeth with a corner of her red, gold-filigreed dupatta, but she couldn't get rid of the grit between her teeth. She gulped down stale water from the glass by her bedside. The sandy taste in her mouth persisted. Her entire body ached as if she were a wrestler who had been flung down at least three or four times during a match. If she clenched her hand, the tips of her fingers hurt, and if she opened her hand and tried to straighten her fingers, sharp cramps tore along the sides of her wrist and her palm. And her neck was so stiff that when she turned her head she could feel the bones cracking.

On the table next to her bed was the sparkling, glimmering necklet, the bracelets, *tika, jhumar,* and the rani-necklace. How many trips she had made during the torrid summer afternoons for all this jewellery. How she had quarrelled over the *kundan,* how angered she had been by the flaw in the rani-necklace, how she had wept on seeing the long white pearls missing from the *jhumar.* Now everything lay on the table unappreciated and neglected, like the peels of a melon. She was overwhelmed by a desire to take the jewellery in her hands and crush it, but for centuries woman has not done everything she has wanted to. For this reason, this woman also merely turned her back, heaved a long sigh, and remained silent.

She blamed her sisters for all this. Theirs was a family where there were four older sisters and each one was more tactless and more of a blabbermouth than the other; how could Mena get married without knowing anything? When Bari Apa came back after her wedding, Mena was still quite young. But as is customary, children always gather around brides, and so Mena too happened to be somewhere nearby when Bari Apa said to her friends between giggles:

'He's even more bashful than I am, I swear. Every night he brings me a jasmine bracelet and a *sanchi pan*. But do you think he places them in my hand? No, he just leaves them next to my pillow, and, with his back turned, starts reading.'

Bari Apa's friends tickled her in the ribs and said, 'Yes, of course he turns his back and starts reading, he's so simple, the poor fellow!'

Cleaning under a nail with a hairpin, Bari Apa replied, 'I swear, if our eyes happen to meet, his face reddens. These are all stories you've heard, men are not what you think they are. By God, he gives me so much love, he praises me so much, he's so gracious that everything happens and you're not even aware that it did.'

Poor Mena had no idea what that 'everything' was that you weren't aware of. But one thing was established: husbands brought you sanchi pans and jasmine bracelets. And anyway, in Mena's house everyone understood the joys of eating bountifully and living well. Mena had also learned that wearing nice clothes and eating well contributed greatly to making life heavenly.

And when Rani got married, more hot *masala* was mixed in with the dreams.

Rani had been married for a year when she had to accompany her husband to England. Her husband was busy all day with visits to the passport office and Rani raced about with him, trying to get all the shopping done. There were comfortable shoes to be bought, gifts had to be selected for their friends in England, or she would be found making lists of things different family members wanted from England. When she and her husband had time they saw film after film because they wouldn't be able to see Pakistani films in England. Rani didn't say much, but looking at her you could be sure that marriage wasn't a dead letter office where all your desires were heaped like a pile of loose dirt.

And what Mena saw at Asiya Baji's *valima* was a blinding revelation. Asiya Baji was applying make-up and Dulha Bhai, sitting near the dressing table, was passing her pins and handing her the lipstick. Later he fastened the long zipper in the back of Asiya Baji's shirt, and God knows what he whispered in her ear because she blushed all over and rocked like a kite. Actually Mena liked Asiya Baji's bridegroom very much. His conversation was so luxuriant that all the family members hastened to share its abundance. The bridegroom's door was never locked; Asiya Baji and Dulha Bhai were never seen sitting alone. The setting was reminiscent of a wedding reception, a poetry reading, the scene at a railway platform. As soon as Dulha Bhai arrives everyone gathers round, a discussion begins, while a television programme is in progress, and Dulha Bhai's and Asiya Baji's glances send out couriers toward each other. When she encounters something she likes, she immediately looks in his direction; receiving a seal of approval at his end, the idea is transformed into a general opinion. They are alone in an assembly of people; their love affair continues in a crowded gathering. Mangoes are being consumed; when a sweet mango finds its way to Baji, it is immediately re-routed to Dulha Bhai, the sweet mango that has just been spotted in Dulha Bhai's hand is seen being squeezed and sucked by Baji. Everywhere there are kisses without any kissing; there is passion everywhere and you don't see anyone touching.

Any deficiency that remained was made up for by Gulabi's wedding. After getting married Gulabi became more of a *gulab*. Her husband was a photographer. He spent the first night of their wedding taking pictures of the bride. With her jhumar, with her tika, standing against the wall, leaning against a window—he photographed her from every angle. A week hadn't gone by before Gulabi's picture appeared on the cover of a well-known magazine. Bickering like children, the two of them would disappear into the darkroom, and when they later emerged Bhaiya Ji would have lipstick marks on his forehead, and Gulabi would be buttoning her shirt front.

Partly it was a question of a difference in environment. Mena's husband's family was not large, but the few family members in the house behaved with each other as if they were ambassadors from enemy nations. Their faces wore expressions of geniality, but their hearts remained dry like withered dates. And Mena had come from a family where everyone battled in the arena of conversation, but when a problem came along, they stuck to each other like teeth. They lived in their own world, and unlike Hindus, didn't believe in the transmigration of souls. The only reason they didn't think ill of anyone was that they had neither the time nor the energy to undergo the physical exertion and mental aggravation such behaviour entailed. Never having experienced loss or deprivation in their own house, they failed to comprehend that the world is filled with all kinds of people, that being able to exist with different types of human beings and to examine viewpoints that are in complete opposition to your own constitutes real living. In Mena's house the biggest tragedy was that insignificant happenings were viewed as life's greatest calamities. Arriving at a movie theatre to find that the show had been sold out, getting back a shirt from the tailor with the neck cut round instead of with the collar that had been requested, or the time when her father had to have three teeth pulled and couldn't eat for a few days—these were disasters never to be forgotten. It's strange, but misfortune had touched this family only mildly, so Mena didn't know that sometimes fate treats certain families as though they were stepchildren. The only unpropitious events were the ones reported in the newspapers, the perusal of these stories resulting in short periods of noisy discourse. But once the chat was over, everyone returned to a life that was comfortably warm like a quilt.

It was the fault of this point of view, or the lifestyle she had adopted earlier in her life, or her small book of poems, or her friends; anyway, whatever it was, the fact remained that the entire courtyard was crooked and she had been sent to dance there without being taught how to.

When she was taken to the bridal chamber at night her back was aching slightly from the effort expended in the six hours of preparation. The two hours of sitting straight at the hairdresser's earlier in the morning was also taking its toll. And not accustomed to wearing heavy jewellery, she had to contend with the burden of the glittering, shimmering jewellery that weighed her down in a strangely pleasurable manner. The fragrance of her perfume along with the scent of the jasmine and *chameli* flowers had created an unfamiliar atmosphere in the room. She had seen numerous brides shut up in rooms like this and had also seen them emerging the next morning trembling, looking coyly sheepish, avoiding looking at anyone with their honeyed eyes. And let's not forget Urdu literature and Urdu poetry which had filled her imagination with sweetness. At this moment she was like the bird that is perched not too far from a food tray, wondering what manner of sailing through the air would enable it to swoop down for a bit of sugar without getting caught. A strange kind of fear, a feeling of having made an open admission of theft for the first time, a vague sense of loss at leaving her parents' house, the warm hospitality extended by her in-laws, a hundred new associations attached to her new life, so many different kinds of handshakes with the life she had left behind—what was there that didn't climb over her like a creeping burden? Sometimes she looked anxiously at the bathroom lit by a blue, zero-watt bulb and so many times she had glanced surreptitiously and with eager eyes at the door from which her bridegroom was to enter.

Mena had already dozed off a few times during the course of her reverie by the time the bridegroom arrived in the bridal chamber. Rehan was better looking, more handsome than he appeared in his picture. Dressed in a brocade *achkan* and narrow payjama, he looked somewhat roguish, but one glance was enough to make Mena realize that the bridegroom was better looking than her.

This was the first blow to her ego.

Mena was among those girls who beautify themselves, dress up nicely, and join the ranks of beautiful women as one of them; attractive clothes, jewellery and make-up enhance her looks. She wasn't the kind of girl whom you wanted to kiss when she had just woken up.

Silently, Rehan took the garlands from around his neck and threw them down on a chair.

'These eastern weddings are so exhausting,' he said with a big yawn. 'And so stupid. Everything is so unreal and silly. Oh, you haven't changed your clothes yet?'

Whatever Rehan was saying was true, and the way he was saying it wasn't objectionable either, but the tone of detachment, weariness, and arrogance in his voice suddenly frightened Mena.

In the same tone of voice, Rehan said, 'Why don't you take off this horse's gear and put on a nightsuit or something. I'll be back soon. Something comfortable.'

The light of the blue bulb disappeared with the closing of the bathroom door.

With mixed feelings of anger, disappointment, and a strange kind of sadness, Mena took off all her jewellery and heaped it on the bedside table. Her friends had secured the *tika* with bobby pins so that when she tore it off she almost ruined her hairdo. In the dark she pulled off her artificial eyelashes, removed the cluster of baubles sitting on the nape of her neck, and taking out her nightsuit from the suitcase she put it on as if it were some medicine her father had instructed her to take.

When the door of the bathroom opened she saw that Rehan was dressed in his pajama bottoms only. The hair on his chest seemed to have co-mingled with the hair on his neck. Everything was strange like a dream, but none of it was all that beautiful.

'That's better,' Rehan said on seeing her illuminated by the blue light of the zero-watt bulb, sitting before him like a geisha girl.

'God knows why brides get dressed up in this idiotic fashion. Do you want the fan on or should I shut it off?'

But before Mena could open her mouth Rehan turned off the switch. In the blue light Mena saw her room as the underworld.

After this, whatever took place didn't take more than fifteen minutes.

All night, while drifting through sleep and wakefulness, she remained suspended in strange places. Sometimes she felt as if she would get up soon and her mother would be calling her to breakfast. Sometimes she felt as if she were dead, or that she was in a cave barred by a steel gate. The hairdresser's Chinese face with long pins held between tight lips kept pressing down over her and she retreated, saying, 'No, no.'

Now she is being bathed in hot water and bath salts, an aroma of *ubtan* emanates from her body, the towel is soaked in cologne, her friends are applying henna to her hands, if there's even the tiniest smudge of nail polish on her fingers a cotton swab soaked in remover is immediately used to wipe it off, just a few dabs of powder on her face draw gasps of admiration from her friends. How important she feels, surrounded by her friends. Everyone's gaze is riveted on her face. 'How pretty Mena looks—she's ahead of all her sisters.'

On the bed next to hers, sleeping on his stomach, was Rehan. The hair spread over his chest reminded her of physical features on a map—evenly spaced, like a caterpillar, extending from north to south. Mena wafted between slumber and wakefulness. Whenever she opened her eyes she found a gleaming, white face bent over her. In the light of the zero-watt bulb this beautiful face was like the face of Dracula pressing down on her to suck blood from her neck.

Frightened, she shut her eyes and dug her nails into the down-filled pillow. She kept wounding the pillow because she was afraid that if her hands were free she might scratch this gleaming face. The room felt airless, like a waiting room. This feeling of being stifled stayed with her until daybreak. The bridegroom's intimate advances had left bruises on many parts of her body, but there wasn't any sign of a kiss on her face.

Mena drank water repeatedly, but each time it seemed to her as if someone had given her soda mixed with sand, and she felt grit between her teeth.

That night Mena felt as if she had dwindled. She thought she should go home and tell her mother everything, then asked herself what there was to tell really. What will people think? And anyway, she wasn't such a dumb, naïve girl, was she? Didn't she know that in the end this was all there would be?

But then her heart tormented her. Was there nothing before the end...before that...before the end, there was nothing? Sometimes the memory of sanchi pans raced through her head, sometimes the fragrance of flowery bracelets overwhelmed her senses, roaming on the pages of the passport were images of Asiya Baji in her high-heeled shoes, circling round and round before her eyes was Gulabi as she had appeared in the picture in the magazine. What should she complain of to her family?

What was there she should tell her mother when she went home and was clinging to her?

How will Ma understand...how will the sisters understand that Mena is like the needle that children leave on the tracks which is crushed as a heavy train goes chugging over the tracks and disappears into the distance.

There weren't any specific complaints she had about life in her husband's house that she could count on her fingers...one, two, three... Everything reminded her of a cinema screen. Beautiful pictures formed and faded out, but there were no imprints left on the screen, which, like unwashed cotton, absorbed nothing. Her susral was like the uncomfortable shoe that, when worn, causes a vague discomfort that one can't pinpoint, but when you take it off the foot swells painfully.

Then, suddenly, some months after her marriage, Mena stopped wearing fancy clothes and jewellery. This made her husband very happy, but her mother-in-law was incensed. Mena had brought over her pre-wedding clothes from her mother's house and now, dressed in a starched white cotton shalwar and crinkled *chanchal* dupatta she looked like a plain, harmless girl, a nice girl. She wasn't one of those who kicked. Awkward, wearing a dupatta that was worn and full of holes, she developed the appearance of a highly-placed servant, but one who had been bought.

Like a chameleon she would have remained unnoticed because of her dull and drab exterior, but she had no control over her eyes. There was a time when her heavy-lidded, honeyed eyes were shiny and sharp-edged. Now, because of her extreme sensitivity she cried constantly and her eyes sank into their sockets. Wasn't she from a family where everyone was determined to remain alive at all costs? But here she was going out of her mind with the thought that she should exercise patience. 'Be patient, Mena,' she kept telling herself, 'better days will come, they will definitely come.' Sometimes she was terrified that God would punish her for spurning his blessings. But when she felt a knife jab at her heart, when during the day she remembered the loneliness she suffered at night, her heart burst and scattered about in little pieces.

In the beginning Mena broke into tears once or twice in her husband's presence. Each time Rehan said the same thing in his detached voice: 'You're very touchy. What is the matter anyway?'

Rehan was one of those men who regard women as dumb creatures, and who, for this reason, attribute a woman's tears to her weakness and stupidity and therefore don't bother to find out what the problem is.

There was only one ploy Rehan had at his disposal to appease Mena. That is, he placed a hand on her shoulder, took her to the bedroom, and locked the door from inside. His manhood was an army that was accustomed to crashing down every door on every rampart, every temple and every castle gate merely with the force of his strength. It was Rehan's conviction that no woman could remain distressed with him or the world after having slept with him. A woman's health, happiness, and satisfaction depended on this one act. He had got to know Mena only through their physical relationship and after this coming together they could sit next to each other like strangers for hours in the same room. When he had appeased her in this fashion he always said: 'There now, you won't cry for at least four days.' The fact of the matter was that this caused Mena's tears to flow with greater intensity.

For a while Mena had no control over her tears, but when she saw that she had to submit to the same thing each time, she became cautious. She still roamed around in Rehan's presence with eyes puffy from crying, but she avoided arousing his sympathy.

Never before had Mena's mother-in-law seen such a simple-looking, simple-minded daughter-in-law. The existence of such an obedient, dutiful, hard-working wife in these modern times was indeed surprising. She was worried that if Rehan and Mena had a falling out their family would lose a good worker. She suspected something was afoot, but the daughter-in-law didn't open her mouth and the mother-in-law didn't have the generosity of spirit to clasp her to her breast.

Seeing Mena's downcast eyes, she would sometimes say to Rehan, 'Why don't you take her to the cinema, take her out—the whole day she's up to her neck in housework.'

Going out produced the same result as crying and complaining, so Mena stopped going out with Rehan.

When Rehan hurled slime at her the first time she felt as if a hit intended to result in a sixer had ended in a catch. She had just come out of the bathroom after a long session of weeping when she ran into Rehan and her mother-in-law in the gallery. Both were chewing *pan* with the same speed.

'Rehan,' her mother-in-law said pityingly, 'Why don't you take her somewhere. Look how sad she looks.'

Rehan, who for some reason had been bursting at the seams, exploded. 'It's not in my power to get rid of her sadness. God knows what lovers she thinks about all day long. Her heart hasn't been with me from the very first day, Amma Ji—she loves her cursed book of poems more than me. She's constantly tucking it away in the suitcase, in the drawer, trying to take care of it all the time and pays no attention to me. She doesn't care if I'm alive or dead.'

Rehan said his piece and left, but to suffer this, this was her reward; the memory of Rehan's accusation plunged into her heart like a spear at every step. The words of her college friends echoed in her heart and flowed from her eyes.

'She's our nightingale. He'll go crazy, just crazy.'

'Our Mena is Scheherazade, she'll tell Rehan such wondrous stories.'

'Her conversation is like sweet candy—our Mena is like a piece of barfi, a piece of barfi, she is.'

She came to Rehan after a struggle. Fireworks exploded between them and then total darkness prevailed. Barring any approach to Rehan's mind were such heavy curtains, such severe guards, such obstacles that each time Mena advanced a few steps and then froze. Like two people who don't know each other's language and begin a long journey together, these two also continued to walk together.

Following this incident the mother-in-law opened her copy of *Bahishti Zevar*.

All of her other daughters-in-law thought her as insignificant as a discarded nail clipping. When the time came to reason with Mena and advise her, she was baffled by her own sense of importance. Beginning with the philosophy of the husband's place as the earthly god and the validation of the funeral rites, to the use of such philosophy as a credit card in heaven and as a visa in society, she explained every aspect in detail. At the end of every remark Mena said, 'But Amma Ji, I have no complaints, why are you explaining all this to me?'

'Yes, daughter, I can see from your face you're not happy. My dear, making your husband happy once procures you seventy rewards in heaven.'

In view of this ratio Mena had already earned innumerable rewards. 'You're just imagining things, I'm like this by nature.'

The mother-in-law assumed a more loving and friendly tone. 'Women have a hundred desires. When it's time for a husband to return from work, they dress up, there's a storm of emotion in the heart, there's a longing!'

'It's just that I've never cared much for all this from the very beginning.'

When the mother-in-law was convinced that her daughter-in-law didn't care for all this she began to feel genuinely sorry for her son. If the wretched wife is a block of ice what's the poor healthy boy to do? Now when she was in the company of others, she said, 'We have an angel, by God, so unworldly, but what can you do? Men don't want to live with angels now, do they? Her conduct is not like that of women. She has not thought of whether her husband is swallowing dirt outside or not, she won't say a word....'

When a few years passed and there were no children, and instead of swallowing dirt at home Rehan began swallowing dirt outside on a permanent basis, the mother-in-law one day placed a hand on Mena's shoulder.

'By God, if you are offended by what I'm saying please tell me so frankly. You are a saint, not an ordinary human being, and I don't want to break your heart. I've heard too many stories about Rehan. If you give me your permission I will find another wife for him. At least that way he'll come home regularly. Only your kindness can save Rehan.'

Mena didn't make a fuss, she didn't shed any tears, she didn't threaten to return to her parents' house, nor did she feel sorry for herself; she quietly agreed to give permission for a second marriage.

The night of the wedding was a strange time for Mena.

Sometimes, tormented by jealousy, she would say, 'Come, dear girl, you come too and get a taste of this fire, see what the fire in this furnace is like.'

Then, feeling bereft, she would think, 'Tomorrow I'll go home. One month with each sister and that's four months taken care of right there....'

Then she wondered if she should congratulate Rehan the next morning or not.

Every now and then the memory of her own wedding night flitted before her eyes. How fair and rosy-complexioned Rehan was, how tall, the hair on his back like the markings of the Ural mountains on a map. She wavered between one memory and the next. When the confines of her thought touched the boundaries of midnight, she got up and walked over to the rear of the bride's room.

The window was shut but everything was clearly visible through a chink between the curtains.

The light was on.

Wearing all her jewellery and bedecked in her shiny clothes, the new bride was propped against the back of the bed like a flamingo, her elbow resting on the *ga'o takiya* as she breathed slowly.

Three-fourths of Rehan's body was hidden from Mena, but she could see a part of his face and clearly hear his voice. 'How beautiful your hands are...who put on this henna with such loving care? Oh, I wish I could devour these hands.'

'I'm not too fond of all this stuff, *ji,* my friends forced me to put it on. Let me take off this tika.'

Rehan quickly grasped the new bride's hand and said, 'Leave it on. How nice it looks on your forehead!'

'I swear by God, my neck is stiff. Let me at least take off this necklace.'

'For my sake, stay as you are tonight. I want to preserve the image of my bride in my mind so that when I'm an old man and grey appears in your hair, I can close my eyes and see my bride as she is today, bedecked like a doll.'

The flamingo glided on the waters of fanciful desires, love, and admiration, while Rehan continued taking the garlands from his neck one by one and placing them in her lap.

The light in the bride's room was not extinguished even once and the blue light of the zero-watt bulb in the bathroom didn't once cross over the threshold to come inside. All night the bride sat up with her clothes and jewellery on and all night Rehan continued to talk lovingly to her.

Early in the morning when sickly yellow sunlight crept over the parapet wall and a mynah silently alighted on the gate, Mena's mother-in-law appeared on the verandah beating her chest, moaning, as she lamented in a loud voice:

'*Hai,* my innocent daughter-in-law, my simple daughter-in-law...I thought she didn't have a woman's heart...hai my Mena is dead...hai the pangs of jealousy killed her, my Mena...hai curse my stupidity. I thought she didn't care about such things...hai my Mena...hai my simple daughter-in-law...hai I thought she ran from a man's shadow.'

The Mena who had gone to sleep by taking just sleeping pills was lying on her bed with her eyes open, as if she were still dreaming, as if she were lost in a dream of sanchi pans and flowery bracelets, a dream in which there was not a single touch, just kisses, all around her, everywhere. God knows how news of this dream travelled to the gate because the mynah perched on the gate lifted up its head, screamed loudly once and then, fluttering its wings, flew away into the air.

Translated by Tahira Naqvi

Ghiyas Ahmad Gaddi

(1928–86)

Ghiyas Ahmad was born in Dhanbad, in the Jharia District of Bihar. He was educated at a madrassa where he learnt Arabic as well as some English and Urdu. But he was mostly self-educated. He loved reading and was a regular at the library at Jharia where he developed a special affinity for literary journals. He was inspired to write fiction in the style of the contemporary writers whom he read with passion. Ghiyas Ahmad Gaddi published three collections of short stories. His second collection, *Parinda Pakadnewaali Gadi* (Bird Trapper's Cart), 1977, received critical acclaim. His third collection is called *Sara Din Dhup* (Sunshine All Day Long), 1985. *Parao,* a novella, came out in 1980. He died suddenly of a heart attack.

In 'Sunrise', which actually takes place at sunset, Ahmed weaves a deceptively simple tale about two boys chasing a white cat. The time could be around Partition, somewhere in north India. The playful abandon of the boys, mixed with their determination to capture the cat, creates an atmosphere of irony, as the chase takes place in the midst of the mayhem of military and paramilitary violence. The story operates on two levels—one senses the possibility that the boys are chasing a young girl. As often happens in Ahmad's stories, the sun plays a central role. Here, in the sun's waning moments, the figure of the cat is transposed, exposing our dependence on the sun, while complicating the denouement of the story for the reader.

Sunrise

'Must be somewhere here...'

The other one did not reply. He simply continued to gaze intently in the weakening light of the tired day at the walls of the ruined building towards which just a short while ago he had seen her running.

It must have been a very old and considerably large building once that now was in ruins. There was rubble everywhere. A wall or two still remained, half standing, awaiting the next rainy season or some sudden blast.

'Let's go back,' the first one said, putting his arm around the second one in a friendly gesture. 'We'll track her down tomorrow.'

'No, tomorrow she might get too far away.' He started climbing one of the dilapidated walls as he spoke.

'Watch out! You might fall.' The first one again expressed sympathy.

'No, I won't.' The second one responded with confidence. Wiping perspiration from his damp neck, he went up the wall. Bits of old mud from the wall crumbled and fell on some dry leaves, and a brick was about to dislodge when the older one stepped forward and stopped it.

The sun was worn out but the day had still to cool after hours of smoldering heat. Any gust of wind that blew was like a slap. It scorched their faces. Neither of them cared that the sun was about to set.

The entire day had been spent just like this. The two lads were exhausted from running after her. From one lane to another, over roof tops they went. When they would climb up on a roof, she would jump down. One time they clearly saw her foot impaled on a nail in the alley and get wounded. They could see the blood pulsing out, and she was lying on the ground unconscious or so it seemed...dead...

'Perhaps she's dead.'

'Don't say that. I want her alive.' The second one silently jumped off the roof as he spoke.

'Alive would be very...what will I do with a dead one?'

She wasn't dead. She wasn't unconscious; simply lying with her head bent, exhausted from running all day, hungry, thirsty, injured from the nail in the alley, tired of being chased by those handsome, hateful boys. As soon as she heard footsteps she raised her head once and she saw that one of them was bending over, about to grab her. She got up with a throb and ran.

'Uff-oh...'

'I say, let's stop chasing her.'

'No.' The second one replied decisively.

'I won't let this be...I want her.'

'I want her too, but I can wait.' Then after a pause he said in a low tone, 'I have my eye on another one!'

'But that one's brown and she growls too.'

'Yes. She jumps to attack,' the first one said. 'But I will tame her. She will become docile.'

'I want this one, just this one.' The other boy said looking in the direction of the road all the while.

'You are really stubborn,' the first one responded.

The second boy did not reply even though he liked what the other had said. He thought of it as praise. A strange feeling stirred him up, putting him on a high and he smiled as an old memory flooded back.

'What is it? You are smiling to yourself?'

'Yes. I remembered an incident.' He stopped and took out a piece of hard candy from his pocket. With his teeth he broke it into two, handed a piece to the older one, popped the other bit into his mouth and began to suck on it.

'Last winter, we, that is Mother, Dad, and Munni were returning from Dad's friend's place. It must have been around midnight. Deep, thick darkness lay everywhere.'

He fell silent. When the silence grew stale the first one prodded him.

'On the way I began to insist that I wanted to drive. At first my parents laughed; then they began to reason with me saying that I was still a child who had no idea of the mechanics of driving a car. How does a car start, get up to speed, negotiate turns, change lanes, and swerve to avoid running over a traveller coming from the opposite direction? They said I would learn all this in due course of time, learn it by myself, each one of those things because behind me, on my back...

'But when I wouldn't take "no" from them, my father brought the car to the side of the road, stopped, and pulled me on his lap. He put my hands on the steering wheel and continued to drive. I imagined that I was actually driving the car. The bright lights of a car from the opposite direction pierced right through my eyes. Then I realized that everything in front of me was becoming hazy and losing its shape and form. I could see nothing; the light was blinding, so blinding.'

One cannot see clearly in very bright light just as one can't in dim light. When a sheet of mist settles everything becomes murky and obscure. A man doesn't look like a human but an unsightly lump or like an animal just like that man who is lying wrapped up in a filthy quilt beneath the old banyan tree by the roadside. The two stare at him. His eyes have a vacant look. His face is deathly pale as if there is not a drop of blood in his veins. He could pass as dead. Lying there motionless like a corpse he stares at them. Then fear like a dark cloud begins to loom in those vacant eyes that were utterly blank a moment ago. His features that seemed frozen begin to distort and he tries to scream but only a gurgle emerges from his throat.

'Have you seen her?'

'She's all white.'

The man shakes his head to say 'no'. He quickly shuts his eyes and hides under the cold, narrow coverlet as though it will save him from the dangers lurking outside.

'The bastard is dead!' the first one said.

'He's as good as dead.'

A man sleeping in the murky haze...is a lifeless lump of flesh.

The second one understood what the other had meant. Just then they saw military vehicles on the road going in the direction of the riots. The first boy quickly pulled the second one to a side and they took cover behind the tree.

'We have nothing to fear,' the second one remarked. 'We are not one of them.'

'No, we're not,' the first one agreed. 'But mistakes happen...its getting dark and darkness can be deceptive, anything can happen.'

Suddenly a blast of putrid air assailed their nostrils. They turn around and see that near the municipal drain that was located below road level crows are busy feasting on the bloated body of a dog. The blast of rotten smell had spiralled and was diffusing now like the dusk, suffusing their bodies and affecting their faculties. Something falls, making the sound of clay crumbling. A murky darkness settles everywhere. They have a sense of foreboding but they quickly dust off nagging doubts and thoughts. Heat lingers even though the sun is in the western sphere of the sky's dome and is slowly descending its steps. Its rays have lost intensity but there is not a speck of relief from the heat and the distress caused by it. The bazaar was tense. It waited wide-eyed, cringing with fear as if in anticipation for the stone to fly from the tensed belt of a slingshot.

Though there was still time for the curfew to begin, it had not become fully dark but people were finishing their work and preparing to rush home. Stores were preparing to pull down shutters. The bustle had diminished. The leaves on the roadside trees and the birds roosting on their branches and on telegraph wires and electric poles seemed to be in a state of suspension, holding their breath.

Fear like a warm breeze touches their being and they are jolted. They blink their eyes and just then their gaze falls on her. She is standing right beneath a big tree, soaking up the dread, fear, and stupor in the atmosphere, scratching the road gravel with her front foot, the hair around her nostrils twitching ever so slowly. The boys move forward silently. She hears the now familiar footfalls and raises her head.

'There she is!' The first boy cries inwardly and presses his companion's hand hard. They both leap forward. She is but a yard away from them but manages to run before they can grab her.

The boys become engrossed in pursuit. She runs weaving through the feet of passers-by, turning to look back again and again she picks her way. They follow close behind pushing people, becoming entangled with them but continuing to run. Now they are out of the bazaar limits, on a lonely road so she pauses for a moment and looks back. She sees her pursuers panting, running desperately as if for their lives, coming towards her. She assesses the distance separating them; suddenly she is overwhelmed but only momentarily. A spark of energy floods her limbs and with a throb she leaps into a nearby ditch. She turns to look at them one last time, plunges into a dense *karonda* bush, and disappears from view.

The pursuing boys come to a sudden stop. Exasperated to have lost her at a point when she was so close to being captured, they pick up stones and hurl them at the bushes, cursing loudly.

The first boy puts his hand on the second one's shoulder with the idea of dissuading him, but the latter pushes him away before he can even say anything and hisses through clenched teeth: 'No!...she...she...' His voice flies sharply through the air like a stone and disappears in the yawning, still atmosphere.

He leaps into the shallow ditch and forces his way into the bushes. The older one follows suit and they both disappear from view. The bushes move for a second, then become still.

The sun has set; darkness grows thicker by the minute, spreading everywhere. The boys have climbed a wall and are on the other side. They peer into the dark. They can make out her form; now here, now gone, suddenly clearly visible again. The second boy's eye catches something. He squints and looks intently. Discerning a shadow hiding behind the murky curtain of darkness his face breaks into a smile.

'It's her!'

Seated on the rubble with her front feet extended, she is licking the wound on her paw. Unaware of impending danger, like a bird on a high secure branch, she is feeling safe and free from troubles. The breeze ruffles through her white hairs. The two observe all this and are thrilled. They softly clutch each others' hands.

'Yes. It is undoubtedly her.' The older boy confirms. His eyes are wide open in the dark. Softly, softly, very carefully, they step forward as if she were a bird that would fly off at the slightest sound. Darkness is creeping forward every moment, making things lose their exact form and shape and seem to be what they are not. Therefore she too seems to be unlike herself.

But it is her. Spotless white, she has not the slightest trace of a brown or black stripe on her body. Not even a spot. It's her whiteness that is so visible even in the lengthening shadows of the night.

They talk among themselves in whispers, of strategies. They make a decision to surround her by moving stealthily forward from opposite sides so as to corner her with the tall crumbling wall in front. Slowly, carefully, they stretch out their hands.

Just then she becomes alert. Her ears perk up to a rustling sound and she turns around in fear and bewilderment. The wall in front of her is too high for her to leap up and get to and this terrifies her.

She turns around and looks at four hands inching closer and closer. Her breathing becomes rapid; she is almost panting.

In a second she makes up her mind, pulls every bit of energy she has left. Just as a horse collects all its strength in its hind legs and lower back, and summons courage before leaping across a large span of water, she does the same and leaps. Her forefeet try to hold on to the top edge of the crumbling wall. She clutches wildly at the crumbling clay, shaking her hind quarters as if she was clawing it, but the dry clay keeps crumbling and falling.

Ultimately she screams in utter helplessness and terror. Her throat emits a sound stranger than a scream of a human being slaughtered, and she falls to the ground.

A grin spreads on the face of the two boys. They utter a shout of joy.

She pulls herself together even after falling from that height. She shakes her neck vigorously in order to gain control of herself. The hands are almost upon her and her courage is dimmed. She emits a deep warning growl, ferocious and terrifying, sharp like the point of a dagger, so sharp and piercing that the two boys stop in their tracks. Fear pierces through their heart like a knife.

'I've heard they become like lions when cornered.' The first boy said to the second in a tearful, terror-stricken voice.

'Yes!' The word slipped out of the second one's mouth, but his stubbornness surged up once more. 'No, that's nonsense.'

The first boy tries to grab her but she takes a big jump past his neck and lands on the ground with a thud. The older boy quickly seizes her legs, picks her up, and tucks her in his lap.

Captured, she strikes back suddenly with all her strength, clawing wildly with her sharp nails. The boy screams, his grip loosens but the other takes her away from his hands and holds her fast.

Squirming inwardly, she is restless in his lap for a while. Finally, having exhausted all efforts to escape, she looks here and there, dejected. She begins to whine and closes her eyes.

The sun has set. Everything is blurry in the darkness. The horizon blooms. A colour, red like blood, spreads and keeps spreading.

'Look at the sky!' The older one says. They both look up at the sky. A shadow crosses their faces.

'Yes.' The younger one replies, a strange emotion soaking his voice. Then the loud piercing tone of a siren from a distance rents the air.

'Quick, come on. Let's go home.' The younger one says, feeling his neck with his hand. He clears the uneven path among the ruins at a running pace and gets to the road. The older one follows him. Military vehicles are making their way down the road, one after the other.

Held tight in their grip she opens her eyes. She looks at their faces in the deepening darkness. There are some shadows mixed with the glow of victory.

Suddenly the beam of a searchlight challenging, pulsating, sweeps past, blinding them.

Muttering, they rush for shelter behind a closed storefront. At that moment she leaps forward from her cowering position in their lap with a throb, and gets free.

As soon as she is free from their grip she looks back agitatedly, rushes across the road, and disappears.

Thundering trucks go by at high speed. It appears as though they are passing over her body, crushing her.

The first one screams: 'Ch..cham...she's dead!'
'She could have escaped....' The second one expressed his doubt while his hand involuntarily touched the spot on his neck where her nails had left scratches.

Translated by Mehr Afshan Farooqi

Hajira Masroor
(b.1929)

Hajira Masroor and her elder sister, Khadeeja Mastoor, are important names in Urdu fiction. They have been called Urdu's Brontë sisters, and also 'literary twins' because they shared the same environment, and wrote about similar subjects. The family, consisting of six sisters and a brother, lived in Lucknow. Their mother, Anwar Jahan Begum, wrote for women's journals. The sisters published their first collections of short stories about the same time in 1944 and came out with their second collections, Hajira's *Hai Allah* (Oh, My God!) and Khadeeja's *Bochar* (Showers) again around the same time (1946). After Partition, the family moved to Lahore.

Hajira, unlike her older sister, who penned two successful novels, only wrote short fiction. She was not so deeply involved with the PWM though she was the co-editor, with Ahmad Nadeem Qasimi, of *Nuqoosh*, a literary journal that was regarded as the standard-bearer of the movement. She has published six collections of short stories and is presently writing her memoirs.

Masroor's fictional subjects are middle-class women who chafe against the barriers that confine their existence but cannot break the restraints that patriarchal society imposes on them. Her narrative style is complex and she writes more in the 'modern' than 'realistic' mode favoured by the writers of the PWM. The story '*Bandar ka Ghao*' (The Monkey's Sore) is a good example of her fictional style.

The Monkey's Sore

She was bundled up on the loose-roped cot on the veranda like a new bride. It was an afternoon of torrid heat and then the fever that wouldn't go up or down—she was feeling miserable. All the members of the household were shut up in the room, comfortably chatting and talking. There were moments when she too felt like seeking refuge from the sun's insufferable heat by getting up and going to the room, but she was afraid that if she did, she would have to face a torrent of vitriolic advice. That was why, despite the heat and her fever, she valued the little privacy she had.

The heat so fierce, and she in the grip of a raging fever. Again and again she felt as if the marrow in her bones had melted and every fibre of her being was being fried in it, and that her ribs, arching like a bow, were being crushed by a strong hand as if they were just straws in a broom. This odd sensation caused her to cough. The same cough—as if someone were beating a rhythm on a hollow, crumbling wooden box! Something came up in her throat as she was coughing and, pulling aside a few loose ropes in the cot, she bent down and spat it out. A tiny gob of blood landed on the floor with a *chup*. Before the sight of blood could generate any thoughts in her head she heard the *khun-khun* of the monkeys and froze. She was terrified of monkeys. Without turning her neck she rolled her eyes and looked in the direction of the noise.

'Oh my God...' The words escaped from her dry, chapped lips, the burning sensation increasing. *Uffoh*! There were so many monkeys leaping about in all directions from the tree in the backyard to the roof. She was suddenly seized with the urge to run into the room, but fear made her immobile. She was afraid all these monkeys would attack her if she moved.

Sitting on the parapet blackened with mildew was a sickly, whimpering monkey surrounded by several fat monkeys busy scratching a black, ghastly sore on his back with their sharp nails. She began to feel sick at the sight of the monkey's loathsome sore. The monkeys were thoroughly absorbed in their activity. No sooner had one started poking around in the abcess than the other bared his teeth, slapped his eyelids, and followed suit. It was a case of a single injured individual surrounded by a thousand surgeons. And all that the sickly, feeble monkey did was fling his head down in pain. It appeared that he was going to die soon. She thought, 'Why doesn't the fool run away from here? What's to be gained from losing his life by having his sore examined?' But he was an animal lacking in reason. Still, the unfortunate monkey's helplessness aroused great pity in her. She wanted to save him from the pack of monkeys who, pretending to be helpful, were merely spectators. But...but suddenly someone placed strong hands over her ribs and pressed her down. Coughs accompanied by a tickling sensation ranging from her chest to her throat. Her chest filled as if she had soaked up the juice of several pans at once. She hastily coughed up spit.

Hee...eeee. Bright red, living blood. Her limbs felt watery and she started rubbing her head against the splinter-ridden cot.

The monkeys were making noises and the people in the room were complaining about her habit of isolating herself. She wearily stretched her legs and placed her hands on her chest. The sound of her family grumbling and the khun-khun of the monkeys seemed to descend into her ears like red-hot rods. 'How similar the monkeys and my family are,' she thought. And she began to feel the veins in her body throbbing. Suddenly it seemed as if someone had said to her, 'You too are like that sickly monkey, deliberately courting deadly diseases.' And as if to offer proof, some images of the past emerged on the surface of her feverish brain.

'A full-grown twenty-three or twenty-four year old, big like a two storeyed house—it's difficult not to worry now,' Amma would mutter anxiously and she would suddenly become overly conscious of the heavy burden of still being single. In her own family, girls her age, actually many who were even younger, had been married for years. Several already had four or five children each, and some, deemed old and worn-out merchandise by their husbands, were back in their parents' homes attempting to repair their tattered youth with the help of amulets and the prayers of holy men. But as for her, God knows what kind of a fate she had come into the world with because no one had bothered to throw a stone at this unique fruit tree. She was not at all bad looking.

She was well mannered and well bred. Yet her marriage could not be arranged. It is true, though, that except for her and her mother no one was very worried about her. As far as the father was concerned, all he could do was gurgle on the hookah all day long or proudly add to his progeny every other year. The older brother was absorbed in his own affairs. Today he's in love with the washerwoman and tomorrow it's the sweeperess who has his heart. And he wasn't doing any of this surreptitiously either; everything was undertaken openly. He didn't show the slightest hesitation in sighing, passing lewd remarks, or scratching himself in proper and improper places in front of his youthful sister.

So this was the environment in which she was spending her life. Her mother tried very hard to keep the vigour of her youth pressed down under the slab of household chores, but God help us! There comes a time when the winnowing basket loses its balance. You must have seen dal cooking on the stove and you must have also observed that when the dal comes to a boil the person watching its progress immediately removes the lid of the pot. This way the bubbling is tempered, is it not? And if the lid is not removed the dal boils over, thereby creating its own release. So a condition similar to a full boil had been created in her life as well. Her eyes, lowered by the weight of modesty all this time, began to look up here and there, as if in search of something. The house next door had been vacant for a long time, but it was said a student was to rent it soon. Well, that was that. The lava churning in the earth's belly found a split in a layer on the earth's surface from which to erupt. While she would be working, her gaze would be drawn to the wall behind which someone was sure to be pacing. Her mother would be scolding her for her lack of concentration, but she didn't hear her; her eardrums would be vibrating, hoping instead to imbibe a strange, masculine voice. Her parents would be quarrelling about something while she would be jumping the wall in her imagination to be held in an embrace. It was lava, wasn't it? It was bubbling inside.

'Why are you going on the roof?' Her older brother was a veritable psychologist.

She squeezed the wet, dyed dupatta tightly between her hands.

'I'm going up to dry my dupatta.' She frowned. Will a hungry person not be angry if a plate of food is pushed away from him?

'Isn't there enough sun here that you feel the need to go upstairs?' He glared at her like an honourable brother and then he lighted a cheap cigarette. Muttering, she threw the dupatta on the cot and sat down. The brother, satisfied, began humming.

Holding your gaze in mine,
O beloved with the fanciful eyes.

Fuming, she silently cursed him.

Today, she looked all around her. No one was there to stand in the way of her desire. Uffoh! How many days she had yearned to peep through this hole. Taking this to be her opportunity she placed her eye on the hole. It wasn't long before a fair-complexioned face appeared before her and then, *chap!* it was gone. Just one glimpse, just one! Her longing swelled. If only he would come before her one more time. She stayed with her eye pinned to the hole. The location of the wretched hole was such that one could neither sit nor stand. She bent as if in a posture of genuflection. Both hands on her knees, eyes on the hole, and her ears directed to the doors of the room. Her back began to ache from the awkward position she was in, her hands became numb, and once or twice the rubbing of her eyelashes against the hole caused specks of dirt from the area around the hole to fall into her eye. But she remained glued to the hole while all kinds of strange longings remained glued to her.

One day. Two days. Three days. For months her body longed to travel through the hole the way her glance did, but finally, exhausted from the effort, she realized that was an impossible task.

'Amma!' Her younger brother was racing down the stairs noisily. 'The wretch cut my kite off.'

'*Arrey* son, who?' Amma was flabbergasted. She had given him four paises only yesterday to buy a kite and today the kite was gone.

'That same person who's living next door. He was saying, don't fly kites on the roof, you'll fall down.' He angrily stamped his foot.

'So, that wasn't so wrong, was it?' she said, pausing in her kneading.

'Come on, you be quiet,' Amma scolded her. 'Who is he to give advice? If the boy doesn't fly the kite on the roof will he fly it on his mother's chest? So, son, why did he cut off your kite?'

'I said, who are you to stop me? I'll fly kites as much as I want, you don't own this place. And that's when he took a cable and cut off my kite string.' The boy then proceeded to spit out three or four heavy curses. She was enraged and felt like leaving the flour she was kneading to go up and give him a few hard slaps. And Amma? She didn't stop him. A little fellow like him using such profanity! She was so much older, but once when she was angry and had used a harmless curse commonly heard in the house, Amma had threatened to hit her with a metal rod, but...

'*Ai hai*, he's nothing, that self-appointed guardian—my son, you should fly kites on the roof when he's not around. One should stay away from low-class people like that and you know, your father is a very strict person—if he gets wind of this no one will be safe.'

'Well, we'll see about that!' she muttered again. Had she been punishing herself all this time for this? That someone should curse him?

'What do you mean when he's not around? He's there as soon as it's evening and he also has his bed there and maybe he also sleeps on the roof. May he die, may I see his funeral...'

Her brother was trying to cool his anger down by cursing. But she was smiling to herself. As if she didn't hear the curses at all. As a matter of fact, she was thinking of something altogether different at this moment. What a delectable thought it was!

The bird in the cage was getting ready to fly.

That night Amma untied the bunch of keys from her waistband and giving it to her, said, 'Here, take these, put the lock on the storage room door and lock the door to the stairs. Today he's gone after the child's kite, tomorrow he'll clean out the house, the wretch!' And then, baring her rotund, shiny stomach, she calmly stretched out her legs on the charpoy. As far as she was concerned, she had made the necessary arrangements to protect her house.

But something else was going on in her mind. She was thinking, as she unbolted the lock on the storage room door, 'The two roofs are adjacent to each other. Why shouldn't I say today everything that has been brewing in my heart all this time?' And she bolted the lock on the door to the stairs. But the key to that lock disappeared from the bunch and was stowed under her pillow.

The police station's tower clock struck two. Everyone in the house was sound asleep. She slipped the key out from under her pillow and began walking in her bare feet. A moist whiff of a breeze gently fondled her emotions. Someone moved a foot and she tiptoed to the water trestle. For a few moments she stared at all the faces in the light of the stars and then, making certain that everyone was asleep, she calmly unfastened the padlock. Now she was faced with the opening of the door. But the door opened easily without any creaking noises, pliant like a hungry beggar woman who turns into a corpse for the sake of a few pennies. How fiercely her heart was beating. As if it would smash her ribs. Dancing in front of her eyes in the darkness of the stairs were all the stars she had been counting since evening fell. The veins in her temples throbbed with the force of her emotions. And on top of this the *bhin-bhin* of the mosquitoes and their little jabs. She laboriously climbed the stairs. She was halfway up. Her body felt like a mountainous weight. Anticipation, fear, darkness, and her stilled breath made her head swim, and then a wave of kaleidoscopic colours radiated before her eyes.

Gada-gad! The full-grown, two-storeyed house, rolling like a ball down the stairs, falling, bouncing, hit the leg of her father's charpoy.

'*Hoho*, hai—thief! Allah!' The radiating colours in her vision suddenly recoiled when she heard the screams. The wick in the lantern was quickly raised.

'Hai, hai, it's her.' The mother beat her own shaking bosom. 'Arrey, I knew this strumpet would be up to no good. Hai, why didn't you die!' The poor mother was about to faint.

'I'll slaughter her, don't anyone stop me, I say—she's just been upstairs, the wretch.' The father lost his senses because his honour had been attacked. But how admirable that although he was out of control he was keeping his voice down—arrey, what if someone in the neighbourhood heard him?

The older brother probably awoke from a dream about his newest paramour. His condition was simply indescribable. He had often in the past tried to explain indirectly to his sister, 'Look, this is a well, no sister should fall into it.' But she had not heeded his advice, so there—he grabbed her plait and began to swing her about. The father's integrity was suffering from inner turmoil and when he saw such an easy way out, he too joined in. Because the mother was in her twelfth pregnancy, she avoided the exertion, but all the singular expletives she could remember she proceeded to spew out at this time.

But despite the pain she was in, she couldn't scream. A failure of resolve makes you a coward and it is the coward who is afraid of the world. She didn't have enough courage to open her mouth in protest against these criminal arbitrators.

Many months passed. She thought that just as her older brother's waywardness was always excused with, 'This is the age for such things,' her great sin would also be eventually forgotten. *But you fool! Did you forget what a woman's status is? A woman is a puppet whose strings are held in society's mangled hands. And when these mangled hands feel an itch, the strings make the puppet dance. But if this puppet comes to life and she begins to act according to her own volition, what will society's inert, decaying body have left to play with?* She thought that just as members of her family had lent a deaf ear to the demands of her youth, they would, similarly, forget this incident and accept their mistake. But this was *her* conviction. In the eyes of her virtuous protectors, however, the sinful scar that marred her life could never heal.

'Tramp,' her brother would say at the slightest provocation.

'*Ari...*' Her mother would take one look at her downtrodden expression and spout hefty curses in one breath.

An ordinary abrasion was scratched by poisonous nails until the scratch turned into a big wound. A wound that would putrefy on the inside and become toxic. Whose poison then engulfed her life with the agony of death. But these horrifying nails still had no rest.

'Why are you stretched out here? The wretch has fever all the time and this scorching heat on top of that and the sunlight. But I know, why sit with the others, everyone will talk and the dear girl's mind will wander.'

The mother continued grumbling, and taking the water-jug disappeared into the lavatory.

Feeling worn out, she curled her legs. On the kitchen roof the villainous monkeys continued with what they thought was treatment of the wounded monkey. Her chest reverberated again with pain. A susurration beginning from her chest travelled to her throat and once more the melting marrow of her bones began to fry her on the inside.

'Allah!' she called out ardently and then raised her pleading eyes toward the blue sky that rested on the world like a vast lid. For a long time her glance attempted to go to the other side of the lid—where she thought a world of justice and compassion existed. But her pleading eyes failed. Wearied, she finally realized that God was content after placing a lid upon His world, just as once she put some leftover dal in a bowl and was satisfied that she had saved it. But when she remembered the dal after a whole blistering afternoon had gone by and went to look at it, she saw that the dal had putrefied and was bubbling.

Translated by Tahira Naqvi

Surendra Parkash

(1930–2002)

Surendra Parkash Oberoi was from Lyallpur in Pakistan. His family migrated to Delhi after Partition. This disrupted Parkash's education and he dropped out of high school. In Delhi he met with writers and poets and was inspired to become a writer himself. He worked as a scriptwriter for All India Radio and later moved to Bombay where he became a professional screenplay writer. In spite of his lack of formal education and professional engagements, Parkash developed into a creative writer of formidable talent and led the way for the movement or tendency towards *jadidiyat* or modernism. His novella, *Dusre Admi ka Drawing Room* (The Other Man's Drawing Room) published in 1968 established him as an important name among Urdu's new writers.

Like many writers of his generation he began as a Progressive but became disillusioned fairly soon. He felt 'extremely bored' with the

Progressive literary scenario and shaken up by his own mental restlessness. Parkash thought that fiction should reflect the mental state of the individual living in the present without the writer's biases being thrust between the truth and the reader. Thus his stories are attempts at self-exploration, in which the reader participates along with the writer so that whatever result may emerge from it can be equally shared by both.

He achieves this effect by keeping close to the quintessential experience, so that it can be exposed in all its stark horror, awesome beauty, and spell-binding freshness. The story '*Bijooka*' (Scarecrow) represents Parkash's narrative technique.

Scarecrow

Hori, of Premchand's story,[1] had grown old. So old that his eyebrows and eyelashes were grey, his back was hunched over, and the veins on his hands stood out in a visible pattern on rough, dusky skin.

During this time, two sons had been born to him. But they were no longer alive. One had drowned while bathing in the Ganges. The other was killed in a police encounter. There is not much to tell about an encounter with the police. When one is at peace with one's inner self, but lives in the midst of restlessness, a confrontation with the police becomes inevitable.

Hori's sons had left behind their wives and their children, five in all—two born to the son who had drowned and three to the son killed in the police encounter. The burden of their upkeep had passed to Hori. Blood flowed with renewed vigour through his aging body.

Old Hori's hands, clutching the plough, relaxed for a moment. Then his grip tightened once more. He yelled to his oxen, and the plough moved forward, rending the breast of the earth.

That morning, the sun had not yet risen. A rosy glow spread across the sky. The five children were naked, bathing at the well in Hori's courtyard. The older daughter-in-law drew the water and poured it on the children in turn as they splashed around joyfully. The younger daughter-in-law was making huge rotis and carefully putting them away in a *changri*.

---

[1] A reference to the hero of Premchand's novel, *Godan* (The Gift of a Cow).

Inside the hut, Hori was already dressed and in the process of tying his turban. Having done that, he glanced at himself in the mirror placed in a niche in the wall. A face furrowed with lines looked back at him. Then he turned and stood in front of a picture of Hanumanji, his head bowed, eyes shut, and hands folded. Coming out into the yard, he called out, 'Is everyone ready?'

'Yes, Bapu!' they replied, in one voice. His daughters-in-law straightened the ends of their saris, their hands beginning to move faster. It was quite obvious to Hori that no one was ready yet. We cannot live without lies, he thought. These lies are so vital to our existence. If God had not given us the gift of lies, we could not live. It all begins with a lie. The effort to pass the lie off as a truth keeps a man alive for years.

Hori's grandchildren and daughters-in-law set out to prove the truth of the untruth they had just uttered. Meanwhile, Hori was busy gathering the tools they would need for harvesting. By the time that was done, the others were, indeed, ready.

The rays of the sun cast a magical aura around the house. Their mood was festive. Today they would reap the harvest. Full of enthusiasm, they were impatient to reach the field, their green, golden field, swaying in the breeze.

These were good times indeed, thought Hori, settling the red and white checked cloth scarf more comfortably on his shoulder. One did not have to put up with the bullying of the overseer or be wary of the grocer, suffer the tyranny of the *angrez* or the greed of the *zamindar*.

Happiness burst like fireworks in their hearts as images of golden crops floated before their eyes.

'Come on, Bapu!' His eldest grandson took his hand, while the others latched on to his legs. The older daughter-in-law shut the door of the house. The younger one put the changri of rotis on her head.

Uttering the name of Bir Bajrang Bali, they trooped out into the lane.

The village was already bustling with activity. Groups of people could be seen moving towards their fields. Others were wending their way back to the village.

Life today was somehow different from yesterday. Or so Hori felt.

He turned to glance at the children following him. What else could children of peasants look like? Dark and sickly, they would probably scurry away at the sound of a jeep. Even the changing seasons would alarm them. His daughters-in-law, too, were no different from the widows of other peasants. Faces obscured behind sari ends, like the wretched lice lurking in the folds of their clothes.

Hori walked on, his head bent. From a distance, he and his family resembled insects of myriad hues, crawling in the dry grass.

Beyond the last house in the lane were the wide, open fields. The water wheel nearby stood still. A dog slept peacefully under a neem tree. Cattle, content after a meal, rested in their enclosures. The fields were a golden expanse in the distance.

Old Hori's land lay beyond these fields, across the canal. It stretched out languorously, waiting for him. Where Hori's field ended began a vast tract of barren land—parched land, with not a speck of green. Your feet would sink in if you tried to walk on that fallow, crumbling soil. The earth there easily turned to dust, just as the bones of his sons had turned into ash when they were cremated; ash which scattered like sand at the merest touch.

The wasteland was gradually moving in, towards his field. Hori noticed that in the last fifty years it had advanced by two yards. He did not want it to swallow up his field before his grandchildren grew up. By that time, he too would have become dust; just another part of some such barren land.

The path ahead seemed endless, but the bare feet of Hori and his family moved resolutely forward...

The sun was peering over the eastern horizon. The long walk had made their feet dusty. Farmers, reaping the crop in the neighbouring fields, called out, 'Ram-Ram!' and continued working with renewed zest, the golden stalks falling under scythes that moved rhythmically.

They crossed the canal, one by one. There was no sign of water, not even enough to create an illusion of it. The water that had once flowed through it had etched strange patterns in the dry sandy soil.

The golden field came into sight and their hearts lit up with joy. Once the crop was cut, their yard would be full of hay, and the hut full of grain. What a pleasure it would be to sit on the charpoy, gorging on rice! And how they would belch!

Suddenly Hori froze in his tracks. Those following him stopped too. Hori stared at the field, horrified. The others looked first at Hori, then at the land, trying to fathom what had happened. Something shot through Hori's body like a thunderbolt. He stumbled forward screaming. '*Abbe*, who is it...?'

Just then they noticed a strange movement in the middle of the waving field. They followed Hori with quick steps. Hori shouted again, '*Abbe*, who is that? Who's in my field? Say something, will you? Who is cutting my crop....?'

There was no reply. They were almost in the field now and could clearly hear the swish of the moving scythe. They stopped, a little unnerved. Tightening his grip on the scythe he held in his hand, Hori challenged, 'Bastard, speak up!'

Slowly, an apparition was seen rising at the far end of the field. A figure that seemed to be smiling at them. And then they heard it speak.

'It's me, Hori Kaka...me, the *bijooka*, the scarecrow!' it said, brandishing the sickle it held in its hand.

Stifled screams of fear escaped them. Colour fled their faces. Hori's parched lips turned white. They were stunned into silence. For how long? A moment, a century, an age? Who knows! They were lost to everything around them. The sound of Hori's rasping voice, quivering with rage, jolted them back to the present.

'You...bijooka...you! I made you from bits of straw to keep watch over my crops. I dressed you in the khaki clothes of an English hunter whom my father helped. The hunter had left them behind as a token of appreciation. I made your face with a pot, discarded from my house. I placed an English hat on your head. And now, you lifeless puppet, you dare to reap my crop?'

Hori advanced as he spoke. The scarecrow, not in the least perturbed by what Hori had just said, grinned at them. As they came closer, they saw that a fourth of the crop had already been harvested. And there the scarecrow stood, smiling, sickle in hand. Where could it have got the sickle from, they wondered. Hadn't it been under their watchful eyes all these months, standing there, lifeless, empty-handed? And today—why, it could be a man! A flesh and blood person, no different from them!

The sight of it, standing there, drove Hori out of his mind. He lunged forward and gave the scarecrow a violent shove. It did not budge. But with the impact of the blow, Hori was hurled to the ground. Screaming, the people behind Hori ran up to him. He was struggling to rise, one hand supporting his back. They helped him up. He stared at the scarecrow, a frightened look on his face, and said 'So you have become stronger than me, scarecrow! I, who made you with my own hands, to stand vigil over my crop.'

Smiling as always, the scarecrow spoke, 'There is no need to be so upset, Hori Kaka. I have only taken my share of the crop—One fourth, that's all.'

'Why? Who are you? What right do you have to a share at all?'

'I do have a claim to the crop, Hori Kaka. Because I am. I exist. And because I have kept watch over this field.'

'I put you there, knowing you had no life. How can a lifeless object have rights? Besides, where did you get that?' Hori asked, pointing to the sickle.

The scarecrow guffawed. 'Hori Kaka, you are talking to me and yet you insist I am lifeless!'

'But how did you get the sickle? And life? You had neither when I made you.'

'Well, it happened on its own. The day you split the bamboo to make my frame, dressed me in an English hunter's rags, etched eyes, nose, ears, and mouth on a broken pot—even that day, life was seething in all these things. When they were put together, I came into being. Meanwhile the crop was ripening, and I stood there, biding my time. A sickle slowly began to take form within me. By the time the harvest was ready, so was the sickle—the sickle you see in my hands. However, I did not betray the trust you had placed in me. I waited patiently for this day. Now when you are ready to reap the harvest, I too have taken what is due to me. What is wrong with that?'

The scarecrow spoke in a slow, deliberate manner. The import of its words was immediately clear to all of them.

'But this is impossible—it's a conspiracy against me. As far as I'm concerned, you are not alive. Don't think you can get away with this, you schemer! I'll go to the village council. Put that sickle down. I won't let you take a single stalk!' Hori yelled.

The scarecrow flung the sickle away, the smile still fixed on its face. The village council met in the barn. It was to take a decision that day. Both the concerned parties had already stated their claims. The council headman and the elders were present. Hori sat in their midst with his grandchildren. Signs of deep anguish were imprinted upon his pale face. His daughters-in-law stood with the other women. They were all waiting for the scarecrow.

At last, they spotted the scarecrow in the distance, ambling along, smiling, of course. All eyes were lifted towards it. There was something about its appearance that commanded respect. As it entered the square, everyone stood up. Involuntarily, they bowed their heads. The sight disturbed Hori. He couldn't ignore the niggling feeling that the villagers had allowed their conscience to be bought by the scarecrow. So had the village council, it seemed. He felt helpless, desperate—like a drowning man wildly thrashing his limbs.

The council headman announced the verdict. A tremor went through Hori as he agreed to give the scarecrow a fourth of his crop. Then he rose to his feet and addressed his grandsons.

'Listen. This is probably the last harvest I will live to reap. The arid land hasn't reached our field yet. My advice to you is this, never set up a scarecrow to guard your crop. When the field is ploughed next year and the seeds are sown, and the nectar of rain brings forth new shoots, bind me to a pole and stand me up in the field instead of a scarecrow. I will look after your crops till your fields are swallowed by the arid waste and the soil turns to dust. Don't ever remove me. Let me stand testimony to the fact that you did not make a scarecrow. A scarecrow is not lifeless as it is supposed to be. Indeed, it acquires a life of its own. And this fact of existence itself invests it with a sickle. To say nothing, of course, of its right to a fourth of the harvest.'

Having said this, Hori trudged towards his field. His grandchildren walked behind him, followed by the two daughters-in-law. Then came the villagers, with slow unhurried steps, their heads drooping low.

They had almost made it to the field when Hori collapsed. His grandchildren immediately set themselves to the task of tying him to a pole, under the curious eyes of the spectators. The scarecrow took off the hunter's hat, held it against its chest and bowed its head.

Translated by Sara Rai

Abdullah Hussein
(b. 1931)

Abdullah Hussein is the pen name of Mohammad Khan, who is among contemporary Urdu's leading novelists. He was born in Rawalpindi and was a chemical engineer by profession until he gave it up to become a full-time writer. He moved to London with his wife in the 1960s and has travelled back and forth between England and Pakistan since then. His first novel *Udas Naslein* (Sad Generations) was published in 1963 and became an instant classic. Since then he has published several novels including *Nasheb* (Downfall), 1982, *Bagh* (Tiger), 1983, *Qaid* (Incarceration), 1989, and *Nadaar Log* (The Indigent), 1996, as well as short stories, and has also won the highest literary honours in Pakistan. All of his short stories are available in English translation.

Hussein translated *Udas Naslein* as 'The Weary Generations' for the UNESCO World Literature Series (2000). The novel, ostensibly a love story about a marriage between two people of different social backgrounds gone awry, is an allegorical saga of the contradictions, disillusionments, and frustrations underlying the events leading to Partition and the painful birth of two nations. The narrative style is deceptively subtle.

The tale of 'The Old Fisherman' is a chapter from *Udas Naslein*, and refers to the tragic and disgraceful Jallianwalla Bagh episode that occurred during the British colonial rule in India.

The Tale of the Old Fisherman

'This is the place,' the old fisherman told them, pointing with his hand.

It was the same place where they had spent that entire day and, before that, many other days. Around an open space with a well in one corner was a brick wall about four feet high. There was just one gate; on the other three sides the entire area was hedged in by tall, multistoreyed buildings. Known as Jallianwala Garden, it looked more like a cattle yard than a public park. They had spent several days here, recording the statements of journalists and political workers, businessmen and lawyers. Today, they happened to run across this old fisherman who, in his eagerness to talk with them, dragged them back to this place, even though they had run out of paper and pencils.

He was short, with small arms and legs, and no one could tell whether nature or age had bent his back. His clothes were in rags and a stench of fish oozed from his body. His face and beard were equally dirty, but an unexpected strength and innocence shone in his eyes. He was one of those men who are born alone and die alone but who, on account of their simplicity and geniality, find frequent occasions to meet and converse with all kinds of people. They looked on as he clambered up the boundary wall like a young boy and perched himself at the top, his feet tucked comfortably beneath him.

'This is the place, my children,' he repeated, waving his hand in a circle again.

The shadows were lengthening in the fading light of the sun, and Jallianwala Garden was totally deserted except for them and the two English soldiers on guard with loaded revolvers in their belts. The companions of the ancient, time-scarred hunchback looked at him with eagerness, feeling as though they were standing on the shore of a desolate ocean which had suddenly gone dry and exposed to view all the broken boats and ships that lay on its floor.

Azra, a little apprehensive, leaned against the wall and said, 'Tell us everything, fisherman.'

'Yes, tell us everything that happened, old fisherman,' the others urged.

'All I've done is sell fish, my children, from the first day—since the day I was born—no—since the day I came of age. For at the time I was born, it was my father who would sell fish, while my mother salted them to keep them from rotting. She was a kind and gentle woman. My father used to beat her, and she would beat me, but most of the year we lived together in peace. The beatings occurred only when my father failed to catch any fish. Summer was always the season of trouble and strife, for the rivers would be flooded and the fish would disappear to the bottom of the muddy water and elude our nets. My father would get mad and start cursing the fish and the net and the boat and the heat of the sun, all the time staring at me balefully, seeking some excuse to beat me. But I always managed to stay out of his grasp. I would turn my back on him and continue to paddle in silence, letting his curses fly in and out of my ears. On reaching the bank I would jump out of the boat, run as fast as possible, and soon get out of his range. The rest of the day I would stay away from the house, knowing it would be in turmoil. I would spend the day away from the fishermen's huts, wandering around holes of muddy water, catching and chewing on small fish. During the days of flood I would always carry a piece of salt in my pocket—it's hard to eat raw fish without salt! At first I had some difficulty, but soon it became a habit and I began to relish eating them. They produced a lot of heat and blood in my body. Then in the evening I would return home and peer into the house from the darkness again. I'd stand there outside the door in the dark, nodding with sleep until in utter disgust I would pick up my pet dog and hurl him to the ground. The dog's cries would tell my mother of my return. But she was a clever woman: she would call to me in a sweet voice to come do an errand for her. For instance she'd say, "The dog must be starving, give him his fish." As soon as I stepped in the door she would grab hold of me. Twisting my ears and glaring with fury, she would call me all sorts of names: "Lazy bum! Tramp! Wretch!"— just about all the names that my father called her. Then she would slap my face again and again. At first I used to burst out in real tears; but later, when I grew accustomed to her temper, I would shriek and shout and make so much noise that my father would wake up and curse us both. Yes, those few weeks of flood used to be really bad.

'Once, when the flood continued for a long time and our poverty became terrible and all our dogs died from starvation, my father became irritable. He began to beat me without even bothering to look for an excuse. Becoming desperate, I thought up a plan. One day, when as usual we failed to catch a single fish, my father angrily threw his net down in the bottom of the boat and, cursing the entire world, towered over my head with his fists raised.

'"Listen, Baba," I said, raising the oar in my hand to defend myself. "First listen to me."

'He let his hands fall, but continued to glare at me, sneezing and sputtering in anger. I said, "If you beat me, I won't row the boat. What will you do then?"

'"I'll row the boat myself," he said like a madman.

'"And who'll catch the fish?"

'"The fish...?" He pulled at his beard in confusion. Then, swearing loudly, he said, "And just where are there any fish?"

"But when the flood subsides? Who'll catch them then?"

'He continued to pull thoughtfully at his beard, and then, without a word, sat down on the net. He got my point all right; after that day he never laid a hand on me. But, as I said, the days of misfortune used to end eventually.

'With the advent of winter the snow on the mountains would stop melting and the water in the river would again become clear and the fish would rise close to the surface. Once again we would have a pile of fish, which my mother would clean and salt and pack in gunny bags. We would find some new dogs for pets, my father would regain his good humour, and all through the winter and spring and autumn we would live in peace and comfort like rich and gentle people. And every evening, my mother would sit warming her hands in front of the fire and say, "Lord, thank you very much. It's good that floods come only during the summer and not in winter, for if you don't get fish in winter you're likely to catch pneumonia or rheumatism—not to mention all the cursing and wrangling. Yes, Lord, thank you very much." She always referred to the beatings she received as "wrangling".'

When the old man stopped for breath, the five listeners looked impatient. They had obviously grown tired of the old man's aimless talk.

'Tell us about the firing,' they said.

'Wait....' The old man raised a hand to quiet them. 'I'll tell you everything. We can sit here until eight in the evening. Let me try to revive my memory. After all these days I have at last found you, people I can talk with. Usually in this city each person is worse than the other. Speak to someone and he remains as dumb as if he had just stepped out of his grave. I have seen many more deaths in epidemics, though... But I was speaking of my mother. She was very kind and God-fearing, and also very clever. But she soon died and all her work fell on us. Then we realized her true worth. Now, somehow or other, my father would go alone to catch fish and, whatever catch he would bring, I'd dry in the sun and put in sacks. At night we would sit on the floor facing each other and eat dry fish with chillies. My father, due to his age, never got used to eating uncooked fish; and as long as he lived he suffered because of it. But there was no way out, for neither of us knew how to light a fire and keep it going. It used to make him quite mad to see me eating raw fish with such gusto. "Son of an animal!" he would shout. "Son of a crocodile! Look at the way he enjoys them!" And I'd laugh and reply, "Baba, you call yourself a fisherman but can't eat fish. What kind of a fisherman are you?"

'"I was born from a human being, not an animal," he would reply. Sometimes I'd add, just to really anger him, "I can eat a live fish. Can you do the same?"

'"Shut up. You're crazy."

'"You think so?" I would reply. "Now look at this." And with that I'd take a live fish from the pail and put it in my mouth. At the sight of the fish thrashing between my teeth he'd get furious and swing at me with a dried eel. Fearing the cane-like lash of the eel, I'd run outside and stand in the dark listening to his angry mutterings, "What an age has come upon us! Snakes and pigs are being born in human families. Did you ever hear of such a thing? A live fish—and a live man eating it!

One life eating another..." Quietly laughing, I would remain safe in the dark and soon finish the fish.'

The old man raised his arms and laughed, showing the three teeth left in his mouth, and as he laughed, the wrinkles around his eyes grew thick. Despite their interest in his ramblings, the listeners were getting concerned about the time. They wanted him to stop rambling and come to the real subject.

In the dim light of the fast sinking sun the old man continued.

'But soon we found out what a failure we were at keeping house. The fish that I'd dry and pack in the bags would begin to stink in only two days, and it would become impossible to keep them in the house. They couldn't be sold either, so we would eat as much as we could in two days and throw the rest of the mess in the river. I also noticed that our daily catch was slowly decreasing, and before long we were eating up the daily catch and having nothing left over. Instead of dried fish, my father began to find fresh raw fish more to his liking, for its fat is soft and salty. So as soon as he'd return with the meagre catch, he would eat it all up. This won't do at all, I thought. Finally one day, getting tired of my father's stupid ways, I closed the door of the hut and followed him to the river.

'It was the month of Magh, or perhaps of Phagun. The snow had not yet melted on the mountains, I remember. The river water was clear all the way to the bottom and one could see the shoals of fish swimming around. I was rowing the boat and my father was standing with his back toward me. I saw that due to age his legs had turned inward and were covered with thick yellow veins. But the day was so beautiful—the colour of the river was a deep blue and so was the colour of the sky. The wind blew around our heads, and my father's hair, flying in the air, was white as snow and caught the light of the sun. Our boat was rocking gently on the ripples that the wind was making in the river. Then we entered the area where fish were plentiful. The river had cut deep into the bank and looked like a lake. Here we saw thousands of fish of infinite hues, big and small, fat and thin, of all shapes and kinds, with the rays of the sun filtering through the water and playing on their colourful bodies. When my father threw his net, the fish swam away in great consternation but still a lot of big ones got caught. Pulling them into the boat, we turned homeward. I was very happy and was rowing with all my strength when suddenly I saw my father put his hand into the net and pull out a fish from the squirming heap. Holding it in his hand he kept looking at it for some time. It was a very pretty fish—deep blue, with golden spots all over it. It kept opening and closing its gills, staring at God knows what with unblinking eyes.

'"The water is beautiful," my father said softly. "My house is ugly. You should go back to your home." He put his hand in the water and let the fish go. Almost losing my temper, I tried to draw his attention by making loud snuffing noises, but he was lost in his thoughts. Then he picked up another fish. It was purple, with black stripes over the long body, red eyes and a red tail. "You are beautiful, but my house is ugly. You too should go home," my father said, and dropped the fish into the water. Striking the water, the fish made a splash with its tail and disappeared. Then my father picked up a third fish, whose skin was white as the whitest silk and which was covered with tiny spots in all the colours of the rainbow. Its head and eyes and lips were also white. My father dropped it too into the water, saying, "You are also beautiful. You too should go home. To fill my belly I need only a few ugly, useless fish."

'By the time we reached the bank, he had thrown away all the good fish in this manner. I was boiling with rage but kept silent, satisfied that finally I knew the secret behind the daily loss. After we reached the bank I said to him, "Look here, Baba, starting tomorrow you'll stay at home and I'll go on the boat."

'"Why?" he shouted angrily.

'"Why?" I shouted back. "You throw away all the fish, that's why!" I was trembling with rage, and though I was then only eleven, he was frightened by my looks. Bowing his head in silence, he led the way home. After a while he said, "You'll understand when you too grow old and your woman dies." I was so furious I didn't bother to answer him.

'After that he remained at home and I went to the river. Once again we managed to store up a lot of fish and once again we began to be considered well-off in that community of fishing folk. But my father was getting older each day, and his sight was weakening. Having spread the fish to dry, he would sit in the shade all day long and advise the fisherman against fighting among themselves, telling those who beat their wives that they ought not to do so or the women would die and then in old age they would have to face the cursed necessity of eating raw fish.

'In this way, by the time I came of age, he was dead.'

The old man stopped to catch his breath, laughed, and then looked around. His three teeth showed again. By now, they were all tired of the old man's rambling loquacity, and Naim had lost all hope of getting any useful details out of him. Only Azra, who had little interest in the work of Naim and his companions, still showed some curiosity.

'Then what happened, old fisherman?' she asked.

'Tell us what happened on the thirteenth of April, fisherman, or else we'll go away,' one of the men said.

'All right, all right. I'll tell you everything before eight, my children, don't worry. For at eight you must leave this place; at that time the curfew starts. I was left alone when my father died. Then I began looking around for a woman to take care of the housework, but unfortunately I wasn't very tall, and all the women that I found were taller than me and didn't want me. The one or two who showed some interest turned out to be very ill-tempered, and as you know, my children, I don't like shrews. After some time I gave up the search; I took my father's basket and began to go around selling the daily catch. Now there was no work to do at home, and there was no need for a woman. I started to live happily all by myself and still do, although I left my village and now live in this city. Raw fish and boiled corn are the only things I have ever eaten. I have now lived in this world five years longer than my father did. I have seen many incidents greater than that of the Jallianwala Bagh—the mutiny of 1857, when my father had just recently died, and the plague at the turn of the century, and...and...But because you are all insisting that I tell you about the Jallianwala incident, I'll talk about that. I can tell you everything that happened on that day and on several days before that.

'You know, some fifty years after the mutiny of 1857, when I told a man all the details of those days, he asked me, "What do you eat?" I said, "Fish and boiled corn." "That's why you're one of the wisest," he said.'

The old man stretched his back and when the listeners caught a glimpse of his three teeth they realized that he was laughing, in his friendly but proud manner.

'The disturbance started on the ninth day of the fourth month, when nine Englishmen were killed in the bazaars of the city. Everything occurred in front of my eyes. They stopped me. There were two of them. I thought they wanted to buy my fish. I gladly put my basket on the ground. One of them stayed with me; the other, with a camera to his eye, backed away. Standing at a distance, he took some pictures. Then, taking a silver coin from his pocket, he threw it toward me. His aim was slightly off and I danced and jumped in the air like a crazy man to grab the coin. He took some more pictures. Finally the coin fell on the ground and when I picked it up they were already going away, laughing and talking among themselves. Then, as I was watching, two men attacked them with drawn swords at the corner of the lane. One sword went clean through the stomach of the guy who had taken my pictures; the other stuck in the ribs of his companion. Both of them were dead by the time they hit the dust. I was thunderstruck by the rapidity of the events. Then it occurred to me that only a few moments earlier I had accepted a coin from those foreigners, and it could be that those two swine might try to attack me too. I quickly put that rupee in my inside pocket, picked up my basket, and slipped away. In the next bazaar I saw three more corpses. They lay in the dust a little apart from each other. Their faces still looked warm. They too were foreigners and their golden hair was dirty with blood and dust. They didn't have cameras. They didn't have anything. Their hands were empty. In the bazaar people were hurriedly closing their shops. A few men stood by the corpses, their faces like children's, pale with fear. Though I felt great pity for those men, I had seen much worse things, so I took the situation in my stride, passing by without showing any interest. I didn't even stop my chanting, and kept on calling, "Fish for sale, fish for sale." In front of the Darbar Sahib I saw another Englishman. He was dying. A thin dagger had gone through his neck and he was clutching its handle as he suffered his death agony. This was the largest square in the city but was completely deserted, even though it was midday. Nothing alive was in sight. I passed through and continued on my way. But that dying Englishman was very young and very handsome. I couldn't restrain myself from taking a second look at him. At the corner of the street I stopped and looked back. The young man's face was lifted toward the sky in death, and his youthful lips were lifeless. Children, you are fortunate that you are still young and do not know much. I'm an old fisherman. But I have lived a long time and know a few things about life. Young faces, young eyes, young lips these are the fairest of all things in this world. But when they are made cold—I have seen fish who continue to smile with open eyes even in death. But young men—that's a different matter. One feels for a young one. To erase his memory I called loudly, "Fish for sale, fish for sale." By the time I reached the court buildings I saw three other bodies, lying by the gutters. And beside the corpses I also saw a fire—a silent and hidden fire flaring among the people scurrying in the lane—a fire that burned in their eyes and in their hearts—a terrible wrath that was billowing over the heads of the people. And I tell you the truth, my children; you didn't see it, but I saw it...I have seen thousands of dead men and animals and fish; and during the red plague I saw three coffins being carried out of the same door at one time; and I have seen women chanting their laments; and I was present when the trains collided and saw one man's head lying near the neck of another; and I have seen hordes of shouting and bloodthirsty people attacking each other; but never was I frightened, never, for there was nothing to be frightened about in those incidents. But when I saw that silent, suppressed anger raging inside every man and animal and tree of this city, I returned home.

'From that time on, all the business in the city stopped, and military trucks and white soldiers began to make rounds in the streets and bazaars. The people of the city, once scattered over every inch of the ground, now began to collect in small groups in the neighbourhood lanes and corners—just like a fishing net, cut in the middle, which begins to collect into small knots. And among these groups there was one which dishonoured a white woman in the middle of the bazaar—the incident that was at the root of the later riots. It happened on the third day after the incident. As usual I was making my rounds, carrying the fish basket. I was feeling rather upset, for by that time the fish had started to smell and there was nothing but hatred in my heart for them. I had stopped shouting my wares—after so many days there was nothing left in them to tout—but I was hoping that some kindhearted person fond of fish might relieve me of them. When I reached the lane that connects the big market with the vegetable market, I was stopped in my tracks. A white woman came running out of the lane and behind her came a baying mob. They caught her in the centre of the market and stood around glaring at her with hate in their eyes. The woman's hair was dusty and her legs were covered with mud. She stood in the middle of that mob, turning slowly on her heels like a mechanical doll, and her face was as colourless as white fish. For some moments those men kept staring at her in sullen silence. Then one of them stepped out, grabbed the collar of her dress, and tore it down to her knees. She screamed and that broke the spell. The pack fell upon her. Right in front of my eyes they kept snatching at her like crows and vultures. I must say though, she was a terrific woman; indeed, she was. Quite remarkable. The moment she got a chance she jumped out from under those men and started running. There was nothing left now of her flowery dress, and only a little piece of underclothing covered her buttocks and hung over her breasts. Her hair was dishevelled and she ran like a witch, straining her legs. I can still picture her well-rounded buttocks and heavy thighs. Ah.... It occurred to me then that if that woman were sitting at my house eating fish, she would look very pleasing. Ah...As she disappeared down an alley, with that mob close behind her, I returned home cursing the bastards.

'That night, for the first time in my life, I couldn't go to sleep. I usually sleep well, for sleep is essential for good health, but that night I just couldn't. I felt parched, as if there was no moisture left in my body. I began to think of my health. I tried heating the room by lighting a fire. Then I got worried about the leftover fish and decided to spread them out against the wall to dry. I lay down on my mat in the corner, but I still felt wide awake. Thinking perhaps it was because of the stink of the fish, I got up again and, gathering the fish in a heap, covered them with my basket. Then I lay down on my right side, since that's the way I usually sleep; but it didn't help. So I dragged my mat close to the fire, a foolish thing to do, for I was already roasting. I got up and was kneeling on the floor, wondering about my condition, when a thought suddenly occurred to me. I removed the basket and selected a rotting fish.

'"I can't seem to find any sleep tonight. So let's have a little chat," I said. The fish remained silent, though her mouth was wide open. "If my father were alive, he'd have let you go before you died. But I don't do such crazy things. So open your ears wide and listen to what I tell you. Don't laugh, for your kids and other relatives may be crying over your death even now." The fish kept her mouth open in a wide smirk which infuriated me. "So you find it funny? You died long ago, you beast, but your dull eyes are still open. You don't sleep yourself, and you won't let anyone else sleep. Here...." and I threw her in the fire. Soon she was crackling and sputtering in the flames; but her eyes were still open and the smirk was still on her face. In my anger I threw another fish into the fire; her eyes were open too but she looked more sober. The smell of burning fish soon filled the room, and you know, my children, how that smell can make your mouth water. But it was past midnight and I didn't feel like eating anything, so I ignored the idea and selected another fish from the heap. "Your skin is so soft and pretty; you might be able to find a customer. You better stay." And I put her aside. This game seemed to help. So after talking awhile with those fish, and burning a few of them in the fire, I fell asleep.

'When I awoke in the morning the sun was already fairly high and people were up and around. But though the streets sounded alive again after so many days of silence, I felt a strange apprehension. Rubbing my eyes to see better, I stepped outside. People seemed to be in a great hurry, and they were all going in the same direction, as though they were headed for some fish auction which had already begun and each of them was eager to buy the best lot. But one thing marked them as different from buyers of fish, and that was their silence. No one seemed to speak to anyone else although among them there were both old and young, big and small, fat and thin. What amazed me more were the looks on their pale faces as they hurried by me with clenched teeth and unseeing eyes. It frightened me and yet aroused my curiosity; I quickly filled my basket and joined them. No one paid any attention to me, so I clenched my teeth like the rest of them and began to walk with my chest thrown forward. Everywhere one looked, lines of people were rushing in the same direction. When we reached the market square we saw a number of white soldiers standing fully armed. As we moved into the square, they took up positions as if in a war and loaded their guns. Then a squad of Indian policemen arrived. They had bamboo poles in their hands and began to beat us with them. Some of us were badly hit and some were not, but we were all pushed out of the square. One stick hit my basket, which fell to the ground, scattering all the fish in the dirt. Trying to retrieve them I was hit a few times on the back, but I didn't give up, and managed to collect most of them. Suddenly loud shouts and slogans filled the air; another crowd had come from the opposite direction and was trying to enter the square. But the police squad stopped them too, and soon they came around and joined us. With their arrival our quiet mob became vocal and began to shout similar slogans. When the noise became unbearable we started marching toward this place where we are now. I was surrounded by people who pushed and fell and shouted, their faces free of any fear and lit instead with passion and anger. Their shouts seemed to make the sky tremble. We kept marching like that, shouting and rushing down the streets and alleys. Lots of small crowds came and joined us on the way, and the few soldiers who tried to stop us were pushed aside.

'When we entered this park it looked like an ocean without a shore. It was already quite full before our arrival, and wave after wave of people kept coming after us, jamming into the park. Under a thick cloud of dust raised by their feet, hundreds of thousands of people were milling around as though it were the day of judgement, and it was impossible to stay in any one spot. The dust filled my nostrils, my feet were crushed a million times, and torrents of sweat ran down my body though it was still spring. I was cursing the mob, and my own foolishness, but it was impossible to get out of there. I was also feeling very embarrassed at being the only one with a basket on my head. Just then I noticed a small boy, hardly twelve, who was crying and seemed lost. Feeling sorry for the poor kid, I took him by the hand and drew him to one side. He kept crying, so I looked into my basket, selected a good-looking fish, and gave it to him. He then became quiet and was soon quite happy playing with the fish, so I told myself that my bringing the basket had done some good after all.

'As the people kept pouring in, the roar of their slogans grew louder and louder. The Muslims were shouting the names of Allah and their religious leaders, while the Hindus and Sikhs were shouting their own sacred slogans. Then I turned around and saw a dark, bearded man standing on high ground, waving his hand to quiet the crowd. But his wild gestures and flying beard seemed to have little effect on the mob. As I watched, a white man dressed like an army officer came up behind him. He shoved the bearded man off the stand and began to shout something to the crowd, threatening with his hands. There was a brief moment of silence when we could all hear his angry voice, and, though it was impossible to understand what he was saying, his gestures and the expression on his face made it clear that he wanted us to get the hell out of there. Suddenly a roar rose from the crowd and someone threw a shoe in his direction. Then more shoes came flying toward him from all sides, looking like flocks of geese rising from the surface of a lake. The people who were near the army officer stood there in silent terror, and most of the shoes fell on them. I kept my wits and held on to my shoes, for you know, my children, I only have one pair. When the shoes were gone, people began taking off their clothes. Now turbans and shirts and undershirts were being rolled into balls and thrown at the officer. Soon about half the people were partly naked, and a few were so shameless they took off everything and ran around completely nude. But soon there was nothing more to throw; only the tumult and noise continued, in which the mob and the army officer both took part. Then someone noticed my basket, and before I could step back, a score of hands reached forward and pulled it out of my grasp. Some of the men glared at me with bloodthirsty eyes when they saw the fish. Then they picked them up and threw them with all their strength toward the white man. The fish that landed short were picked up by the men at that spot and thrown forward, and then farther and farther until one fish hit the army officer right between his eyes. He caught it as it slithered down his face and looked at it in disbelief. Then raising his head, he looked at the crowd, then at the fish again, then back at the crowd, and suddenly with a jerk he smashed the fish in the face of the man standing in front of him. Next he threw his arms in the air, shouting like a maniac, and then suddenly the firing began.

'In a man's lifetime, he's seldom likely to see a scene like the one that followed. People were running in mad confusion like fish caught in a net; but the pursuing bullets were faster than the fleeing men...There was one man who was running with a hand on my shoulder when he was hit. He jumped into the air like an acrobat and was held there for a moment by another bullet, and then another bullet, until he turned a somersault; and when he hit the ground he was already dead, though his face had lost none of its passion. His body was soon hidden by other bodies. In my panic I kept running even when I saw my ancestral basket rolling on the ground as bullets kept hitting it. Then suddenly my feet went cold and a shriek escaped my lips, for in front of me was that well...that dry well...do you see it over there?...that same one. It was only a few yards away from where I had stopped. Some people running by me had fallen into it, then many more people, and soon the well was so filled with dead and the dying that the fleeing men could run over the human bodies. Running along crouched under the pursuing bullets, I passed the spot where we are sitting now. You see this wall? It's empty now, but at that time human bodies were hanging over its entire length. Their legs were on the inside but their arms hung over the other side with bellies resting on the wall. These were the people who had tried to escape over the wall, thinking it was low enough, but as they reached the top they were hit by the bullets. And as I stared at them from inside the park they looked like pieces of laundry strung out by some washerwoman to dry in the sun. Did you notice these holes in the wall? Ah.... You who go around asking people for the news, what do you know! You can never know the punishment that was given to this ill-fated city! Ah...

'As I came out I saw some dogs pulling at a fish. It was that fat white fish I had put aside the night before in the hope of finding a good buyer. Now, as I saw these strange "buyers", I felt like laughing, but it was no time for laughter. I had to get away from there as quickly as possible to save my life.

'Stumbling and falling, I finally reached the spot where they had attacked that white woman the day before. The escaping people had been stopped at the mouth of the street, and after much pushing and pulling, when I reached the front, I saw the strangest sight. On both sides of the street white soldiers stood ready to shoot, and a river of human bodies seemed to be flowing through the middle. These were men like you and me lying on the ground and crossing that twenty-five yard stretch on their bellies. They were not allowed to use their knees or elbows. They were told—all of us were told—to crawl like snakes, for at that spot we had behaved like snakes toward their white woman. Anyone who tried to raise himself on his knees or elbows was immediately shot. Then the soldiers thought up something even better: they lined up on one side of the market and began to shoot just six inches above the heads of the crawling people. The slithering cowards buried their faces in the ground and inched forward with the help of only their toes and nails. In the meantime wave after wave of fleeing people kept coming, for this was the only route of escape from the park. As soon as a place became free, someone from the crowd would fall on his face and begin crawling in the dirt. As you know, my children, crawling is not very difficult for us fisherman. My father, may God bless him with peace, had taught me when I was only six to float on the surface of the water without moving a limb. So when my turn came I had to drag my head on the ground which injured the side of my skull so that it remained swollen for many days. I went across with greater agility than most men, however. There was one old man crawling along side of me, with not a single hair on his head; his skull was bleeding and one cheek dragged a wide line behind him in the dirt. This old man was crying bitterly, though he was also somewhat ashamed of his tears. At the end of the passage, when we got up to run, I recognized him. He used to buy fish from me every Thursday and had three grown-up sons and a large grocery store.

'For many days after that I stayed away from that place, but from a distance I saw people being forced to crawl over that stretch of ground—though crawling is unbecoming to human beings. I never recovered my ancestral basket.

'Now you'd better leave this place, my children. The curfew will be starting any moment and then for twelve hours anyone found in this area will be shot at sight. I've tried your patience a lot, I know, but you yourselves asked me to tell you everything. "Old man, tell us everything." So I've told you every bit of it—But you don't need to be dismayed, my children, for I have seen worse things.'

'Aren't you going to leave this place?' one listener asked.

'No.'

'Are you a Muslim or a Hindu?' Naim asked quickly.

'Aha, that's a nice one.' The old hunchback gestured with his index finger and laughed. 'Yes, that's a nice question. Frankly, I don't know. You see, well, I was too busy to ask my father, and my father was too busy to tell me. The fisherman only knows how to toil; he doesn't have time for such questions.' Then he pointed toward the white soldiers. 'I've also told them everything. They don't bother me any more. They know I'm not interested in those things. I'm only an old fisherman, somewhat hunchbacked.'

On their way back they kept turning their heads to look at that small dark figure who, tired after the long discourse, now sat quiet and alone on the wall, while a desolate night spread around him. The barrier of night gradually thickened until he disappeared from sight. But for many years after that evening, that dark and lonely figure kept coming back before their eyes.

Translated by C.M. Naim and Gordon Roadarmel

Asad Muhammad Khan

(b. 1932)

Asad Muhammad Khan was born in Bhopal, India. While in college he got into trouble because of his leftist leanings and spent a fortnight in jail. His father pressured him to move to Pakistan in order to start afresh. He began his literary career as a poet but later switched to writing short stories. His first published story '*Basode ki Mariam*' (Miriam from Basoda), 1971, established him as an outstanding prose stylist. His stories are about city people who expend most of their energy coping with the formidable stresses of urbanization as a result of which their lives have become abnormally disarrayed; yet they are human too. He has published three collections of stories so far: *Khirki Bhar Asmaan* (Windowful of Sky), *Burj-e Khamoshan* (Silent Terraces), and more recently, *Ghusse ki Nai Fasl* (Harvest of Anger).

Khan is a brilliant prose stylist. He brings his expertise as a scriptwriter to create sparkling dialogue and a cinematic touch to the unfolding of the story. He is probably the first writer in Urdu to write historical or quasi-historical fiction set in the era of the Pathan kings in fifteenth and sixteenth century India. The story, '*Ghusse ki Nai Fasl*', presented here is set in the era of Sher Shah Suri (1486–1545), the Afghan ruler of north India who defeated the Mughal emperor Humayun. The *mardoozi* sect in the story is entirely imaginary as is the character Hafiz Shukrullah Khan, but Barmazaid Kor was indeed Sher Shah Suri's prime minister.

Harvest of Anger

Hafiz Shukrullah Khan preferred brevity in his speech.

He was a quiet, intellectual sort of person. Perhaps this was why he liked to be brief in what he said; he considered detailed explanations a waste of time and such things caused him great anxiety.

He had a thickset, muscular body and, although he was an educated gentleman, he was known in the neighbouring villages as a man with a temper. Perhaps this was why people referred to him behind his back as 'Hafiz Gainda'.

Although Hafiz Shukrullah knew that he was called Hafiz Gainda, he reacted to it with restraint and disregard. So far he had only thrashed those people who called him by that name to humiliate him or who deliberately used it to his face. He ignored anyone who called him Gainda without meaning it, or when children and friends used it in an informal, good-natured manner.

Hafiz Shukrullah Gainda had another strange trait. He would treat atheists, as well as those who belonged to other religions, in a gracious manner. It was his opinion that being courteous cost nothing. How do such people harm us if they disagree with us? Indeed, they were lost in any case. This kind of attitude in an elder of the village should have been quite enough to astonish the common Muslims, but people were not surprised. They were aware of Hafiz Shukrullah Khan's nature.

Hafiz Shukrullah Khan lived in a village called Rohri, situated on the banks of the River Gomal which skirted the bottom of the Sulaiman Mountain Range, the *Koh-e Sulaiman*. He had heard from his elders that Rohri was the homeland of the ancestors of the benevolent and all-powerful Sultan, Sher Shah Suri. The Sultan's grandfather, Ibrahim Khan, had set out from Rohri with his young son, Hasan Khan, and had never returned. Ibrahim Khan had died in Narowal in the Punjab and Hasan Khan had died in Sassaram in Bihar.

Like everyone else, Hafiz Shukrullah Khan believed that since the grandfather and father had not come back to this now-forgotten village, there was no reason to think Sultan Sher Shah would do so. Having reconciled himself to this, Hafiz Shakarullah Khan resolved that if the mountain would not come to him he would go to the mountain. Thus, after consulting his family, Shukrullah Khan Gainda decided to go to the capital to see the Sultan and he began making preparations for the journey.

Shukrullah Khan had heard of the stability and prosperity lying beyond the Punjab and Multan in Sirhind, Bihar, Bengal, Malwa, and Khandesh. He had also been told about the intellectuals and philosophers found there. He had heard many stories about that distinguished son of Rohri, Sher Shah Suri, who had, in a very short time, constructed highways stretching for eight hundred miles, introduced land reforms, and brought peace to many troubled areas of Hindustan. Using his sword and his wisdom, Sher Shah had annihilated the mischief mongers and troublemakers and made this God-given land fit for mankind to live in.

Shukrullah Khan Gainda wanted to see all of this just once with his own eyes. He wanted to behold Sher Shah, the great Sultan, 'The Wielder of the Sword, The Just'. Therefore, in the name of God, he saddled up his horse, tied in a thick cloth those books which he couldn't bear to be parted from for long, and set off to meet Sher Shah.

Hafiz Shukrullah had learnt from his elders and had heard from those who had visited the royal court that when one presents oneself in front of a royal personage, one pays obeisance and offers gifts that are invaluable to both the giver and the receiver. After a great deal of thought, Hafiz decided on the gift he would take for His Exalted Majesty, the Sultan of Hindustan.

Shukrullah went to the mound in the village where, according to the elders, the Suris had had their hearth and home in the past. From here he took three fistfuls of earth and tied them up in a brocade cloth which a soldier had given him to make a satchel for his books.

With the earth tied up in the brocade cloth and his favourite books, Hafiz Shukrullah Khan set off, going first to his aunt's house in Hasan Abdal. After staying there for seven days, he travelled to Lahore with a group of *bafinda*s or cloth weavers. Lahore was a city of fun-loving, carefree people, but Shukrullah had a modest nature and was an introvert. For five days, he rested from the fatigue of the journey in the lodgings of the bafindas. He didn't venture out even once to see the laid-out gardens or the hustle and bustle of the city. On the sixth day, he set out again, this time in the company of gypsy grain traders, the banjaras. Travelling in a caravan of bullock carts and taking care not to tire his horse, he continued on towards the capital.

Hafiz Shukrullah had left Rohri with some money. In Hasan Abdal, his aunt, out of love for him, added a handful of silver to his pouch. On the way to Lahore, the bafindas with whom he was travelling refused to let him spend any money. They said it was an honour for them that such a venerable and learned gentleman was journeying with them. Therefore, Shukrullah Khan proceeded toward the capital with a substantial amount of money on him. The banjaras tried their best to deprive him of some of it along the road, but Hafiz Gainda didn't give them any opportunity to succeed. It wasn't his intellect and wisdom, which in any case didn't impress the banjaras very much, but his muscular body and sword that kept them in check. Nevertheless, he thought it best to part company with this caravan of gypsies.

Lahore was now left far behind, and the capital was still some distance away. The crowds were growing larger at the government-run *sarai*s, or inns. Although these inns were very cheap, Hafiz was not comfortable with crowds. As they drew closer to the capital the number of villages along the road was also increasing. There were mosques in these villages as well as private sarais and guesthouses. Hafiz Shukrullah knew that the caretakers of the mosques would gladly let him stay with them. But he decided that instead of sharing bread with the *pesh-imam*s and the *muezzin*s, it would be better if he spent some money and stayed in private guesthouses. After just a few stops he would reach the city. Then, if need be, he might even find himself a job since there are thousands of them in the capital. Thus, stopping and resting in private sarais and guesthouses along the way, Hafiz Shukrullah arrived at the capital.

He intended to stay in a sarai which was close to the city library. He had decided there was no point roaming around the city. All cities were the same anyway. Since he had only a few days here, why not spend them in the library. What better way to pass the time than by looking at books and copying whatever he wished!

He met with the manager of one such sarai and found out the cost of room and board. The rent was not too high, considering facilities offered, and the cost for food was also about as much as in any of the bigger sarais in the city. There was, however, a major problem. There was no private single room available. The manager suggested, 'If you want you can take one bed in a four-bed room.'

The Hafiz said, 'Oho! my brother! If I wanted to live in a crowd I might as well have stayed in the government-run sarai.' The manager looked at the pile of books and surmised that this intellectual from the region of Roh was either going to burn the oil, reading books, or engage in a *chilla*, a forty-day meditation; this was not the place for him. He gave Hafiz Shukrullah the address of a nearby sarai and said, 'You're a learned man. There you'll find a vacant room as well as people of your ilk.'

'People of your ilk,' the manager had said with a smile. At the time Hafiz Gainda didn't understand, nor did he dwell on it too much. Holding onto the reins of his horse, he walked along until he reached the sarai. He was quite happy with what he found. Here an entire room was vacant. The place was neat, clean, and inexpensive, and compared to other places there wasn't even much noise, almost none at all.

After tethering his horse in the stable and depositing his satchel of books, his brocade bundle, his weapon, and other luggage in his room, Hafiz Gainda took out his pen and paper, and headed towards the library. He was a tough, rugged mountain man. As far as eating was concerned, he had no need for formalities like people in the city. Since he planned to spend the whole day in the library, he had put several handfuls of roasted chickpeas in the pocket of his quilted coat before he settled down to read. Just after noon, Hafiz Shukrullah got up to perform his obligatory *zuhr* prayer. He offered the prayer in the small garden of the library under the shade of a green, leafy, fruit-laden tangerine tree. Then he ate a handful of chickpeas and drank some water.

A coffee-vendor came by and sat down in the sunshine on the stairs of the library. With his utensils tied to a coal burner which was hanging from a shoulder sling, he roamed the streets and bazaars selling Arabic coffee. Coming upon this pleasant spot, the vendor sat down to rest. His weary demeanour appealed to Shukrullah Khan. He had no great desire to drink coffee; nevertheless, he bought some and sat down on the stairs near the vendor and began to drink it. The coffee was good and it refreshed Hafiz Shukrullah so he purchased a few more of the small cups. He finished his coffee and was just getting up when he saw a young man come out of the library and walk towards him. The newcomer, who must have noticed the Hafiz sitting among the books, greeted him and said, 'O learned one! Sit by me for a while and drink a cup with my compliments.'

The newcomer had spoken fluently in Persian. Gainda smiled, 'Okay, one more cup!' and thanked him as he sat down. He took the coffee, told the newcomer his name and asked what his was. The young man was from Isfahan and he said that his name was Feroze. They indulged in some light conversation. Feroze was studying history and logic and had left home with the intention of becoming the student of a scholar from Jaunpur.

After drinking their coffee, the two climbed the stairs and again sat in the library.

Hafiz Shukrullah sat leaning against the huge window of the library and read till the sun went down. A short time before the evening call for prayers, he got up and left. Sitting in a corner on the far side, near a small pile of books with papers spread around, Feroze was busy taking notes.

Shukrullah Khan's first day had been a fulfilling one. After his meal at the sarai, before the late evening prayers, he went out to look around the bazaar. In the centre of the city, attached to the newly-constructed *madrasa* of the Afghanis, was a small mosque. The Hafiz offered his prayers there. Then, roaming around, losing his way and asking for directions here and there, he managed to return to the sarai. He was tired so he went to sleep at once.

God only knows how long Gainda had slept when, half-asleep and half-awake, he began to think that screaming, bellowing, man-eating demons-of-the-desert were chasing him. He tried to run and save himself but it was as if the earth was holding onto his legs. With all the strength of his body he tried to free himself but was unsuccessful. Raving like a horde of hunger-crazed camels, moaning and lamenting like creatures being tortured, the demons-of-the-desert came within a few steps of closing in behind him. Those man-eaters could reach out with their claws and touch him, and one of them even extended its sharp pointed talons and lacerated his back. Hafiz Shukrullah let out a muffled scream and woke up. He got up and sat on the bed.

'My Goodness! What kind of dream was that?' he thought. But it wasn't exactly a dream; there was some reality in it too! The room seemed to be filled with screams and shouts and voices of rage. The hair on his body stood on end. 'God help me! What kind of sounds are these? What demons have entered this room!' He stood up, raised the wick of the lamp, and then took his dagger out from under his pillow and tucked it in his belt. But there was no one else in the room; only this hair-raising noise all around, from above as well as from below.

Hafiz Gainda wrapped himself tightly in the quilt, picked up the lamp, and came out of the room with his sheathed sword. He thought that perhaps hooligans had raided the sarai. But this was a densely populated city, and no ordinary city but the capital. How could thugs and robbers dare to raid and terrorize neighbourhoods during the reign of Sher Shah? Criminals only have their way when a ruler is weak or corrupt and Sher Shah was neither weak nor corrupt.

Then Hafiz Shukrullah Khan thought that perhaps a fire had broken out in the sarai and people were running to save themselves. He came out into the veranda and looked, and even went towards the courtyard, but there was no smell of burning. From the veranda he saw that there was light in every room but the occupants were nowhere to be seen. There was a fire burning in the courtyard but no one was sitting there—no stablehand, servant, sentry, or fellow citizen, no resident or traveller. There was no sign of anyone for miles.

Then Hafiz Gainda noticed the light of torches on the roof. The sound of voices was also coming from there. He found the staircase to the roof and went up holding the lamp and his sword. There he beheld a strange sight.

The roof had been illuminated with many lamps, torches, *diya*s and *shama*s. It seemed almost as if it was daytime. Forty or fifty men and women were sitting in a circle emitting strange sounds of rage and anger. At times, it seemed as though they might get up and tear each other apart. But in spite of the rage and the fury no one moved from his place or attacked anyone. They were only intimidating the person in front of them with angry noises, glaring at them with wide-open eyes, and gnashing their teeth.

Hafiz Gainda set the lamp down, put his sword behind him and stared in amazement at all these people ranting and raving.

He recognized many of them. The owner of the sarai—who during the day would sit with his elbows leaning against a pillow, looking with half-closed eyes at all the guests coming and going—was present. The manager, who considered every guest his master, even his mentor, and who would prostrate himself in front of everyone, was sitting there as an equal. So was the chef, who spent his entire day cooking and tasting and who had grown quite fat with all his eating. Many other staff were also there, including the stablehand and the groom. Most surprisingly, even the guests staying at the sarai—who could be recognized as privileged by their clothes and their contented looks—were present. What was so amazing was that these guests, like everyone else, were sitting with their faces contorted, their teeth bared, and their eyes wide open, ranting and raving at the person in front of them.

'What kind of people have I stumbled on to?' thought Shukrullah Khan, 'Or is this a dream?'

But this was not a dream. All those people whom Hafiz Shukrullah had seen behaving very normally, standing, sitting, eating, and drinking, were here, and they were wild and seemingly scared out of their wits.

'Are they in the throes of some delusion? Are all of them experiencing some sort of madness simultaneously? Is a secret society having its meeting? Or is some satanic cult revelling in its macabre rituals?'

Hafiz Gainda was about to move away from there and return to his room when a man from the assembly stood up and, rubbing his face as if he had just woken up from sleep, came towards him. The Hafiz recognized him at once. It was the groom under whose care he had left his horse. After that, a woman, who from her features and the colour of her skin looked like she had come from some cold country, got up from the circle, rubbing her face the same way and walked towards the Hafiz. The groom and the woman each gently took one of his hands and pulled him towards the circle. Then the woman's eyes fell on his sword and she exclaimed, 'Goodness! Why have you brought a weapon? This is an assembly of rage. Of what use is a sword? Leave it here and come with us.'

Shukrullah Khan freed his hand from the woman's grasp forcibly. The groom was still gently holding his other hand but when the Hafiz managed to free one hand from the woman's clasp the groom took hold of both of his wrists and held them tightly, pulling him towards the gathering. 'Come! Come *Agha*. Don't delay any more. You're already late.'

'What kind of quandary have I gotten trapped in?' thought Hafiz Gainda. With an angry jerk, he freed his hands from the groom's, motioning to them to stay away. Then he picked up the lamp and quickly walked towards the stairs.

Everyone saw him forcibly freeing his hands and they expressed their displeasure by making a very dreadful sound.

Climbing down the stairs he felt as though forty or fifty savages would soon swoop down on him and tear him apart. Hafiz Gainda had never before seen such shocking fury, or such a ferocious expression of rage. Wrapped in the quilt and ready to face any violent situation, he descended the steps one by one. Who knows when he might need to put down the lamp and pull out his sword. But no one came down the stairs, and he thanked God that these demented people, the staff of the inn as well as the guests, stayed on the roof, frothing at the mouth with rage and emitting terrifying sounds within their assembly.

On reaching the courtyard, Hafiz heaved a sigh of relief. From the veranda he could see the small room belonging to the manager and the row of guest rooms. All the doors were open and all the rooms were empty. Hafiz Shukrullah walked slowly to his room and sat down on the bed, placing the lamp on its stand.

So this is what the supervisor of the first sarai had meant to say. He had said that the Hafiz would meet people of his own ilk. That dolt thought that I was a crazed maniac and so he sent me here. Shukrullah Khan Gainda became so angry that if it had been daytime he might have marched over to the first sarai, grabbed hold of the supervisor and given him such a thrashing with his horsewhip that the dolt would have remembered it all his life. But circumstances dictated that, for the time being, he gain control over his anger and analyse the situation.

'I'm not in the wilderness. I'm in a city, an overpopulated city in the heart of Sher Shah's kingdom, its capital. The Minister of Police and the Minister of Law are here. The night patrol passes through the streets. What reason is there for me to take any action? I'll just go register a complaint right now against these maniacs who disturb the sleep of humanity; my sleep has been spoilt but God's other creatures should be allowed to complete theirs peacefully.'

Hafiz Gainda began dressing to go out when the voices of anger and rage coming from the roof suddenly ceased. He opened the door and looked out. He saw the movement of shadows and lights in the courtyard and one or two guests passed by in the corridor.

A beautiful child holding his mother's hand came by. When the child smiled and looked at him, the woman also turned her eyes towards Hafiz Shukrullah and smiled.

Things had slowly begun to improve.

First the child smiled, then his mother smiled; then in a sing-song voice she greeted Hafiz Gainda, '*Salam-alaikum* learned one! How are you?'

He didn't know what he should say to this beautiful, smiling elegant woman. Softly he said, *'Behamdil-Lah,* by the grace of God, everything is fine.'

Holding onto her child's hand, smiling at him and lowering her big sparkling eyes, she walked past. A servant of the sarai, carrying some utensils, also went by the open door. Now he too was smiling. He greeted Hafiz Shukrullah with a nod of his head and went by. As soon as the servant left, the same middle-aged woman who had tried to stop Hafiz on the roof came into the corridor walking slowly with two smiling travellers. When she passed in front of his door she offered her salutations with great affection and affability and then she walked on, whispering a prayer.

'My God! What is this? All these people who are now smiling at me, greeting me, and offering their blessings were worse than enemies for me and for each other only a short while ago. They were glaring at each other with meanness and hatred, with extreme anger and rage, and they were roaring like bloodthirsty beasts. Look at them now, with affection and love, with grace and courtesy they're going towards their rooms hand in hand.'

While walking through the veranda, an overweight kitchen worker cleared his throat and came towards Hafiz Shukrullah with great respect saying, 'Your servant has prepared some fresh soup. If the master commands, I'll serve it. *Insha-Allah,* God willing, you'll like it.'

Hafiz Shukrullah looked at him coldly, 'Imagine. This fool is asking me if I want soup! These godforsaken souls wake me up in the middle of the night and now he wants to offer me soup, damn!' Hafiz got up from his bed and slammed the door right in the broad shiny face of the fat, comical cook.

The courtesy of this employee of the sarai caused Hafiz Shukrullah Khan Gainda's anger to fall flat like soapsuds in the sun. He changed his clothes and tried to sleep. And strangely enough, he did!

In the morning, the attitude of the staff and the manager was as good-mannered and businesslike as the day before. At daybreak they had informed him that hot water was ready so the Agha might take a bath. And the abundance of food and the hospitality with which almonds, sweets, coffee, etc., were served was also more than expected. There was continued goodwill among the guests and travellers. Who could imagine that in the middle of the night these people had been after each others' lives with their threatening looks and gestures?

Hafiz was late. Today, following the afternoon prayers, he was to present himself before the Master of Ceremonies, the Lord Chief Minister, Bermazaid Kor, to give him the petition requesting an audience with the King of Hindustan, His Majesty Sher Shah Suri, to pay his respects because he was not only one of the king's subjects but also an inhabitant of the king's paternal village, Rohri.

He had until the afternoon to sit in the library. With his bundle of papers and his pen, Hafiz Shukrullah set off in that direction.

As before, he went and sat by the window. He wanted to have the books of his choice retrieved and then lose himself in them, but today was not like the day before. The shouting and screaming of the previous night kept coming back to him. He remembered the terror and anguish that he had felt on the stairs when he was coming down from the roof.

Leaving his pen and paper behind, Hafiz Shukrullah went out into the garden for a walk. After being out in the fresh air he felt calmer and decided to go back inside. He saw Feroze, his acquaintance from the previous day, coming towards the library. Shukrullah Khan stopped to greet him. Feroze Isfahani asked, 'O learned one! You seem deep in thought today? Don't you feel like reading?' Hafiz said something evasive.

Feroze then said, 'You seem tired? Didn't you sleep well last night?'

Again, Hafiz was noncommittal, but when Feroze persisted, he thought about the worrisome incident of the night before and the fact that he had to stay a few more days in this city. He should ask Feroze the address of some reasonable sarai.

The Isfahani youth gave him the addresses of many sarais, with details about their costs and their facilities. None of these were suitable for Shukrullah Khan; some had rents that were too high, some were far away from the library, and others were situated right in the middle of noisy markets.

Feroze wanted to know what problem had occurred in the sarai where he was staying that made him so anxious to change to some other. Hafiz Shukrullah Khan had no alternative but to tell him the whole story.

Instead of being sympathetic after hearing the whole story, Feroze began to laugh. How strange! Feroze had experienced the very same thing on his first day in the city. He said, 'But learned one! The heavens were kind to me. Early in the evening I found out that it was a sarai belonging to the mardoozi so I took my baggage and left before nightfall.'

Hafiz Shukrullah Khan was not familiar with any group by the name of mardoozi. The truth was that he was hearing this name for the first time. When he asked, the Isfahani explained to him that, after centuries of distortion, urbane materialism had now manifested itself in the form of the mardoozi sect. 'I don't know who their Supreme Teacher is or where they're based. All I know is that people in power find this ideology very useful and enlightening in the pursuit of their goals so these beliefs and practices are flourishing in the capital. And in imitation of the privileged, those of lesser status and even servants have now begun to join the sect.'

Shukrullah Gainda wanted to know something about the basic teachings of this sect, so the Isfahani explained that. the mardoozi believe that man's nature consists of a combination of love, anger, faith, and hatred. But man's culture, education, and social obligations make it imperative that he not expose his anger and hatred and this, they believe, leads to destructive tendencies; the hatred seeps deep down into the mind and begins to fester there. Then it keeps on breeding inside. A man thinks that he has been purified of hatred and that his mind is without anger or abhorrence.

But the mardoozi say that this is not actually the case. Anger remains inside a man all his life, but is hidden. However, if at the end of each day he is given a chance to express it, and in the process get rid of it, then a day will eventually come when that man is able to purge himself completely of his hatred and anger. The mardoozi call this the state of 'completion'.

'That is why,' Feroze continued, 'to attain this "completion" every member of the mardoozi sect sits with his group at the end of each day and rids himself of all the hatred he has accumulated and all the anger he has nursed throughout the day. For the remainder of the night and the next day he becomes a civilized, loving, and complete human being.'

Feroze also told him in passing that Sher Shah's Minister of Court, Amir Bermazaid Kor, was a mardoozi.

'*Inna lil-Lahe wa inn a ilaihe rajeoon!*' Shukrullah exclaimed after hearing this long explanation. He found such detailed discourse tiresome. 'Indeed we are God's creatures and unto Him do we return! These cuckolds have managed, at last, to find a way to systematically waste valuable human assets like anger and hatred.'

Here the saga of Hafiz Shukrullah Khan's incomplete journey ends.

As we know, Hafiz Shukrullah Khan Gainda preferred to be brief in his speech.

He was a quiet, intellectual sort of person. This is why he shunned details and was frustrated by any waste of time.

He did not write an elegy on the futile waste of the anger that exists within a man. However, before returning home he addressed a few lines on a piece of paper to His Excellency, Minister of the Court, Bermazaid Kor, in a manner which cannot be duplicated here.

When it was time to leave he gave Feroze the piece of brocade cloth he had used to carry the earth from *Koh-e Sulaiman,* from Rohri.

Hafiz Shukrullah had opened the bundle and scattered that earth from the mound of the Suris over the bed of white flowers which stretched from the stairs of the library down to the walls of its courtyard like a foamy stream gushing by.

Early the next day, when Feroze was climbing the stairs to the library, he happened to glance at the bed of flowers and received such a jolt that it seemed like a physical blow had caused him to sit down on the stairs.

The flowerbed, which was awash with soft, white flowers the day before, was now glowing angrily with brightly burning red roses.

Translated by Aquila Ismail

Iqbal Majeed
(b. 1932)

Iqbal Majeed is from Moradabad, India. After receiving an M.A. in politics, he taught at the local college for several years before moving to All India Radio, Bhopal as producer of Urdu programmes. His new job restricted his literary output considerably. Nevertheless, Majeed is recognized as a leading writer of contemporary short fiction in Urdu. His work has been translated into several Indian languages and English. He also writes radio and stage plays. He has published two collections of short stories so far. Recently, he has brought out a novel, *Namak* (Salt).

The story presented here, *'Do Bhige Huey Log'* (Two Men, Slightly Wet), 1970, from the collection bearing the same name is a classic of modern Urdu fiction. A man who claims to be 'not different from others' is completely discombobulated to learn how different he actually is and that he is not even aware of this! As the story progresses a slow tension builds up, leading to an unexpected ending.

Two Men, Slightly Wet

The rain started quite suddenly. The fat drops came down with such force that they hurt. No one had thought it would rain. It wasn't the season and the weather hadn't been changing. When a big change occurs unexpectedly we are at first merely startled, then find our lives totally disturbed. In just a short time the rain turned everything topsy-turvy. People had come out without raincoats or umbrellas, now they scurried around seeking shelter.

I am not different from others. I too was momentarily stunned when the first raindrops hit me. But the next moment I decided to do what the others had done. I was walking down the road; I ran and took shelter under the first roof I could find. I was still trying to catch my breath after the sudden dash when another man came staggering in. We glanced at each other once, then continued with our efforts to compose ourselves. I wiped my face with my handkerchief, looked over my shirt and pants, then began to watch the road.

'Now who could have known it would rain!' the other man remarked, perhaps to get my response. But I was in no mood to start anything, I remained silent. Nothing got started.

I had thought that the shower, being unusual for the season, would peter out in a few minutes, but a glance at the sky killed that hope. I couldn't understand how so many clouds had gathered overhead without anyone noticing. By now it was really pouring. The dark clouds covered the entire sky. The road in front of me, crowded a moment ago, was filled instead with water. I was still reviewing these matters when I was startled to feel some cold drops fall on my shoulders. For the first time I noticed that it was a roof above our heads and not the sky.

I guess something similar happened to the other man. Simultaneously we glanced at each other again, then together our eyes turned upward.

Where we had taken shelter was a broken-down porch, jutting out in front of the main door of a rather old house. It was barely five feet square. The door behind us was bolted and locked. The termite-eaten beams of the old-fashioned roof sagged; they now glistened with the water that was seeping in. Slowly the moisture would accumulate into drops, which would fatten and, unable to hold their weight, fall like ripe mangoes. Suddenly the wind brutally turned in our direction and one water-laden gust left us drenched to our knees. I stepped back, furious. The other man seemed almost to jump. There was really no space in the back, but he struggled as if the wall itself would move back against his onslaught. The wind receded, but increasingly drops of water kept falling down on us from the beams and from the cracks in the ceiling. My companion had now started to twist and turn, as if trying to shrink into himself.

I glanced at the wide road. Once in a while some car would go splashing by, its windows rolled up. One or two men went by on bicycles, grim-faced, drenched to the skin, furiously pedalling away. I liked the attitude of those bicycle-riders, but the rest bored me. I looked toward my companion. He was dressed in a long shirt and payjamas; the shirt was wet at the shoulders. The drops from the ceiling had not left his back dry or his arms either. The payjamas, of course, had already been taken care of by that big gust a moment ago. Seeing the condition he was in, I surveyed my own clothes. It was obvious we were in the same mess. I could barely suppress my anger.

'Well, it doesn't look like it will stop,' I remarked, shifting my pose and looking at my companion as if I wished to be forgiven for my previous indifference.

'Yes, the clouds mean business.'

'And this place doesn't look very safe either,' I said, glancing at the ceiling.

He too looked up. Then our eyes met again, briefly. Frankly, I was feeling a bit peeved; I now wished to get away from that place. I could see a man or two making slow progress on the road. While I was struggling to decide, a few more drops fell on my head. I quickly shifted to another spot. But now the entire ceiling was leaking; the drops of water followed me whichever way I tried to shrink. The same thing was happening to the other man; he too was constantly moving from one spot to another. Finally, in exasperation, I turned to him.

'Come, let's get out of here.'

He looked at me and quietly smiled, but then merely shrank into another corner. Perhaps my remark struck him as too silly to deserve any attention.

But I was enraged. It was suffocating under the porch. The drops dripping from the beams pierced through my clothes. The unpaved floor was now all mud, and in a few depressions water had formed puddles. I looked at my companion with some intensity, but his face showed no sign of boredom or anxiety. I kept looking at him, expecting him to change his mind any moment, but I was disappointed. He stubbornly remained where he was, as he was. I could no longer control myself; this time I addressed him irately.

'You think you can save yourself from getting drenched by standing here?'

'Seems rather doubtful,' he replied without enthusiasm.

'Do you think this rain will stop in the next ten minutes?'

'It doesn't look like it,' he replied, stressing every word.

'Then why put up with this misery?' I said with some heat. 'If we must get drenched, why here, so abjectly?'

'Let's wait a bit more, it may stop,' he said, shifting his position, and began to wipe his face with the hem of his shirt, now clinging to his body like a second skin.

I drew in a deep breath, then exhaled, to relieve some of that suffocating feeling, then turned to watch the road. No change had occurred in the rain; it still came down in torrents. In anguish I looked to the left and to the right once again. No other shelter was close enough. There was a gas station, but quite far away, and beyond that the compound wall of a house. I knew that house. A lady doctor lived there, and its gate had a big sign, 'Beware of Dog'. I was still stretching my neck, trying to peer through the sheets of rain, when a dog came panting onto the porch, and flapped its ears. It was immediately shooed off by both of us.

'Look, it's silly to stand here like this,' I addressed my companion once again.

'What should we do then?' he asked.

'Let's get out of here.'

'But the rain is pretty bad.'

'So what?' I said, flaring up. 'We are already dripping from head to toe. Don't tell me you still think you're protected by this roof?'

'But...still...,' he stopped short.

'Well, I won't stay here a minute longer. I'm leaving.'

'As you wish.' He tried to shrink further into himself.

I was secretly burnt up by his reply. I had thought there was much in common between him and me. Going out of the house. Getting suddenly caught in the rain. Taking shelter under a roof that was veined with cracks. Getting drenched in that miserable manner. With so much in common, I had expected our thoughts would also be the same. But I could make no sense of the stupid way he was behaving.

Pushing out my chest I lifted one foot off the ground and began to roll up the leg of my wet pants. I was perturbed. I was angry. The discovery that my assumptions had been wrong had left me with a bitter feeling. There was so much difference in the way we thought! Our paths were far apart! Even our notions of gain and loss didn't coincide. He wanted to get wet little by little, standing under a leaky roof. His entire body would get drenched; the roof would not give him respite. It would continue to rain drops on him. And the drops would fall on his hair, roll down the back of his neck, down his back, to the tip of his spine. No doubt the process was slow, it needed time, but he was not such a fool as not to know what the result would be. Then why was he clinging to this porch? Perhaps he had persuaded himself to be satisfied with what he had managed to get at his very first attempt?

Lazy!

Stupid!

Coward! Dead!

I spat on the ground and, pushing back my shoulders, swaggered out into the torrent. I didn't look back once. Gusts of wind and sheets of rain welcomed me.

Struggle! Explore! Search! That is life.

I belong to the new generation. I think differently. That roof was leaking and he was getting more and more wet. To stand in wet clothes, exposed to the wind, was very dangerous. He could catch cold. Sorry, but each of us would rather die his own way. We make our own selections. Not everyone wants to die of cancer, just as not everyone prefers to jump under a train. But if that man was to catch cold and die of double pneumonia, just imagine what the gossips would say:

Fool! Stood under a leaky roof all day long, hoping that the rain would stop!

Such is the end of all wretched, useless people. It all depends on the way we think, the way we look at life. We all die. And how we die, that is also insignificant. Good, we can have a good talk on this subject. It is a good topic. I will go to the coffee house and stand there under a fan. My shirt and pants are made of Terylene, they will dry in a few minutes. Then I will ask my companions there, what they would like to die for. How they die, that is their business. I only want to know the goal for which they can accept death. To catch pneumonia under a leaky roof and die, is that a great goal? I know they will listen to me. They will say, 'In you speaks the new awareness of the Sixties.' I shall answer, 'You are right, that is the big difference, the way we think.' And then I will tell them more. That there is still a man standing on that porch; he doesn't want to get wet under the heavens, nevertheless he is getting drenched.

He has not come with me. But I did choose to walk and get drenched under the wide sky. The clouds burst over me, but my body withstood their onslaught. It is only now that I have reached the comfortable seat and the solid roof of the coffee house. I have explored and asserted. Suffered the buffets of rain in this pursuit. I was not scorned by the rain; I felt attached to it.

Attached!... They will sit up at this word.

That the attacking gusts of wind and water aroused in me amazement, inspired me to seek.

Amazement!... To seek!

And after my companions carefully take hold of these words I will tell them that there was this very strong belief within me that attaching myself to that rain and moving with it I would definitely reach a new and better state.

Belief!... They will quickly take possession of that word too. Afterwards, completely forgetting that man caught in the rain, they will bring out slowly, like misers, the four words they had grabbed from me.

Attachment, curiosity and wonder, and belief.

Then their eyelids will droop and shift, like a parrot's, and in soft tones they will inform me that in the Rigvedic age, man in fact had these four great things:

Attachment, wonder and curiosity, and belief.

We have none, and that is the problem. None of us can write a Veda, any Veda...But what was it that I was saying about that man caught in the rain?

But the rain...

Suddenly I realized the rain had stopped. My thoughts began to sag. I looked up at the sky; the clouds were fleeing. The coffee house was still pretty far away. Without my willing it so my feet were making rapid but bumpy progress on the long rain-washed road. My pants and shirt clung to my body; the lines of the undershirt could clearly be seen. I recalled there was still one cigarette in the packet of Char Minar in my pocket. I took the packet out and glanced around. A bit ahead there was a roadside tea shop; its stove seemed full of glowing coals, fanned by the wind. The wind was quite chilly.

Stopping outside, by the blazing stove, I took out the cigarette. It was wet through. Putting it to my lips, I first shook off some of the water from my clothes, then borrowing a match from the vendor, lit the cigarette. But I could get only a couple of puffs. It sort of dissolved into pieces; only a whole lot of tobacco crumbs were left sticking to my lips. Spitting them out furiously I asked the vendor for a cup of tea, and moved closer to the coals to dry myself. The road was again full of passers-by.

'So now you're drying your clothes here!' someone said by my side.

I looked up. That same stranger was going into the tea shop, his face wide with laughter.

'Come, have a cup of tea,' he called to me after he sat down at a table. I went over and sat down beside him. The wind was still gusty. My clothes felt a bit drier.

'You were in too much of a hurry, for the rain stopped only ten minutes after you left,' he remarked while squeezing water out of the hem of his shirt.

I looked at him without much enthusiasm and mumbled, 'And if it hadn't stopped?'

'Then there was no choice.'

I felt sorry at his answer. To misuse precious words is as saddening as using a bullet to kill a tiny bird.

'You are a common man,' I retorted.

'Oh? And how is that?'

'The same as all the other common people.'

He wasn't a bit put off by my remark; he merely laughed. When the tea arrived he began to stir his cup with gusto.

'I would like to tell you in all seriousness that you, and all people like you, are a handicap to themselves.'

Instead of appearing hurt at my remark, he gave a short laugh and looking straight into my eyes, said, 'I guess you're angry because I didn't keep you company.'

'Don't be silly,' I said heatedly. 'Who needed your company? I wasn't Napoleon going off to some battle and in need of followers. I had merely made a simple observation.'

'What observation?'

'That if you were already getting wet why not move on in the rain. I ask you now, did you succeed in staying dry?'

Instead of a reply he intently looked for a moment at my shirt and then asked with a smile, 'This fabric is called polyester, isn't it?'

'Yes. But it can also get wet.' I tried to be sarcastic.

'Your pants are of the same fabric perhaps?' He scrutinized my pants.

'Yes.'

'There isn't any pocket in your shirt, is there?'

'No, there isn't.'

He remained silent for a while and finished the tea, then said, 'I know I have no right to ask you this, but if it is all right with you tell me if you have anything else on you?'

'What do you mean?'

'I mean do you have anything in your pant's pockets?'

'I have got some change.'

'Any paper money?'

'No.'

'Any picture...that you wish to carry with you?'

'No.'

'Any letter or document that you consider precious and want to protect?'

'No.'

'Any medicine? I mean pills or capsules that you may be carrying to give to someone seriously ill and waiting for them?'

'No, I have nothing of that sort on me.'

'Perhaps some talisman on which you rely and which is expected to bring you success so long as you carry it on you?'

'Now what sort of nonsense is that?'

'That means you don't carry a talisman?'

'No, I do not.'

'That means you have on at this time only pants, a shirt, a pair of shoes, and some change?'

'That's right.'

'And your shirt will dry sooner than mine?'

'True.'

'Likewise your pants will dry quicker than mine?'
'Indeed.'
'Well, there it is.'
He began to smile.
'What?' I asked, incensed.

'You have nothing else on you but your clothes, your shoes, and some change, but I do. The things that you have, it won't matter at all if they got wet—but even if my clothes and shoes get soaked I want to protect that one thing.'

'What thing?' I shouted.

'The thing that I have and you don't.'

'Well, what is it?' I was quite angry now. 'Stop trying to trap me like some smarty lawyer. Nothing is that important in the world. You are only talking rubbish.'

He didn't reply immediately. Leisurely he counted out the money to the vendor; after we had both come out of the shop, he patted me on the shoulder and said, 'When you have something in your pocket that you may badly want to protect you too will prefer to get soaked under a roof rather than outside. At that time that will be your handicap.' Then he walked away.

My polyester clothes were now completely dry.

Translated by C.M. Naim

Jeelani Bano

(b. 1936)

Jeelani Bano, daughter of the poet Hasrat Badayuni, lives in Hyderabad (India) and represents the generation of short story writers who came to the fore after the Progressives had declined and were therefore free from the ideological compulsions that dominated Urdu literature in the 1930s and '40s. She is married to Anwar Moazzam, a poet and scholar of Islamic studies.

Jeelani Bano has published several collections of short stories, novellas, and radio plays. She writes about the struggle of the transition from the glamorous feudal society in the erstwhile princely state of Hyderabad to the present state of stressful progress and uncertain values. She won the prestigious Sahitya Akademi award for her novel *Aiwan-e Ghazal* (Gallery of Ghazals), 1977, which is again an exploration of the flow of past culture of Hyderabad into the present.

The story here, translated as 'Some Other Man's Home' (*Paraya Ghar*), is from a collection by the same name.

Some Other Man's Home

All the houses look terribly alike—I'm afraid I might end up in some other man's home. That fear kept haunting me as they took me away from the hospital.

The doctors at the hospital had said I had been badly hurt in an accident—they must have lied—otherwise I should hurt somewhere—they seemed to look at me with suspicion—they kept watching me as if any moment I'd jump out of my bed and run away.

And then it happened—what I was afraid of.

God knows what strange house they have brought me to!

No sooner had they forced me down on a bed than some woman began shrieking, 'Ooooh! How terrible! He can't be my Hamid. Nothing could've happened to him.'

Then some child asked, 'Who's that, mummy? Who's that all coiled up in daddy's bed?'

Now there couldn't be any doubt: I had been brought to the wrong house—that's what I was afraid of all along.

What's going to happen next? What if the man of the house comes back and finds me here?—run...run...

But there were people around me, holding me down. 'Calm down, bhabi, calm down,' I heard someone say in the next room. 'He'll get crazier if you don't. Try to make him happy. Get him to like it here.'

Make me happy?—Like it here?—what imbecile won't take care of his family himself but force another person to sleep in his bed?—I must've fallen among robbers—they want to rob me—where are my keys?

What fool's house is it, anyway? There's hardly any light in this room...

Why hasn't the sun come out today? I hope they didn't lock it up too—perhaps it's night now—how did that happen?—but if it's night there should be stars and the moon—'Uncle Moon, so far away; Uncle Moon so far away'—who's there?—come in, come in—is it Mr Sun?—yes, the sun ought to be up now—but suppose one morning it doesn't come up, what would I do then?

I won't be able to shave—nor would I be able to drink my tea—how can anyone shave in a dark room? I might cut my neck—that fool doctor at the hospital had said, 'Don't ever try to shave yourself!'—why did he say that?—did he think I had lost my hands in that accident?

How would I get my shaving things now?—I seem to have lost my keys—all my things are gone—I've been robbed—there must be robbers living in this house—how they stare at me!—their eyes bulge—they whisper to each other all the time—then there's that boy Fazlu, who brings me my meals—every time he sees me he grins like an idiot—the fool.

Perhaps they've all gone mad due to some accident—perhaps they were going somewhere in their car and suddenly...

God, how my head hurts!—did someone hit me with a rock?—I must retaliate—I must hit back with a bigger rock—I should give someone a good thrashing...

But I just don't feel like getting out of this warm, soft bed right now—also, I'm scared of the man who keeps peeking at me through the transom—he gives me such mean looks—he seems to gloat over my troubles...

'Go away! Get away from me! Leave me alone!'

My shouts brought Nimmo waddling to my bedside—she's a plump woman...

I'm not sure how I happen to know her name—she pretends I'm her husband—that's a good one, isn't it?—I'm sure I've never seen an uglier face, or a more hateful woman—I flatly told her I won't touch her, not even with my slippers—but she keeps coming back, again and again—she tells me to shut up and lie quietly—it makes me wonder: was she the wife of some poor beggar like me in her previous birth...

Nimmo came into the room and asked, 'Whom are you shouting at?'

'That fellow up there, why does he keep staring at me?' I pointed at the man in the transom.

'God have mercy!' Nimmo shouted, striking her forehead with her open hand. 'That's no man—that's you. Don't you even remember yourself?'

Now how can that be true?—how can that man be me?—and if he is indeed me then who am I?—which of us is the real me?—this is just terrible—it could get pretty sticky for me if these strange people found out that the real me was someone else—I had better find some hiding place for myself—where's my blanket?—now I won't respond, no matter how hard someone calls...

'He isn't insane,' someone speaks angrily in the next room. 'Why don't you folks get him some medical treatment? Doesn't anyone want him to get well—to give all of you a hard time again?'

'...so much property...big savings account...seven hundred rupees per month in pension...'

That must be Nimmo's husband—probably he's gone mad—or are they conspiring against me?—they want me to go mad?—did they cut me into two...put one part in the transom?—they must have kidnapped me from the hospital...

Who's here now?—who's pulling at my blanket?—I'm not here—I'm over there, in the transom...

It's Nimmo again—with a plate of grapes in her hand—who are these other people with her?—perhaps she's brought them to watch the show...

With great affection she puts a grape in my mouth—and says, 'Come on, Hamid, be nice. See, your aunt's here, also Nishat and Akhtar. Or have you forgotten them too?'

'How're you feeling now?' a man asks, sitting down on the bed.

'Aha! I begin to see now,' I say to the man—I've recognized who he is—'You're that man in the hospital—you must've come to give me a shot'—I quickly grab a vase to defend myself—'Get out of here—or I'll let you have it in the mouth.'

Nimmo starts to cry, but I give her a kick—I say to her, 'Stop acting! You think I'm some pet monkey to show to your friends. If you aren't careful in future I might make you dance for them.'

It looks like I'll have to get away from this place—now that would be something—one day they'll come into the room and find I'm gone—then they will have something to cry over...

But this other me, he's really spoiled everything—he has his eyes fixed on me all the time—now why did that happen?

Why did I break into two?—what can one-half of me do?...

One day Nimmo sent two children into my room—a boy, Pappu, ten or eleven—very suspicious—very much on his guard—he seemed to think I had a rock in my hand—and a very pretty little girl—like the doll that goes chun-chun when you turn the key in its back.

'Come here, Chun-Chun,' but she ran up to the bed before I could finish—Pappu tried to stop her, but she threw her arms around my neck—her lovely hair spread on my chest...

'Daddy, daddy,' she said, 'how did you hurt your head? Pappu's scared of you, daddy. You're not going to spank us, are you?' Then she cupped my face in her hands and whispered, 'Get me a little airplane, daddy, then both of us will fly away.'

'Yes, we'll fly away, very far away. Grrr, grrr, zoom, zoom.'

Suddenly the two of us were flying around in a small airplane.

'Ta-ta,' Chun-Chun waved to those contemptible people below us. 'Ta-ta, ta-ta,' I shouted too.

'Stop, stop! What do you think you're doing?'—those curs have got hold of me again—'Don't be so wild. You're not well'—Nimmo grabs from the back—'Get down, Munni. You can't ride on daddy's shoulders anymore. He's not feeling well, you know.'

'Let go of us'—I try to free myself—'We're flying to Delhi. We're going way far away. Ta-ta, ta-ta...'

But Chun-Chun had to get down—I too was forced back on the bed—then Nimmo came and sat down near me.

'Thank God,' she said, her voice all cream and honey—'Thank God, you still remember your children'—then she touched my face and snuggled closer—'I swear to you I was so scared you might have forgotten your children too. I don't know what we'd have done then.'

'Why? What's the problem?' I push her away from me.

'Why! You think I'd go out and get a job at my age. Thanks to your pension we still somehow manage, but only barely. What else do we have now? Just a little bit of property. I tell you, I envy Imtiaz's mother. She lived in luxury till the day she died. Why did you then marry me? Where would I go now with these small children?'

Nimmo must be crazy—one moment she's crying, the next she begins to giggle—so unpredictable.

Suddenly she puts a piece of paper before me. 'Here, sign it'—she coyly says.

What's this now?—something to make me her slave for life? What if it made my split permanent?—one part peeking through the transom—the other lying here snared by these thugs...

'What are you looking around for? Hurry up and sign the paper.' Nimmo must be standing on hot coals—she is so agitated—I closely look at the paper—1000—1000—numbers come into focus, then disappear...

'Aha! So that's what it's all about—money!'—I quickly sign the paper.

'Mummy, what would you've done if daddy had forgotten how to sign his name?' That's Pappu—next to Pappu, Fazlu—behind Fazlu, Shimmi—then some other Ummi—Pummi—they form a circle around me...

'Just think, all the money would've been lost if the sahib had forgotten how to write!' That's Fazlu—he has teeth like the seeds of a rotten melon...

'Shut up!' I pounce upon him. 'Who the hell are you to talk of money? And why the devil must you flash your teeth every time you see me? Am I a clown? Are there horns sprouting from my head?' They burst into laughter...

A suspicion crosses my mind: has my appearance changed in some way?—do they know I'm split in half?—that one half of me sits in the transom?—perhaps that's why they keep staring at me—what's more amazing, the I in the transom also stares at me like them...

Perhaps I shouldn't act so wild—the other day I chased a fly all over the house—so many light bulbs got smashed—the glass cabinet was knocked over—Nimmo said everyone was watching my show—you might have thought all the movie houses had closed—that all the people looking for entertainment had come into this house—there were so many of them.

Some of them even put on their own shows—a matinee was going on in the dining room—that cute girl, Shimmi, was the heroine—a tall, dark man was the hero—quite a romantic show it was—plagiarists!—I've seen such cooing couples in every Hindi movie—they seemed ready to burst into a song—'You're my moon, I'm your moonlight'—God! I'd have gone crazy if they had—'Cut, cut!' I shouted—they were so frightened they actually stopped—the hero leaped out the door and ran away—the heroine threw herself at my feet—'Daddy, please forgive me'—now she was shedding false tears...

I pulled her away—the way the father does in that movie—'And you forgive me too, for I can't play in your trashy movie.'

Just then Chun-Chun came into the room—the lap of her frock was filled with paper cuttings—'Quick, daddy, I've brought you lots of money'—she dropped the strips of paper in my lap—they turned into currency notes—then she started picking them one by one—'With this note we'll buy a big cake, with this, an airplane—with this, some cigarettes for daddy and with this we'll buy a daddy...'

'You're silly!' That was Pappu again. 'You don't buy daddies with money.'

'You can too. Didn't you buy us all with money, daddy?'

'Of course, I did. I bought all of you with money. You're all my slaves. Here now—line up all of you!'

I gave the order, but no one listened.

'Pappu's stupid,' said Chun-Chun. 'Mummy says if one has money one can buy anything.'

That gives me an idea—perhaps I should try to buy back that other I. I grab all the money and push her away. 'Get Out! This is my money.'

'No, it's mine,' Chun-Chun begins to whimper. 'Daddy's taken all my money. I want my money back.'

Nimmo comes into the room.

'What'll you do with those scraps? Let Munni have them.'

'I'll buy my other I with it. You want me to remain split in half for ever?'

'God have mercy!' Nimmo's frightened by my scolding. 'Go on, children, go and play outside. Your daddy's about to have another of his fits.'

She locks me inside the room and goes away...

I'd also like to kill all my enemies, but I don't have my gun—it was borrowed by the man who killed Kennedy—he hasn't brought it back—would I otherwise let so many wild and useless people run around freely?—particularly Nimmo and Fazlu, and that Imtiaz?—the three ought to be shot—you'd see how brightly the sun shines that day—how people laugh...

'Bang...bang...bang!' I make my fingers into a gun and begin to shoot—those who come within my range fall—right and left—Nimmo—Fazlu—that pig-faced doctor who sent me by force to another man's house—the clerk in the pension office who smirks every month when he sees me—they're all dead—now we can have some fun—eat and...

How hungry I am today!—I haven't eaten anything for the last twelve months—I'll have some kababs today—hot and spicy—and if I don't get to—that day he's so concerned about 'what people might say'...

People—people!—who are the people the residents of this house are so afraid of?—if I ever find out I'll give them all the dirt—that other day when Nimmo had gone out, Imtiaz opened the safe with a key of his own and took out some jewellery—that any day now Shimmi will run away with that swarthy fellow—she too has plans to open the safe—every day I hide behind this curtain and watch what goes on—one day Pappu was picking pieces of meat out of the dish on the table and gobbling them down when I surprised him—later they were all muttering: 'How did he get in there?' 'How long was he hiding there?'...

And that Fazlu—what a rascal he is!—he brings me my meals, then sits down and gobbles them himself—one day, after he leaves the room, I put my ear to the door and listen—he tells Nimmo that he had fed the sahib...

'No, no. I haven't eaten anything. I'm starving. Give me some food.' I run into the room and shout at them.

'God Almighty! What does he want now?' Nimmo says to Shimmi. 'Just now Fazlu fed him and now again he's hungry!'

'You might get sick from eating too much,' Shimmi tells me, pushing me towards my room.

'No. I'm starving. I haven't eaten anything. You can ask Fazlu.'

Instead of an answer, Fazlu looks at Nimmo and starts laughing.

'But why did you have to come here? You'll only make a mess on the table. Go to your room. I'll send you something to eat.' Nimmo pushes me into the room and bolts the door from outside.

'Don't push my daddy—don't hit him,' Chun-Chun shrieks outside the door—she is crying.

'Shut up! Be quiet! Daddy's darling!' Nimmo starts spanking her.

'Open the door.' I beat my head against it. 'Open the door.'

It is opened.

Have they killed her?—wiping the blood from my face I look for Chun-Chun—she's standing in a corner scared to death—we run into each other's arms...

Nimmo has thought up another trick to keep me confined to this room—she brings all sorts of people to talk to me—to keep me happy, she says.

Two days back she brought a crazy man to see me—he had a false beard which flapped in the air—he kept grabbing at it as if he were scared of being exposed—the moment he saw me he clasped me to his breast—as if we were old buddies.

'Well pal, how are you?' he asked heartily. 'Feeling better now?'

'You tell me, how're things with you? Care to sell this beard of yours?'

He jumped back, but I grabbed his hand and pulled him down beside me—no harm in having some fun with a loony.

He pulled himself free and moved away to sit on a stool.

'I thought of coming to see you several times, but I was afraid you might not even recognize me,' he said, smoothing his beard.

'That's true,' I reply, 'You have changed a bit since you went crazy.'

I don't know why he started to laugh—they say mad people always consider others to be mad—perhaps the old rascal thinks I've gone crazy?

'You know, pal,' he says after a few moments, 'you know, I do feel bad about you being sick. But what can we do? It's as God sees fit.'

'And I just adore this beard of yours. Won't you let me have it for just one day? Chun-Chun and I want to play cops—and—robbers.'

At that he jumps up and starts for the door—then stops and remarks somewhat pompously: 'Talk some sense. I understand your wife didn't even bother to get you treated. Anyway, did you hand over all your pension to these people or did you save a little for yourself?'

Again that damn word!—it seems I'm only the name of a pension—no one sees me as a human being—they see only an amount of cash—none of them talks of anything else—I wish I could peel this pension off my face and throw it away—but in that case, would I even be visible to anyone in this house?

I don't remember how or when I got rid of that nut—I heard Fazlu say that when I tried to pull at that guy's beard he was scared out of his wits and ran away—what else could I've done—how else do you treat a loony?

Another such character came into the room the other day—he too acted as if we were old buddies—started telling me of all our good times together—all lies—then on the sly slipped into his pocket my expensive Parker—he smoked all my cigarettes too—then, as he was leaving, he made a great show of telling me how he had been looking after Nimmo—trying to cheer her up so she won't be heartbroken by my illness—finally he proudly declared that it was he who had brought me here from the hospital—when I heard that I couldn't restrain myself any longer.

'So it's you who threw me into this hellhole! But why? What did you gain from torturing me so?'

'Nothing yet,' he replied with a smirk, 'but I will, soon enough.'

'I'm calling the police. I'll expose you.' I twirled the dial of the telephone. 'Hello, hello.'

'Give me my telephone.' Chun-Chun came and pulled it out of my grasp—it is her telephone—'Here, let me do it,' she said, 'Whom were you calling?'

'The police. Get them to come quickly or else the criminals will get away.'

'Hello.' Chun-Chun put the receiver to her ear and sat down on the floor—she had a serious look on her face—'Come quickly. They're bothering my daddy. They're not giving him food.'

After a while both of us got tired of that game.

'That's it. Now let's go and catch the thief.' And we earnestly set out in pursuit.

'Sssh! Don't make any noise,' Chun-Chun said, putting a finger to her lips.

We crawled on our knees from room to room—suddenly my head struck the foot of a bed—someone jumped down—'Thief, thief,' I started shouting, and grabbed his leg—'Hurry, bring my pistol. I've got him.'

'We caught the thief! We caught the thief!' Chun-Chun began to clap and shout.

'Let him go, please let him go. The children might come. Please don't shout so.' That was Nimmo.

I looked more carefully—how amazing—the thief was the man who a moment ago had been talking to me!—by now the whole house had gathered there—Shimmi—Pappu—Imtiaz—Fazlu—they looked flabbergasted—first they looked at me, then at the man—then they walked out of the room without saying a word—what cowards! They don't even have the guts to tell off the thief.

That night I could hear Nimmo muttering in her room: 'No, he isn't mad. He's just shamming. He pretends to be careless about himself, but he never stops watching me...'

One day an amazing thing happens.

What do I see but that the night has ended—the people are up and around—there is light in the room—but I don't see any sun—did the thief steal the sun?—my anxiety grows—then Chun-Chun comes in with her telephone—I immediately tell her the terrible news: 'Someone stole the sun last night.'

'What! Where did it go?' Chun-Chun is horrified—in this house none is smarter.

'Who knows! Didn't you notice how dark it was? Now I'm lost. Without a sun how can there be a day? When can I now get out of bed?' I start crying.

When she sees my tears Chun-Chun throws down her toys and rushes to cling to me—she spreads her golden hair on my chest.

'I'll buy you a sun this big,' she says, spreading wide her arms—then she opens her hand, 'See, I've two paisas.'

'Silly! No one can buy the sun.' I laugh at her foolishness.

'Then how did it come to you?' she asks, with wide open eyes.

Well!—now we had another problem on our hands—how did the sun come to me in the first place?—and why did it come?—did the sun also know about my pension?—did it hear about that other I too?

'Who's he?' I ask Chun-Chun, pointing with my finger.

'That?' For a long time she stands there looking at the other I—her neck stretched upward—then she says, 'That's daddy.'

'Whose daddy?' I'm glad—he turns out to be someone else.

'My daddy,' she says, putting her palms on her chest for emphasis—then she adds, 'That's you.'

Me?—a shiver goes up my spine—even these children know that I've been cut into two!

Do you know who hung me up there, Chun-Chun?' I ask her furtively—first making sure no one was listening.

'Mummy did,' she likewise whispers into my ear. 'One day she put you behind the glass, tied a cord, and hung you up there.'

She put me behind the glass?—tied a cord?—in other words, I've been executed!—hanged till dead—I'm no longer alive—I have nothing to do with this world now—why am I then lying in this bed?

I get up and quietly stand against the wall, but just then Nimmo barges into the room—she's been cross with me ever since I caught the thief—however, now her voice is soft as butter—first she tries to pull me away from the wall—then, when she fails in her efforts, she flops down on the floor near me.

Even so she starts acting very important—she refers to my pension as her pension—to her children as 'my children'—she says she needs thirty thousand rupees—she wants to sell the house and also take out all the money in the bank—so that Shimmi can be married off—so that Imtiaz can be given his share and then kicked out for good.

I listen—like some real-life, hapless husband—these talks of pensions and bank accounts bore me to tears—but after a while I couldn't take it any more—I start scolding her—'Be quiet! I won't listen to you any more. You've killed me. You put a cord round my neck and strangled me. I'm dead.'

She falls at my feet. 'Please forgive me, Hamid. Please forget what happened that night. I'll never deceive you again.'

'Ha! Why should I forgive you?' I kick her away. 'You stole my sun. It was never so dark before.' I kick her again. 'And you took away my pistol. Now I can't shoot the thieves. Do you know how many thieves are lurking in this house? What kind of a place is this anyway? Some film studio where people constantly act out romantic scenes? No, I refuse to take part in your stupid plays.'

Just then I happen to look up. 'Who put that noose around my neck? You cut me up and hanged me. Now I can't even show my face anywhere.'

Nimmo begins to shriek—I keep hitting her with anything I can get hold of—some people rush into the room—they try to stop me—I hit them too and they run away—I chase them—today I'll kill the whole lot—I'll shoot them all.

'Come! Come everyone! See what this man is doing!' Nimmo is shouting to the neighbours. 'Today I'll have all the property transferred to my name!'

'Go ahead and try.' Imtiaz enters the room. 'I'll take daddy with me.'

'You think so? You'd better not even come near him.' Nimmo shrieks at him, waving her hands. 'Some lover of his daddy! I know why you want to take him with you. So you can swallow all by yourself the seven hundred of his pension. You'd better not even try it. He's all the support left for my little ones.'

The two are fighting so loudly it's impossible to understand them—

I drop the rock in my hand and start to think—will Imtiaz really take me away from this crazy place?

That other I shouldn't get a whiff of it, I tell myself—I want to give him the slip—now it should be his turn to tackle this bloodthirsty bunch.

'Come Chun-Chun, let's get out of here.' I pick her up in my arms—she seems scared by the fight raging around her.

'Where are we going?' She drops her doll and its tiny bathtub—she makes herself comfortable against my shoulder.

'We're going far away...very far away...where the sun is.'

I open the gate of the house and step out on the street—the people inside keep fighting—they don't even try to stop us—perhaps they weren't fighting—perhaps they were mourning someone's death—the sun's death, perhaps, or my pension's...

'Daddy, daddy,' Chun-Chun is saying, 'Imtiaz Bhai was hitting mummy. He wants your pension.'

So my pension is not done with yet?—what should I do now?—I'm scared—Imtiaz might start hitting me too.

'Daddy, you must throw away your pension,' Chun-Chun advises me. 'Throw it into the river. Then no one will fight.' Then she starts clapping her hands. 'Look daddy, we found the sun! There it is, trying to hide in the river. Let's hurry and catch it.'

It's indeed the sun—so it wasn't stolen after all!—it only tried to hide away from us in the river.

'Run faster, daddy. Mummy is coming behind us. She's coming to catch you.' From her perch on my shoulders, Chun-Chun keeps me informed.

What should I do now?—I begin to run faster—but I see no place to hide—there is nothing but water in front of us—where can we hide from Nimmo?—'Come Chun-Chun, let's hide in the water. Let's see how they catch us then...'

Translated by C.M. Naim

Enver Sajjad
(b. 1934)

Enver Sajjad is from Lahore where he practises medicine. But, more importantly, he is a fiction writer, painter, writer of radio and television plays, and an actor. He is also active in politics. His first anthology, *Istiarey* (Metaphors), published in 1964, established him as a leading exponent of the *tajridi* (abstract) and *'alamati* (symbolist) short story. Sajjad self-consciously strives to narrate experience in the most excruciating detail which imparts it a relentless directness. His prose has a visual art-like texture. His subject is mostly protest against all kinds of oppression and tyranny but his stories cannot be classified as social documents because he assiduously maintains the creative distance between writer and subject and keeps the experience at an abstract level. Many of his stories use animal metaphors; well known among them are '*Parinda*' (The Bird) and '*Gae*' (The Cow).

The present story belongs to the same genre as those mentioned above but its symbolism is more complex because the event narrated is something that a female scorpion is known for, yet her action becomes poignant because she is carrying five babies on her back.

Scorpion, Cave, Pattern

If a scorpion is trapped in a ring of flames, it stings itself to death.

This statement has already been proven false.

In the corner is a long table against the wall, with a piece of blank white paper lying on it. If the gaze is lowered along the right rear leg of that table, then on the floor, one foot from the table leg, is a covered drain that opens into the bathroom. Water from the bathroom does not enter the room through that drain. Sometimes, just sometimes, when the water flows rapidly, then right beneath the roof of the drain, where there is a hole, a drop gathers and runs down the walls of the small cave. Little by little like this, little by little, under the roof of the drain, a small swamp has formed, it is like looking at a big swamp through the wrong end of a telescope. When the current of air moving along the floor strengthens for a moment, then from the trembling surface of that stagnant water a few mosquitoes fly up and sit on the wall of the drain.

The length of this tunnel between the bathroom and the room is eight inches.

If the gaze is lifted from the table in the corner against the wall, with a piece of blank white paper lying on it, to the wall, then on the wall's surface, two fingers' width above the table, is the sill of a closed window with half-broken, blind panes, on which an empty pineapple jar lies overturned in such a way that the sun's rays, despite being cut by the sharp lines of the half-broken blind panes, fall vertically on the jar.

Where the wall with the window in it rises and meets the ceiling is a rectangular pattern of light shaped like the window. The side of the pattern further from the window is three-fourths as long as the side nearer to the window. The rectangle of light, this half-transformed brightness of the intact portions of the window, is so perfect that even the sharp lines of half-broken panes show in it. In this rectangle of light the inverted shadows of people passing outside fall from one direction, merge into the sharp lines of the half-broken panes and the rectangular lines of the window frame, and emerge in the other direction. On the ceiling the warp and woof of the motionless window, with its entering, merging, separating shadows, has been woven by rays refracted from the stagnant water outside.

In the background, sounds of the city.

In the air the merging, separating sounds of the city; the people entering the frame of light on the roof, merging, separating; the jar lying overturned on the window sill; the piece of blank white paper on the table; the eight-inch-long tunnel one foot from the right rear table-leg, its surface rippling when the current of air moving along the floor increases; all this, all this mixed in together, blended in this union of vision, on which the present eye's curtain has fallen.

The curtain rises.

The air entering through the half-broken panes of the window, with the sounds of the city mixed into it, slides the piece of blank white paper off the table, the piece of white paper hangs halfway off the table, hesitates for a moment, is pulled entirely off the table by the weight of its hanging half, flutters, falls on the floor one-and-a-half feet from the tunnel.

Now a scorpion's head emerges from the tunnel, pauses at the threshold of the tunnel and looks around for a moment, comes out. Its body is wet with the oily muddy water of the little swamp that has come into being at the bottom of the tunnel. On its back ride five small microscopic scorpions dyed with the same muddy water.

The female, bearing on her back the burden of five small children, advances. Three broken parallel lines are marked on the floor by her wet feet. Five inches from the pieces of blank white paper, a spasm runs through the female's body, the oiliness of the children's bodies slides on the oiliness of the female's body, the children slide off her back and fall to the floor. The female feels the burden on her back lightened, she turns and looks at the undulating, crawling children for a second. In this way her face turns toward the wall, with its closed window, its blind, half-broken panes, its shadows which enter the frame, separate, and are reflected on the ceiling. The female, after looking at the undulating, crawling children for a second, runs straight to the wall, and climbs it. She heads for the window sill on which an empty pineapple jar lies overturned.

Five microscopic scorpions, because of their bodies' helpless trembling, slither along the floor very rapidly toward the piece of paper which lies spread out blank and white on the floor one-and-a-half feet from the tunnel.

Now there is a tumult in the reflected moving shadows on the ceiling, and the waves of vibrating sound in the air.

In a dark corner enveloped in darkness, a male emerges from his hole. At first he lets his tail hang loosely, then he stiffens it, waves the sting like a rose-thorn at the end of his tail, grinds together the teeth of the pliers-like claws at the ends of the arms which emerge on both sides from the point where head and body join; he advances. His gait is not normal. The juice and scent from the erect thorn in the prominent thorny surface beneath his stomach have made him feel intoxicated, the juice and scent which want to leave his control and enter the control of the female.

Looking around, he moves along with this gait.

Some distance away, the female, enveloped in the same darkness, is absorbed in searching for worms, her gaze falls on the intoxicated male. To entice her, his behaviour becomes even more intoxicated. The female becomes fully attentive to him. When the male comes near, she, intoxicated with his scent, allows him to touch her. The pliers-like claws on the male's and female's arms clasp each other. Then the male begins to move backwards, it seems as though the female is pushing him.

Then another male appears out of the blue. The couple, clasping each other in their claws, keep moving in the same way. The second male makes a dash, clutches the female's tail in his claws, and a tug-of-war begins. At length the second male tires, gives up, and lets go. The first male, clasping the female in this way, continues his journey.

Then the foreheads touch each other, the mouths press each other, then moving over each other's faces like the touch of a breeze, they begin to pursue their pleasure. The female is not bored by all this activity, so the result of boredom, the female's tail lashing the male's head, does not occur.

Crowded close in scent and juice, this dance of utter intoxication continues.

Now they arrive in the shelter of a big stone in a dark corner enveloped in darkness. The male, collecting his remaining strength, pulls the female toward him. The prominent thorn in his juicy, scented, thorn-bearing surface, lodges in the female's juicy, scent-squirting hole, around both parts, the erect teeth grip each other.

The male opens the pliers-like claws on his arms and releases the female's claw. Once more he gathers all his strength and prepares to flee. But not enough strength can be gathered for him to free the teeth on his stomach from the teeth on the female's stomach, remove the thorn from the hole. He becomes helpless. The female's tail, like a whip, lashes the male. The sting like a rose-thorn lodges in his body, then she frees herself from the corpse, looks at it for a moment, then slowly advances and gradually takes his head in her mouth, begins to chew, begins to swallow. Eventually she eats his whole head. Leaving the rest of the body, she sets off at an extremely slow pace.

From dark corners enveloped in darkness a crowd of worms advances toward the headless male.

The female, moving at the same slow pace, arrives under a tub which has one side lifted up by a brick beneath it. Under the tub, reaching the shelter of the brick, she pauses, rests, continues to rest.

The magic of this event of the darkness becomes an ocean wave in her stomach and raises its head, flings her whole being against the hard surface. Then from the central hole in her stomach five microscopic children emerge one by one. After some time, when they begin to move around they come crawling and climb onto her back. With her pliers-like claws the female helps them to mount, then without any special purpose she sets out toward the place where the eight-inch-long tunnel connects the bathroom to the adjoining room.

Arriving at the mouth of the tunnel, she slides off the edge into the swamp which has grown up in the bottom of the tunnel. After sinking into the stagnant water she comes to the surface, her feet, pliers-like arms, and tail wave crazily in the air. She turns on the axis of her stomach, a typhoon arises in the swamp, tumult grows among the larvae, the mosquitoes fly up, the children quietly cower on her back, gripping her tail and quivering. In this state of going under and coming up, going under and coming up in confusion, her serrated claws happen to touch the edge of the floor. With immense difficulty she grasps the edge, plants her feet firmly, collects her body, and gradually reaches dry land. For a moment she stops at the threshold of the tunnel to look around, then comes out. Her body is wet with the oily muddy water of the pond, the bodies of the five microscopic scorpions on her back are dyed with the same oily muddy water.

Now the female, moving very swiftly along the window sill, suddenly pauses. Lifting her head, she looks around. Turning, she moves in the opposite direction from the jar, then pauses. She moves to the right, pauses, moves to the left, then turns and swiftly, involuntarily, runs and enters the overturned jar, in which the sun's rays, although cut by the sharp lines of the half broken blind panes, fall vertically. The moment she enters the jar she becomes frightened and tries to get out, but on the high walls of the jar's round mouth her hands and feet can find no purchase.

Meanwhile those five microscopic children, slipping because of the helpless trembling of their bodies, fall to the floor and land at the edge of the piece of blank white paper.

In the jar, the female, trying to escape from the constant attack of the vertical rays, beats her head against the walls of the jar.

The five microscopic scorpions cross the border onto the piece of blank white paper, separate, and in the boiling madness of their veins begin dancing, begin jumping.

Then the tumult of the reflected moving shadows on the roof, and of the waves of vibrating sounds in the air, reaches a crescendo.

At this moment of crescendo the attacks of the vertical rays perforate the female's body. If a scorpion is imprisoned in a jar tike this, it dies from the sun's light and heat.

This statement has already been proven true. Without regard to this truth, five microscopic scorpions dance, jump, one by one impress like a pattern on the piece of blank white paper the burden of the oily muddy colour of the water on their bodies, feet, arms, claws, tails, and stingers, a pattern into which the poison in the stingers like rose-thorns at the ends of their tails has fully dissolved.

The dancing, boiling poison of the pattern on the piece of blank white paper; the lifeless body in the jar, a target for the sun's rays; the sounds of the city merging, separating in the air; the reflections entering the window-frame on the ceiling, merging, separating; all this, all this joined together, blended together in this unity of vision on which the present eye's curtain has fallen. Now the curtain rises.

Translated by Frances W. Pritchett

Balraj Mainra
(b. 1935)

Balraj Manra (this is how he spells his name now) is an extremely visible and influential writer despite his small output. He worked as a paramedic, and was an active member of the Communist Party-supported All India Trade Union Congress. He now lives a semi-reclusive life in the south Delhi neighbourhood of Greater Kailash.

Balraj Manra was among the pioneers of modernist fiction in Urdu. He emerged on the literary scene in the 1960s with a deliberately muted, plotless narrative that was inward-looking and abstract. His early stories were about individuals who felt estranged from their environment because they perceived the boredom or absurdity of existence. Manra started a journal called *Shu'ur* (Awareness) in the 1970s that continued to be published intermittently up to the 1980s and made a strong impression for individuality of style and production. A small collection of his stories in English translation was published many years ago, but no collection in Urdu has come out so far.

The story presented here, 'Composition One' (*Kampozishan Ek*), is the first of a series and was written in 1966.

Composition One

WHAT AM I TO THE SUN?

I—ignorant, helpless, sick—unable to say a thing.

In those days the question WHAT AM I TO THE SUN? was locked in the prison of my mind.

I had no keys with which to fling open the gates to this mind-prison and let out the question and, with it, free myself.

Who has the keys?

I—ignorant, helpless, sick—whom could I ask?

In those days living under a spell.

Here the sun would rise; there I would awake. The sun would start its journey, I would start mine. We would move forward, onward, leaving milestone after milestone behind along the way. Here the sun would set; there I would fall asleep.

How did it happen?

I don't know. I have never looked full face into the sun.

When first I fell asleep in the sunset, I was facing it. A cool breeze flowed softly, very softly, while the sun smiled through the rustling foliage of the neem tree. I was sunk deep in my armchair, soaking up the balmy weather. Every now and then I felt a gentle, mysterious ebb and flow, sweet sensations—sweet, mysterious sensations—the sun smiling through the rustling neem foliage. The shadows of the neem waltzed on the cool, emerald velvet of the smooth, mowed lawn. The mellow, absolutely charming drunkenness of three successive glasses of Diplomat whiskey.

The smiling sun began its gradual descent.

I pulled the chair behind the neem trunk and fell drowsily into it.

The sunshine lay as a pale sheet over the emerald turf.

Suddenly it began to shrink.

Lifelessly, my hands dropped, my legs dangled lazily, my eyelids began to droop. The last bit of sunshine flickered for a moment and shrank completely as I felt drowned in a compulsive, heavy sleep.

When I opened my eyes, it was a pale sun smiling sadly on the eastern horizon.

Never before had I slept so long.

From that time it became a routine. Here the sun would rise, there I would awake. The sun would start its journey, I would start mine. We would move forward, onward; milestone after milestone was left behind along the way. Here the sun would set, there I would fall asleep.

In the mind-prison something uneasy began to stir.

Something I had never experienced.

I failed in trying to give some meaning to the stir, but my efforts continued. The sun would rise, I would awake; the sun would go down, I would sleep. It went on and on. Only after the passing of an age was I able to give some meaning to that strange stir.

What Am I To The Sun?

I—ignorant, helpless, sick—unable to answer.

Strange to say, that stir came to resemble a question locked in the mind's prison.

WHAT AM I TO THE SUN?

I—ignorant, helpless, sick—unable to say a thing.

Ignorant because I was unable to answer.

Helpless because I could neither overwhelm the sun nor overcome myself—for here the sun rose, there I awoke; here it sank, there I slept.

Sick because—desperately and continuously—all my veins needed the sun's rays.

To rise with the sun, to sleep when it set became a torment—a torment because my relation to the sun was beyond comprehension. I knew I could not rest until I had determined the precise nature of this relation, for WHAT AM I TO THE SUN? echoed and re-echoed in the prison house of my mind.

The pity of it, I had no keys to this prison so that I could fling open the gates and let out the question and, with it, free myself.

Who has the keys?

I—ignorant, helpless, sick—whom could I ask?

And so it went: Here the sun appeared on the eastern horizon, there wakefulness touched my lashes. The sun, pale and sad; I, withered and gloomy. The sun far, far away while my taller shadow spread obliquely westward. The sun would begin its course and my slanting shadow would keep it company. When the sun began to rise slowly from the eastern horizon, my shadow began to dance slowly round and round me. As the sun came towards me, my shadow would shrink. The sun atop my head; my shadow under my feet. The sun moved slowly westward; my shadow lengthened towards the east. The sun sank here, and there I was overcome by sleep.

Is my shadow my bond to the sun?

I would try to grasp the basis of this all.

Is my shadow my own?

Filled with misgivings, I would falter, feeling unable to go on.

Is my shadow the shadow of the sun?

Are the sun and I twins?

After thinking so hard and so often, all I knew was that I was ignorant, helpless, sick. But the realization of my ignorance, helplessness, sickness was no answer to my misery—the mystery remained inscrutable.

One day, as the sun moved forward on its course, a stranger, a complete stranger, the wind, whispered past my ear:

'Innocent friend! You are the centre of sun and shadow—shadow and sun revolve around you.'

Thenceforth it was so: Here my eyes opened, there the sun rose; here I set out on my journey, there the sun set out on its journey; moving forward, onward, leaving milestone after milestone behind; here I fall asleep, there the sun goes down.

Translated by Muhammad Umar Memon

Shamsur Rahman Faruqi
(b. 1935)

Modernist critic, poet, and fiction writer, Shamsur Rahman Faruqi was born in Pratapgarh, Uttar Pradesh, and earned his master's degree in English literature from Allahabad University. Faruqi joined the Indian Civil Services from where he retired in 1996. He presently lives in Allahabad, the city from where he launched the literary journal *Shabkhoon* in 1966, a landmark in the trend of modernism or *jadidiyat*. Faruqi's thought has evolved strongly in the direction of interpreting and putting into new use the ideas and practices of pre-modern, especially eighteenth-century Urdu literary practice. He is the author of more than a dozen books on various aspects of literary criticism, and the recipient of numerous awards and honours.

It is a lesser known fact that Faruqi started his career as a short story writer and planned to write a novel; a dream that he recently fulfilled with the publication of the historical romance *Kai Chand the Sar-e Asman* (There were Many Moons in the Sky, Karachi, 2006), a novel of truly epic proportions in every sense of the term.

After completing his critical investigations of the entire range of Urdu poetry in his four-volume study of the soul stirring poetry of Mir Taqi Mir (*Sher-e Shor-Angez*), Faruqi perhaps felt that he still needed to put down in writing more of the enormous knowledge he had filed away over his thirty-some years of critical thinking, although, this time, in a different medium. As he says in the introduction to his first collection of short stories, *Savar aur Dusre Afsane* (The Rider and Other Stories, Karachi, 2001), he had written so much on Ghalib by way of literary criticism that if he was to write something more on Ghalib, it had to be in a quite different vein, and what could be more appropriate yet different than an *afsana* or story about Ghalib and his times; hence, the short story '*Ghalib Afsana*'. He published it under the assumed name of Beni Madhav Rusva in the journal *Shabkhoon*. The story created a stir among Urdu readers because of the sweep of its scholarly and linguistic brilliance. There was speculation about who could have penned this remarkable piece of fiction. The '*Ghalib Afsana*' is the second in the series of his reappearance as a fiction writer. The first, '*Lahaur ka ek Vaqia*' (An Incident in Lahore), was published under the assumed name Umar Shaikh Mirza. '*Lahaur ka ek Vaqia*' is a story that is suspended between a nightmare and an actual incident.

An Incident in Lahore

It happened in 1937. In those days I lived in Lahore.

One day it occurred to me that I should go visit Allama Iqbal. I used to own a beige coloured Ambassador car. I drove in it to Allama Sahib's bungalow. I didn't know the house number or the exact directions for how to get there, but I had a good idea where McLeod Road was and also that he lived on that street. So I was able to find his house without much difficulty.

The street seemed unusually dusty. The footpath, or let's say the broad strip of land on either side of the road, was dry and covered in dust. The gate of the bungalow was made of wood and very high. It was plated with a grey tin or maybe iron sheet which made it seem heavy and mysterious. The gate was open and I could clearly see the short driveway curving towards the main house. The house was big and grand but old and rundown. One could, even from the street, discern the signs of patchy repair and the one new addition to the building. I recalled Ihsan Danish's poem '*Allama Iqbal ki Kothi*' (Allama Iqbal's House) that had been published a couple of months ago in one of the magazines, *Khayyam* or *Alamgir*. The poem expressed sadness and regret at the dilapidated state of the bungalow. The last couplet was:

Ihsan, I hear the house has now been repaired,
I will go sometime and visit there once again.

I stood debating with myself whether to take the car inside or leave it by the sidewalk. I thought that there might be another car parked in the portico and if I left mine in the driveway it might block someone's path. So I left my car by the side of the street and got out. At that point I noticed that there were two or three stalls, the kind that cigarette or pan shopkeepers have, on the sidewalk across the street from me. There was a crowd of young men and loafers gathered around them. There were some fairly young boys there too. I was displeased to see them wasting their time at pan shops instead of studying at school.

I was locking up my car when five or six young boys suddenly ran across the road and came towards me. From their demeanour and the way they were gesturing, I presumed they were asking for something. I said to myself that this was worse than wasting time. These kids seemed to be professional beggars. They must be under the control of some organized criminal group that made beggars of children and ruined their lives. Before I could pull my car keys out of the lock some four or five kids and a thin, mean, evil-looking man had come up right by my side, their hands barely inches away from my jacket.

I was horrified to see that these boys were not beggars or illiterate vagrants from the neighbourhood. They seemed professionals; the sort that sell their bodies. I said to myself, God have mercy, what's going on here? Am I dreaming? It was broad daylight in a decent neighbourhood of a busy city; and these criminal boys?

Now it dawned on me that those hands were not angling for my coat pockets, they wanted to grab the edge of my jacket; they wanted to strike a deal with me. These ten or twelve year olds' eyes held no innocence, but had the glint of a strange, evil look; their faces bore a maturity and unattractive insipidity that even adults seldom possess. Disgusted, I pushed them aside and moved away from them quickly, but they followed behind. God forbid! Such things don't happen even in the most sensational fiction. Is this really happening or am I going mad? I thought to myself. Then I made practically a gigantic leap, got away from that crowd and went through the gate towards the Allama's bungalow.

Thank God, those rogues didn't dare to come inside. The gates were open, yet those boys stopped by the post as though struck by an electric current. I ran towards the portico, flicking dirt off my clothes and hands in hate and revulsion.

I honestly can't recall the details of my meeting with the Allama. All I remember, and that too vaguely, is that he received me with great kindness.

When I rang the bell, an old man from whose appearance I figured him to be something between a distant relative and a butler, answered the door at once. I gave him my name and he went inside and came back within seconds with the information that Allama Sahib was receiving visitors in the drawing room (called, for some reason, 'the round room' in Urdu) and asked me to step inside. I have no recollection of what we talked about. I was an engineer with the railways, was interested in poetry (still am), knew many poems of the Allama by heart, but besides my fascination with poetry I possessed nothing else that would make me worthy of having a conversation with the Allama. I do remember very well that the Allama took care not to make me feel that our meeting was a waste of his time. Nor did he broach a subject that would make me aware of my own ignorance.

My visit lasted half an hour. Then I made my salaams and took leave. Allama Sahib stepped out of the room to bid me farewell. It did cross my mind to request him to do something about the crowd of evil urchins who hung out just across the street from his bungalow gate, but I couldn't summon the courage to say it. How did it concern him anyway? This was a matter for the police to take care of. Perhaps the Allama wasn't even aware of the kind of crowd that hung around those stalls across the street.

When I emerged from the portico, I noticed a grey-coloured, somewhat weather-beaten Austin A40 car parked in the driveway. It couldn't have been the Allama's because I had heard that he owned a large Ford. Anyway, it must be some visitor, I said to myself. So it was good that I had parked my own car outside, I thought.

I came out, euphoric from the meeting with Allama Iqbal. For a moment, I had forgotten that there was a possibility of encountering those urchins again. But upon reaching the road, I was stunned, completely taken aback. A number of those urchins stood by my car, they had even pushed the car around, for it was now facing in the opposite direction from which I had come. I was still in something like a state of shock when I picked up the courage to walk towards the car while those wicked boys nearly clung to me. Their bodies emitted a strange animal-like odour, mingled with the smell of rancid oil. I hadn't yet made up my mind how to deal with them, when a tall, thin man dressed in a long yellow shirt, quite soiled with use, and a matching shalwar, leapt towards me. Barefaced insolence and lack of morality was writ large on his face, so large, in fact, that I instinctively recoiled as if I had touched a wet, gooey substance. At that time, I was facing the road and he was on my left, facing the sidewalk.

When I tried to turn around and kick him, he sought to trip me by putting out his leg. But, God be praised, his leg entangled with mine in such a way that he lost his balance and fell with a splash into the deep drain below the sidewalk. Grabbing this opportunity, I quickly opened the car door and prayed in my heart that the car would start without trouble. My prayers were heard. The engine turned over smoothly as soon as I turned the ignition key. I put the car in gear and stepped hard on the accelerator.

The car moved forward with a jolt. My intent was to move quickly from the first gear to the second because the second gear has both pushing as well as accelerating power. But when I went into the second, I realized that we weren't moving forward much. It seemed as if some force was holding the car back and was in fact dragging it in the opposite direction. I looked back and found that a number of the urchins were holding fast to the bumper and the trunk with all their might, preventing it from moving forward. So here I was, flooring the accelerator with full strength, and there were ten or twelve boys pulling in the opposite direction, and with so much success that the car was barely able to crawl forward at a snail's pace.

I hunched my shoulders and bent my head as if the danger was in front of me and not behind me, as if I was about to slam into something with full force. Bending my head and narrowing my body into a stoop, I put all my mental and physical resolve into putting so much acceleration in the car it should shake off the group of boys and get away. But God alone knows how much strength those filthy devils had mustered at that time. My fifteen hp engine coupled with my own determination were proving futile, the car was crawling, only just. Before I'd covered barely fifty or a hundred yards, I was convinced that the car was going to stall very soon, or the power of those urchins themselves would simply prevent it from moving ahead.

By now I was close to a breakdown myself. I kept thinking over and over that this car which I had imagined would be enough to protect me and be the vehicle of my deliverance could become a noose around my neck or a net of death and destruction. If I remained inside the car, in the space of a few minutes this devilish horde would stop me from getting away, they would pull me out of the car and God knows what they would do to me then. The man whom I had pushed into the gutter, might actually cut me into pieces and scatter my body all over the place.

[Now after many years, as I write these lines, I realize that my logical brain, which the physiologists call the 'right brain', was numb and I was in the control of my left brain. The left brain which is also called the 'reptilian brain' is common to humans, and to crawling and egg-laying animals.

It has been said that in the process of evolution, it took tens of millions of years for this brain to evolve, because it evolved from crawling to egg-laying animals to humans, and that's why it is also called the reptilian brain. Our fundamental and baser emotions are the product of this brain: lust, fear, hunger, oppression, safety, the flight instinct, etc., all are a product of this brain. It has been determined that in most criminals, especially murderers and rapists, the left brain is more dominant than the right brain. Because it is located in the lower left part of the skull, it is called the 'left brain'. The right brain evolved over tens of millions of years: logic, far-sightedness, and intelligence are its abilities. The left brain has no interest in logic, intelligence, remorse, and when it becomes dominant it suspends the ability to think or reason. It has also been found that in some types of mental illness, the left brain becomes dominant over the right brain.]

Anyway, right now my only concern was to get out of the car and escape. If the car is no longer a sanctuary, there must be a way to escape by getting out of it—or this was my logic. But how will I leave the car and where, I had no idea.

Suddenly, I felt strangely apprehensive. The street was totally deserted. The empty, virtually desolate road seemed deafeningly silent. A line from Kabir came to my mind: *An empty city stood awful all around*. McLeod Road had never been a busy thoroughfare, but it was never entirely deserted either. One or two cars would certainly pass by every other minute. A short distance from the Allama's place was the grand mansion of his well-known friend Sir Joginder Singh. There were always one or two guards posted at his gate. At a short distance from Sir Joginder's bungalow was Bahramji Khudaiji's store, located in a residential type of building. They stocked high quality foreign liquor and cigars. Whiteway-Laidlaw's sumptuous two-storeyed storefront was a couple of furlongs from there. Several cars and many carriages were always seen parked in front of this store. God knows why neither those mansions nor stores were in view. In fact, there wasn't a traffic policeman at the crossroads.

[Now that I think about it, it occurs to me that my speed was so slow that it can only be described as 'a snail's pace'. The buildings and stores that I have mentioned above must have been several furlongs ahead. So how could they be visible from where I was? But as I have said, at that time it wasn't my human brain but the reptilian brain that was in control. I am convinced that had I found the courage and continued to keep driving at whatever speed was possible, I would have certainly reached some safe or populated neighbourhood within five or ten minutes; my pursuers would not have been able to touch me. They couldn't have entirely prevented the car from moving. If they had tried to attack me through the windows, they would have had to let go of the car, and in the meantime I could have increased my speed and been able to free myself from the danger. But at that time I felt that the car was like a death cell; if I remained in the car, I would surely be killed.]

I thought to myself that if I could find a stout pole or a wall somewhere, I could dash the car against it. The sound of the collision would attract a few people at least, maybe even a policeman, or perhaps I would be injured or become unconscious, and then this gang of ghouls would surely let go of me. At that time, it did not occur to my reptilian brain that in order to have a real accident, one has to have speed. My speed must have been around five kmph, and one needs to be going at least twenty to twenty-five to gain a satisfactory accident. It also did not occur to me that I would be completely at their mercy if I was injured or became unconscious. They could take me anywhere, on the pretext of going to the hospital. Or, they could further injure me right there itself. I consider it my good luck that I didn't see any object against which I could crash my car and carry out my plan.

At this moment, I realized that the repulsive man, clad in the grubby yellow shirt, was also helping the urchins, and was assisting them in stalling my car. Now I will never be able to escape, I thought to myself. Although the speed of the car had not been much affected yet, I was convinced that the man in the dirty shirt would risk his very life to stop the car.

How long can a mother goat hope to keep her kid? I thought to myself. I was reminded of a servant of my late father's who had an appropriate albeit slightly comic couplet for such occasions:

How long will the baby mangoes shelter behind the leaves?
One day after all, they'll grow into full mangoes
And be sold in the market.

In normal situations, I would smile when I called the couplet to mind, but today I felt like crying. Furthermore, at that time I saw my childhood in a rosy-pink- and-orange light, full of hope and arousing desires of success, even though in reality, my childhood had been rather unhappy and not worth remembering at all.

[It is said that once Bismil Sa'idi said to Josh Malihabadi, 'Josh Sahib, were your poetry was not lacking just a little bit in the moods of pain and sorrowful thoughts, you would have been an even greater poet.' Josh replied, 'Certainly not. My poetry is not lacking in pain and sorrowful thoughts. Just listen to this couplet:

The best days of my life,
Those that tell of my weeping.'

On hearing this, Bismil Sa'idi burst out laughing and said:

'By God, Josh Sahib, I never heard a better couplet on the theme of childhood!'

Anyway, forget about Josh Sahib and Bismil Sahib, the truth is that *my* childhood was spent in being thrashed by those who were older than me and me howling at the thrashings.]

On the verge of tears, I thought to myself, 'I wish I was seven or eight years old, so that I would not be in this car, in this state, where my honour and my life are at stake. After all, I haven't harmed anyone, have I'?

I was then reminded of my childhood days when I would be scolded or beaten for every little thing, and often without reason. And if there was a reason, then my innocent little brain was unable to understand what it was. There doesn't have to be a reason for everything, was the conclusion that my small brain had arrived at in those days. Later on, when I understood the difference between cause and reason, I concluded that that if one knows the cause of something, it doesn't follow that one can find out the reason too. For example, someone is murdered, and after examining the dead body we reach the conclusion that his death was caused by a bullet from a pistol. Then this is simply the cause of the murder. It doesn't tell us the reason for the murder.

At this moment, the cause for my life being at risk is that I was present at a certain place at a certain time. If I hadn't been here, this wouldn't have happened. But there was some reason for my being there, and there must have been a cause for that reason, and again, a cause for the cause...

So is the whole world merely a tale of causes? Is there no reason? Or, perhaps, we've come here for some reason? Mir Taqi Mir whispered in my ear:

Conditions arose that caused me to be here for many days now

What causes? Why were we brought over here? So that I should become a victim of these young flesh traders, even as I rode in my own car? To become the target of the unholy activities of their leader? I said to myself in a state of near-hysteria.

Suddenly I heard a noise from behind the car in the street. It seemed that some more people had come out to help my enemies. The car's speed decreased further. Or perhaps it was my imagination. But I decided that remaining there for even another moment was as good as inviting some big misfortune. I recalled that my devilish pursuers had stayed away from the Allama's bungalow. Perhaps they were afraid of going into homes? Therefore the best thing for me would be to stop the car by the side of some gate in such a way as to block the gate, and jump out, and run for it. But how will I run? Won't these people pounce on me instantly and grab hold of me? I was thinking about these possibilities when on my side of the road, that is, on the left side, I saw just what seemed to be a safe bungalow. Gotcha! I said to myself with joy in my heart.

With a forceful jerk to the steering wheel, I turned the car into the gate at an angle and stomped on the brake with all my strength. The force of my swinging to the left and the clamping of the brakes made the car stall and stop at an angle in the centre of the gate. My pursuers also were unable to bear the centrifugal force of the sudden movement and fell off, and were thrown about. I looked back and saw that my nearest pursuer was at least ten, twelve feet behind me. I grabbed the ignition key and ran blindly toward the bungalow, that is, I entered what I thought was my refuge.

A biggish bungalow, though somewhat dreary-looking. There was no servant, or watchman, or even a gardener at the front. A verandah with a high plinth, in it there were old-fashioned easy chairs and frog chairs and a dressing table with a full-length mirror against the wall. A hat-stand stood beside it. I hadn't the time or the courage to stay and observe more and dashed down the length of the veranda. I saw what seemed to be a room at the end of the veranda. The door leading to it was slightly ajar, I stepped quickly inside and drew the bolts.

There was a faint smell of disinfectant in the room. I opened my eyes wide and looked around and realized that I was in a bathroom. I felt for and found the light switch. A yellowish light came on and I saw that it was a space seven or eight feet in length and about the same in width, with a toilet seat and an area for bathing. Instead of a dry commode there was the new-fashion flush system with an iron cistern above; a chain was suspended from the cistern. There were very few bathrooms of this style in India at that time. I was however, familiar with them because two big railway companies, the G[reat]. I[ndian]. P[eninsular]. Railway and the B[ombay]. B[aroda]. & C[entral]. I[ndia]. Railway had ordered such bathrooms to be installed in the first-class waiting rooms. I worked for the G. I. P. Railway myself.

I had a terrible urge to pee. Perhaps it was on account of fear or maybe I really needed to go. I didn't feel quite safe but the urge to relieve myself was very strong and I also didn't know when next I would get a chance to do so. I had barely touched my trouser belt when there began a loud incessant pounding on the door. God knows if they were my enemies or some member of the house who suspected that an intruder was in the bathroom. Anyway, I was in no condition to open the door and come out. There seemed no possibility of remaining hidden in the bathroom either. Where would I go if I came out? Then I glanced at the opposite wall and noticed a door there. I didn't care where it led, it was a route for escape.

Softly, I slid the bolts on the far door. Thank God, the door isn't locked on the other side, I thought to myself. It'll take them longer to break down two doors and the pandemonium created by the breaking doors will surely attract someone's attention. At that moment I forgot that the devil-horde couldn't enter any homes and therefore it was very likely that the person or persons beating at the door were connected to the owner of the house.

When I emerged from the door I saw that I was back in the same veranda and that it in fact extended much further down. On my right was an enclosing wall so the veranda was now a corridor. Right next to the bathroom door was another door in the wall that must open directly outside. The door was partially open and there I could see three servants clearly. They sat on the doorstep and on the threshold, and were so absorbed in gabbing away that they weren't aware at all of my presence. I did not want to draw their attention either.

I must have crept along stealthily, cat-like, for some ten yards when I saw a door that opened into the house. Just then I heard the muffled sound of the bathroom door caving in. I didn't linger any longer but stepped inside the house.

Once again, I was in a hall; a spacious hall with archways. It gave the impression of a house of busy inhabitants. Two women sat on a wide bedstead fine-chopping some betel nuts. I can't recall their faces or their dress now. Near the bedstead was a large padded frog chair in which sat a plump, soft-bodied, fairly good looking middle-aged woman wearing a sari. Across from her, two relatively younger women sat on chairs, knitting. I judged that the middle-aged woman was of some authority among them. I offered my greetings to her. I think that from my body language and speech and air of being totally confused and rattled she sensed that I wasn't a vagrant or a housebreaker. The other women certainly seemed a little nervous but they didn't raise an alarm or protest. Perhaps they felt safe in the presence of the older woman. The older lady didn't return my greeting; instead she inquired in a cold voice:

'Who are you? How did you get in here? Get out of here at once.' She seemed more annoyed than afraid.

'For God's sake, give me shelter. I am in grave danger.' I replied in a whisper.

'Why? Is the police after you?'

'I'll explain later. There is no police. I'm a respectable engineer. Some rogues are after me.'

'Rogues chase rogues. Respectable people have nothing to do with them. Now get out. At once. Or I'll call the servants.'

'How will you face God if I am killed?' Suddenly the idea flashed into my mind that this woman, even though she looks highly respectable, is not the lady of the house. 'For God's sake take me to some responsible person!'

My arrow had found its mark. She changed her posture and said, 'Responsible? Who else is responsible here? What is your story?' Her tone was sharper now; the emphasis was on the pronoun 'your'.

Haltingly, I began to tell my story. I was afraid that the incident was so bizarre that they would not believe me. If someone narrated such a tale to me I would regard it as madman's chatter. This apprehension made the sound of my voice unconvincing even to my ears and my story seemed more impossible than ever. Anyway, those people seemed to listen attentively. The tale wasn't exactly long. It would take only a few minutes to finish it. So I continued, and prayed in my heart that they would believe me.

The door through which I had entered had remained open as before. Everyone was engrossed in my story. Suddenly the man in the grubby yellow shirt walked in, quite casually. He had a long barrelled pistol in his hand.

I ran and tried to hide behind the older woman's chair. The man pointed the gun straight at the woman and said in a strangely aloof, cold, harsh, and extremely derisive tone: ' Come, tell me, what am I to you?' Instead of 'you', he used the Urdu equivalent of the French *tu*, indicating familiarity or contempt.

A sensation of terror gripped my body. Were they all in it together? I said to myself in terror and amazement. None of us was in a state to do something to dispel this new danger. The women were frozen as if carved in stone. There was a door right behind the place where I was trying to hide ineffectually. But some instinct told me that there was somebody behind the door.

Before I could make up my mind whether there was really someone behind the door or not, or if he was friend or enemy, the door opened with a thunderous clap and something black came out with a loud soughing whooshing sound, swept into the courtyard, and established itself there like a whirlwind or dust-devil.

I saw that all the women lay almost unconscious, their faces covered with their dupattas. The gunman was on his knees, his face bowed. His hands were folded at his chest in a manner that suggested obeisance. His pistol had fallen from his hands and lay at the feet of the middle-aged woman. But the lady herself seemed completely detached from everything. She had covered her head and face with the hem of her sari, and she had collapsed in the frog chair like a rag doll. My feet weighed a ton. My heart had sunk into my shoes. But my brain (the reptilian brain) was still somewhat alert. I said to myself that there couldn't be a better chance than this to make good my escape. Perhaps I would even be able to get my car out of the gates of this house.

Full of fear, almost dragging my feet, I came out of my refuge (pah! what a sanctuary!) like a thief. That black funnelling whirlwind remained as it was in the courtyard. I could hear the whooshing sound it made. It now seemed almost like a wail. I don't know why but I felt that I should not make the slightest noise. Was it a dust-devil, or some bad spirit, or a scourge from God? But what effect could my silence have on it? Perhaps that too was an idea of my reptilian brain; crawling animals often freeze when faced with danger, as if they were dead.

As I crept by the man wearing the dirty yellow shirt, I had an urge to deliver a solid kick at his ribs. That bastard was now dead anyway. But what if he wasn't? And the black whirling funnel? I restrained myself. Then it occurred to me to pick up the pistol just in case those fiends were waiting for me outside. But whatever sense remained in me cautioned that I did not know how to use firearms, nor did I have a firearm license, so why invite more trouble? I had died a thousand deaths before I survived this one ordeal, I should get out without committing any more follies.

'But suppose those women and the man in the grubby yellow shirt are actually dead? The police might pursue me...,' I said to myself fearfully.

'Stupid,' I scolded myself in my heart. 'If you hang around here any more, the police will surely come even if they weren't coming in the first instance. So what if these people are dead? It is none of your business. But if the police catch you here, you're in trouble. You'll be taken around everywhere in fetters. You'll lose your job too. Move your feet and get out from here at once.'

I walked out of there gingerly, as if I was walking on egg shells. It was dark by the door in the corridor. Perhaps the three servants had fallen asleep or they were unconscious, who knows? I stepped over their bodies and came out of that house of ghosts and fears.

The street lamps were lit up. A vehicle or two passed by slowly. Everything seemed normal yet somehow changed. I couldn't put my finger on how exactly the place had changed. In a little while it suddenly occurred to me that McLeod Road was not as deserted as it had been this morning. Also, when I had entered that bungalow for refuge it was broad daylight, perhaps eleven o'clock or so. I was sure that I hadn't stayed in that house for more than fifteen minutes. Then why was it dark outside?

Nervousness and fear made me feel nauseous. My mouth was filled with brackish watery saliva and before I could control myself I threw up with a reflex, emitting a deep-throated buffalo-like noise. Only a mouthful of bitter blackish-yellow substance came out. I had had a very light breakfast and many cups of tea in the morning, and that was several hours ago (or perhaps an entire day had passed), so what else could I expel from my stomach? Panting like a heat-struck dog I tried to control my heaving chest and stomach. My nausea hadn't subsided despite the vomiting. I recalled the beginning of the novel *Taubat-un Nasuh* (Nasuh's Repentance) when Nasuh vomited with great force and the vomit was black like a crow's feather. I also recalled another story I had read as a child in which the vomit was as black as a crow's feather. 'Am I suffering from gastroenteritis then? Or have I put poison in my mouth somehow?' I asked myself anxiously.

My head spun uncontrollably and I crashed against a nearby wall. My hand struck the wall as if to break the fall, or to save myself from injury. I felt a sharp pain in my palm, like the sting of a scorpion. Anxious, I examined the palm closely and found out that a thick nail that was perhaps jutting from the wall had pierced my palm, making a wound half an inch deep. The gash bled profusely. My shirt sleeve and my trousers were spotted with blood. Dizziness and fear together with this wound made me more distraught than ever before.

I had no alternative but to stay where I was, so I leaned against the wall after checking it thoroughly. I bandaged my palm tightly with a handkerchief to stem the bleeding. After a long time I felt a little better. I said to myself that all this was surely the work of the djinns, or evil spirits and I must recite the Quranic verse of 'The Chair' to ward off evil. But I couldn't remember the words so I began reciting the short chapter called *Ikhlas* (Indivisible Oneness of God) and another Quranic verse *la haula wa la qu'uata illa bi'allah* (There is no Force and no Power except God) over and over again. After sometime my heartbeat stabilized. My throat felt parched. But where was water there? I said to myself that

I should be brave, cross the road, get into my car and make a run for it. This wasn't the time to look for water or worry about getting proper medical treatment for my hand.

I dragged my tired feet and walked towards the gate of the bungalow where I had left my car. I was a little afraid that those vicious urchins might still be there. But their leader lay inside (presumably dead), so those dirty bastards must have gone away too. Having voiced these thoughts to myself, I hastened towards the gate.

The bungalow had seemed extremely large when I was running towards it for refuge. I had imagined the front veranda and the inner corridor to be at least two hundred and fifty feet long. Contrary to my expectations, the distance now was much less. I had barely walked a dozen steps when the gate came into view but my car was not there. I was shocked for a minute but then I remembered that I had left my car at such an angle that it had blocked access through the gate, so someone might have pushed and moved it to one side.

But the car had disappeared, and so thoroughly that there was no sign even of tyre marks at the gate, no tell-tale signs or drag marks scored on the earth by my sudden application of brakes in order to stop and make a sharp turn into the gate. My car had vanished as if it had never existed. Did someone steal it? I thought to myself. But people didn't steal cars in those days. Where would a car thief sell the vehicle? Few people kept cars then, and they were mostly lawyers, doctors, or Government officers. Anyway, even if a thief had stolen it I didn't have the courage or the time to go lodge a report of the theft. What story would I give to the police? What was I doing there in that bungalow? There was no sign that there ever was a car parked there. All I had were the keys in my pocket. I checked my pockets; the keys were there.

To have his car stolen was not an ordinary event for a railway assistant engineer. I should have had the matter investigated immediately. Obviously, it would not be easy for me to buy another car; perhaps I would never own another car at all. But at that time, I had no option. I also thought that a car was not like a needle that could get lost and never be found. At that time the best thing for me was to leave as soon as possible. Often, the human brain cannot comprehend simple things and this was certainly beyond the natural and normal. It was best not to investigate this any further. I was saved by God's grace. I've heard of people losing their minds in fear, even dying in such circumstances. I ought to think of myself, not of the car.

Convincing myself that this was the best route to take, I came out on to the road under the street lamps. For some reason, my clothes seemed yellowish to me. Perhaps it was the dim, semi-blind municipal lighting. A *tonga* was approaching, I hailed it and got in. My clothes seemed even more yellow now. God forbid, did I have jaundice? Just then the coach driver turned and looked at me with a meaningful expression in his eyes. Perhaps he had noticed the splotches of red on my clothes. Or were my clothes really yellow? Suddenly I was wracked with a feverish tremor. In a tremulous voice I asked the coach driver to hurry up and take me to the railway station because I had to catch a train. The Mughalpura station was nearby. I was there in minutes. The Pathankot Express was pulling into the railway platform as I got there. I bought a ticket for Pathankot, boarded a compartment, and sank into a seat. So what if I did not know anyone in Pathankot; the grubby yellow-shirted man and the black whirlpool funnel were not there either.

A friend of mine read all that I have written above and said:

'What nonsense have you written here? Are you writing a memoir of your life, or made up stories and events from your dreams?'

'You know that I have sworn not to write even one false word in my autobiography. That's why I make you read every page so that if there is any error or untruth you can help me correct it.'

'That is as may be. But what the hell do I correct here? Dammit, you've crossed all limits this time. You say that you had an Ambassador car in those days. You idiot! That car was manufactured for the first time by the Birlas in 1957, well after India's partition in 1947. They bought the blue prints of the English Morris Oxford and manufactured a car called Hindustan 14. When the Morris Oxford model changed after a couple of years, the Birlas came up with a copy of the new model and called it Landmaster, and then after some more years the Hindustan Ambassador was built according to the latest design of the Morris Oxford.

How on earth could you have driven an Ambassador and gone to meet Allama Iqbal in 1937?'

'I must have forgotten the model!' I retorted irritably. 'You know I always had a car from the time I got a job.'

'How could you forget the model? You forgot the model of your very first car so well that you created something that didn't exist? And, brother, tell me, how could the Allama live on McLeod Road in 1937? In October of 1936 or sometime thereabouts, Allama Sahib got the construction of Javed Manzil completed on Muir Road and moved there soon after. In which life did you meet him on McLeod Road in 1937?'

'Maybe it was Muir Road, not McLeod Road,' I was nettled. 'There's not much difference in the names. Can a person remember such minute details? Perhaps that's why I didn't see Sir Joginder Singh's bungalow and those big shops there.'

'Doubtless, one can't remember every minute detail. But we are talking about important details here. Well, if one were writing an oral romance like the *Amir Hamza* in the name of autobiography, then that is something else again.'

'Don't drag the *Amir Hamza* into this. There can't be a better historical narrative,' I said, enraged.

'As you wish; but don't say this in front of everyone or they'll send you to the lunatic asylum. And my dear, the urchins that you talk about, you must have read about them in the newspapers. They belonged to a migratory tribe called Kanjar and practised crime as a profession. A band of Kanjars got into Lahore at one time and members of their community, especially the young children, were often nabbed while committing petty thievery. They had set up camp in the Baghanpura neighbourhood, not on McLeod or Muir Road. You may have passed that way at one time and must have had a dream about them later. Now you are embroidering your autobiography with their tale.'

'Okay, have it your way. But look at this!' Saying this, I thrust my palm right under my friend's nose, almost into his eyes. The old wound's scar was still very clear and deep on my palm. 'You bastard, what is this then?' I said through gritted teeth. 'I can even tell you the name of the doctor in Pathankot who treated this wound.'

My friend was shocked into silence for a moment. It was quite apparent that he was at a loss. But he was no less adamant than me. After a while he said, 'The scar doesn't prove that this wound was inflicted at the time and place you mentioned in your st...I mean in your memoir.'

'Okay, maybe not, but if the doctor is alive, at least he can verify the time and the year.'

'It's been more than fifty years. God knows where the doctor is, or whether he is alive or dead.'

'Even Galen didn't have a cure for doubt, and even Socrates couldn't treat obstinacy.'

'Granted. But I am arguing because you youself asked that I read the book like a hostile critic. I don't want even one erroneous thing to find its way here.'

'So okay, because you didn't really find anything so far, you begin to invent false charges against me.'

'The fact of the matter is that there were many things in your narrative that bothered me, but they weren't so important or noticeable. In this particular chapter, you haven't written even a word that could be counted as a factual incident.'

'Other things, such as?' I asked, suppressing my anger with a great effort.

'You haven't mentioned anything about the Allama's voice. By then, his voice had become completely hoarse.'

'I've already said that I don't remember any details of that meeting.'

'But such an important thing...'

'Shut up. Do you know that the word "incident" [*vaqi'a*] also means "reality" and "dream", and even "death",' I said with great pride, as if I was disclosing a great discovery to him.

'Then I have nothing to say. But tell me, why did you give credit for Munir Niazi's line to Kabir?'

'What nonsense are you spouting?' I yelled.

'Well, nothing, just that the line of verse "*An empty city stood awful all around*" is Munir Niazi's and you can find it on page 25 in his book of poems titled *Dushmanon ke Darmiyan Sham* (An Evening in the Midst of Enemies) published in 1968. You've attributed it to Kabir in 1937. Where did you see it in Kabir? Come now; accept the fact that you have inserted a story in your autobiography!'

'All stories are true! All stories are true!' I screamed after a moment's silence, and then began to sob uncontrollably.

Translated by Mehr Afshan Farooqi

Naiyer Masud
(b. 1936)

Naiyer Masud, one of Urdu's finest contemporary writers, was born in Lucknow to a reputed family of *hakim*s. His father, Syed Masud Hasan Rizvi 'Adeeb', was a professor of Persian at Lucknow University and a distinguished scholar of Persian and Urdu. Masud followed in his father's footsteps, earning doctorates in Persian and Urdu. Now retired, he lives in his ancestral home in Lucknow. He has been writing fiction since 1971, and has published three collections of stories.

A remarkable quality of Naiyer Masud's writing is its restraint; it is subtle, muted, and low-keyed, free of even the slightest trace of sentimentalism, yet steeped in a deep sense of loss. Most of Masud's stories are narrated in the first person and are about individuals living in communities that have now become marginalized. They could be threnodies of a fading culture that unfolds through a dream-like ambience, calm on the surface but turbulent beneath. Masud's stories seem vague on a casual reading and that may be because the plots themselves are vague, the connectedness is at a level more profoundly rooted in the cultural subtext of which this fiction is made. He admits to his penchant for reworking plots of earlier stories and 'nudging them forward'. His stories often feel incomplete, 'needing to be continued'. Many of his stories can be categorized as 'fantastic', though he contests the idea of their being so. He says that his stories are not fantasies, because one cannot say that such events do not occur in real life. However, he does acknowledge the influence of Kafka—whom he has also translated—and Poe on his fiction.

'*BadNuma*' (The Weathervane) represents his fictional stance very well. The weathervane, which resembles a bird, or a fish, or both, is a metaphor for transience; the events that unfold as the young narrator grapples with its significance can be perceived as 'fantastic'.

The Weathervane

Our weathervane, which looked at once like a fish and bird, had stopped pointing windward for quite some time now. However, it stayed put on the roof of our house as long as my father lived. On different occasions it was suggested that it be taken down from the rooftop, because it no longer worked. But, each time my father would give the same reply, 'Its place is on the roof, and if it doesn't stay there, where else can it be placed?' Sometimes he would also say that this was a distinguishing feature of our house and that was its real purpose, for who needs to find out the wind's direction anyway?

But I needed to find out. I loved to fly kites, though I was not dependent on the weathervane. Throughout the day I would often look up at the colorful kites flying in the sky. Just by looking at the kites, near or far, I could tell in which direction the wind was blowing. I could also tell, which the weathervane couldn't, whether the breeze was strong, or mild, or erratic. In the evening, after it became dark, the kites were brought down and the sky would be almost desolately silent. From then until morning, one might need the weathervane to point out the wind's direction, but once kite-flying time was over, I really did not need this information, and even if I were to require it, one couldn't see the weathervane in the dark.

Occasionally, I would shift my gaze from a flying kite to the weathervane and would find that it was working accurately. I would, in fact, make it a point to look at it on a hot summer day when I noticed all the kites slowly drifting in one direction, and would intuitively know that the wind was changing direction in mid-flow. On such occasions the weathervane would also, very slowly, almost as it were against its will, nevertheless silently and smoothly turn left or right and position itself in the direction of the wind. On these occasions I felt myself being drawn close to it.

It was on one such occasion that I heard its voice for the first time. I felt even closer to it, though now it was fixed in the wind's direction and quiet. That day, I examined it up close and for a long time. From a distance it resembled an animal in between a fish and a bird, but now I observed that there was nothing bird-like in its structure. It only resembled a fish, though its architect had perched it on its axis in a manner quite similar to that of a bird's perching on the tip of a branch. Its tail and side fins were just like those of a fish but from a distance gave the impression of a bird's outstretched tail and wings.

At first glance, it looked like a bird, not a fish, perhaps because it was associated with the winds and not with water. From a distance, it also looked fragile and delicate but up close it appeared somewhat ugly and not so delicate. Anyone could tell that it had been made to weather rough seasons and all sorts of breezes.

I kept on scrutinizing it and just when I was convinced that it looked like a fish it occurred to me that it was actually a bird which had been strangely transformed into a fish. And at that very moment my eyes fell on a kite flying straight ahead of it, and I realized that the gentle breeze was once again changing course. When I turned my attention to the weathervane, I saw that it was still fixed in the same direction as before but shuddering softly. Very slowly, I turned it in the direction of the changing course of the wind and once again I heard the weathervane's murmur. I couldn't tell which component produced that sound. I also did not realize then that its breakdown had begun. I was paying more attention to its murmur, which sounded familiar, but I just couldn't remember where I had heard it before. I scrutinized each part of the weathervane. Its shuddering had ceased, and it was pointing in the direction of the wind.

After this, I noticed the weathervane pointing in the wrong direction many times, and on each occasion I thought that I must inform my father that our weathervane was not working. But sometimes it would point in the right direction, so I kept my counsel. Nevertheless, now, as soon as I got on the roof, I would glance at the weathervane first and then look up at the sky, searching for a kite to determine which way the wind was blowing. Mostly, the wind was in another direction. Sometimes the wind would change and blow in the direction to which the weathervane was already pointing. On such occasions I would think: our weathervane does not follow the wind's direction, the wind follows its lead. And then all kinds of strange thoughts would cross my childish mind, the strangest one being that not only did the weathervane point in the wrong direction but that it could turn the winds in the wrong direction too.

Eventually, it faced a direction in which the wind never blew. It was the time of year when hot, strong winds blow and the kite-flying season is over. The early afternoon hot breeze had begun to blow, and I could feel its breath on my body but it had not picked up enough force for me to guess its direction. On such occasions, I did not really need the weathervane. I raced down the staircase, tore a sheet from my reading and writing material and picked a shard of a broken clay water jug from the garbage in the courtyard. Then back on my way to the roof I tore the sheet of paper into circular bits, we call that *takal,* and made a small pile out of it. Standing close to the weathervane I placed the shard under the pile and tossed it straight into the air. The shard went up a short distance with the pile, was suspended in the air for a moment and then, leaving the paper pile suspended, began its descent. The paper pile was frozen for a split second and then its scraps began to disperse and fly here and there. Just then, I heard the hollow noise made by the earthen fragment as it fell on the weathervane's back and I was sidetracked from watching the scraps of paper. The weathervane's shuddering was fading. I gently massaged its back just as one would pet a hurt child or reward a pet animal. Then I looked up. All the scraps, fluttering and whirling, were moving in the one direction, west to east. Then they fell below the roof of my house.

I looked at the weathervane. It was stationary, still pointing in the direction the wind never blew. I cautiously tried to turn it around, but it was frozen in its position. Then I tried carefully twisting it in the opposite direction but it did not budge. When I exerted some pressure to make it move, it murmured and shuddered and I was afraid if I exerted more force I might break some part or ruin the weathervane itself. I stepped back to look at it. Just then I heard a voice:

'Is it broken?'

A young girl was standing on the terrace adjoining our house. The wind was making soft ripples in the thin-textured long scarf she wore and her gaze was fixed on the weathervane. Then she looked at me. This girl and other girls of the neighbourhood would come out on their terraces when the weather was nice and talk to one another in low suppressed voices. Sometimes, one or more friends accompanied her. And then they would laugh and talk loudly. On such occasions they would also stare at our weathervane and point it out for others to see. I was more interested in my kites than in the girls, but their voices reminded me of the tiny little birds which chirped in the evening, around sunset, in the vines clasping the columns in our courtyard.

There was no fixed time for these girls to come out on the terrace. Watching this girl standing alone on her terrace, staring at our weathervane on a deserted afternoon, made me feel as if a family secret had been uncovered. And she again asked:

'Is it broken?'

'No,' I replied. 'Its okay.'

'Why?' She addressed me while gazing at her scarf, 'the breeze is...'

'The breeze is in the wrong direction,' I replied, interrupting her in mid-sentence.

After that, she stood for a while looking sadly at the weathervane, then turned and, walking slowly, went down the stairs at the opposite end.

I thought that now I must tell my father that the weathervane is broken, but on second thoughts decided to watch and wait for a few more days. Now, I would go on the roof several times during the course of a day and upon seeing the weathervane rooted in the same direction, come away. I would definitely go on the roof in the early part of the day and observe it until the sun's rays would grow stronger and the air become hot. Sometimes I would fall asleep momentarily, but then some clatter nearby would put me on alert. On one such occasion I was taken aback on hearing rustling noises. I looked up. Kites in myriad colours were flying in the sky, just as they fly on certain holidays. I stared at the bunch with interest for some time. I was abruptly reminded of the weathervane and glanced in its direction. It was bearing in the direction in which flying kites were pointing towards the wind. I looked at the sky, the kites were now slowly moving towards the right. I looked at the weathervane. It was slowly turning towards the right. As I was about to go near it the hot wind sort of slapped my face and I woke up. There were no kites flying anywhere. However, from the searing slaps of the hot gusts of wind, I could tell that it was blowing from west to east. But the weathervane was fixed in that strange direction. I got up and went very close. Gusts of wind striking on its right side seemed intent on pulling it out of the roof, but it was frozen in one spot like a statue and did not even shudder. Then I was convinced that it had become useless and I began to scamper down the stairs to break the news to my father. I was feeling a little happy as children do; in fact I can now say even adults feel that way when they get a chance to beat others in breaking special news, even bad news.

Coming down the stairs, I remembered how angry I had been at the weathervane in my dream, but on waking I couldn't remember what it was that made me so angry.

I went straight to the visitors' room in the front of the house where my father used to recline on a long, low, cane armchair. I had been seeing him reclining on this very chair and in this room for a long time now, but I do remember that earlier he used to reside in the inner part of the house, though he had to often go and sit in the visitors' room because there were many people who called to meet with him. Still, each day there were many visitors, but right now only my mother was sitting with him. And I didn't see her right away either. I was coming inside from being out in bright sunlight and initially all I could see was a darkness suffusing the room. I couldn't see the cane chair, but I was sure that my father would be in it, and several visitors would be in the room, so with a lot of enthusiasm, like an announcer, I reported the news of the weathervane, and also added that it was fixed in the wrong direction for several days now, and that its parts were probably mixed up. Meanwhile, the darkness in the room dispersed and I saw my mother repeatedly putting a finger on her lips, motioning me to be quiet. I shut up. I would have shut up anyway because I had said all that there was to say. I looked at my father. He was covered with a sheet up to his waist, his eyes were closed and he was literally lying on the chair. The look of contentment on his face made it obvious that he was in a deep sleep.

I was quiet, but my mother once again put a finger on her lips, silently drew me closer and whispered: 'He had a hard time falling asleep.'

Just then my father spoke: 'What happened? What broke down?'

My mother again motioned me to keep quiet and whispered: 'He is sleeping.'

My father's closed eyes and facial expression showed the same look of contentment as before. We both watched him for a while, then my mother said softly: 'Do you need something done?'

The kite-flying season being over, I had nothing much to do. I shook my head to tell her that I was not looking for anything to be done.

'Then sit by his side for a while,' she said. 'I will join you in a moment.'

I sat near my father. My mother got up and was leaving the room when she paused and turned, signalled me to come near and in an even lower whisper asked: 'Is it really broken?'

I was about to nod in reply when my father tried to turn on his side. This was difficult for him and he needed help. He opened and shut his eyes a few times. In the meantime my mother drew near his chair and carefully helped him take a turn and he again fell asleep. My mother bent forward and whispered in my ear: 'Don't tell him.' And she left the room.

I sat silently gazing at my father. He continued to lie with his eyes closed and the contented look on his face, and just like that, without opening his eyes he asked: 'How long has it been since it broke down?'

Was he speaking in his sleep? I asked myself. But just then his eyes opened and his facial expression indicated that he was in pain. He was trying to turn on his side again. When I tried to help him he stopped me from doing so and said: 'Let your mother come.'

'Shall I call her?' I enquired, rising.

'No, she must be coming,' he said and then asked, 'How long has it been broken?'

I found myself being compelled to answer, and was happy for the compulsion. I recalled the first day when the weathervane began to malfunction, the wind had begun to change its course but it was steadfastly pointing in the same direction. I narrated all that had happened from that day to the present. And what I did not tell him, he asked anyway: 'Did you try to fix it?'

I denied flatly. He kept looking at me silently with half-closed eyes. I guessed that he did not believe me and I began to feel uncomfortably like a culprit. And just like a culprit, I was thinking of making up another lie when he said: 'Alright, don't play around with it, and...' he covered my hand with his, 'Don't tell your mother.'

He was about to say something when, hearing a footfall at the door, he stopped himself. My mother had brought something for him to eat. But before she got near his chair my father pressed my hand softly and said: 'Don't tell *anyone*.'

But the very next day he was surrounded by visitors and all of them were talking about the malfunctioning of the weathervane.

(2)

Visitors, as I mentioned earlier, came to see my father in large numbers. Among them would be new faces I would see once or twice and never see again. But, besides these interim visitors, there were people who would regularly come by, almost every day. If any one of the regular visitors missed a turn, my father would, sometimes in an admonishing and sometimes anxious manner, enquire how they had been. Most of these visitors were from our neighbourhood, and their houses were close to ours. But I rarely saw them walking on the streets or in the lanes. However, when I went on the roof to fly my kite, I would see some of them on the roofs of their houses, mostly in winter, and they would be sunning themselves. At that time they would be dressed in ordinary plain clothes. But these very people when they came out to visit us would be dressed from head to toe in highly formal clothing as though they were invited for a special occasion. And my father too did the same. Whenever some one came to call on him he would get dressed in full formal attire and then go receive the guests in the visitor's room. But when he started virtually living in that room, he gave up that custom and now instead of changing clothes he would draw his wrap right up to his shoulders when a visitor came.

I often had to escort visitors to that room. Sometimes mother would send me in with sherbets, etc., to offer the guests. On such occasions I would get to hear the conversation going on in the room. I liked the sound of their talk, but I couldn't pay close attention for I didn't stay long enough in the room. I just knew that they and my father were great talkers and there was laughter and joking. But they would become quiet in my presence and I would come away from there hastily.

But that day when I went in with a tray of eatables all the visitors suddenly became silent and turned towards me in such a way that I became nervous and for no reason I began to feel like a culprit. But all of them and my father too were looking at me with gentle smiles in the manner considerate grown-up people adopt towards younger persons. After some moments one of them asked:

'My boy, that thing on the roof, the one that gives the direction of the wind...'

'That is broken,' I chimed in, and having said that became uneasy and glanced at my father, but he still had a smile on his lips. He said very gently:

'Tell them the whole story.'

'Yes, son, from beginning to end.' Another visitor said.

I told them all that I had told my father, and held back from them too the fact that I had tried to correct the weathervane's direction.

The room was silent was a long time, and slowly the smiles vanished from their faces. Then someone said to my father:

'That is why I say that you should have it brought down.'

In reply, my father said the very same things I have mentioned in the beginning. Then they began to talk of other matters and I came away with the empty tray.

After this I heard them in that room, many times, talking about the weathervane. But gradually, the attention ceased, perhaps because the number of daily visitors was also dwindling.

During the course of two winters the numbers had diminished considerably. And those remaining faded away one by one. Ultimately, only one visitor was left who would come by occasionally. He had difficulty walking. Some family member of his would help him walk to our house and come back later to take him back. But even in those days the visitor would be dressed from head to toe in elegant clothes. One day, I was there when this last visitor was talking about the weathervane with my father. They were the same old questions and my father was giving the same old replies. That day, for the first time, I interrupted my elders and asked the question that had crossed my mind several times: 'Can't it be repaired?'

'By whom?' my father answered in a dejected tone.

'My son, only he could have repaired it,' the visitor responded in an even more dejected tone, 'the one who made it.'

My father nodded dejectedly in agreement and then added: 'Others will ruin it even more.'

The visitor agreed, nodding in the same dejected fashion, and then both remained silent for a long while. Yet the silence seemed to be silent communication and they stayed this way until a servant arrived to help the visitor back home.

After he had left my father asked me to come to his side.

'Forget about it my son,' he said, 'and think about your mother. Can you see how she is wearing herself out caring for me?'

At that moment my mother who had probably been waiting for some time for the visitor to leave, came into the room. She was clutching a round copper tray with both hands. Right in the middle of the tray was a brazier in which coals were burning and on the coals was placed a small pot in which some paste was being warmed. The aroma from the paste filled the room and I began to feel warm and safe. My mother put down the tray on the floor near the chair, and clasping the pot with the end of her dupatta she took it off the coals and put that on the floor as well. My father observed her all this time and then said: 'Aren't there other people at home? You have to do all the work.'

Without replying, my mother removed the sheet draped on him and began to fold it.

There were other people in our house, but my mother did all my father's nursing. She never mentioned her own health problems, so we had no idea that she was steadily wasting away. But one morning it was late and she did not wake up, and later in the afternoon her dead body was kept in the midst of relatives, close and distant.

That day, other people nursed my father and we did not tell him anything. But later at night, instead of inquiring about mother he announced her death himself and then said: 'I had said this would happen.'

For several days he did not speak to anyone, and family members were nursing him. Visitors had stopped calling on him now. No one called on him when mother died, or maybe some did call, and I did not know. But now a family member would always be by his side and I too went to his room many times during the day and stayed by his side for hours.

One evening, when the birds were chirping in the vines in our courtyard, I entered the visitors' room and found my father's last visitor there. I was barely able to recognize him. And I couldn't reckon after how many days he was visiting us again. He was sitting at a decidedly crooked angle on the visitor's chair and an attendant who looked as if he needed aid himself was standing behind him. And in standing right behind the chair he was preventing the visitor from falling sideways. This time the visitor was dressed in ordinary plain clothes and now I recalled that he was the same man who would sit on winter afternoons on the roof of the house adjoining ours, and he would have only a piece of cloth around his waist, and at that time I did not perceive him as one of my father's visitors but as some other person.

He sat silently with his head bowed, quivering. My father was silent too and it seemed that they were unaware of each other's presence. I stood silently too. Gazing at them I once again began to feel that they were communicating wordlessly. I was by my father's head and the visitor was in front of me. His body was still trembling and the attendant would support him with both hands and sometimes support him with one hand and fan him with the other as if he was chasing away flies. I gazed intently at my father and the visitor's faces one by one; I subconsciously began to presume that they were talking about the weathervane. And this presumption turned into conviction when suddenly my father said: 'Advantage, there is no advantage, but then it is not harming anyone is it?'

The visitor sat for a long time, nodding his head in agreement. Eventually, the old attendant helped him and took him back, and in the process stumbled and nearly fell twice himself.

By the time the rainy season was getting over, all at home realized that my father did not have much time left. His caregivers grew more attentive and every need was taken care of. Whenever someone did something for him he would respond with blessings and his tone was a happy one. Yet he was deep in thought too. I now spent most of my time in his room, and watched, as he lay absorbed in thought. His eyes were sometimes wide open and sometimes half open, but did not appear to be focused on anything. When I saw him gazing blankly it would cross my mind that perhaps he was thinking about my mother or perhaps he was thinking about our weathervane. But his health was deteriorating speedily now. I forgot all about the weathervane and even my mother.

There were no clouds in the sky now. But occasionally the cloudless skies would silently light up with a flash of lightning and people would make predictions on the possibilities of rain. One night, on the last day of the lunar month, the silent flash of lightning became purposeful. I was in my father's room. It used to be almost dark there in daytime, but tonight it seemed as if many bright lights were flashing on and off. I would see my father lying on his armchair and then he would be lost in darkness. The display of flashing lights which filled me with delight in childhood now filled the space with dread as sporadic illumination revealed the tussle going on there. My father was lying still. Suddenly it occurred to me that he was struggling with his last breaths. I thought that I should alert the rest of the family when I heard the tired, faint voice of my father: 'Who is on the roof?'

I drew near him.

'On the roof?' I asked, bending towards him.

'On the roof,' he said, 'I can hear someone.'

I strained my ears to listen. All was quiet, only the lightning was flashing. I listened even harder and now I heard a low voice. It was like a groan, somewhat like one hears from the lips of older people when they stand up or sit down. But it didn't seem that it was coming from the direction of the roof.

I heard the low voice again, and it struck me that I had heard that voice before from the weathervane when the wind was changing direction, and again when I had forced it to turn windward.

There was a flash of lightning and I saw my father straining to hear the voice. I said:

'I'll go on the roof and check.'

He did not reply. I ran out of the room and crossing the courtyard, went up the stairs and was on the roof in a trice.

I saw the weathervane gleaming, on and off. With each flash of lightning it came into view, looking like a delicate thing wrought in silver. I went up close to examine it. It was still frozen in the strange position. There was no shuddering or any other sound to be heard coming from it. I was in the process of examining it from different angles when I became aware of someone standing on the roof adjoining ours. Her face was sporadically lit up by the flashing lightning.

She seemed to be a woman advanced in years. I couldn't recognize her and tried to look at her carefully with each new flash. Eventually, I recalled that she was the one who would stand on the roof with her friends and sometimes by herself. At the moment, she was alone on her terrace and stood gazing at the weathervane. She seemed unaware of my presence. I pretended that I wasn't aware of her presence too, and slowly walked away and came down the stairs.

In the room my father was lying on his side. I had tiptoed in but my father heard my footsteps nevertheless, and asked:

'Was anyone there?'

I reported that there was only the weathervane, and that it was silent and frozen in one direction. My father continued to lie on his side and was quiet for a long time. Just when I was convinced that he was sleeping, he drew a deep breath and said: 'Arrange for it to be brought in.' And he drew another deep breath.

I glanced in the direction of his voice. Lightning had ceased flashing now and far away in the sky some cloud was rumbling. I looked at my father's face in the lone dim light burning in the room. He was sleeping soundly and the sheet covering his chest was heaving gently.

After this, as we had expected, my father did not live long. He was conscious to the very end and would even talk a little. Mostly he would shower blessings on those of us nursing him. Sometimes he expressed regret for bothering us. But he never mentioned the weathervane again. This did not surprise me as much as the fact that he never talked about my mother. On the last day he did take my mother's full name, and then died before completing his sentence.

(3)

After my father's death I was caught up in the everyday chores of domesticity. During these years several houses in my neighbourhood built upper storeys and these new constructions surrounded my house in such a manner that it became quite impossible to spot the weathervane from below. At first I wasn't aware of this but one day, returning home, I paused at the turn from where one could spot the weathervane on the roof of my house. The new top floor of an adjacent house had eclipsed both my house and the weathervane. I tried various angles but could not catch sight of the weathervane.

After several unsuccessful attempts, I came home and went straight up to our roof. The weathervane was set in the same position as before, and there was no apparent change in its form. Looking at its discoloured body and crude design, I was amazed how it could possibly have seemed so delicate and silvery in the flash of lightning.

The following day, a mason was digging the small platform on which the weathervane had been affixed. Before starting the job the mason had informed me that he would extract the weathervane carefully from its base but he wouldn't be able to set it back on its axis in the right position. Upon hearing this I said: 'It doesn't have to be put back.'

After this, the mason began working with assurance. He scraped off the layers of cement from the platform. Finally, the pivot was loosened and began to wobble. Working steadily, the mason turned towards me and said: 'Where will you store it?'

I hadn't thought of this. I made a quick decision and said: 'In the loft or in a big box.'

'It will spoil if you simply store it,' he said, and then added after a pause, 'I have an idea if you agree.'

I went along with his idea.

(4)

I don't get as many visitors as my father did. These visitors keep changing and they only come to my place when they need something done or I need something from them. Every visitor, at least at first, looks with interest at the crude fish that is affixed on a platform, built in one corner of the visitors' room. Its head and tail are almost at the same distance from the floor, making it appear that it is lying flat on the tip of its axis. And looking at it, no one can think that it could be a bird and could be related to winds. Everyone thinks it is a decorative piece and probably that is why no one asks me what purpose it serves. I, too, don't tell them that this is our own weathervane and it no longer points windward.

Translated by Mehr Afshan Farooqi

Khalida Husain
(b. 1938)

Khalida Husain started writing fiction in 1963 under her maiden name, Khalida Asghar. She emerged at this time as an extremely moving, complex, and profound fictional voice in Urdu. She wrote stories charged with a feeling of menace, loss, and alienation, for example '*Hazar-paya*' (The Millipede) and '*Savari*' (The Wagon); these stories almost became symbols of what *jadidiyat* or modernism had to say about the human condition. After half a dozen brilliant stories she stopped writing. Apparently her marriage in 1965 and the subsequent move from India to Pakistan in 1967 had something to do with that. She began writing again after twelve years—a more mature, restrained writer than before. She works and lives in Rawalpindi and has published three volumes of short stories. Her stories in the second phase of her writing career are mostly about female identity in the traditional society of present-day Pakistan.

The story presented here is important in its urgent immediacy; it represents a sensitive writer's response to sufferings caused by the so-called war on terrorism being waged in the name of democracy. Though based on a news report and following closely on actual events, the story still succeeds as fiction, invoking disgust and horror in the reader, more so than the newspaper story.

Adam's Progeny

The helicopter's huge rotor had not yet stopped whirling—sand was blowing all around. Perhaps it was not intended to be shut down. But no, maybe it has stopped and I am imagining it still running. Because events keep following one another continuously, sometimes an image of something meant to be forgotten is engraved in one's eyes for a long time. Then, he rubbed his eyes and found them full of burning sparks. In his palms, between his fingers, and beneath his nails, nostrils, and ears, everywhere, the sand burned like sparks. There was a menacing dryness all over the place. Everything was at the point of cracking. He curled his toes inside his heavy boots; a sticky dampness there. The stench rose from his feet and stuck in his throat.

He saw all of them...one, two, three...all five standing in front of the helicopter in a semicircle. He narrowed his eyes in the intense black heat of the sunshine and tried to catch a glimpse of the new arrival. To his surprise that lithe-bodied, uniform-clad man kept his flaming red face straight up. After exchanging salutes, they began to move in the direction of a convoy of vehicles. Now they were so close that he could see the glassy-blue marble-like eyes of the new arrival. They were not eyes but marbles, as is the case with their eyes generally. Actually he couldn't see any special quality that would have recommended this man being sent from overseas. When the group got closer, the expert cast a cursory glance at him. Then the inspector said, 'He's our man.' After that, as was his habit, he twisted his mouth and laughed. 'I would say he has become our man. Such people are very useful. We can't do without them. If we hadn't found such people our work would have become very difficult, almost impossible.'

So far the inspector was under the impression that he did not understand their language very well. They had learnt a few words of his language. Those words were enough for everyday needs and also for some specific requirements. But he could understand their language really well, though he did not want them to know this. What a language it was—its words slithered hissing and spitting on one's lips like the sting of a snake, always filling his mouth with a poisonous taste.

Now they were all seated in the vehicle. He sat with the driver.

'So what is the particular challenge that is bothering you all?' the expert inquired, cigarette in mouth.

'We are not killing ourselves in this accursed desert to be driven mad by these reptiles. There is definitely something, some great mysterious, satanic power in them which refuses to be extinguished. Something like the dreams one has of men who live on even after they are dead. These men spring back to life moments after they are killed, following us, threatening to choke the life out of us. Such are the nightmares of this desert.'

From his front seat he could recognize that this was the voice of the captain who had gotten the habit of kicking with his thick military boots the groaning, emaciated men who lay prostrated in the barracks. Once, when he thrust his hand in his pocket searching for a cigarette, a maroon wallet fell out with a thump and lay open. In it was the picture of a girl with corn-coloured hair and blood red lips which were parted in a lustful way.

'Oh.' The captain had immediately picked up the wallet and, leaning back against the burning wall of the barrack, delivered a solid kick on Hamza's chest, as he lay gasping for breath. Then he broke into peals of uncontrolled laughter. Hamza, who used to be so healthy that we called him 'Hercules'. But, after he was injured, the poison spread throughout his body, and in a few days he was reduced to a heap of bones. Now as the jeep drew close to the jail, he thought of all this, all the while sitting straight and unmoving in the seat.

'Crushing a man's masculinity is an art. And until you extinguish it, the weakest of the weak will keep troubling you, making life difficult, in other words driving you mad.' The expert still clutched a cigarette between his lips.

Two soldiers who stood on guard opened the huge iron gate of the jail and saluted, smartly clicking their heels together. The jeep came to a halt near the barracks. The inspector gestured, indicating that he wanted him to come up nearer to him. Now he was standing amongst the five.

The inspector was explaining (even though he thought this man didn't understand much of the language) that he was a key man among the insurgents, and that he had fallen into their custody by a stroke of luck. He knows that one cannot live without food. And that nothing is more priceless than life itself. Death, in fact unalleviated death is an unbearable state of affairs. Everything else is empty imaginings that go up in smoke. He's cooperating with us—that is why we have given him our uniform to wear. He has provided us intelligence about the biggest insurgent group. Then the inspector uttered a dirty expletive.

'Hey, Amin ibn Sayeed. Your mother-father's lamenting your death will be your only self identification.' Voices were boiling inside his head, unsolicited.

'So he's a very useful man, is that it!' The expert dug an iron finger in his chest as he spoke. This sudden movement pushed him from his position. Those around him bared their teeth.

'What's his name?' The expert's eyes were made of stone. In fact his mouth was like a slit in blue rock. His lips barely moved when he spoke. Perhaps he always kept his teeth tightly clenched.

'His name is Amin. He was a university student and the organizer of an insurgent group. Others like him are in cell number "000". You will be happy to see them and appreciate our work.' The captain gave him a solid push, throwing him viciously against the wall.

'Okay. I don't have much time. I want to start work immediately,' the expert said, stepping out briskly. Then, the five men began marching. The captain pushed him along as they moved forward. All this time, the wound on his toe had been oozing blood, soaking his sock completely. Sharp waves of pain were coursing through his leg upwards to his neck like an electric current. Despite this, there was a strange feeling in his innards. A black churning was spreading through his stomach. It had been two full days since he had had anything to eat or drink. And all this because of Hamza.

Abu Hamza, who was preparing himself that day for a suicide attack. Laila and Quddus were there too. They were in a small, airless room, in a ruined building surrounded by rubble, well hidden from the street. That day, after a lot of difficulty, he was able to salvage a few pieces of mouldy bread from the garbage. There was a bunch of people scouring the garbage for pieces of bread.

On Laila's cheek was a long deep scar. A shard had embedded itself there in the course of an explosion. Abu Hamza had pulled it out with his dissection forceps. Laila's hands were icy cold with the intense pain, and her body was trembling. That day her father and younger sister had been driven out of their house and arrested. The arrestors were actually looking for Abu Hamza and Laila.

Entire neighbourhoods had been stuffed into prisons on charges of terrorism. Before this, they had no idea that prisons could outstrip neighbourhoods. No one was permitted to go near the prisons.

Abu Hamza put a bit of mouldy bread in his mouth and nearly vomited.

'It's full of bacteria. It's better to choose your own death than to die from a bacterial infection.' Laila said, tying that belt around her waist.

'But what will you get out of this? You will die and some of them. You don't even know who among them or how many? Probably some innocent or untargeted people would get killed in this blast. Above all, what will your father and sister gain from this?' he had said to Laila.

'Nothing can bring them any relief now.' Laila had replied.

'I know. If Sakina is still alive, what state would she be in and my father...' She lapsed into silence.

'Do you want me to suffer the same fate as Sakina?'

'No. No.' He had immediately replied, and at once got up to help her adjust her belt and set the device. Laila was very calm. He took both her hands and held them between his. At that moment there was a soft warmth about them. Her brown eyes seemed darker than ever. Suddenly he felt embarrassed. He let go of Laila's hands. She calmly lit a cigarette. She had become addicted to smoking in her university days. She leaned back against the wall, and closed her eyes composedly, taking deep drags from her cigarette. Smoke continuously drifted through her full lips. Abu Hamza flung the remaining part of the mouldy bread at the wall.

'I find all this unbelievable. Sadaam Husain, the Protector of the World, emerges like a rat from a six-foot deep hole in the ground. In spite of that, nothing has changed for you and me. Amin, you didn't believe in the power of divine intervention. Do you believe in it now? For centuries, Nature has been intending this event. In fact, centuries are mere passing moments in this master plan. Since eternity this land has been saturated by the blood of innocents. The curse it bears is coming to pass word for word.' Abu Hamza got up and started pacing. There wasn't much room to pace in that small area.

'Abu Hamza I'm surprised at you, such fatalism. You're a medical doctor and yet you believe in all of this. But this is nothing. The world is overflowing with the blood of innocents. This is the history of humanity. There must have been countless curses; and blessings or curses, what are they after all?' He spoke agitatedly.

'I didn't believe in this. But the winds of this land are wailing and have been wailing interminably. This land produces gold, gushing forth like a torrent. But that doesn't seem to matter. Starvation and repression have been stretched on generations like tight clothing. At this time my only concern is my need. I want to choose a better death.'

'But it doesn't necessarily have to be this way. One doesn't have to die. Definitely not. Staying alive is a natural urge, more acceptable.' An inner voice had whispered this to him, and he had flushed with shame. When and how did this weakness arise in him, he wondered? Perhaps this is inherited.

Abu Hamza's father was a farmer and Laila's worked at extracting oil from the earth. They were working-class people who knew how to live with physical discomfort. They found pleasure in hard work and pain. And he? He was the son of a professor who had spent his life amid books and words. His father taught others the philosophy of life and existentialism but never had the chance to test his own principles. All of this had blended in his son's blood. 'Books turn a man into a coward'. He felt more ashamed at this explanation. His father loved cleanliness and beauty. He could not tolerate even a speck of dust or dirt in the house. He walked barefoot on the marble floor of his room, the soles of his feet white like marble itself. Every object in his room was spotlessly clean and sparkled like glass. In this clean environment he lived in dread of physical pain. Suffering and the thought of death always made him fearful. Therefore in his old age he spent considerable time in prayer and meditation. But for him? His share was only the fear of physical pain and terror of death. He bore no allegiance to any ideology except what was obvious and true. And this indeed was the truth, he thought: that existence is just another name for keeping one's body alive under all circumstances. All of humanity's efforts were to get rid of sorrow, pain, and suffering. These sorrows and sufferings are physical, only physical.

But at this time, Laila was in front of him. Her beautiful body wrapped in that full-length black dress. He had failed miserably to control the desire to touch her, to see her undressed. He knew that Laila was engaged to Abu Hamza. This was another reason for him to feel ashamed. It was as if shame and regret were coursing through his body instead of blood. Then Abu Hamza said: 'Laila, you will be at the crossroads by the Bank at five past ten and Quddus and I will be at the market street at the same hour.' Abu Hamza produced a small camera from his shirt pocket.

'Amin, Gibreel al Amin.' He spoke affectionately like old times. 'Here, take a picture. Bring it to the media folks after we are gone so that they can see how happy we were at the time.'

Abu Hamza put his arm around Laila. She rested her head against his shoulder in such a way that their cheeks touched. He saw this scene through the lens of the camera and clicked. The three of them silently left the room and went outside. It was bleak outside. At some distance, dogs were scouring through a rotting garbage heap. The sky was full of the thunder of airplanes flying.

He sat in that empty cell of a room till five after ten. He sat leaning against the wall at the same spot Laila had rested her back. Cigarette butts lay scattered in front of him, some silver-grey ash on the floor. He stood up at six after ten. He saw parts of Laila's beautiful body floating in the air and Abu Hamza's strong arms and broad chest reduced to lumps of burnt flesh sticking to the walls. That is the acute suffering, the pain, and terror that every human has to bear when life ebbs out of the body. He was reminded of one particular lecture by Professor Abdul Hamid: How does one define death, that itself is debatable. What is death? The Professor was explaining that this is the truth, the absolute truth, and not make-believe that death comes like a piece of fabric getting caught in the sharp thorns of an acacia tree, and one tries to free it, but in the process it rips into shreds. The acacia tree remains, but the fabric doesn't. The tree will always remain. Just then, while straining his ear in anticipation of an explosion, he lifted his nose to test the air for any possible odour of explosives. But instead of that sound and smell, there was the tramp of heavy boots, and a man fully armed was standing in front of him.

Then the man kneed him in the groin. He doubled over in pain. The man twisted his arms behind his back and tied them up. Then, in his tongue, he uttered the foulest obscenities that were beyond anything imaginable; nothing worse could ever be conceived in any language.

'Where are they? Where is the rest of the group?'

That was a bizarre moment. Certainly, skin being scraped, nails pulled out, private parts crushed is irrelevant. Certainly, fresh and wholesome food and bodily comforts are necessary. Absolutely necessary. As soon as he entered the cabin, he told them that at five past ten the group members were at the market street and near the bank by the crossroads. How easily the images had been printed from the camera. He could see Laila's beautiful eyes and feel the soft warmth of the touch of her hands as if she was alive. Unaware, tears streamed down his cheeks and mingled with stinking spittle that had been spat on his face and clung to his lips.

That day, a beautiful girl named Laila merged with the elements in such a way as if she never existed. But Abu Hamza, Abu Hamza was rounded up, while he was semi-conscious, still breathing. Such injured, semi-conscious victims are like gold to interrogators, easy to get confessions from. As are faithless, unprincipled people like him.

'Gibreel al-Amin!' A name he was not worthy of. He thought about this. But trusting and cheating on trust, these are only concepts, when the body and its senses and their satiation are primary. Now he was following them into that cell where Quddus lay on the floor with his hands chained behind his back, and a black attack dog, his long red tongue hanging out, with pointed teeth bared, repeatedly growled and pounced at Quddus, then was pulled back by the collar. In the cell next door, Abu Hamza, who had been picked up in a semi-conscious state, and despite being subjected to his skin being scraped, limbs stretched, eyes blinded with the brightness of a thousand suns, and relentless, unremitting high-pitched noise, had not uttered a single word.

It was beyond belief! The ones with the heavy boots and weaponry, blue glassy eyes, and merciless lips uttered all possible obscenities. Abu Hamza's ribs stood out. His chest was a mass of blue bruises and raw, red wounds. Yellow pus oozed from the gashes on his legs. White, thread-like larvae slithered in the wounds. His handsome jaw was marred with blue, lumpy nodes, and his hair jumbled like knotted string hung over his eyes. His thick beard and nails had not stopped growing. His fingers were swollen like yams, and a watery substance oozed from them.

'So this is the leader!' The expert looked at Abu Hamza closely and then turned towards him.

'You know him?'

'He was the one who told us where to find him.'

Abu Hamza moved the thick fringe of hair from his eyes with his yam-like fingers and looked at him. There was no complaint, no surprise in his eyes, or on his face. No hate either. After the expert had been briefed, he sat down in a chair and the other four sat around him. He stood alone in a corner. Abu Hamza kept watching him all the while.

He was getting bits and pieces of the expert's conversation. The expert was telling the rest of the group the importance of conditioning prisoners before interrogation and extortion of sensitive information. 'And their masculinity is the biggest hurdle to overcome. In fact, the quality of maleness itself is problematic among men in general, and especially among these Arabs. Until you convince them they are not even men, they are of no use. Tomorrow morning at nine-thirty, put up a pavilion in the enclosure outside the barracks. You have a lot to learn yet.'

The expert left, whistling a tune.

So the pavilion was erected and was ready exactly at nine-thirty. All residents from the barracks were collected together. So many people, he was amazed at the numbers. People who had been missing for months; those who had been counted amongst the dead. He wanted to look at each one carefully. Was this a gathering of dead people? Maybe that is why there was an eerie silence amidst the crowd. Nothing but stillness. Then a drum was beaten. Boom. Boom. It was followed by a bugle, and the huge iron gate was flung open. The entire corpus moved as one whole body, and came into the pavilion. That woman soldier, dressed in a soldier's uniform, her breasts pushed upwards by the belt strained against her shirt; her brown hair was creeping out from the confines of the army beret. She held a thick leash in her hand and the leash was attached to the neck of a moving creature—what kind of a creature, one couldn't tell. Was it man or dog, it wasn't obvious. But it was moving on four legs, larger than a dog, stark naked. Like an animal, its nakedness exposed its sex. It crawled on all fours, carrying its skeletal frame. Its face was held in front like a snout, and a tangled beard hung down. Do dogs have beards? He tried to remember. The female soldier forcefully jerked at the leash, making the four-legged creature's neck twist and turn. Then she would deliver a powerful kick on its posterior with the heel of her thick military boot. Then she would give a triumphant glance, waving at the onlookers.

Now the expert was standing in front of the row of officers. He lifted his hands, forming his fingers in a 'V' and shouted 'Bravo. Keep it up.'

The female soldier became more energized, hearing this praise. The expert cast a triumphant glance at everyone and shouted, pointing at the creature with the collar, kicking its snout with his heavy boots.

'Dog. Dog. Brr-Brr. Woof, woof.' Half the crowd laughed, the others remained silent. Then the expert gestured and a bunch of photographers came running, carrying with them all sorts of cameras. Then two soldiers walked up, unzipped their pants and begin to urinate on that four-legged creature. The four-legged creature stood squirming beneath the stinking cascade, trying to protect its face and eyes.

'Hey, hey!' The female soldier pulled at its collar, demonstrating her extraordinary strength and endurance. Abu Hamza collapsed on his hands and feet, an animalistic scream emerged from his throat. The cameras began moving fast, click, click.

Suddenly, the drum was beaten, and the crowd dispersed. They disappeared inside the barracks within moments. In the black pavilion, the four-legged creature lay on the ground, and the female soldier tugged at its collar.

Translated by Mehr Afshan Farooqi

Muhammad Mansha Yad
(b. 1938)

Modernist fiction and radio/television feature writer, Mansha Yad writes both in Punjabi and Urdu. Muhammad Mansha was born in Shekhupura, Pakistan. A civil engineer, he was employed in the corporation that supervised the construction of Islamabad. Mansha has lived in Islamabad since 1963.

He was an active member of the Halqa-e Arbab-e Zauq, serving as its secretary for nearly ten years. He began writing for children's journals when he was quite young. Some of his collections are *Band Mutthi Mein Jugnu* (Fireflies in a Clenched Fist), 1975; *Maas aur Mitti* (Flesh and Earth), 1980; *Khala Andar Khala* (Void Within Void), 1983; *Vakt Samandar* (Time, Ocean), 1986; and *Darakht Admi* (Trees, Men), 1991.

Mansha Yad revisits the Partition in his stories again and again. As a modernist, he relies upon allegory rather than abstraction. The story presented here from *Khala Andar Khala* is a fine example of his style.

The Show

They cover a long distance in the dark and arrive at the river bank at daybreak.

Here and there the bank is littered with dead and half-eaten fish. 'Father, this is the work of otters.'

'Yes, son,' says the older man, 'this is precisely what they do. They keep killing the fish and piling them up. But when the time comes to eat them, they fight among themselves and ruin the game and bloody themselves.'

'All these fish!' says the boy. 'Wouldn't the river run dry of fish if they kill so many in just one night?'

'This could happen, if the otters keep multiplying.'

The two put their bags down on the bank and look across the river at the village they are headed for. The minarets of the village mosque are clearly visible, but there is neither a boat nor a bridge to cross over to the other side. Troubled, they look at the river. It appears uniformly deep and wide at every point. The older man broods a while and then says, 'Son, let's place our trust in God and plunge into the river.'

'Whatever you say, father.'

'What if we drown?'

'We won't repeat the mistake.'

'You've turned out to be quite smart, Jamura!' the older man laughs and says.

'But, of course. I'm your son—am I not?'

'We certainly would have plunged,...' the older man stops, thinks some, and then says, 'but for this dream I had last night.'

'What dream, father?'

'It was a very frightening dream, son.'

'What did you see?'

'Oh Jamura, I saw that there was a big crowd. I'm standing in the middle of that crowd with the spotted snake curled around my neck. The children are clapping and older people are throwing coins onto the sheet spread on the ground. Just then the snake, whom I've nurtured with the same loving care as I have you, suddenly bites my neck and empties its poison.'

'And then?'

'And then darkness begins to fall before my eyes. People's faces begin to dim and their voices fade out. I feel I'm falling deeper and deeper into the well of a deathly sleep. As I'm drowning, I muster all my ebbing strength and call after you in the darkness.'

'Then?'

'Then I wake up with a start, hearing my own cry and, lo, I see it's midnight, the moon has gone, the dogs are howling ominously, and the breeze, heavy with dew, is moving about balefully.'

'What happens next?'

'My eyes fall on you. You are lying all curled up from the cold. I throw the sheet over you, just as I always do in the arena, when I slash your throat and then make you leap back to life. But at that melancholy hour of the night I felt that the manner in which I threw the sheet over you was distinctly ominous. And my sleep left me.'

'Just from that,' the boy says, 'you concluded that we should not enter the river?'

'Yes, son. It doesn't look like a good day for us.'

The older man sits down and stretches out his legs to rest. The boy, still full of energy, starts clambering up and down the hills at a run. Suddenly he shouts: 'The bridge, father, I can see the bridge! It really isn't all that far!'

The word 'bridge' sends a current of fresh energy through the man's decrepit old body. He stands up and sprints off to the hill and gazes at the water flowing downstream. Then, overwhelmed by a sudden rush of happiness, he says, 'Yes, the bridge isn't all that far. But...the path is riddled with difficulties.'

'That hardly matters, father.'

They pick up their gear and start walking along the river on the path which takes them through formidable cliffs and steep slopes, hills, ravines, dangerous fjords, thick jungles, prickly brambles, and dry grasses that injure their feet. But they keep moving along. And the tall minarets of the village mosque across the river move right along with them. They are exhausted from walking on what looks like an endless trek. Morning turns into noon, noon into afternoon, but the bridge still looks just as far as when they had started. Which prompts the older man to say, 'It is very strange, Jamura—the bridge keeps moving ahead.'

'And the village too,' the boy says. 'The minarets are walking right along with us.'

'Strange, isn't it, Jamura?'

'Very strange, father.'

'I'd say, son, it's some kind of spell.'

'Want to know what I think, father? We make fun of people all the time. Today, well, today, we are being laughed at.'

They keep trudging along. The afternoon dwindles. They are exhausted from walking. Their lips are crusted from drinking the river's muddy water over and over again. Their clothes are torn to shreds and their feet are bleeding from walking through the thorny brush. Still the bridge and the minarets of the village mosque beyond remain as distant as ever.

'Stop, son,' the older man says. 'Perhaps we are not fated to reach the village across the river. We'll keep walking on and on but will perhaps never reach the bridge.'

'What shall we do then?'

'Let's go back.'

'No, father. What good will it do to go back? We've aimed for the village across the river, haven't we? Besides, men don't give up easily.'

'You've a point there, son. Even our womenfolk don't easily get frightened by the fury of the waves. They plunge right into the river with nothing but pitchers of unbaked clay to keep them afloat.'

'Good, father, then let's jump into the river.'

'No, son, you'll tire. Besides, we've all this gear to carry.'

'Don't worry about me, father. As for our things, we'll have new ones made once we get there.'

The older man says nothing. He puts the stuff back down and gazes off into the river waters. Then breaks into a song:

Deep is the river
the boat rickety and old
And fearful tigers stand watch on the river bank...

The boy chimes in, completing the lines:

I too must visit my lover's abode
Would that someone came along.

Suddenly they hear the sounds of dogs barking and cattle lowing.

'These sounds—right in the middle of the jungle?' the boy says.

'Looks like there's a village nearby—I mean a different village.'

'Looks like that.'

'Let's spend the night in this village. We'll have a good night's rest and then we can start off again early in the morning. What do you say, son?'

'As you like.'

The older man thinks for a bit and then starts off after the sounds. The boy trails behind him, casting furtive glances every now and then back at the village across the river. Gradually they pull farther and farther away from the river bank and come upon a small village.

Abruptly the older man stops short. He looks overhead at the jujube tree and asks dumbly, 'Jamura, it couldn't be—'

Jamura too looks into the tree, then picks up a rock and hurls it at the foliage. Berries come tumbling down. He picks one up, tastes it, and quickly spits it out. 'Yes, father,' he says, 'it's only neem. Horribly bitter.'

'God take care,' the older man says. 'Neem right along with the jujube. It doesn't bode well. Son, it's some spell.'

The boy just gawks at the sky without speaking a word.

'Those are swallows, son.'

'Yes, a whole flock of them.'

'Must be looking for food.'

'Or something else—who knows?'

'What else, son?'

'Elephants.'

'No, son, no. They are not those swallows. These are the kind who just sit on the backs of elephants, have a good time and chirp.'

'Let's get out of here, father. This place doesn't look right.'

'God will take care, son,' the older man says. 'Let's do a little business here in this village. We'll spend the night here and be on our way early in the morning.'

'Whatever you say, father.'

They step into the village, dump their gear in an open space, and scan the area. The boy spreads out a sheet and sits down on one of the corners. The older man yanks out his small kettle drum and flute from the gear and begins to play them both.

In no time a crowd of children materializes and begins to gather around them. The faces of father and son light up with hope and satisfaction. The older man looks at the boy meaningfully and shakes his head, as if saying, 'Fine, now we'll earn enough to spend the night splendidly.'

The older man continues playing the flute and drum, becomes tired and says, 'Son, it's a strange village. My arms are frozen stiff from playing the drum and my chest has gone dry from blowing into the flute, and we have yet to see an adult man or woman with a coin to spare.'

'They might be deaf, or they might have plugged their ears with cotton. Who knows?'

'Why so, son?'

'Because if one never gets to hear good news, a time comes when he's so fed up he doesn't want to hear anything at all.'

'Bravo Jamura, you've learnt your lesson well. Now tell me this: what makes you think they have never heard good news?'

'I see it written on the faces of these children, father.'

'Jamura, you're a smart boy.'

'Look who is my teacher.'

'You are right, son. They do look like orphans.'

'It even occurs to me that they have themselves driven their parents out of the village.'

'I wonder if we haven't tumbled into the wrong place.'

'Yes, it looks like that.'

'Not a single adult man or woman in the whole village! Looks as though all the adult population has gone away to other villages to perform shows as we do.'

'Then they will surely come back. We must wait for them.'

'Why?'

'Just to find out who is the better showman: you or they.'

'No, Jamura, no. These children scare me. They look so strange.'

'Well then, let's get out of here.'

'Yes, son, that makes better sense. But let's just ask these children where all their elders have disappeared to.'

'We are elders ourselves,' a brat blurts out from the crowd. 'Do we look like youngsters to you?'

Father and son are taken aback and exchange uncomprehending glances. They still haven't quite recovered from the shock when another tiny child addresses them in a perfectly adult voice: 'The Scribe has spoken the truth. Now you two get on with your show and be on your way. We don't permit those who think they are bigger and older than us to stay in our town a minute longer than is necessary.'

'You mean to say that not a single person of adult height lives in this village?'

'We don't let them,' a boy chuckles and says. 'We get rid of them right away.'

'So this village...' the older man stammers.

'Yes, this is our village and I am its chief. But don't waste our time. If you can perform some very good tricks, why, we will surely reward you. Enough. Now get on with your show.'

'We are not quite done watching the show before us,' the boy remarks.

'You! Mind your manners, boy!' the chief shouts angrily. 'Or else...'

'My, my,' the boy breaks into a laugh, 'you do behave like a chief's son.'

'Chief's son? Damn it, I am the chief!'

'Yes, yes, he is our chief!' a whole bunch of small ones affirm vociferously. But the boy keeps laughing. Then, edging close to the older man, he says, 'I wonder whether we haven't wandered into the land of dwarfs.'

'Showman, what's this nonsense?' the chief screams. 'He is calling us dwarfs? Tell the impudent brat to shut up, or get the hell out of our village.'

The older man looks about in numbed silence, then says to the boy, 'Jamura, be quiet. This is some spell.'

'What spell, father? These kids...'

'They're not children, my son,' the older man cuts him short.

'Then what are they?'

'Take a close look at them, Jamura. They have grey hair and they have wrinkles on their faces. They are advanced in years but their brains are still unripe. I'm afraid they could be quite dangerous.'

'Strange.'

'Very strange, son. God help us.'

Presently a few dwarfs walk in, carrying cots and wicker stools. The chief, along with crowds of his midget population, sit down on these. The chief says in a commanding voice: 'Let the show begin!'

The older man throws a perplexed look at the spectators, then begins to take things out of the bags.

First, he produces three balls and sets them on the ground. Then he covers them with three bowls, mumbles 'abracadabra', and blows over them. One by one, he lifts the bowls. Presto, the balls have disappeared.

He looks at the audience, expecting applause. But they are unmoved. They just stand or sit in motionless silence.

Next the old man puts the bowls back on the ground face down. When he picks them up one by one, each reveals a ball underneath. Again he looks at the chief and others among the audience, again expecting applause. But they seem totally unimpressed by the trick. They neither move nor applaud.

Then he takes a rupee coin out of his pocket. He turns it into two rupees, then the two into four, and exclaims, 'Gracious gentlemen! True lovers and connoisseurs of art! I'm no magician. This is merely sleight of hand. Were I a magician, I wouldn't have come here; I would've just stayed home minting money.'

'We know that,' the chief interrupts him. 'Just get on with the show.'

'Well, then, get into the act yourself,' Jamura says. 'What are you waiting for?'

'Showman, this impudent brat...' the chief snaps, bristling with rage.

'Chief, I beg your pardon,' the older man implores and, with a gesture of his hand, tells Jamura to be quiet. He then pulls out trick after ingenious trick to amuse them: he makes a perfectly empty glass become filled all by itself; turns the filled glass over without spilling a drop; closes his hand over a handkerchief and when he opens it, lo, the handkerchief has changed colour; swallows a lighted cigarette and makes the smoke come out of his ears; wraps a spotted snake round his neck and makes it bite him; swallows a knife clean and then makes it come back out...

But none, including the chief, is amused. No one claps or applauds.

'Strange.'

'Very strange, son. God help us.'

In desperation, he makes an announcement:

'And now for my grand finale I shall slit Jamura's throat and, after I've killed him, bring him back to life.'

Suddenly the chief and his subjects break into wild applause. The man is simply shocked. Earlier, whenever he made the announcement for this trick, which he usually saved till the end, the greater part of his audience reacted with horror and tried to persuade him not to do it. But these folks—what kind of brutes were they that they went into such ecstatic applause at the mere mention of slashing a throat?

He makes Jamura lie down on the ground and, as usual, pulls a sheet over him. Then he jerks out a butcher knife from his bag and, running his hand along the blade, says:

'Gracious gentlemen! True lovers and connoisseurs of art! What father can slash the throat of his own son? Only prophets have the guile and the courage to do so. This is but a game, a trick, an optical illusion. All for the sake of this wretched stomach which must somehow be filled...'

'Don't waste time with your prattle!' the chief thunders.

'Plunge the blade,' shouts someone in the audience.

'Yes, plunge the blade, plunge the blade,' the audience chime in, shouting at the tops of their voices.

The man tries to overcome his nervousness, then comes up to Jamura, wielding his butcher knife, and slashes the boy's throat.

The audience breaks into ecstatic screams, applauds widely, whistles and boos, throws coins on the sheet, and without bothering to observe his being brought back to life begins to slink away.

Slowly the place empties out.

The older man calls, 'Get up, son, and collect the money.'

But Jamura doesn't respond.

The man nervously uncovers the sheet and is horrified to see Jamura lying in a pool of blood, his neck actually severed.

The showman's cries begin to echo throughout the village.

Translated by Muhammad Umar Memon

Salam Bin Razak
(b. 1941)

A fine contemporary writer of fiction and translator, both in Urdu and Marathi, Razak retired from teaching in 1999. He has also written scripts for films in both languages. His work has been widely translated into Indian and foreign languages. Some of his collections are *Nangi Dopahar ka Sipahi* (Guard of Naked Afternoons), 1977; *Mu'abbir* (Interpreter of Dreams), 1987; and *Shikasta Buton ke Darmiyan* (Among Broken Idols), 2001.

He won the Sahitya Akademi Award for translation in 1998 and for creative writing in 2004.

Ekalavya—The Bheel Boy

Hiranyadhanus, the Bheel, with his only son Ekalavya in tow, traversed jungles and deserts, crossed rivers and ravines, mountains and valleys, and, after enduring great hardship for weeks and months, finally reached the outskirts of Indraprasth.

The day was far along by the time they entered the city, and the shadows had begun to shorten. The streets were sparkling clean and shops opened for business, vibrant with jostling crowds of shoppers. Priests—their colourful ceremonial marks pasted across their broad foreheads, hair neatly braided, and their sacred threads hung diagonally across their bodies from the left shoulder to the right hip—came clip-clopping out of temples on their wooden clogs. People would see them and immediately prostrate before them reverentially, while the priests accepted this obeisance by raising their heads. Every now and then, a mounted soldier, his sword hanging from his waist, a fringed diadem on his head, passed by. A few beggar boys, heads completely shaven except for a short, thin braid resting on the neck, and bare-bodied, except for a saffron-coloured dhoti draped around their waists, their foreheads smeared with ashes, went about collecting alms in their begging bowls.

Just then Hiranya, the Bheel, appeared on the street, holding his son's hand. As soon as the priests saw him, their foreheads creased with displeasure. People busy shopping momentarily turned around to look at the Bheel and his boy. By chance, the eyes of a mounted soldier also fell upon him. He spurred his animal on and promptly overtook Hiranya. He cracked his whip in the air and asked in a thundering voice:

'O Chandala! What brings you to the city this early? It isn't even a Thursday.'

'I haven't come to buy or sell anything. I have merely come to see the illustrious and the mighty Gururaj Dronacharya.'

'Gururaj Dronacharya?' repeated the incredulous people who had promptly crowded on the scene.

'Yes, him.'

Hiranya's throat was fast drying up; he was finding it hard to bear the lance-sharp eyes of the people.

'You are a wretched Sudra,' the mounted soldier rumbled, 'yet you talk about meeting Gururaj. Don't you know that's a sin?'

'Yes, Scion of a Kshatriya, I know that it is a sin. But a child's fancy has driven me to commit it.'

'Whose child?'

'My own, O Guardian of the Kingdom!' Hiranya replied, looking at Ekalavya who stood holding his finger.

'And what is his fancy?' the soldier asked, looking closely at the skinny, dark-coloured little thing who stood, holding a small bow in his other hand, with a quiver full of arrows hanging from his shoulder.

'Son of a Kshatriya, this fortunate one insists on learning archery from none other than Dronacharya himself, the Most High.'

Hearing this, the soldier looked at the people gathered around them. They all appeared positively shocked by the diminutive Bheel's insolence. Then he cleared his throat and said, 'O Wretched Man, Guruvirya Dronacharya teaches archery only to sons of Brahmins or Kshatriyas. You are neither. What makes you think you can get him to teach you archery?'

But this time it was Ekalavya who raised his head and answered, 'I'll persuade him with my skill.'

'Well then, show us your skill,' the soldier said, smiling with ridicule, as he looked at the people who also nodded derisively.

Quickly, Ekalavya straightened his bow, took out an arrow from the quiver and scanned the area with his restless eyes. He spotted a waterfowl in the sky. The Bheel boy strung his bow, slightly stretched out his left foot, rested his right knee on the ground, took aim and released the bow. The arrow whizzed out. The next instant the waterfowl fell right at the boy's feet, its body skewered by the arrow.

Everyone—the soldier included—peeled their eyes and gawked now at the bird, now at the boy. Some even cheered, 'Bravo! Well done!' in spite of themselves. The bird fluttered briefly and then the life ran out of it. People, overcome by both surprise and adulation, began to whisper:

'What perfect aim!'

'Who is this son of a Bheel?'

'Where are the two coming from?'

'Whom have they come to see?'

'Rajguru Dronacharya.'

'Rajguru? Really?'

'Yes. This son of a Bheel has come to learn archery from Rajguru. Or so it's said.'

'Son of a Bheel and wanting to learn archery from Rajguru—that's an outrage!'

'Rajguru won't teach him. No, never!'

'Of course he won't. This man's just a Bheel. And Rajguru Dronacharya is of such elevated status!'

'Well, let's just see.'

The soldier, as immobile as a statue, stared at Ekalavya for a while, and then after clearing his throat once again, said, 'Well, all right, you can go and see Rajguru if you must. But I'm telling you, he's not going to teach you anything. How will he teach you the art which princes no less than Bheema and Arjuna are learning from him?'

'But if I could just see him once,' Hiranyadhanus pleaded, 'my visit to the city, all the hardship I've had to endure, will have paid off.'

'Gururaj must be instructing the princes in the woods of the royal palace. If you can betake yourself there somehow, you'll be graced with a sight of him.'

Thereupon the soldier spurred his horse on. The horse lurched forward. The crowd moved to let the horse pass, and the soldier trotted off.

Hiranya seized Ekalavya's hand and the two began to walk towards the royal palace.

At the gate of the enclosure behind which lay the woods they were stopped by the gatekeeper, who said, 'O Chandalas! Watch where you're going. Don't you know evil spirits are not permitted here?'

'Lord, have mercy! Permit us to see Rajguru Dronacharya Ji. Just once! Please! For the sake of God, do us this favour!'

'Shut up, Vile Man! You're but an infernal being, yet you want to have a vision of Mahaguru Dronacharya? Don't you know, by merely uttering Mahaguru's name with your vile tongue, you've already defiled it, which is an unpardonable sin. That's crime enough to stick a red hot rod into your mouth.'

'Mercy, Son of a Kshatriya, mercy!' Hiranya joined both hands, begging for the gatekeeper's forgiveness, and then promptly touched the ground with his forehead.

Seeing Hiranya humble himself thus, the gatekeeper's anger subsided some. He raised his eyebrows and offered the question, 'Why do you want to see Acharya Deva?'

'For the sake of this obstinate brat. He has gotten it into his head to learn archery from Acharya Deva.'

The keeper of the royal gate burst into laughter, and went on laughing for a while. Then he said, 'You look a little crazy too. Oh dear! What makes you think that Acharya Deva will consent to teach archery to a Bheel's son?' He raised another resounding guffaw, 'Ha-ha-ha!'

'Lord, I know I'm being very impudent. But I felt helpless before a child's insistence. I had to come here. If only I could see Acharya Deva once, I will fall at his feet and implore him. I'd do exactly as he says. But I must see him.'

'And you there, wretched son of a Chandala,' the gatekeeper suddenly accosted Ekalavya. 'Do you know how to shoot arrows?'

'Lord, he knows but a little,' Hiranya Bheel said quickly.

'That tree over there,' Ekalavya pointed. 'Pick out any of its fruit, any at all, and I'll pluck it down by your feet.'

'Lord,' Hiranya quickly intervened, 'please don't mind; he doesn't mean it.'

The gatekeeper ignored Hiranya. He stared at the boy and said, 'Look, if you are unable to fell that bunch of three mangoes over there in one shot, I'll seize your bow and arrow and have you and your father beaten about the head with a shoe ten times over. Agreed?'

'Agreed!'

Hiranyadhanus froze. 'Lord, please let it go. Forgive him. He's just an ignorant little boy.' Then he grabbed the bow and chided the boy, 'Ekalavya! you argue with the Lord, where is your shame?'

'No, no! Don't stop him! Let him shoot. And if he misses, be prepared to receive ten blows over the head with a shoe.'

'Lord, you are the master. You can strike me now. You don't need an excuse.'

'No, the deal's struck. He must shoot.' Then looking at the boy, the gatekeeper said, 'Go on, shoot!'

Ekalavya strung the bow, took aim, and pulled the bowstring all the way to his earlobe. The arrow shot out with a whiz and the next moment the bunch of mangoes plunked down near them. The gatekeeper's mouth fell open at such superb deftness, his eyes riveted incredulously on the bunch.

Ekalavya bowed and saluted him reverentially.

Just then some commotion was heard inside the enclosure. The gatekeeper started and turned round to look. 'Well, well, what do you know?' he said. 'Acharya Deva's palanquin is coming along.'

He beckoned Hiranyadhanus and Ekalavya to step aside and unsheathed his sword with a flourish and stood at attention with the sword held before his face.

Shortly four palanquin-bearers briskly strode out of the gate carrying a golden palanquin in which sat Rajguru in all his pomp and glory.

Clad in a silken dhoti, his sacred thread in place, caste mark on his forehead, crown on his head, ears strung with jewelled ornaments—Rajguru's face emitted such radiance it was impossible to behold him. Two bodyguards holding tall lances came trailing behind the palanquin. Suddenly Hiranya threw himself in front of the carriage and, joining his hands in a gesture of reverence, touched the ground with his forehead. The armed guards made a dash for the Bheel and tore him from the ground.

'Guru Deva,' Hiranya implored. 'Please listen to my petition, I beg you.'

The guards began to drag him away to one side, but the Bheel kept on his humble litany, 'Guru Deva, hear me out. Please. Just once. Then punish me however you will.'

The Rajguru kept looking at Hiranya with his shining eyes for some time and then raised his hands, making a gesture for the guardsmen to let go of the man. And the guards released him accordingly.

Once again Hiranya prostrated himself on the ground and, joining his hands in a gesture of extreme humility, entreated, 'Devaraj, I am Hiranyadhanus, the Bheel. And this is Ekalavya, my only son. He's dying to learn the art of archery. If Your Highness would just so much as give him a place by Your feet, he'd be able to satisfy his heart's desire. Lord, don't be angry. I know this is an outrage, but what could I do? I'm powerless before this childish insistence.'

Rajguru Acharya lifted his eyes and looked at Ekalavya. The boy immediately made his obeisance. The Rajguru beckoned him to come close.

'Why do you want to learn archery?' he asked.

'So that I may protect myself against beasts in the jungle and against enemies in the village.'

'You do know, don't you, that archery is taught only to sons of Kshatriyas? You are a Bheel, and yet you talk about learning archery. Such insolence is punishable with your life.'

'Guru Deva, just give me the permission and I will sacrifice myself at your feet.'

Rajguru Dronacharya smiled artlessly. 'Son of a Bheel,' he said, 'you are very clever. But we really cannot take you as our pupil. This is forbidden by our laws. All the same, we give you our blessing.'

Guru Deva Dronacharya made a sign. The guards promptly withdrew from the Bheel, and the bearers moved on with the palanquin. Ekalavya and his father kept looking at the palanquin carrying Guru Deva

Dronacharya away. When it had disappeared from view, father and son withdrew to their forest.

Subsequently—the story goes—Ekalavya made himself a clay image of Guru Deva Dronacharya and made it into a living mentor before whom he persevered in perfecting his skill at archery. The day came when none could equal him in that art.

Then thirty-five hundred years later, it so happened that Ekalavya was reborn in the household of a poor labourer, who also went by the name of Hiranyadhanus. When Ekalavya became five years old, Hiranyadhanus put him in a municipal school. The boy turned out to be an exceptionally bright student. Day and night, he worked hard at his studies, always securing the highest marks in his exams. He very much wanted to become a doctor. After he graduated from high school with top honours, Hiranya took him to a medical college.

As luck would have it, the self-same Guru Deva Dronacharya turned out to be the principal of that college.

Ekalavya filled out the admission form. His scores were so good that Guru Deva Dronacharya called him into his office cubicle. He recognized the father and son right away. He smiled and said, 'Come in, Ekalavya, do come in.' Then, looking at the father, 'Well Hiranya, how are you?'

'I am fine, by God's grace, Maharaj.'

'So what do you do these days?'

'Lord, I work as a day-labourer in a mill.'

'I see. A menial worker, huh, yet you want to make your son a doctor—why?'

'He certainly will become a doctor, Maharaj, that is if you're kind and willing to do us a favour.'

'Don't say that, Hiranya, please don't. You don't know that we are still quite as helpless today.'

'How can you possibly be helpless?'

'Dear God, thirty-five hundred years haven't taught you a thing! Poor Hiranya, still the same old idiot!'

'My Master, I certainly don't wish to sound impudent, but back then we were considered Sudras. Today we are no longer considered quite as servile a caste. So what possible obstacle could there now be in accepting Ekalavya as your pupil?'

'That's precisely the problem, Hiranya. Times have changed. If you were still a Sudra, or a Harijan, I'd have had no difficulty admitting Ekalavya against the Backward Caste quota. Today your not being a Sudra is the biggest stumbling block. Ekalavya couldn't be more unfortunate: when he should've been born to a Brahmin or a Kshatriya, he chose a Sudra; and when he should have been born into the family of a Harijan, he chose a non-Harijan household. You tell me now, what should I do?'

'Do what you will, Master, but don't send us back in disappointment. I've come to you full of hope.'

'We are truly helpless, Hiranya.'

'Lord...Master...'

'Peon!' Principal Dronacharya called his servant, who promptly appeared. 'Show in the next candidate!'

Dronacharya turned his face away from Hiranya and Ekalavya. The peon made a gesture for them to exit the room, as he called out the name of the next candidate.

Translated by Muhammad Umar Memon

Syed Muhammad Ashraf
(b. 1957)

Syed Muhammad Ashraf belongs to a notable family of sufis and writers from Marehara, in the Etah district of Uttar Pradesh. Since 1700, each generation of the family has produced a writer of distinction. Muhammad Ashraf was born in Sitapur and received his education at Aligarh Muslim University. He works for the Indian Revenue Service and lives in Bombay.

Ashraf has made a mark as fiction critic and short story writer. His first collection of stories, *Dar Se Bichre* (Separated from the Flock), published in 1994, won wide critical acclaim. His second book, *Nambardar ka Nila* (1997), is a novella and his most recent collection of short stories

Bad-e Saba ka Intezar (Awaiting the Morning Breeze) was published in 2000. He won the Sahitya Akademi award for creative writing in 2003. His work has been translated into several Indian languages and English.

Ashraf's fiction engages with the deeply felt sense of loss of the instinctive, mutual trust shared by communities before Partition, and memories of the past that continue to play a role in the lives of Muslims in contemporary India.

The Man

He stood there, watching them pass below his window. Then, abruptly, he closed the window with a bang, turned, and pressed the fan's switch—now on, now off—before leaning against a chair near the table.

'Their numbers increase every day,' he said softly.

Sarfaraz raised his head from his open palms to look at him.

'You've only seen it for two days. I've been watching this for weeks. If I keep the window shut, I feel suffocated. If I open it, it gets worse. All of them seem to be heading this way.' He fell silent for a moment. Then he said, 'I'm meeting you after such a long time. I feel so happy. Yet...these people...'

'I've told you what happened on my way here. And it isn't as if I've just noticed it. Back in the village it's the same. I can't say what this might lead to.'

Sarfaraz looked at his childhood friend with affection. He was meeting Anwaar after fifteen years. How many memories they shared! As a boy, Sarfaraz had been sent to his uncle's home to study. Khalu lived in a large village. Two miles away, in the district headquarters was an Inter College. On his first day there, a boy of about his own age had casually taken Sarfaraz's eraser to rub out the balloon-like flowers he had drawn in his exercise book and replaced them with a duck which looked like a lamp. Then he had returned the eraser. During roll call the teacher had called out, 'Sayyid Anwaar Ali?' And that boy had said. 'Hazir Janab.'

'Sayyid Anwaar Ali,' Sarfaraz muttered.

'Hazir Janab. Thinking of school, are you?'

'Yes. How did you guess?'

'Yar, you still speak like a villager. Only the Art teacher called me by my full name when taking attendance.'

Sarfaraz smiled. He did not like being called a simpleton. But then, he reasoned, he was a senior officer and this childhood friend of his, an Urdu teacher in a primary school. He calls me names because he feels inferior, Sarfaraz told himself, and this thought made him feel better.

It was at that same moment that his mind leaped back in time. But for Anwaar, he would have never been able to get home from school, not one day! Without Anwaar, he would have been half-dead with fear by the time he crossed the dark jungles, the deserted orchards, and the silent fields that lay between the district headquarters and the village.

Sarfaraz rested his head on the back of the chair and closed his eyes. How pleasurable it was to remember that childhood terror!

In early winter, classes ended at four p.m. When the last bell rang, a chattering crowd rushed out of the classrooms, bags on shoulders, feet dancing homeward. He was the only one from his village, in this college. He would leave the college gates with slow, hesitant steps, afraid of the terrifying journey home. Sometimes Anwaar would be with him, walking up to the lake. But even he would not go beyond that. The road turned sharply at that point and if you looked back from there, the district headquarters had disappeared. Before going his way, Anwaar would reassure him. 'Don't be scared, Sarfaraz,' he'd say always. 'Once you cross the canal and enter the grove, you'll find someone there.'

Feeling helpless, but too embarrassed to show his fear, Sarfaraz would put on a brave face. 'What is there to be afraid of? Sometimes I meet someone in the orchard and that's good, but even if I don't, it doesn't worry me.' With an air of nonchalance, he would head for the village, but he remembered how both of them would keep turning to look at each other.

The moment Anwaar disappeared from sight Sarfaraz would touch the *taweez* around his neck and quickly start reciting the *ayt al-kursi*. Before reaching the canal he would have also chanted the four *quls* and blessed himself. Praying each step of the way, he would then move towards the grove. It was usually dark—the sun set early in winter.

On the dirt track, before he turned onto the tow path by the canal, a solitary cyclist or a bullock-cart would occasionally pass by, bells tinkling. But once he reached the embankment, it was totally deserted. The eerie sound of a vulture shifting perches high above on the *shisham* or rearranging its rustling wings made the desolation even more frightening. He would not be able to recall the *ayt al-kursi* sometimes, and would start reciting the *qul-o-wallah-o-wallah-o-ahad* instead. Sometimes he even managed to repeat the first *kalima*, the *kalima-e-tayyab*.

The grove would then appear, its aging mango trees shrouded in the mist of fading day. One Sunday, he discovered that it was perpetual dusk inside the grove, even at midday. In the evening, of course, it became darker. It was as if the tips of trees had crowded together in a conspiracy. Passing under the *fajri* tree he would hear his heart pound. It would seem as if Jinnat Baba would, that very instant, descend from the tree.

After the grove lay the sugar cane fields. Walking past them, he was certain that at any moment a lurking wolf would spring out from the fields which came next. At last, over the *pilkhan* trees, the minars of the masjids and the *kalash* of the village temples would appear. His body would relax, strength slowly returning to his legs. And he would break raucously into a film song.

Once or twice a month, when entering the grove, he would see a man walking towards his hut, a spade in his hand. On those days, a relieved Sarfaraz would start singing in the grove itself, breaking off only to greet the man—with great familiarity. The man would put down his spade when he heard Sarfaraz's loud, 'Salaam huzoor'. He would squint at him and say, 'Ram-Ram, beta. Aren't you Patwari sahib's nephew? My greetings to him.' Not that he met the man every day. But it was the hope of meeting him that gave Sarfaraz the courage to return home from college. Otherwise, he would have given up his studies and returned to his own village.

One day it was late by the time he left college. He had been so engrossed in watching a volleyball match that he did not realize the time. When he looked up, the sun had turned red. He set out in a hurry.

As he turned on to the path along the canal, he shuddered at the thought of not seeing the man on the way. He wiped the sweat of his forehead as he walked past the shisham tree. Suddenly he was sure someone had slid down the branches and was following him. His mouth went dry, he could not breathe. With slow, scared steps he moved on. Then the sounds behind him stopped. Maybe Jinnat Baba was taking aim now to shoot a magic ball at him. Feverishly reciting the kalima, he peered over his shoulder. It was a large monkey on all fours, growling at him. He was afraid of monkeys too, but not as much as he was of Jinnat Baba. Clutching his bag, he hurried on. His pace slackened only at the edge of the grove. Ahead was the deserted grove where he had no hope of finding the man this late. Behind him was the monkey.

The sun had set quite a while ago. The trees of the grove had begun their evening whisperings. He entered the grove. Walking towards the old fajri tree, his heart beat fast. This was the real abode of Jinnat Baba...

Then he heard a voice. 'You are very late today, beta.'

Arrey, the man was there after all! Sarfaraz was more pleased to see him than he was when the English teacher had given him a Very Good for writing 'My Cow'.

He looked at the man. He was standing among the trees near his hut. He was leaning on his spade, one hand resting on it, the other pulling his *angochha* over his ears. Wrapped in mist, the man in an ordinary dhoti, kurta, and angochha looked like an assistant of Hazrat Khizr, the prophet who had drunk the water of immortality.

'Salaam,' Sarfaraz said happily. 'Salaam huzoor!'

'May you live long, my son. Say Ram-Ram to Patwari sahib. And try not to be so late.'

That night, Sarfaraz ate his dinner and then went and sat with his aunt in the hall. Impulsively, he hugged her and told her the whole story. He wanted his Khala and Khalu to know what he had to brave every day to attend school. But when she heard that he had got late because of a volleyball match, Khala was furious.

Snuggled into his quilt, he lay in the hall, worrying how he would ever return from school if the man were to die. But the man looked younger than Khalu. Surely, he was unlikely to die soon! Anwaar's voice broke in on his memories.

'Your cousin is getting married,' Anwaar was saying. 'Your Khala called to complain that you have totally forgotten them. She said I should tell you that they are eager to see you. And that you must attend the wedding.'

Sarfaraz felt contrite, but he did not want to show it. In a grave but hollow voice he told Anwaar that one found little spare time when working for the government, especially as he was in a responsible position. Then he remembered Ayesha. He used to play with her when she was a baby. How quickly she had grown up!

'When is the wedding?'

'The wedding party arrives the day after tomorrow.'

'Arrey! Why has Khala gone and fixed a date now? Hasn't she seen the madness all around? Hordes of people, their faces blazing red, are out there in their trucks and tractors. They always carry weapons and there's such hatred in their eyes...'

'Yes, I did tell Khala that this is not the time for celebrations. Every village has been infected by the madness. Attitudes have changed in her village too, but she has no choice. The boy they have chosen for Ayesha is Khalu's brother's son. He is returning to Jeddah in three days. Besides, Khalu has not been too well. He is anxious to see Ayesha settled. You must leave at once, Sarfaraz. Ring up Bhabhi and tell her to get ready.'

'Don't you read the newspapers, Anwaar? Just the day before yesterday, people were dragged off a train and...'

Anwaar too was silent. Then he said in a brisk voice, 'Achha then, leave Bhabhi and the children here.'

'Yes, I won't be able to take them along.'

'It is eleven o'clock now. Even if we start at twelve, we should reach by seven, before it gets too dark.'

'Yes. It's about two hundred and fifty kilometres, right?'

They were on the bridge across the canal when some people suddenly stepped in front of the car and motioned them to stop. A procession of trucks and tractors was coming their way. The crowd was shouting frenzied slogans and seemed driven by a strange passion.

Sarfaraz's heart sank. They were carrying no weapons, nothing to defend themselves with. They sat still in the car. Sarfaraz found himself silently repeating the *ayt al-kursi*.

The procession went past them. The people who had stopped the car started shouting slogans and as the procession moved on, they joined it, still shouting.

Sarfaraz sat frozen, unable to start the car. Anwaar sat quietly beside him, each instinctively aware of the other's fear. When finally he started the car, Anwaar said, 'I have always found that they never do anything to individuals on an open road. For that they have trained people in each village and town. Last Friday when Ahmad the shopkeeper turned on to the path by the grove, someone came from behind him and...'

A chill ran down Sarfaraz's spine. He drove on mindlessly, as Anwaar continued to talk. 'It wouldn't look good if a crowd were to attack isolated people. But then, we are well prepared too,' he added in a conspiratorial whisper.

Finally when they turned along the canal road, the sun was already setting. How terrifying these places had seemed once, this silent canal, the deserted path, and the whispering groves, Sarfaraz thought. Had it not been for that man with the spade....

He braked suddenly. Caught in the headlights of the car was a huge monkey, its palms resting on the ground, making the growling sound he remembered so well.

They smiled as they watched the monkey run up a tree. In the branches, a vulture moved. A sound of fluttering wings. How that sound used to scare me, thought Sarfaraz.

'When was Ahmad attacked?'

'Four days ago.'

'Arrey...' Sarfaraz's hands that gripped the steering wheel were damp with sweat.

'What's up?' Anwaar asked, though he knew what the matter was.

'Nothing. So the incident was recent. Did they find anything?'

'What could they find? Right after the burial, the police officer scolded us for letting people walk through the grove alone after sunset in times like these. Attackers find it easy to operate at night. Stop, Sarfaraz. The road ends here, remember?'

They got out of the car. They walked past the embankment. Sarfaraz was stepping into the mist-shrouded grove after a long time. Today, it held no fear, yet a strange quiet had entered both of them. It didn't go away even when they spoke loudly to one another.

And then as they passed the ancient fajri tree, Jinnat Baba's haunt, Sarfaraz suddenly clutched Anwaar's hand so hard that Anwaar almost cried out in pain.

He looked at Sarfaraz, who was staring at a large mound. In the dark Anwaar could not even make out what Sarfaraz was pointing to.

Sarfaraz squeezed his hand harder. Then, abruptly, he turned around and ran. Dragging Anwaar along and, stumbling, slipping.... Scrambling up, they rushed out of the grove; Sarfaraz pulled the car door open, pushed Anwaar in, and drove off at full speed.

Soon they were speeding across the bridge and on to the familiar dirt track.

A nerve twitched in Sarfaraz's cheek. He was bathed in sweat.

'Tell me,' said Anwaar finally. 'Whatever it was, we have left it behind. Tell me what happened?'

Sarfaraz stopped the car.

'There was that man standing on the mound in the grove, among the trees. Did you see what he had in his hand, the thing on which he was leaning? It was a....rifle.'

Translated by Saleem Kidwai

GLOSSARY

achkan   a long coat or jacket buttoned in front
Alha   *Alha* was a certain Hindu hero whose stories of bravery are sung in many parts of northern India. These stories are also called *Alha*
Alif Laila   the tales of Alif Laila, also known as the *Thousand and One Nights* or the *Arabian Nights*, is a collection of amazing and startling stories that mostly originated from Arabia, Persia, and India
Amir Hamza   *Dastan-e Amir Hamza* or *The Adventures of Amir Hamza* is an epic from the Islamic cultures of the Middle East which is rooted in the legends of Prophet Muhammad's uncle, Amir Hamza and his companions
anchal   the last yard or so of a sari which covers the breast and shoulder
angochha   a towel-like cloth which people fasten around their waist while bathing and afterwards wipe themselves with
angrez   an Englishman
apa   an elder sister
auz o billah   'Refuge in God'—the key words in the sentence, 'I seek refuge in God from accursed Satan'
ayt al-kursi   the Quranic verse known as 'the verse of the chair' in which God describes Himself as the creator of the universe
azan   the Muslim call to prayer
babu   a title of respect, used as a courtesy title for a man
bafindas   cloth weavers
Bahishti Zevar   a collection of small books containing religious

Glossary

	instructions for men, women, and children by the great Sufi and theologian, Maulana Ashraf Ali Thanvi of the Deobandi School
Baital Pachchisi	a collection of twenty-five ancient Indian stories narrated to a king by a ghost named Baital who lived in a tree
Bande Matram	also 'Bande Mataram' and 'Vande Mataram'; 'Hail to the Mother', a poem/song composed by Bankimchandra Chattopadhyay
banjaras	itinerant tribals who purvey and convey goods
baqarkhani	crisp bread made of butter, milk, and flour
barat	marriage procession
barfi	a kind of sweetmeat made of condensed milk cooked with sugar
bhin, bhin	buzz, humming sound (of mosquitoes, flies, etc.)
bidi	a thin cigarette made of tobacco wrapped in a tendu (*Diospyros melonoxylon roxb.*) leaf, secured with coloured thread at one end
bitiya	a loving form of address for daughters
burqa	an all-enveloping outer garment with veiled holes for the eyes worn by many Muslim women in India, Pakistan, and Afghanistan
chacha abba	paternal uncle, father's elder brother
chadar	a sheet, a bed linen; to offer a chadar is to present a sheet as an offering to be spread over a tomb of a saint. It can also refer to a sheet-like wrap worn by women to cover the upper half of the body
chambeli	gardenia or jasmine flowers
champayi	of the colour of orange-yellow flowers of an Indian evergreen timber tree (*Michelia champaca*)
changri	a basket made of woven twigs used to store *chapattis*
chapatti	flat, unleavened, disk-shaped bread of northern India, made of wheat flour mixed with water
chela	disciple

chilam	part of a hookah/sheesha (multi-stemmed, often glass-based water pipe device for smoking), which holds the tobacco and the fire
chilla	forty-day vigil of meditation, forty day prayers
chowki	a square, low seat made of wood
chust	tight
dal seo	a salted snack made of ground pulses
Dabistan-e Urdu	school of Urdu
dahi-bara	a snack or fast food prepared by soaking bara (or vada, a doughnut shaped snack made from lentil or potato) in thick yogurt
dauri	platter made of palm leaves
degh	a large meal cooked in a huge metal pot also called degh
dhamin	a large snake which is said to suck milk from cows and is said to be harmless
dharma	the principle or law that orders the universe in Hinduism
dhobi	washerman
dhoti	a cloth worn round the waist passing between the legs and tucked in behind
diya	a slender form of light given by a small earthen pot with a wick made of cotton and dipped in oil
doli	a small, portable, enclosed cot, used by women to travel short distances
domni	a woman singer or dancer belonging to the caste of Indian Muslims who converted from the Hindu *dom* (scavenger) caste; the males mostly play musical instruments for a living
dupatta	a long scarf that is essential to women's suits in most parts of India and Pakistan
falsa	tiny, purple, cherry-like fruit
faqir	a dervesh, a religious mendicant
faqir (of Imam Husain)	a dervesh devoted to Imam Husain, grandson of Muhammad, who was martyred in the Battle of Karbala in 680 CE

Farvari	the month of February
fatwa	a legal pronouncement in Islam made by a *mufti*, a scholar capable of issuing judgments based on Islamic law
ga'o takiya	a large pillow or bolster that supports the back of a person sitting
garba	a dance, originated in the Gujarat region in India, similar to Western social dancing; however, garba is religious in origin
ghalta	baggy, loose women's pants
gharara	a large sacque
ghee	clarified butter
gitpit gitpit	talking quickly in a foreign-sounding accent
gole ke kebab	small rounded chunks of meat that are usually marinated before being threaded on a skewer and grilled over coals
gulab	rose, mostly associated with pink colour and freshness
gulab-jaman	a sweet dish comprised of fried milk balls in a sweet syrup flavoured with cardamom seeds and rosewater or saffron
gulal	dry form of colour (usually red), which people apply on each other on the festival of Holi
gurbani	various sections of the Holy Text that appears in the several Holy Books of the Sikhs
gurdwara	Sikh place of worship (meaning 'the doorway to the Guru') and may be referred to as a Sikh temple
gurmukhi	Gurmukhi script was standardized by the second Sikh guru, Guru Angad Dev, in the sixteenth century for writing the Punjabi language
hadis	generally written as 'hadith' in English, these are traditions relating to the words and deeds of Prophet Muhammad and are regarded as important tools for determining the Muslim way of life
hakim	a physician, doctor
halim	a dish prepared with grain, lentils, and meat

halvai	one who makes sweetmeats, a confectioner
hamzad	a genie said to be born at the same time as a child and believed to stay with him/her for life, often playing malevolent tricks on him/her or others
henna	the plant *Lawsonia inermis* used for dyeing the hands, feet, and hair
Holi	the festival of colours in India held at the approach of the vernal equinox
houris	beautiful women who will be at the service of believers when they go to paradise
hujoor	My Lord, Your Majesty (the right Arabic pronunciation is 'huzur')
ikhlaas	declaring the Indivisible Oneness of God
imam	head of a religion, minister of a mosque, priest, one who is followed
inquilab	revolution or upheaval
isha prayers	the night prayer of Muslims; its time varies from the end of the first third of night till midnight
Jal tu jalal tu	a colloquial kind of SOS prayer usually recited to oneself in times of crisis
jalebi	a sweetmeat made of deep-fried, syrup-soaked batter shaped into a large pretzel shape, and is mostly bright orange in colour
jamavar	a special type of (originally hand-made) shawl made in Kashmir
jamun tree	an evergreen tropical tree in the flowering plant family *Myrtaceae*
jharu	a broom
jhumar	an ornament consisting of a number of chains forming a fringe which is attached to the top-knot of a woman's head and falls on the forehead
kachori	a round flattened ball-shaped snack made of fine flour filled with a stuffing of yellow moong or urad dal

	(pulses), gram flour, black pepper, red chilli powder, salt, ginger paste, and other spices
kahar	a caste of Hindus whose business is to carry palanquins and the like, and also to draw water
kajal	lamp black, applied medicinally, and as a collyrium to the eyes
kalavah	a raw thread as it is wound from the spindle
kalima	Islamic declaration of belief; it serves as a kind of minimal creed for Muslims and is one of the five pillars of Islam
kalima-i-tayyab	the first and foremost *kalima* meaning 'there is no God but God, and Muhammad is the messenger of God'
kaliyug	the 'Iron or Evil Age' of Hindu mythology. Since a year of the gods equals 360 years of men, the extent of Kali Yuga is said to be 432,000 years. During kaliyug, righteousness has diminished by three-quarters, and the age is one of devolution, culminating in the destruction of the world prior to a new creation in an endless cycle of time
kamini	a lovely and beautiful woman; name of a flower
karonda	a small acid fruit of the *carissa carandas* family
keora	scent made from the strong scented flower of a plant (of the same name) of the *pandanus odoratissimus* family
khaddar	a very thick and coarse kind of handwoven cotton cloth
khaja	a sweet delicacy prepared from refined wheat flour, sugar, and edible oil
khasdaan	a portmanteau, a betel dish or box with cover
kheer	sweet dish made of rice, milk, and sugar
khicari	a popular Indian dish made of a mixture of rice and lentils, it is supposed to be easy on the digestive system
khirni	yellow sticky gum-fruit
kirpan	a ceremonial sword or dagger worn by all initiated Sikhs
kothi	a warehouse, mansion
kulvadhu	the proverbial woman, the family's symbol of fecundity

kundan	very fine gold
kurta	a traditional piece of clothing, a loose shirt falling either just above or somewhere below the knees of the wearer
laddu	a kind of ball-shaped sweetmeat made of the meal of chickpea with the addition of sugar and butter (ghee)
Lakshmi pooja	worship of Lakshmi, the Hindu goddess of wealth and fortune
laung chire	a dish prepared from peas meal
luchi	a type of deep fried pancake made of wheat flour
madrasa	an Islamic place of study, a school, an academy
maghrib prayer	the evening prayer, the fourth daily prayer in Islam, offered at sunset
mahfil	get-togethers or a lively gathering of people
maika	parental home of a married woman
majnun	madly or desperately in love, passionate
malaa'ii	milk cream
manjha	a feast given by the bride and bridegroom's family prior to the wedding
mannat	vows
marsiya	an elegy, an elegiac poem written to commemorate the martyrdom and valour of Hazrat Imam Hussain and his comrades at Karbala
masala	a spice blend with myriad variations. Generally, it could be a simple combination of two or three spices or a complex blend of ten or more ingredients
mirasin	a woman singer belonging to the hereditary caste of musicians; these women only sing in front of women
missi	a powder (composed of yellow myrobalan, gall-nut, iron-filings, and vitriol) used for tinging the gums to a black colour
mohallah	a neighbourhood or locality in cities or towns
mubarak	blessed
mulmul	a fine, soft muslin
munsif	a subordinate judge

mushairah	a term used to describe an event where poets gather to recite their poetical work
namaz-e janazah	a prayer carried out for Muslims at funerals, after the wrapping of the body and before the burial
nauha	a genre of Urdu poetry depicting the martyrdom of Imam Hussain, it is a sub-part of *marsiya*
nazm	an Urdu poetic form that is not a ghazal
neem	a tall, usually evergreen East Indian tree (*Azadirachta indica*), widely cultivated in tropical Asia for its timber, resin, bitter bark, and aromatic seed oil, which is used medicinally and as an insecticide
nihari	a beef or lamb stew made from hooves (a dish cooked by simmering or boiling slowly) and is a typical, and popular, Muslim dish
pan	a type of Indian snack, which consists of fillings wrapped in a triangular package using leaves of the betel pepper (*Piper betle*) and held together with a toothpick or a clove
pan daan	a pan box
payjama	loosely fitted trousers tied with a draw string
pani ki phulkiyan	a popular street snack in India comprising a round, hollow *phulki* (made from a dough of wheat flour, water, and salt by rolling it out into discs) fried crisp and filled with a watery mixture of tamarind, chilli, and potato
papad	a thin wafer typically made from lentil, chickpea, black gram, or rice flour and is served both baked or fried in oil
paratha	flaky East Indian bread made with whole-wheat flour and fried on a griddle. The basic version simply has clarified butter brushed between multiple layers of dough that are then folded and rolled out again. More exotic versions of *paratha* are stuffed with various vegetables, fruits, herbs, or spices
pindi	a kind of ball-shaped sweet made of flour mixed with several kinds of nuts, almonds, raisins, etc.

pipal	a fig tree (*Ficus religiosa*) in India, having broadly ovate leaves with a long terminal projection, is regarded as sacred by Hindus and Buddhists
pugly	a mentally unstable woman
puri	a light unleavened wheat bread, usually deep fried in oil
qazi	a judge or magistrate who has authority in all cases of law—religious, moral, civil, and criminal
qibla	direction towards Mecca, to which Muslims turn their faces when at prayer
qorma	a highly spiced and flavoured meat curry whose sauce may be thin or thick depending on the recipe
qul ho vallah	'Say, God is one', but there is a play upon words here. The Arabic words are thought to sound like the rumbling of an empty belly
qulfi	an iced sweet generally made of milk, cream, and sugar
Quls	*qul* is the first word of *suras* (chapters) 112, 113, and 114 of the Quran with the meaning 'say'. *Qul* or *quls* are used to denote any one or all of these *suras*
raita	a salad with sliced cucumbers beaten in sour milk or yogurt
Ramacharit-manas	An epic poem based on the story of prince Rama of Valmiki's Ramayana, composed by Goswami Tulsidas, a sixteenth-century Indian poet, is considered one of the greatest works of Hindi literature
Ramayana	An ancient Sanskrit epic, attributed to the poet Valmiki, holds a very important place in Hindu tradition and culture, and narrates the story of Prince Rama of Ayodhya, whose wife Sita was abducted by the demon Ravana, the king of Lanka
razai	a quilt
roti	unleavened bread
rubai	a four-line poem or quatrain, with rhyme scheme AABA
rudraksha	seeds of rudraksha tree (*Elaeocarpus ganitrus*), which grows on the foothills of the Himalayas. In Sanskrit,

	rudraksha literally means 'the eye of Rudra' or 'red-eyed'. God Shiva shed a tear on viewing the misfortunes of humanity. This single tear became the first rudraksha tree. Sacred garlands of rudraksha beads (108 in number) are used for keeping count while reciting or chanting a mantra or name/s of a particular deity
salam	salutation, greeting, parting salutation, the general meaning of which is peace
salamat	safe and sound
samadhi	a structure in memory of the dead. It looks like a tomb, but it is without remains. The term also describes a non-dualistic state of consciousness
samosa	a common snack in South Asia consisting of a fried triangular-shaped pastry shell stuffed with potato, pea, onion, garlic, etc., often savoured with tea
saqi	wine bearer
sari	a traditional Indian garment worn by women. The sari is a very long strip of unstitched cloth, ranging from five to nine yards in length, which can be draped in various styles
sarkar	a reverent form of address suggesting authority
sasural	the home of the in-laws with whom the newly-married woman lives after marriage
seth	a title of respect given to merchants
shagird	disciple or student
shalwar	a loose-fitting lower garment usually worn by women
sharbat	chilled sweet drink flavoured from fruit juice or flower petals
sharina	casuarina tree
shastra	a treatise or text usually written in Sanskrit in explanation of some idea, especially in religious matters
soz	dirge
Subhan Allah	'Perfect Glory is to God', is commonly used as an exclamation of joy or relief

surma	antimony, collyrium
tahmad	a coloured, full length cloth worn round the loins
takhallus	the nom de plume assumed by poets
takht	platform or wooden seat
tandoor	clay oven
tanpura	a type of string instrument
taqcha	a niche
tasla	a deep dish
taweez	an amulet
taziya	the miniature replicas of the shrines of Hasan and Husain, martyred sons of Ali, the Caliph, which is carried in procession at Muharram by Muslims
tika	a forehead ornament, usually rounded in shape and intricately crafted, popularly worn by brides in the Indian subcontinent
tikka	a forehead ornament or a coloured circular decoration on the forehead made of vermillion
tonga	a light two-wheeled cart/vehicle pulled (generally) by a horse
topi	a cap
ubtan	a paste made of chickpea flour, turmeric, oil, and rose essence rubbed on the body to clean and soften the skin
ustad	a master, teacher/preceptor
valima	a marriage feast generally hosted by the groom's side after the consummation of the marriage
vihara	a Buddhist or Jain temple or convent
zamindar	a landed estate-holder, a lord of manor

TRANSLATORS

VISHWAMITTER ADIL published English translations of Urdu poetry and fiction and was a screenwriter, director, lyricist, and film actor. He was a prominent member of the Progressive Movement in Urdu literature, an active participant of IPTA during its heyday, a radio broadcaster, and he wrote lyrics, screenplays, and scripts for many Hindi films (like *Shagird, Junglee, Geet Gaya Pattharon Ne*, and *Joru Ka Bhai*), and radio and television plays and serials. He published *A Chronicle of the Peacocks: Stories of Partition, Exile and Lost Memories*, a selection from Intizar Husain with Alok Bhalla.

AHMED ALI was a Pakistani novelist, diplomat, and scholar who was responsible for arguably the greatest novel ever written about Delhi. Born in Delhi, he was involved in the Progressive literary movement as a young man. He contributed to *Angarey* (Embers), 1933, a collection of short stories that caused an uproar among fundamentalist Muslims. His other books include *The Golden Tradition* (translations of Urdu poetry), *Ocean of Night, Of Rats and Diplomats, Twilight in Delhi*, and *Al-Qur'an: A Contemporary Translation*.

ALOK BHALLA is Professor Emeritus of the Central Institute for English and Foreign Languages, Hyderabad. A scholar and translator, he has many books to his credit including *Contemporary Indian Literature* (1999), and *The Life and Works of Saadat Hasan Manto* (1998). Between 1993 and 1996, he published six volumes of *Yatra: Writings from the Indian Subcontinent* with Nirmal Verma and U.R. Ananthamurthy.

MEHR AFSHAN FAROOQI holds a doctorate in History from Allahabad University. She teaches South Asian Literature and Cultural History in the Department of Middle Eastern and South Asian Languages and Cultures at the University of Virginia. Her research interests are in language and its literary uses. Her current book project is a history of Urdu prose.

SYEDA S. HAMEED is a feminist and writer who is widely recognized for her passionate engagement with public affairs and social issues, especially for women, minorities, and peace. She holds a PhD in literature at the University of Alberta. She has served as member of the National Commission for Women (NCW) and has written extensively on the atrocities and injustices faced by Indian women.

NEELAM HUSAIN is a social activist, fundamentally involved in the lobbying for legal protection of women in Pakistan. She heads the organization 'Simorgh'. She is also a translator of Urdu fiction.

AQUILA ISMAIL holds a degree in Electrical Engineering and was Associate Professor at the NED University of Engineering and Technology, Karachi. She does freelance editing for City Press and Oxford University Press. Her book reviews and essays on women's issues have appeared regularly in many Pakistani publications. She is also a noted translator.

SALEEM KIDWAI, medieval historian and gay studies scholar, and translator, taught history at Ramjas College, University of Delhi for many years, and is now an independent scholar. His other areas of interest include Mughal politics and culture, the history of *tawaif*s, and north Indian music. With Ruth Vanita, he is co-editor of *Same-Sex Love in India: Readings from Literature and History* (2000). Kidwai has also translated singer Mallika Pukhraj's autobiography, *Song Sung True*.

JONATHAN LOAR received his master's in Religious Studies from the University of Virginia in 2007 and is now pursuing a PhD. His academic interests include contemporary Hinduism, nationalism, violence in religion, and Hindi and Urdu languages.

MUHAMMAD UMAR MEMON is Professor of Islamic Studies and Urdu Literature at the University of Wisconsin-Madison. He edits *The Annual of Urdu Studies* and has published several collections of Urdu short stories in English translation, the latest being *Snake Catcher* by Naiyer Masud (2006).

C.M. NAIM is Professor Emeritus, South Asian Languages and Civilizations, University of Chicago. A selection of his academic essays, *Urdu Texts and Contexts*, was published in 2004.

TAHIRA NAQVI teaches Urdu in the Department of Middle Eastern and Islamic Studies at New York University. Her short stories have been widely anthologized, and she has published two collections of short fiction, *Attar of Roses and Other Stories from Pakistan* and *Dying in a Strange Country*. She has just completed her first novel. She has translated extensively from such authors as Manto, Chughtai, Khadija Mastoor, and Hajira Masroor.

FRANCES W. PRITCHETT is Professor of Modern Indic Languages, Department of Middle Eastern and Asian Languages and Cultures, Columbia University. Her research interests include Urdu and Hindi literature and language, especially the classical ghazal. She maintains a substantial research site on South Asia, at http://www.columbia.edu/~fp7.

A. SEAN PUE, a PhD in Middle Eastern and Asian Languages and Cultures, and Comparative Literature from Columbia University, is currently a postdoctoral research associate at the South Asia Language Resource Center at the University of Chicago. He is preparing a book manuscript on the modernist Urdu poet, N.M. Rashid.

ALOK RAI holds a PhD from University College, London. Currently, Professor of English at the University of Delhi, he is the author of *Orwell and the Politics of Despair* (1988) and *Hindi Nationalism* (2001). He is the grandson of Premchand.

SARA RAI, a creative writer and translator, lives in and works from Allahabad. She has published several volumes of her translations and edited others. She is the granddaughter of Premchand.

GORDON ROADARMEL was born in India in 1932. He took his master's degree in English and Asian Studies at the University of California in Berkeley, and his PhD in Hindi literature at the same institution. Roadarmel was a pioneer in introducing modern Hindi literature to the Western world.

RALPH RUSSELL is the doyen of Urdu Studies in the United Kingdom. Teaching at SOAS, he has published diversely in pedagogical materials, translations, and critical studies, as well as his autobiography. Some of his well-known titles are *Three Mughal Poets* (1968), *The Pursuit of Urdu*

Literature (1992), *Hidden in the Lute: An Anthology of Two Centuries of Urdu Literature* (1995), *How Not to Write the History of Urdu Literature* (1999), and *The Oxford India Ghalib* (2003).

GURIQBAL (BALI) SAHOTA teaches Indian literary and intellectual history at the University of Minnesota's Department of Asian Languages and Literatures. He is currently working on a manuscript entitled 'The Late Colonial Sublime'.

ACKNOWLEDGEMENTS

The editor and publisher are grateful for permission to include the following copyright material in this volume:

Abdullah Hussein, 'The Tale of the Old Fisherman', translated by C.M. Naim and Gordon Roadarmel. Reprinted by permission of the Translators.

Asad Muhammad Khan, 'Harvest of Anger', translated by Aquila Ismail. Reprinted by permission of Oxford University Press, Pakistan.

Aziz Ahmad, 'The Shore and the Wave', translated by Ralph Russell. Reprinted by permission of the Translator.

Balraj Mainra, 'Composition One' translated by Muhammad Umar Memon. Reprinted by permission of the Translator.

Bano Qudsiya, 'Within the Circle of a Wave', translated by Tahira Naqvi. Reprinted by permission of Unistar Books Private Limited.

Enver Sajjad, 'Scorpion, Cave, Pattern', translated by Frances W. Pritchett. Reprinted by permission of the Translator.

Iqbal Majeed, 'Two Men, Slightly Wet', translated by C.M. Naim. Reprinted by permission of the Translator.

Khadija Mastoor, Extract from *Angan* (Inner Courtyard), translated by Neelam Husain. Reprinted by permission of Simorgh Women's Resource and Publication Centre.

Krishan Chander, 'Irani Pilau', translated by A. Sean Pue. Reprinted by permission of *The Annual of Urdu Studies*.

Muhammad Hasan Askari, 'The Bitch', translated by Mehr Afshan Farooqi. Reprinted by permission of *The Annual of Urdu Studies*.

Muhammad Mansha Yad, 'The Show', translated by Muhammad Umar Memon. Reprinted by permission of the Author and the Translator.

Rashid Jahan, 'A Visit to Delhi', translated by Syeda S. Hameed and Sughra Mehdi. Reprinted by permission of Women Unlimited, an associate of Kali for Women.

Surendra Parkash, 'Bijooka', translated by Sara Rai. Reprinted by permission of the Translator.

Syed Muhammad Ashraf, 'The Man', translated by Saleem Kidwai. Reprinted by permission of the Author and the Translator.

Although every effort has been made to locate and contact copyright holders prior to printing this volume, this has not always been possible. However, if notified, the publisher will be pleased to rectify any inadvertent errors or omissions at the earliest opportunity.

SELECT BIBLIOGRAPHY

I only list works of authors who appear or are discussed in the two volumes of this anthology. The anthologies cited here have been ordered by year of publication. In some cases, I have excluded the listing of compilations and selections that I did not consider useful.

Anthologies

Nagi, Anis (ed. and tr.), *Modern Urdu Poems from Pakistan*, Lahore: Swad Noon Publications, 1974.

Bakht, Baidar and Kathleen Grant Jaeger (eds and trs), *An Anthology of Modern Urdu Poetry*, Delhi and Ontario: Educational Publishing House, 1984.

Jamal, Mahmood (ed.), *The Penguin Book of Modern Urdu Poetry*, New Delhi: Penguin Books, 1986.

Ahmad, Rukhsana (ed. and tr.), *We Sinful Women*, London: The Women's Press, 1991.

Memon, Muhammad Umar (ed.), *The Tale of the Old Fisherman: Contemporary Urdu Short Stories*, Washington, DC: Three Continents Press, 1991.

Khwaja, Waqas Ahmad (ed.), *Pakistani Short Stories*, New Delhi: UBS Publishers, 1992.

George, K.M. (chief ed.), *Modern Indian Literature, An Anthology*, Vols. 1–3, New Delhi: Sahitya Akademi, 1992.

Memon, Muhammad Umar (tr.), *Fear and Desire: An Anthology of Urdu Stories*, Delhi and New York: Oxford University Press, 1994.

Rehman, Samina (ed. and tr.), *In Her Own Write: Short Stories by Women Writers in Pakistan*, Lahore: ASR Publications, 1994.

Hameed, Yasmin and Asif Farrukhi (eds), 'Special Issue on Women's Writing', *Pakistani Literature*, 3 (2), Winter 1994.

Bhalla, Alok (ed.), *Stories About the Partition of India*, Vols. 1–3, New Delhi: Indus and Harper-Collins, 1994.

Rahman, Anisur (ed. and tr.), *Fire and the Rose: An Anthology of Modern Urdu Poetry*, Calcutta: Rupa and Co., 1995.

Russell, Ralph (ed. and tr.), *Hidden in the Lute: An Anthology of Two Centuries of Urdu Literature*, Manchester: Carcanet, 1995.

Cowasjee, Saros and K.S. Duggal (eds), *Orphans of the Storm: Stories on the Partition of India*, New Delhi: UBS Publishers' Distributors Ltd., 1995.

Hameed, Syeda S., and Sughra Mehdi (eds), *Parwaaz: A Flight of Words*, New Delhi: Kali for Women, 1996.

Paul, Sukrita Kumar and Muhammad Ali Siddiqui (eds), *Mapping Memories: Urdu Stories from India and Pakistan*, New Delhi: Katha, 1998.

Farrukhi, Asif (ed.), F.W. Pritchett and Asif Farrukhi (trs), *An Evening of Caged Beasts: Seven Post Modernist Urdu Poets*, New Delhi and New York: Oxford University Press, 1999.

Iqbal, Muzaffar (ed.), *Colors of Loneliness*, Karachi and New York: Oxford University Press, 1999.

Hussein, Aamer (ed.), *Hoops of Fire: Fifty Years of Fiction by Pakistani Women*, London: Saqi Books, 1999.

Siddiqi, Safia (ed. and tr.), *The Golden Cage: Urdu Short Stories by Asian Women in Britain*, New Delhi: Sterling Publishers, 2002.

Jalil, Rakhshanda (ed.), *Urdu Stories*, New Delhi: Srishti Publishers and Distributors, 2002.

Habib, M.A.R. (ed. and tr.), *An Anthology of Modern Urdu Poetry*, New York: Modern Language Association of America, 2003.

Dutt, Nirupama (ed.), *Half the Sky: Stories by Women Writers of Pakistan*, Chandigarh: Unistar Books, 2004.

Sheikh, Moazzam (ed.), *A Letter from India: Contemporary Short Stories from Pakistan*, New Delhi and New York: Penguin Books, 2004.

The Oxford India Premchand, Introduction by Francesca Orsini, New Delhi: Oxford University Press, 2004.

Memon, Muhammad Umar (ed.), *The HarperCollins Book of Urdu Short Stories*, New Delhi: Harper Collins Publishers India, 2005.

Asaduddin, M. (ed.), *New Urdu Fictions*, New Delhi: Kali for Women, 2006.

Asaduddin, M. (ed.), *The Penguin Book of Classic Urdu Stories*, New Delhi: Penguin Books, 2006.

Selections from a Single Author's Work: Fiction

Abbas, Ghulam, *Hotel Moenjodaro*, translated by Khalid Hasan, New Delhi: Penguin Books, 1996.

———. *The Women's Quarter and Other Stories from Pakistan*, translated by Khalid Hasan, Islamabad: Alhamra Publishing, 2001.

Ahmad, Zamiruddin, *The East Wind and Other Stories*, translated by Shamoon Zamir, New York: Oxford University Press, 2002.

Bano, Jeelani, *A Hail of Stones*, translated by Rajinder Singh Verma, New Delhi: Sterling Paperbacks, 1996.

Chughtai, Ismat, *Lifting the Veil: Selected Writings of Ismat Chughtai*, edited by M. Asaduddin, New Delhi: Penguin Books, 2001.

———. *My Friend, My Enemy: Essays, Reminiscences, Portraits*, translated by Tahira Naqvi, New Delhi: Kali for Women, 2001.

Hosain, Attiya, *Translating Partition*, edited by Ravikant and Arun K. Saint, New Delhi: Katha, 2001.

Husain, Abdullah, *Stories of Exile and Alienation*, translated by Muhammad Umar Memon, Karachi and New York: Oxford University Press, 1998.

———. *Downfall By Degrees*, translated by Muhammad Umar Memon, New Delhi: Katha, 2003.

Husain, Intizar, *The Seventh Door and Other Stories*, edited by Muhammad Umar Memon, Boulder, Colorado and London: Lynne Rienner Publishers, 1998.

———. *A Chronicle of the Peacocks*, translated by Alok Bhalla and Vishwamitter Adil, New Delhi and New York: Oxford University Press, 2002.

Hyder, Qurratulain, *The Sound of Falling Leaves*, New Delhi: Sahitya Akademi, 1994.

———. *The Street Singers of Lucknow and Other Stories*, Karachi: Oxford University Press, 1997.

Khan, Asad Muhammad, *The Harvest of Anger and Other Stories*, translated by Aquila Ismail, Karachi and New York: Oxford University Press, 2002.

Premchand, *Deliverance and Other Stories*, translated by David Rubin, New Delhi: Penguin Books, 1988.

———. *Widows, Wives and Other Heroines*, translated by David Rubin, New Delhi: Oxford University Press, 1998.

Manto, Saadat Hasan, *Kingdom's End and Other Stories*, edited and translated by Khalid Hasan, London and New York: Verso, 1987.

———. *Stars from another Sky: The Bombay Film World in the 1940's*, translated by Khalid Hasan, New Delhi and New York: Penguin Books, 1998.

———. *Partition: Sketches and Stories*, New Delhi and New York: Viking, 1991.

———. *A Manto Panorama: A Representative Collection of Saadat Hasan Manto's Fiction*

and *Non-Fiction*, edited and translated by Khalid Hasan, Lahore: Sang-e Meel Publications, 2000.
—. *Mottled Dawn: Fifty Sketches and Stories of Partition*, translated by Khalid Hasan, New Delhi and New York: Penguin Books, 1997.
—. *Black Milk: A Collection of Short Stories*, translated by Hamid Jalal, Lahore: Sang-e Meel Publications, 1997.
—. *Black Borders: A Collection of Thirty-two Cameos*, translated by Rakhshanda Jalil, New Delhi: Rupa and Co., 2003.
—. *Letters to Uncle Sam*, translated by Khalid Hasan, Lahore: Alhamra, 2001.
—. *A Wet Afternoon (Stories, Sketches and Reminiscences)*, translated by Khalid Hasan, Islamabad: Alhamra, 2001.
—. *Stories and Sketches*, edited and translated by M. Asaduddin, Karachi: Oxford University Press, 2001.
—. *Black Margins: Stories selected by M. Asaduddin*, edited by Muhammad Umar Memon, New Delhi: Katha, 2004.
Manzar, Hasan, *A Requiem for the Earth: Selected Stories*, edited by Muhammad Umar Memon, Karachi: Oxford University Press, 1998.
Mastoor, Khadija, *Cool Sweet Water: Selected Stories*, translated by Tahira Naqvi, New York: Oxford University Press, 1999.
Masud, Naiyer, *The Essence of Camphor*, translated by Muhammad Umar Memon, New Delhi: Katha, 1998.
Masud, Naiyer, *Snake Catcher: Stories*, translated by Muhammad Umar Memon, New Delhi: Penguin Books, 2006.
Qasmi, Ahmad Nadim, *The Old Banyan and Other Stories*, translated by Faruq Hassan, New York: Oxford University Press, 2000.
Riyaz, Fahmida, *Zinda Bahar Lane*, translated by Aquila Ismail, Karachi: City Press, 2000.
Singh, Balwant, *Selected Short Stories*, edited and translated by Gopichand Narang and Jai Ratan, New Delhi: Sahitya Akademi, 1996.
Yad, Mohammad Mansha, *Mansha Yad's Tamasha and Other Stories*, edited by Jamil Azar, New Delhi: Sterling Publishers, 1994.

Selections from a Single Author's Work: Poetry

Amjad, Amjad Islam, *In The Last Days of Autumn*, translated by Baidar Bakht and Leslie Lavigne, Lahore: Sang-e Meel Publications, 1991.
Faiz, Faiz Ahmad, *Selected Poems of Faiz*, translated by Daud Kamal, Karachi: Pakistan Publishing House, 1984.

——. *An Elusive Dawn: Selections from the Poetry of Faiz Ahmed Faiz*, translated by Mahbubul Haq, Islamabad: Pakistan National Commission for UNESCO, 1985.

——. *The True Subject: Selected Poetry of Faiz*, translated by Naomi Lazard, Princeton: Princeton University Press, 1988

——. *The Unicorn and the Dancing Girl*, edited and translated by Khalid Hasan and Daud Kamal, London: Independent Publishing Company, 1988

——. *The Rebel's Silhouette*, translated by Agha Shahid Ali, New Delhi: Oxford University Press, 1992.

——. *Poems by Faiz*, translated by V.G. Kiernan, Karachi: Oxford University Press, 1973.

——. *O City of Lights: Selected Poetry and Biographical Notes*, edited and translated by Khalid Hasan and Daud Kamal, Karachi: Oxford University Press, 2006.

Farooqi, Saqi, *A Listening Game*, selected and introduced by Shamsur Rahman Faruqi, translated by Frances W. Pritchett, London: Lokmaya Press, 1988; reprint, London: Highgate Poets, 2001.

Faruqi, Shamsur Rahman, *The Color of Black Flowers*, translated by Baidar Bakht, Karachi: City Press, 2002.

Hali, Altaf Husain, *Hali's Musaddas: The Ebb and Flow of Islam*, translated with a critical introduction by Christopher Shackle and Javed Majeed, New Delhi: Oxford University Press, 1997.

Iman, Akhtarul, *Taking Stock: Selected Poems*, translated by Baidar Bakht, Leslie Lavigne and Kathleen Jaeger, Lahore: Sang-e Meel Publications, 1991.

——. *Query of the Road: Selected Poems*, edited and translated by Baidar Bakht, Leslie Lavigne, and Kathleen Jaeger, Calcutta: Rupa and Co., 1996.

Iqbal, Muhammad, *Poems from Iqbal*, selected and translated by Victor Kiernan, London: John Murray, 1955.

——. *A Selection of Urdu Verse*, translated with comments by D.J. Matthews, New Delhi: Heritage Publishers, 1993.

——. *Tulip in the Desert: A Selection of the Poetry of Muhammad Iqbal*, eited and translated by Mustansir Mir, Montreal: McGill-Queen's University Press, 2000.

Jafri, Ali Sardar, *My Journey: Selected Poems of Ali Sardar Jafri, Urdu Poems with English Translation*, translated by Baidar Bakht and Kathleen Grant Jaeger, Delhi: Sterling Publishers, 1999.

Kazmi, Nasir and Basir Sultan Kazmi, *Generations of Ghazals*, selected and translated by Debjani Chatterjee, Bradford: Redbeck Press, 2003.

Komal, Balraj, *Selected Poems of Balraj Komal*, translated by Baidar Bakht and Leslie Lavigne, with an introduction by Shamsur Rahman Faruqi, Delhi: Educational Publishing House, 1989.

———. *A Sky Full of Birds*, translated by Balraj Komal, New Delhi: Sahitya Akademi, 1992.

Naheed, Kishwar, *The Price of Looking Back: Poems of Kishwar Naheed*, edited and translated by Baidar Bakht and Derek M. Cohen, Lahore: Book Traders, 1987.

———. *The Scream of an Illegitimate Voice: Selected Poems*, edited and translated by Baidar Bakht, Leslie Lavigne, and Derek M. Cohen, Lahore: Sang-e Meel Publications, 1991.

———. *The Distance of a Shout*, selected and translated by Asif Farrukhi, Karachi: Oxford University Press, 2001.

Niazi, Munir, *A Cry in the Wilderness*, edited by Asif Farrukhi and Salman Tarik Kureshi, with an introduction by Muhammad Ali Siddiqi, Karachi: Oxford University Press, 2002.

Rashid, Nun Mim, *The Dissident Voice: Poems of N.M. Rashed*, translated by M.A.R. Habib, New Delhi: Oxford University Press, 1991.

Riaz, Fahmida, *Four Walls and a Black Veil*, edited and translated by Patricia Sharpe, Karachi: Oxford University Press, 2004.

Shahryar, *The Gateway to Dreams is Closed*, translated by Baidar Bakht and Leslie Lavigne, New Delhi: Sahitya Akademi, 1990.

Novels in Translation

Ahmad, Aziz, *Shore and the Wave*, translated by Ralph Russell, Islamabad: Alhamra, 2003.

Chughtai, Ismat, *The Crooked Line*, translated by Tahira Naqvi, Oxford: Heinemann, 1995.

———. *The Heart Breaks Free, The Wild One: Two Novellas*, translated by Tahira Naqvi, New Delhi: Kali for Women, 1995.

Husain, Abdullah, *The Weary Generations*, edited and translated by the author himself, UNESCO Collection of Representative Works, Pakistan Series, London: Peter Owen, 1999.

Husain, Intizar, *Basti*, translated by Frances W. Pritchett, with introductions by Muhammad Umar Memon and the translator, New Delhi: Indus and Harper Collins, 1995.

Hyder, Qurratulain, *A Season of Betrayals: A Short Story and Two Novellas*, translated and introduced by C.M. Naim, New Delhi: Kali for Women, 1999.

———. *River of Fire*, translated from the original Urdu *Aag ka Darya* by the author, New York: New Directions, 1999.

———. *My Temples, Too: A Novel*, translated by the author, New Delhi: Women Unlimited, in association with Kali for Women, 2004.

———. *Fireflies in the Mist*, translated by the author, New Delhi: Sterling Publishers, 1994.

Mastoor, Khadija, *Inner Courtyard*, translated by Neelam Hussain, New Delhi: Kali for Women, 2001.

Premchand, *Nirmala*, translated with an afterword by Alok Rai, New Delhi: Oxford University Press, 1999.

———. *Courtesan's Quarter*, translated by Amina Azfar, with a foreword by Ralph Russell and an introduction by M.H. Askari, Karachi: Oxford University Press, 2003.

———. *The Gift of a Cow*, 2nd edition, translated by Gordon C. Roadarmel, with an introduction by Vasudha Dalmia, New Delhi: Permanent Black, 2002.

———. *Gaban: The Stolen Jewels*, translated by Christopher R. King, New Delhi: Oxford University Press, 2000.

Rusva, Mirza Muhammad Hadi, *Umrao Jan Ada*, translated by David Matthews, Calcutta: Rupa and Co., 1996.

(Auto)biographies and Critical Studies

Ahmad, Nazir, *The Repentance of Nussooh: The Tale of a Muslim Family a Hundred Years Ago*, edited and translated by M. Kempson and C.M. Naim, Delhi: Permanent Black, 2004.

Bhalla, Alok (ed.), *Life and Works of Saadat Hasan Manto*, Shimla,: Indian Institute of Advanced Study, 1997.

Blackburn, Stuart and Vasudha Dalmia (eds), *India's Literary History: Essays on the Nineteenth Century*, New Delhi: Permanent Black, 2004.

Coppola, Carlo, *Urdu Poetry: 1935–70, The Progressive Episode*, Unpublished PhD Dissertation, University of Chicago, 1975.

Dryland, Estelle, *Faiz Ahmad Faiz, Urdu Poet of Social Realism*, Lahore: Vanguard Books, 1993.

Faruqi, Shamsur Rahman, *The Secret Mirror: Essays on Urdu Poetry*, Delhi: Academic Literature, 1981.

———. *The Flower-Lit Road: Essays in Urdu Literary Theory and Criticism*, Allahabad: Laburnum Press, 2005.

———. *How to Read Iqbal: Essays on Iqbal, Urdu Poetry and Literary Theory*, edited and compiled by Muhammad Suhayl Umar, Lahore: Iqbal Academy Pakistan, 2007.

Flemming, Leslie A., *Another Lonely Voice: The Life and Works of Saadat Hasan Manto*, Lahore: Vanguard Books, 1985.

Hansen, Kathryn and David Lelyveld (eds), *A Wilderness of Possibilities, Urdu Studies in Transnational Perspective*, New Delhi: Oxford University Press, 2005.

Iqbal, Javid, *Encounters with Destiny: Autobiographical Reflections, A Translation of Apna Gareban Chaak*, translated by Hafeez Malik and Nasira Iqbal, Karachi: Oxford University Press, 2006.

Issar, Devendra, *Memoirs of Fragrance*, translated by Riyaz Latif, Delhi: Kritika Books, 2000.

Kumar, Sukrita Paul (ed.), *Ismat: Her Life and Times*, New Delhi: Katha, 2000.

Minault, Gail, *Secluded Scholars: Women's Education and Muslim Social Reform in Colonial India*, New Delhi: Oxford University Press, 1998.

Mir, Mustansir, *Iqbal*, Makers of Islamic Civilizations Series, London and New York: I.B. Tauris, 2006.

Naim, C.M., *Urdu Texts and Contexts: Selected Essays of C.M. Naim*, New Delhi: Permanent Black, 2004.

Patel, Geeta, *Lyrical Movements, Historical Hauntings: On Gender, Colonialism, and Desire in Miraji's Urdu Poetry*, Stanford: Stanford University Press, 2002.

Pandey, Geetanjali, *Between Two Worlds: An Intellectual Biography of Premchand*, New Delhi: Manohar, 1989.

Pritchett, Frances W., and Shamsur Rahman Faruqi, *Ab-e Hayat: Shaping the Canon of Urdu Poetry*, New Delhi and New York: Oxford University Press, 2001.

Pritchett, Frances W., *Nets of Awareness: Urdu Poetry and Its Critics*, Karachi: Oxford University Press, 1995.

Majeed, Sheema (ed.), *Culture and Identity: Selected English Writings of Faiz*, Karachi: Oxford University Press, 2005.

Mir, Ali Husain and Raza Mir, *Anthems of Resistance: A Celebration of Progressive Urdu Poetry*, Delhi: India Ink/Roli Books Pvt. Ltd., 2006.

Qadiri, K.H., *Hasrat Mohani*, Delhi: Idarah-e Adabiyat, 1985.

Rab, Syed Fazle, *Sociology of Literature: A Study of Urdu Novels*, New Delhi: Commonwealth Publishers, 1992.

Rai, Amrit, *Premchand: His Life and Times*, New Delhi: Oxford University Press, 1992.

Raipuri, Hameeda Akhtar Husain, *My Fellow Traveller*, translated by Amina Azfar, with a foreword by Mushfiq Khwaja and an introduction by Asif Farrukhi, Karachi: Oxford University Press, 2006.

Riaz, Fahmida, *Reflections in a Cracked Mirror*, translated by Aquila Ismail, Karachi: City Press, 2001.

Rockwell, Daisy, *Upendranath Ashk, A Critical Biography*, New Delhi: Katha, 2004.

Russell, Ralph, *How Not to Write the History of Urdu Literature and Other Essays on Urdu and Islam*, New Delhi: Oxford University Press, 1999.

——. *The Pursuit of Urdu Literature, A Select History*, London: Zed Books Ltd., 1992.

Sadiq, Mohammad, *Twentieth Century Urdu Literature*, Karachi: Royal Book Company, 1983.

Schimmel, Annamarie, *Gabriel's Wing: Study into the Religious Ideas of Muhammad Iqbal*, Lahore: Iqbal Academy, 1989.

——. *Classical Urdu Literature from the Beginning to Iqbal*, Wiesbaden: Otto Harrassowitz, 1975.

Sharar, Abdul Halim, *Paradise of the Assassins: A Translation of Firdaus-e-Bareen*, translated by Tariq Mahmud, with an introduction by Asif Farrukhi, edited with chronology and notes by Amina Azfar, Karachi: Oxford University Press, 2005.

Sohail, K., *Literary Encounters: Interviews with Urdu Writers Living in the West*, Lahore: Pakistan Books and Literary Sounds, 1992.

Suhrawardy, Shaista Akhtar Bano, *A Critical Survey of the Development of the Urdu Novel and Short Story*, reprint with an introduction by Asif Farrukhi, Karachi: Oxford University Press, 2006.

Varma, Pavan K., *Ghalib: The Man, the Times*, New Delhi: Penguin Books, 1989.

Zaheer, Sajjad, *The Light: A History of the Movement for Progressive Literature in the Indo-Pakistan Subcontinent*, translated by Amina Azfar, with an introduction by Ahmad Ali Khan, Karachi: Oxford University Press, 2006.